Sabrina in Space

Sabrina in Space

The Early Years

Dennison R. Love

Order this book online at www.trafford.com
or email orders@trafford.com

Most Trafford titles are also available at major online book retailers.

Print information available on the last page.

ISBN: 978-1-4269-9756-3 (sc)
ISBN: 978-1-4269-9755-6 (e)

Trafford rev. 08/24/2015

www.trafford.com

North America & international
toll-free: 1 888 232 4444 (USA & Canada)
fax: 812 355 4082

This book is dedicated to:

Miss Sabrina G. Pasterski

And, to the Future that didn't happen yet!

Preface:

I am Sabrina Pasterski I was born in Chicago, Illinois where I went through my early school years with a perfect attendance record. I was introduced to speed at a very early age, when I noticed that airplanes can fly much faster than cars. At the age of 5 years old. I ran into my first barrier of flight, as I discovered that my legs were too short to reach the rudder pedals in an airplane.

So, by the time that I had turned 6 years old I was re-building my own Cessna 150 airplane from the wreckage of two others, Cessna 150's. This is when I discovered that I could build an airplane that not only had a set of operational rudder pedals that reached the bottom of my shoes. I also had a set of working brake pedals that I could also reach with both of my feet.

Due to my high test scores I was able to earn my pilots license in Canada by the ripe old age of 7 years old. I became a very active member of the Experimental Aircraft Association as well as their youngest Aviation adviser on my 8th birthday.

That's when I met my friend Dennison who decided to write my premature biography. In this story line at 14 years old I launch myself all the way to the Planet Mars just to make a single touch-and–go to get a few soil samples.

I became the first 7th grade Girl on Earth to have an actual jar full of Mars to bring into my class for "Show & Tell." I also became the first girl on Mars to be trapped inside a jar full of Earth after I was shot down by a meteor storm that discovered me all at once.

That's when I started to have some very interesting adventures. I keep getting asked "Is the rumor true, did you really make a V.T.O.L. landing with a SR-71 at Oshkosh?" My reply seems to shock him when I informed him that I had landed at Pioneer Airport as it was closer to the museum. But most of these adventures have not happened yet. But then we can only hope. Be sure to check your Book Store for more of my Adventures.

These are Log Entries:

Log Entry #1.
My First Around the world flight:

When I was in the first grade the entire school had a paper airplane contest. I did my own research to discover that it was not the lift, weight, thrust or drag that made the airplane fly, it was the poor little things aerodynamic balance as well as the center of gravity that caused flight.

This bit of knowledge enabled me to build mass centers into my paper airplane designs. This enabled me to win every paper airplane flying contest all the way up to the national level. When I was 8 years old, I started to build real airplanes.

The secret of my spaceflight success is simple when I looked at the history of spaceflight, I discovered that a single person spacecraft built to my standards was the only way at our present level of technology to get off the surface of the Earth and operate in outer space. To do his I had to be able to do it all, I am not only my own pilot I am also my own Historian, Designer, Programmer, Builder, Mechanic, Engineer, Navigator, and Astronaut.

I build all of my own equipment as well as operate it all by myself. It took me six years to design and build "Sabrina No. 5" she was my first operational rocket-ship, she is a basic vertical launch type with a landing skids that need lots of run way to land on. She was able to taxi on her own without causing grass fires. It takes a little more power to move but, the metal skids will not melt or blow out on landing.

Besides, if I ever get her to Mars I will definitely need skids to land on its surface as I do not think that there are any usable runways on the surface of

Mars. I started out with the basic lifting body design. I even went back to the Wright Brothers ideas and came up with a way to adapt wing warping to high speed supersonic flight, after all a girl has to able to maneuver no matter how fast she can move. Needless to say I built all of the flight controls to fit my body measurements. A full grown adult definitely would not be able to get into her cockpit.

Despite the speed that I was traveling at I would have to stay inside the Earth's atmosphere, I experimented with all the other liquid rocket motors and gave up.

Therefore, I decided to use the basic Aero-Spike Rocket Motor. I used the wet shield method as long as liquid is in contact with the inside surface of my heat shield it will displace the heat and keep the outer surface from melting or burning. Any kind of liquid would do, so I decided to use water so that I can also use it as a radiation barrier, if nothing else I could drink it.

Ultimately, I could float whales in it. I also had to make my own flight gear, parachute, pressurized flight "G" suit and all. For it to count as a world record I would have to stay inside the Earth's atmosphere, and maneuver from point to point. I set everything up for a vertical launch out of "O'Hare Airport "as I figured my touch down speed I would need a lot of runway to slow down on. So I decided to let "Sabrina Five" skid to a stop, I even carried a spare drag chute as I didn't want to end up in downtown Bensenville.

Due to my inability to taxi to the active runway with a full fuel load I had to launch from my current location. I extended the balance strut from my vertical stabilizer then activated the keel-lifting device that works out of my nose wheel strut. This makes Sabrina No. 5 into a tail sitter. I made my pre-launch safety check then requested and got permission for a vertical take-off, from my starting point. I activated my space suit it took less than a second for my gray flight suit to morph into its white space suit mode helmet and all.

The air traffic controllers were a little hastened when I added in the part about going directly to 100 thousand feet while I was still over the active runway. They must have though the world had ended when I launch off with my Aero-Spike only at 39%. I couldn't go to full power until I had put at least 4,000 feet between the end of my rocket engine and the runway.

As I started to move I manage to burn off most of the touchdown marks that had accumulated on the runway without starting a grass fire.

I managed to reach my operational altitude of 100,000 feet before I made it to the other end of the runway. I started to throttle back as I noticed that my fuel flow meter was still skipping numbers as it tried to display correct figures.

Log Entry #2.
Touch and Go on Mars:

There I was sitting in my own backyard the first person to do a touch and go on the surface of Mars about to be late for school. I was trapped in my pilot's seat waiting for the top surface of my space craft to cool down enough to allow me get out, without melting the bottom of my tennis shoes.

I had gone through all three of my space suits during this trip, my Sunday go to meeting space suit ran out of power just as I touched down in my backyard. As my Space suit shut down it collapses my helmet, pulled back my space boots and gloves, last thing it did was to form into a Gray Flight suit. It seems that residual heat had leached into the top surface of my Sabrina No. IX causing it to overheat.

I can tell you for a fact that on my next space ship Sabrina No. X the hatch will not be on top of the space craft. As always, the first thing I had to do was get permission from both of my parent to fly to the Planet Mars. I had to take advantage of "Mars Closest Pass to Earth". After all 34 ½ million miles is as close as the planet Mars has ever come to the Earth.

I had my Mother Ship No. IV transport ship, pick me up in the school parking lot just after school last Friday, with my Sabrina No. IX Space ship loaded aboard and ready to go to Mars. As the pre-flight program was getting my spacecraft checked out as well as ready for launch.

I got into my spaceflight gear; actually, I was already wearing it all. I had to command my school outfit started to morph my skirt start to get longer and formed pants. Then space boots, my blouse started to morph sleeves and a hood.

The sleeves extended to my fingertips then formed mittens that tighten up to form fitting gloves. My hood filled out and became my space helmet. Then I climbed up the ladder walked across the top of my Space ship and got down into the cockpit. Once inside my Command POD, I activated my flight systems computer.

I called the Elgin TRACON to request a vertical assent to 100,000 feet with a Northern exit out of their air space. As I reached an altitude of more than twenty-seven miles high, thanks the Aviatrix Jacqueline Cochran all political boundaries ended at an altitude of 50 nautical miles above the surface of the Earth.

I didn't need to wake up the Canadians. I had my mother ship IV dropped myself off at 300,000 feet while traveling around Mach 10 over the North Pole. She is the only mother ship that I have that was designed for V.T.O.L. operations. This allowed me to use the parking lot without for launch without wasting all that fuel taxing all the way out to Sullivan Road. I activated the auto return button on the auto- pilot part of my newly built Command Computer before bailing out with n my Sabrina No. IX Space ship.

I used the full power descent method to get up to orbital speed. It seems odd to dive towards the surface of the Earth at full power only to miss it by a couple thousand feet. Then to zoom out the other side of the Earth's atmosphere directly into outer space. The knack lies in knowing how to throw yourself at the ground and not getting any of it on your nose cone. As I was heading for the Earth's only Moon I checked back with the Elgin TRACON for a vector as well as landing permission back at the school for Mother Ship No. IV. The time lag in communication didn't seem to confuse them.

All of my Sabrina Space ships are equipped with a movable cockpit pod that is allowed to move. So that it will change its orientation to lessen the effect of pulling lots of G's while I am maneuvering or changing speeds. The Command POD also has the capability of floating and being moved around as needed to correct for changes in the center of gravity as I use fuel.

In an emergency, I can use it as an escape & survival pod. As soon as I was in deep space past the Moon I used the "Solar Gravity Assist Method" to make a record-breaking trip to the planet Mars. I had to dive my space ship directly at the Sun while accelerating under full power. I used my higher math skills to calculate the precise moment, to pull past the orbits of Venus and Mercury.

To use the mass of the sun to gain just enough speed to be able pull out of the dive after using its gravity to accelerated towards, then meet up with the planet Mars as it orbited around from the other direction.

Mars was so close that I arrived there in record time. It was fortunate that I made an "A+" in math as I did not have a problem doing space flight calculations. I did all the navigation calculations in my head without the need to figure on my knee pad.

The real trick was to calculate how to fly an arc in outer space to make the nose of Sabrina No. IXs meet up with the correct part of the Martian atmosphere at the correct angle. I was able to move my cockpit and living area to the extreme end of Sabrina IX and use the rest of the mass to spin at six R.P.M.s. This enabled me to live under one "G" as I was traveling to Mars. I went into full station keeping mode, I got caught up on my E-mail, as well as homework, had lunch and dinner.

I noticed that my GPS locater in my E-mail was giving the exact location between Mars and Earth. When I began to close in on Mars, I stopped the ships rotations and made sure to avoid both of Mars moons and I flew straight into its upper atmosphere. I had to performed several orbital passes high in its upper atmosphere to slow down, I was able to deploy my speed brakes just enough to allow me to skim its surface.

I could only make one high speed pass where I was actually able to touch its surface. I lowered a sampling hook to scrape up several hundred pounds of Martian surface samples, then pulled up and went directly back into outer space.

I used Mars forward speed to help throw me back towards Earth, then the last of my fuel to power-dived back towards the Sun, to zoom into Earth's atmosphere. I went back to station keeping mode for the trip back to Earth. I used the vacuum of outer space to keep my newly acquired samples from the planet Mars from being contaminated; I stored and cataloged all 233 pounds of them.

After avoiding the Earth's Moon, I dove directly into the Earth's atmosphere at over 60,000 miles per hour I had to perform four orbits inside the ionosphere to help the ship slow down. I had feathered the body of Sabrina No. IX to make maximum aerodynamic drag, I took a minute to think back to my first round the world flight, it took only 60 minutes, this time the first orbit only took 15 minutes, next orbit 35, then 75, 150, finally 310 minutes.

As I was coming out of my communication blackout on my way to my touch down point in Elgin, Illinois. It was a pleasant change to see something other than my external fireball on my sensors cameras. My traffic collision avoidance system instantly located and identified all the local traffic that was flying 90 miles below me.

My communications system picked up several radio transmissions that were occurring while crossing the California coast for the last time, my altitude was only 82 miles. I was decelerating with the cockpit turned around so that I was really flying backwards. And I was only pulling four "G's. I wasn't in their control space but, they were monitoring my movements on their radar screens. I listened in as the Cessna Pilot asked for readout of his ground speed, "90 miles per hour" the Center replied.

A moment later, the Pilot of the twin engine Beech requested the same, "120 miles per hour," the Center answered. I wasn't the only one that was proud of my ground speed that day as almost instantly an F-22 Pilot. Who I saw flying below me, smugly transmitted," Center, Dusty 52 requests my ground speed readout. There was a slight pause, then the response, "525 miles per hour on the ground, Dusty 52".

There was another silent pause I was thinking to myself how unique a situation this was, I activated the communication system and announced "Center, Sabrina No. IX, "do you have ground speed readout for me?" There was a long pause Sabrina Nine, your ground speed is "12,889 miles per hour". That was an interesting response because I had been out of fuel for the last 35 million miles, and I was doing my best to slow down.

No further inquiries were heard on that frequency. While I continued monitoring it until I was over the east side of Texas. My lack of speed was starting to cause my Space ship to fall vertically. I didn't want to alarm any one, as my rate of descent was dramatic so I contacted Houston center to request a vector to Chicago and to request that all traffic below 160,000 feet be cleared.

A skeptical air traffic controller, with some disdain in his voice, asked me, "How do you plan to get to 160,000 feet?" I told him that I was planning to descend and added the fact that it would take me a while to get that low.

I was cleared directly to Chicago although he didn't like the idea of me "booming" everyone in his controlled air space. It would take me a while to decelerate to an air speed below Mach one so I didn't stop emitting sonic booms until I was over Davenport, Iowa. I was just getting the hang of supersonic aerobatics when I ran out of air speed.

I deployed my drogue parachute as I was now going so slow my aerodynamic controls were useless. I deployed the main parachute canopy as soon as I slowed to terminal velocity at around 60,000 feet. I deployed my main landing parachute early to give the skin of my space ship a little more time to cool down. The external air temperature was 100 degrees below zero so I decided to put it to good use as my surface temperature gauge was still off its scale.

I got in touch with the controller from the Elgin TRACON to get a vector to my touch down point. He was just returning from his break and wanted to know if I was still falling"? Since he had been monitoring my communications since my first contact with the Los Angeles Air Traffic Center. I informed him that I wanted clearance from 60,000 feet and below and that I was not falling anymore. I had to have a lot of main parachute out there because of the altitude. I had to make sure to stay clear of O'Hare's traffic patterns, as my only lifting surface did not like jet wakes or wing tip vortices.

The controller told me that I had to wait my turn as some "pilot" had just opened a giant size parachute in the center in his control zone! I informed him that I was that pilot and that I needed directions. The Air Traffic Controller wanted to know why I was using a parachute and if I wanted to declare an emergency. I told him "No" it would make me late for school if I declared an emergency.

I informed him that I was flying a Lifting Body type space craft that did not have any wings. The only airfoil I had was a very large parachute. He gave me permission to descend and the heading to Elgin, Illinois. I wanted to land as close as I could to my home. I lowered the landing skids and steered into the wind. I had lots of control by pulling on key shroud lines.

After holding, back as long as I could I finally put Sabrina No. IX down in the sand filled landing pit in my back yard. I decided not to touch down in the driveway as I didn't want to crack the concrete surface again.

Because the surface of Sabrina IX was still glowing white, hot from the heat of my atmospheric re-entry, the outer skin of my space craft was too hot to allow me to get out.

I had to wait until the lawn sprinkler system went off and the constant spray of cold water finally cooled enough of Sabrina No. IX's skin to allow me to walk across its top. To make matters worse my Sunday go to meeting suit had closed itself down as it went into the school uniform mode.

I was able to pull the canopy of my main parachute over the top of Sabrina No. IX this would make the neighbors think the swimming pool had a cover on it. As soon as sun light hit my closed down space suit it automatically powered itself up just enough to morph into my school outfit No.6.

I checked out my now bottled Martian samples and removed a small one to take to school. I now had enough time to prepare for school and catch the School Bus. That morning at school, I was the only 10th grader that had her very own jar full of the planet Mars, for show and tell. So far none of my class mates believe that I obtained them myself.

Log Entry #3.
My Flight Gear:

I have always made my own flight gear, space suits and all. I started out by using memory material that enables me to alter the color and softness of the material as the need arises. I am still growing so the material has to be able to expand as well as stretch.

It also has the capability of serving as a "G" suit as well as all the plumbing necessary for space walks it has to be waterproof as well as meteor-proof. The suit is programmed to form the smart material around every part of my body including my hands, feet, knees, elbows & shoulders. The suit also has self-contained heating and cooling systems.

I use the heating system more because the temperatures on Mars can reach -200 F. When activated my school blazer hardens up and forms a hood which expands out to become my space helmet. The sleeves extend to cover my hands and then form mittens that tighten up to form fitting gloves.

My skirt divides in half and forms pants that extend their legs to form space boots. On the occasions when I have to change the suit it's designed to fold itself into a shoebox size container for cleaning and recharge. I designed all of my space suits to operate at 15 PSI the same pressure at sea level on Earth.

I try to keep at least three suits online at the same time, they are my primary, back-up, and Sunday go-to-meeting suits. Because of the morph cycles I do not need to have any interchangeable parts. They don't come with an extra pair of pants.

However, I can have it make extra thick layers of outer surfaces as needed. Its surface can change colors for several different reasons, its programmed to start out a very bright white then to change color as its consumables get used up when it's time to recharge it turns into a bright red color. When it's deactivated and I am wearing it as a flight suit it turns a basic gray color.

I can even create emblems as well as ID patches. Due to my latest upgrades in programming I can get it to change into any of my schools outfits, name tags and all, it also can form into a Windbreaker with a hood, for rainy days.

I can display my company logo "Sabrina Aviation" on the back of my space suit. I can even have it flash large format words on the suit to give instruction to other astronauts. I have a built in extra power system that will allows me to carry the extra mass of the suit when I wear it on Earth, when I am still under one "G". I have added some extras, to my suit program that will make it easier to work underwater, webbing between my fingers & thumb in my glove program, as well as swim fins for my boots in any type of liquid that I might be submerged in.

If submerged in water, my suit systems can separate the water back into hydrogen and oxygen to fuel my suits built in fuel cells. I also have a new He/3 reactor that I can use to power my space suit.

All of my space suits also have to be meteor proof, as they are a bigger problem than most people think the best analogy is similar to being hit by a golf ball moving at a very high speed. I can tell you from experience that it's not very funny when anybody gets zapped by one. All asteroids have a gravity field as such it attracts other meteors.

The problem comes from the smaller "Want-a-bees meteors" orbiting around the asteroid, to stay in orbit it has to be moving at a very high rate of speed usually a whole lot faster than a Golf ball. To make matters worse the Want-a-bees meteors will descend and sooner or later hit or land on the asteroids surface.

Size is relevant! I have seen meteors as large as small cars orbiting asteroids. Therefore, the space suit has to be able to harden up in a micro second to stop a bullet the size of a Volkswagen from making a hole. Each suit also has an emergency deployment system so far my only problem is when somebody in my chemistry class does something stupid I am the only person in the room wearing an operation full pressure, fireproof, space suit helmet and all.

When I first met up with Pinger-5, I used the morph program to enhance the space suits so that I was able to modify my operation to make it automatically adjust to fit a full size Humpback Whale.

My main problem with my Whale suits was beefing up the cooling properties as whales have evolved to live in extremely cold water, the only time that I have noticed them using any of the space suits heating systems, was when they were scooting around the surface of Mars. After seeing all my Whale/naut's expanding the use patterns of their space suits I think that it's about time that I got into the act.

My latest modification adds the capability of personal "Powered Flight" this way when I want to play Super-Girl I can just fly off all by myself with the use of a space suit mounted rocket system, add in a He/3 reactor and I am good to go any time and for any distance. Even Mom likes my latest modifications as if I am ever forced out of one of my space ships I will have a way to get away.

Log Entry #4.
One Morning at School:

I just found out that the internet search company Google is offering $20 million dollars for about a gigabyte of digital data from the Moon. Google is sponsoring a contest to see which private group can be the first to land a robot on the Moon and send images back to Earth it says the high-resolution "Moon cast" should contain panoramic shots of the Lunar X Prize. An executive wrote that Google thinks space is "cool".

Adding space exploration has led to such break- troughs as abrasive heat shields, as well as millions of other inventions, that make life on the Earth possible. Contestants have until 2012 to complete the expedition and can earn a $5 million bonus for finding such things as water and equipment left behind by earlier Moon missions.

It's not like I was doing another touch & go flight to the surface of Mars. My first problem was coming up with enough stuff to hit the Moon with, I checked around school and found closets full of potential lunar impactor objects some of them already had TV cameras installed. I came up with a targeting program designed to earn some extra money by landing near enough to see all of the old early Apollo landing sights.

I discovered that with a little programming a GPS unit could be programmed to find any spot on the Moon. All I would have to do is program for the time delay and direction. Mrs. Topson my Science Teacher was glad to give me all of their leftover stuff that I could use. She really loved all of her newfound empty spots in her closets. Her only request was that I not to bring any of it back. It's a good thing because I plan to scatter every one of them all over the face of the Moon.

It only took a couple of hours to modify and update enough of the impactors and cameras to find each of the Apollo landing sights on the Moon. I loaded them all into several of Sabrina No. IX's Meteor collection buckets and started to load her into good old Mother-ship number IV. Sabrina No. IX was not going as far as the last trip, so I could put more fuel aboard Mother ship number IV.

I checked with the navigation computer and noted that I could not use the solar gravity assist trick for this flight. I would have to use my on board rockets to return to Earth and that I had a chance to catch Mother ship number IV. If I would program her flight computer to stay in flight during my rapid climb out of the Earth's atmosphere.

I had made modifications to my primary space suit so that it would look like my school uniform, on command. My skirt extended to form pants then space boots around my shoes, at the same time, my school blazer expanded into the top part of my primary space suit helmet and all. I asked my Principal if it was OK for me to launch a couple of tons of lunar impactors towards the surface of the Moon. He said I could do it as long as I was back before lunchtime. Then I called the Elgin TRACON and requested permission for a vertical climb-out to 100 thousand feet with a western vector.

I started out with Mother four's vertical Lift-Fans, just to start everything moving. I only fire up the center parts of her Aero-Spike Engine, just enough to stay under Mach one, and I went for altitude, as I didn't want to "boom" everybody in the country again. I had to do a lot of climbing turns to get up high enough so not to startle everyone.

I finally got to a point where then I fired up my Aero-Spike Rocket Motors to 100% it would boost me up to orbital speed. I checked with my old friends at the L.A. Center they wanted to know if I was having a problem seeing, as I was only moving at Mach 8. I informed them that everything was A-OK and not to worry I was only in second gear.

I fired my Aero-Spike Rocket Motors again to take me up to the edge of space where I would be able to launch Sabrina No. IX. I had to wait until the last minute to program her flight computer and put her in the proper location to pick me up in a couple of minutes. This was easier than I ever imagined. Not to mention the time I would save by not having to pack up Sabrina No. IX's landing parachute.

I waited until I was well out over the Pacific Ocean. As soon as I was at my required altitude & speed, I pushed the launch button and Mother ship Number IV ejected me into outer space. It's a good thing that I brought Sabrina No. IX's along with me.

The first thing I did was to put Sabrina No. IX into her customary full power dive to attain the speed that I needed to put me on a direct solar orbital flight track towards the Moon. I was only going on a lunar course. I did not have to dive as close to the surface of the Earths as last time. I shot through the Earth's atmosphere and out the other side into outer space. This maneuver allowed me to accelerate to well over 25,000 miles per hour.

I checked my calculations and discovered that I was right where I needed to be. I opened the meteor collection buckets and made one last check. Then I fired one of my retro rockets. This slowed Sabrina No. IX just enough to let all of the cargo that I had loaded into the meteor buckets to moved out in front of me.

I let all the lunar ballistic impactors get a safe distance away before I turned Sabrina IX around. I fired my retro-rockets again to reduce my speed enough to fall back into the Earth's atmosphere. I entered the atmosphere like a shooting star.

Because of all of the variables, I had to calculate everything in my head as it happened. My timing was perfect after a half orbit. I came out of my communications blackout precisely where I wanted to be flying formation with Mother ship No. IV. I checked in with her flight computers and found that everything was fine. Then requested her to open up and take me aboard.

As soon as I took control, set my course back to the school parking lot. I put her down in her usual parking spot just in time to get the last lunch tray in the cafeteria. My primary space suit morphed back into school outfit No.15 as I walked in from the parking lot. Over the next four days I kept track of all my lunar travelers, I didn't have to make many course corrections.

Because all of the Lunar GPS impact sights were dead on, a little too dead on. They all landed right where I told them too. My only problem was they hit directly on all of the historical landing sights, all the standing descent stages of each Lunar Modules, everything from Apollo 11 to 17, I took out all 3 of the parked Lunar Rovers, as well as Apollo 12 & 14's Golf Cart.

They also re-hit all the S-IVB impact locations as well, all the lunar module assent stage impact points. My favorite was a photograph taken looking down the ladder of Apollo 11's "Eagle" descent stage just a micro-second before impact. I turned a whole folder full of pictures into the "X-prize folks" I'm still waiting for the check.

Log Entry #5.
My Command POD:

The Command POD is my home when I am off planet. It houses my Cockpit, Command Computer, homework center & workshop as well as my living quarters and my flight kitchen. I built it as a sphere. I can change its orientation as required for Flight. I also use it to change the center of gravity of my space ship as it uses liquid fuel.

The Command POD also serves as my escape pod which has its own heat shield and atmospheric re-entry & ballistic control system. The Command POD also has its own adjustable tracked landing gear that I use to change its orientation inside the space ship, to keep everything level as I travel over rough ground. It's waterproof, insulated and equipped with a fully functional life support system that can heat as well as cool. I can use it as an emergency shelter on the surface of the Moon, Mars or anywhere on the surface of Earth.

I designed the landing gear to be able to be used to move the Command POD around on the ground for maintenance and re-supply. I plan on driving it into town for shopping trips when I am old enough to get a driver's license. I might have a hard time fitting in into a parking space or getting under a bridge. I have a folding gangway-boarding door that exits from my workshop to ground level. That I use when the Command POD is installed in any of my other operational aircraft or spacecraft.

My Sabrina No. X ships are able to have the whole Command POD extend for egress as I recently discovered that leftover heat from my Heat shield ascends and re-heats the top of my ship to the point where it almost made me late for school. Like my cockpit, my homework center has a full wall sized special shape flat screen that makes it look like I am sitting in the classroom.

I have a 360-degree view so that I can see and communicate with other students as needed. I can even spot paper clips on the floor. My only problem is the communications time lag. The greater the distance between my Command POD and the Earth, the longer the lag time.

When I am on the other side of the Sun my signal won't reach Earth at all. It's nice to know that the internet works anywhere in space. However, it does get a little inconsistent close to the surface of the Sun. It even works on Mars as long as I have a direct line of sight with the Earth. My only problem is the time delay.

My workshop has to be small my main tool is an instant prototype machine that I use to make spare parts. I built the living quarters and the flight kitchen to be usable under one "G".

I can change my ships movement to create a one "G" environment or more. So that I can get good night's sleep in my bed without worrying about waking up floating around in Zero "G". I have also modified them in size to accommodate any of my Whale Astronauts.

Log Entry #6.
First Time I saved the Earth:

If your wonder why you have to go to work today, it's all my fault. As you remember last week, everybody got the word that the world would end at noon Sunday when an asteroid would hit the Earth and make a very large crater where the city of Chicago is now located. It's lucky for you that I am the only 10th grader that had an operational space ship.

I am also the only 10th grade student that has her own fleet of space ships. They let us out of school early, all the emergency sirens were screaming, all the radio stations started with the same "seek shelter warnings" as soon as I got home I turned on my computer to find out the bad news. A large asteroid was detected coming from around the Sun heading directly towards a verified impact on Earth.

To make matters worse the primary impact point was Chicago less than 20 miles from my back door. The impact was supposed to happen in less than 80 hours. This news was very bad as I had lots of homework due at school during that time period.

The first reports had its size rated as an Earth Leveling Event 5 miles high, 8 miles wide, and 10 miles long. It had traveled very close to the Sun and was burned black in color. This also makes matters worse as a black on black object is very hard to see. I had played "Killer Asteroids" on my computer and won but, not against anything that large.

I decided that I was going to stop this real life space monster myself. As nobody knows what we were dealing with. N.A.S.A. had hit it with several of their Heavy Metal Impactors, all without any effect. Then all the Major

World Powers that had them, Nuked it several times, over and over again, all without any effect.

The Air Force flew a whole squadron of their brand new LA-1s to line of sight points all over the world and fired their lasers until every aircraft was out of its "joy juice" all with no effect. Then it looked like everybody on the whole planet Earth was just standing still like a deer staring into oncoming headlights, the world was just waiting for the impact. The one thing everybody did know was that Chicago was going to be ground zero for the BIG Impact.

This made the worst case of gridlock possible. I checked back with the school only to hear the recording that said, my school was closed pending the destruction of the Earth. This seemed to open up my time schedules, now I had time to save the planet myself.

So far, I had gotten nothing but conflicting information. So with both of my parents' permission I decided to fix this unearthly problem myself. I came up with several plans of my own. I had the automated loading computer now hard at work out fitting Sabrina No. IX with all the equipment needed to launch and tame this "Space Monster".

I had just finished building my first series of PAM rocket engines that I had planned to use to capture asteroids. I had them all quickly loaded into Sabrina IX's cargo holds, as well as plenty of extra cable connectors. There was so much information coming and going that I finally decided at 75 hours to impact that I would launch off Earth and find out for myself.

This time I had Mother ship No. 4 pick me up in the backyard. As I climbed aboard Sabrina No. IX, I got a real shock when it noticed that my automatic food loading system had stocked me up food wise with lots of extra-large bags of M&M's. I didn't have time to change anything I figured, what's the problem with bring along a few extra bags, so I started my launch sequence.

I activated my primary space suit and went to work. I launched off the Earth solo to find out what was going on. Plan "A" would be a reconnaissance flight to see for myself what was happening. Plan "B" called for lots of Steel Cable and PAM rocket motors that I will be used to change the Space Monsters trajectory, as to not hit the Earth.

According to my navigation computer, the only way to intercept this VERY LARGE ASTEROID was to do a gravity assist off the Moon. The Elgin TRACON was so busy directing evacuation flights that they hardly noticed Mother ship Number IV's, arrival much less her vertical launch and climb out.

I made contact and requested my usual vector, and went to full power. I reprogrammed the flight computer for a trip to the Moon. Then had Mother four drop me off at the proper coordinates, due to all the extra equipment loaded on board it took longer than planned. The power dive was normal and just like that I was finally on my way to the "Space Monster" with less than 70 hours until impact.

I had always planned to go to the Moon I had already sent a load of Lunar Impactors & Mobile Camera RCVs' to it surface. I couldn't get past the fuel problem. This would not affect me on this trip, as I did not plan to stop.

The Moon is not the best choice for a gravity boost, but it was the only ride that was going my way. I re-oriented my Command POD and started my station, keeping rotation. I had to trade lots of fuel for speed it took me 4 hours to make it to the Moons Orbit then with the speed assist from the Moon, then another hour to intercept the "Space Monster".

I settled down and checked the internet. I started to make plans, my first good news was that my "Mother ship number IV" had made it safely to my base in Texas, and was being turned around by base automation for its next use.

I was getting hungry and decided to check out the galley for something to eat, only to discover that M&M's were the only thing to eat in my galley, the food systems had even frozen a large supply for future use. I re-checked its program to discover why M&M's, are so abundant. Only to find a reference to the movie "Mission to Mars".

Then I noticed some good news, one-half of the on board food supply was made up of peanut M&M's with the other half plain M&M's. If I failed this space mission at least I wouldn't starve to death.

As I watched the destruction of human civilization from a front row seat. I was traveling under one "G", I kept monitoring the communication net for more information. I had timed my trajectory angle to the point where I used the gravity of the Moon to sling shot me in the direction of the Intruder.

After 5 hours of gravity my flight computer stopped my ships rotation and started scanning with Sabrina No. IX's external cameras. As soon as my onboard system started to detect objects, then lots of objects! Then millions of objects! I finally found out what my space monster was made of, the news was not good.

The Space Monster was a gravel pile it was held together by micro gravity only. With all the smaller, want-to-be-me asteroids trying to rotate around themselves, a mass of meteors all trying to find a bigger meteor to combine with. They all seemed to be following a large iron meteor that I named the LEADER at first sight I noticed that "She" was potato shaped 10 miles long, 10 miles wide and eight miles high.

This asteroid was spinning on all three of its axis, and acting like the flipper arms in a giant pinball machine hitting all of the smaller meteors back into the swarm. I also discovered that things were bad, as the Human World Powers that had Nuclear Weapons had wasted lots of them trying to destroy this Intruder.

They turned a large single asteroid into millions of smaller Meteors all trying to go to Chicago. I could see large empty spots where the Nukes had gone off, this made it worse, as now gravity was pulling all the very small radioactive sand and dust size fragments back into the swarming micro gravity field.

This was very bad news; as I was not dealing with a single problem that was now due to take out Chicago in less than 64 hours. Now I have millions of meteors that would leave millions of city block size craters all across the surface of the Earth led by the LEADER who will make the largest meteorite strike since the arrival of the Dinosaur Killer.

I decided to tame the largest asteroid that was left. I officially designated her "The Leader" as its gravity field was pulling all the scattered pieces towards it surface. I had to land on the LEADER to install my control system.

So at 60 hours until impact I fired the first Docking Harpoon into The Leader's surface. I let the cable play out until in made several rotations. It didn't take long to wrap up the LEADER in cables, after letting out more than 500 miles of cables.

I locked the spindle and let the LEADER pull me down to its surface. I aimed for a hard spot that had several layers of the cables intercepted each other. This was the first time I got to play Super-Girl, in its micro gravity field I could fly. After reprograming my space suit to space walking mode I made my exit through the cargo bay.

I discovered that I could all the large rocket motors with ease. It took less than an hour to set everything up and get it operational. I did have a problem following all the control cables back to my Command POD on board Sabrina No. IX.

I could fly and lift like Super-Girl but I sure didn't have any of her super vision. I had a hard time following the wires back to my Command POD, I turned on all the systems then fed all the data into the flight computer, on my command the LEADER instantly stopped its spinning and the system stood ready for me to move the LEADER where ever I wanted it to go.

As soon as I took control of her I tried to play "Pied Piper" only to lose the rest of the swarm, I figured that would never do as the "Swarm" had lots more mass that the LEADER. My maneuver proved a little troublesome I decided to use the LEADER as a magnet to attract as much of the swarm as I could. It took most of my fuel supply to slow him down so that the rest of the meteor swarm would catch up.

I planned for all the swarm to impact the back side of the LEADER, as it turn out the entire swarm went in to orbit around the LEADER, this caused the swarm to go crazy billions of different orbital tracks all trying to come to a stop on the surface of the LEADER. My first warning came when the PAM unit on the backside of the LEADER stopped working.

Then everything blacked-out, it was the first time that I had to go to back-up emergency Power. It took more than an hour for me to get the fuel cells back on line and to find out that most of my cameras were working. My only problem was that they were buried in Micro-Meteors.

The maintenance program also had lots of problems as there were thousands of various size holes in my pressure hull. All the liquid in my entire Space ship was now gone, this meant there wasn't any radiation shielding, or control over the LEADER with everything was still heading towards Chicago.

So there I was buried alive on an asteroid that was still on its way to Chicago, the good news was that I still had plenty of M&M's to eat. Chicago was still getting closer so I had to get back to work. I was out of water, this left plenty of empty space inside what was left of Sabrina No. IX.

I disconnected the Command POD and extended its landing gear then drove to the interior of the ship where the engine room used to be.

I disconnected the Aero-Spike engine from the back panel, laid it on the deck. I had to determine what direction was up. To do this I took off one of my tennis shoes and held it up by its laces, then I turn the engine to fire away from the LEADER's center of mass. I set the controls for a full throttle blast as I had to give the newly covered surface of the LEADER its very first crater.

I moved the Command POD back to its flight position and close to as many internal blast doors as I could. Then I fired the engine, it took me an hour to clear a way back to where I had repositioned the Aero-Spike engine. The view was great this was the first time I had actually taken the time to just look outside when I was in outer space.

I morph my space suit into operation, ballistic control system and all. I extend my emergency shelter from the Command PODs lower ramp door, set up my antenna array and got back to work. It seems that the Atomic Oxygen cloud that was released when my Pressure Hull was breached had settled back to the surface and it had frozen all the various size meteors into a single unit for miles. Now that I had opened my emergency supplies, I checked for anything eatable only to discover more M&M's.

I checked to see if my last maneuver had brought Chicago anymore time, as I had done nothing to divert the LEADER' s mass. Now that I was back in business, I called up my Base Control and had all my Space worthy Mother ships loaded with water and readied for a direct flight to me as, Chicago was still getting closer. This was my first emergency non-crewed launch of all my mother ships,

I had a plan. To make it work I needed every drop of water that I could get. I sent all the proper commands to reconfigure all the mother ships. To dump all the jet engines, install Aero-Spikes all around, and fuel them with extra fuel as well as water. I lucked out as both of my parents and a large number of their friends had shown up and served as my Mother ships ground crew, so in record time all four of my heavy lifters were made ready to launch.

It must have been quite a sight to see four Aero-spikes all firing at full power all under my control at the same time this was the first time that I had flown formation with myself.

I set the trajectories and shutdown all of the engines, as soon as they all cleared Earth's gravity field. Then I sat back and waited until they got to me. I spent the time cataloging meteors and eating M&M's.

I managed to fill a few boxes full of smaller meteors as well. I packed up the Command POD and drove it out of its first crater so I can take a look around, all this time the countdown clock had been running down. I found out that all the swarm had caught up with the LEADER. I checked the trajectory twice despite all the pain and anguish I had only managed to move the LEADER's touch down point to, You Got It! All the way to downtown Bensenville. This goes to show you what an aviatrix will do to keep out of downtown Bensenville.

Everything was very dusty I figured the only chance I had was to get all four, of my mother ships up to me with all the water they could haul. By that time, I had figured out where I want them I programmed all four of them to nudge themselves as slow as possible into the surface of the newly reformed LEADER. All two- miles away from my location on the dark side of the LEADER, 90 degrees apart from each other.

I used my location as the center they all impacted as directed, and then released their water supply in to the surface mix. I set e-mails to the Air Force letting them know that I had everything under control. I gave them the orbital track, and requested a cease-fire, as I did not want to have to add dodging laser hits to my navigation problems. I had to wait until everything passed close to high Earth orbit,

I used the dark of the Earth, and this gave lots of time for all the released water to freeze the LEADER together. The change of direction burn went off well, there was a little spillage that traveled on and made a spectacular meteor show over Chicago, all without making a single meteorite strike.

Due to all the changes in its center of gravity & mass I had to move the Earth's second Moon into its first parking orbit without the aid of a computer, you could say that I was flying it by the seat of my pants.

I had to correct for all the variables as they happen. Later as I was driving around on the surface of Earths newly formed second Moon, I got lucky and found pieces of one of my PAM Rocket Motors. I had to work on it for a time I eventually was able to use it to launch myself back to Earth.

I had enough fuel to slow may decent to the point where it hardly burned my heat shield. Its hit me all of a sudden despite everything I was the now the first 10th grader to capture her own Moon. Not to mention saving the City of Chicago, and kept the whole planet Earth from being punished harder than Shumaker/Levy 9 did Jupiter.

Before I left, I carved out a sign large enough to see from the surface of the Earth, it was cut into several miles of the LEADER's surface it read:

"Meteors for Sale"

Some toasted,

Some frozen,

None radioactive,

Various sizes,

Will deliver call:

Sabrina Aviation

Ask for the Asteroid Farmer. Me!

I landed a mile or so out of town, as the Command POD's parachute landing system is not as flyable as I would like it to be. I shut down my last serving PAM motor and saved its fuel system. I had lost a lot of equipment including my "Sabrina No. IX" I don't think that there was enough of her left to salvage.

Not to mention being buried under several miles of the still shifting surface of my newly formed Moon II. As I was driving my Command POD back Home I stopped at the first open restaurant and had my first balanced meal since my emergency launch several days ago.

I had the four course dinner that came with a dessert you guessed it, Ice cream with M&M's. As soon as I got home my parents wanted to know what I had been up to. So I told the nothing much just saving the planet!

Log Entry #7.
Meteor Mining:

The first thing I had to do was to get Sabrina No. X operational. I designed her to turn inside out to protect the heat shields from being perforated by the thousands of drifting meteors that were still roaming around the LEADER, this way it could load lots of meteors at the same time. I also made the POD's emergency shelter longer and wider.

This also puts the heat shields out of the away from my Command POD when it is in its landing mode. My plan is to use it as a temporary sorting station for loading and cataloging meteors for scientific study. I also built in a vertical take-off & system. On the ground, in the open position, the POD was moved to the front and out of the way.

The lower gangway would point towards the stern making a relatively safe work area that I could use to load meteors directly into travel containers. It only took about an hour to build my first He/3 saving device, the first thing that I did to every meteor was to extract all the helium three that it may have captured during its life in outer space.

In time things settled down on the surface of my Moon I had to start building Sabrina No. X space ships as fast as I could. Tides caused by the Earth, Sun and the Earth's original Moon helped the process. The end result was a round smooth surfaced sphere that was about 15 miles wide.

That wasn't bad for my first try, as luck would have it most of the microscopic radioactive fallout caused by all of the nuclear detonations managed to fall harmlessly into the Earth's Atmosphere and burned up as micro-meteorites just as I made low Earth Orbit.

The last of the radioactive fallout managed to spill out the top, as the thrust from all of my Retro-Rockets managed to move the LEADER just enough to make Low Earth Orbit. So far, I have not found any leftover nuclear warheads that might have gotten caught up in the LEADER'S gravity well.

Who wants to be known, as the only 10th grader that has her personal Nuclear weapon, even if it is a dud? If I do find any, I plan to launch them into the Sun, after all, who would want a roasted, frozen, dented and very perforated nuclear bomb lying around her hanger.

I did find all of N.A.S.A.'s impactors, I asked them if they wanted them returned and they refused. It took a few flights but I finally got it down to a science using a remote control system, first I would launch one of my new Sabrina No. X Meteor Farmers off the Earth from my base in Texas.

It flies directly to my newest Moon and docks itself into one of the four stranded Mother Ships on its surface. Then it transfers fuel and water into each of my stranded mother ships depleted systems. As soon as they get enough water and fuel moved up to make them all operational, each mother ship would go into station keeping mode to wait for their next mission. The thought of using any of my mother ships in outer space never occurred to me.

That's the reason that none of them has ever had a heat shield. I couldn't be able to return any of them to Earth until I had invented my Sabrina No. 39 series space ships. The Sabrina No. X Space ship would then move over to the other side of the LEADER to pick up a load of meteors. Where it would open up, turn itself inside out, and then close back. This process would scoop up and fill all of the internal hoppers.

After an internal check for anything radioactive, as well as a weight and balance check, the Sabrina No. X ship would launch herself back to Earth and fly to my Space base in Texas where it would use aerodynamic drag to slow the meteor loaded space ship for landing. It would then use the largest Ram-Air Parachute on the planet Earth, to make a controlled landing at my base in Texas where it can be unloaded then refueled and used again.

I finally got the whole flight operation to a point where it would be under computer control, as I had to get back to school. I finally realized that I need to do something different, as it would take hundreds of Sabrina No. X space ships hundreds, of years to recover all the meteors that I had to move.

Log Entry #8.
Space Elevators:

I thought about all the options and decided to go into the elevator business. Therefore, I decided to make my first Space Elevator from the top down. So I built the first automated factory to build all the structures that I would need to make the elevator work on the surface of the LEADER. It wasn't that hard to design and build Elevator Shaft Components. Then with everything aboard, I moved the LEADER 33,000 miles out to its geosynchronous orbit location directly above my base in Texas.

It took a while to build a 32,999 miles 5,279 foot tower all the way down to Texas. Everything got containerized as I started to haul equipment up and meteors down in a continuous train of elevator cars. It seems that everybody on Earth wanted to have a pet meteor. As the LEADER got consumed back to its original ten mile long potato shape. I hollowed it out with tunnel boring machines and made it into the system's largest warehouse that could change its mission by replacing its internal modules.

I open the first "Zero G' hospital, all the patient has to do is survive the 33,000 mile elevator trip. I also set up my first He/3 extractor to capture this energy source. Whenever they want He/3 I will have tons of it for sale.

It took a while to recover all the pieces of Sabrina IX along with the rest of her PAM rocket motors. It took even longer to weld her back together and patch all her holes. I had her original Command POD brought up from Earth.

After converting my Mother Ships into Space tugs I launched them back out into Outer Space to grab, several meteors and asteroids that were close by, just to make room for all the work crews.

I decided to keep several tamed large iron meteors on station where I could use them to destroy any of the other millions of rogue asteroids that could destroy Earth. I took several of the larger iron meteors to use for my Lunar Space Elevators I figured that I would have to start out with five operational shafts just to handle the volume.

Take a large metal meteor add a couple of Aero-Spike Rocket motors installed on each end and a ballistic control system and I was ready to colonize the Earth's Moon with space elevators.

Before I could build on it I had to clean up its orbital tracks, the worse problems were the leftovers in orbit, locating and tracking the Eagle and part of Snoopy was not a problem, however catching them without making a major space-junk problem around the moon.

I started out with three separate elevator operations, one on the back side with an up orbit as well as a down orbit sight. My plan was for all of my Human Colonies to first get settled at my Rocket Base in Texas at the foot of the Earth Space Elevator.

Then when they were self-sufficient I would move them up the elevator through the LEADER. Then on to a large Asteroid Ark Ship send them off to the Moon. To a pre-made location structure under the Lunar surface near the base of one of my lunar space elevator shafts that were ready for new arrivals.

Each Asteroid Ark Ship is a one of a kind structure I gave each one its own model number. The ship that I decided to use to move my first "Space City One" was my Ninth Asteroid Ark Ship.

She is a potato shaped Iron Asteroid that three miles wide, two miles high and five miles long at this time she was the largest Asteroid Ark Ship that I had, I only made one hole in her, where the docking hatch was located this was to make it pressurize to 15 P.S.I.

This enables me to match the Earth's sea level pressure wise; I had an internal rotating section to transport Plants & Animals that need gravity to survive. I also build in rotating rest rooms that were equipped with regular gravity operated toilets & showers so as to not make life hard on all the Green Horn Space Colonist.

Log Entry #9.
Study Hall:

As soon as everything got ironed out operationally, my parents decided that I needed to get back to school. I had to admit that having other human students around me really felt good after my adventures in outer space.

I was working at my laptop during study hall when my incoming alert went off there was a truck size," fan blade shaped" meteor on its way to impact somewhere close to St. Louis, just west of the Mississippi River. I could tell from Sabrina No. X's telemetry that it was really a nasty one.

I diverted one of my new Sabrina No. X's who was on the current Meteor Farming Mission, to intercept and capture it. Because I was on Earth in school she was free to pull all the "G"s' needed to capture it in a couple of minutes. Mr. Jenkins, my study hall teacher, came over to see what I was doing.

He asked me, "How come you don't have anything better to do than playing video games in my study Hall?" I told him that I was not playing a computer game and informed him that, "this is not a video game this is happening now in real time in outer space".

The radar dish on my destroyed Sabrina No. IX space ship is still running under miles of meteors that are stuck to the surface of the new Moon that I had left parked in low Earth orbit last week. My ships warning system had picked up this meteor on its way to strike within the city limits St. Louis, Missouri.

He said, "Yea, sure you can park it in my parking spot", find something better to do in my study hall!" I put in a few commands and changed my laptop to another subject.

The next morning guess what Mr. Jenkins found in his parking spot. One fan blade shaped 11,000 pound meteor, courtesy of Sabrina Aviation.

Needless to say, it was a nasty one that would have broken up during its entry into the Earth's atmosphere and would definitely have caused more than one house size crater to be blasted out of the ground, in several different locations inside the City Limits of St. Louis, Missouri.

Log Entry #10.
Was to do the same on Mars:

When I was still in elementary school I met up with the various Mars Societies that were having a convention in Chicago at the same time. The National Space Society as well as the Mars Society and their Martian City design team; whose job was to design the first city that was to be built on the surface of Mars.

They were having a fun time with various different schools that were trying to come up with a Martian surface type city design. I got a last minute invitation to meet the head Martian at the River Rose Restaurant in Des Plaines, the dinner was an evening meal set in the restaurant's southern dining room. As everybody was ordering for themselves the meal time discussion was obviously Martian City's.

I had seen all the entries and none of them had made any since as they all had the distinct lack of a space ships or landing pads. My friend Dennis had started out the discussion by asking the official expert what generation of Martians had built the Martian City in their official design as their design had a distant lack of a space port or for that matter any surface roads of any kind.

I jumped into the conservation to suggest that there must have had to be a large section of EAA members living in their city as there was not an airport as the aircraft owner were dismantling their flying stock and taking it home with them.

It seems that none of the experts had discovered that it was impossible for humans to live on the surface of Mars. First off the local weather would continually bury the city and then dig it up long before its population had time to die from radiation poisoning.

Dennison's next suggestion was even better when he asked the Martian expert, what he would sell the landing rights to me for. As I was asking him about the construction of his landing pad, he pulled out a ball point ink pen and started to write calculations in the restaurants table cloth, just like he was Howard Hughes drawing his first sketch of his Constellation Airliner.

I could tell from his math symbols that this was the first time that he had decided to figure out the amount of dynamic thrust as well as the amount of fuel burn that would be needed to make a soft ballistic landing on the surface of Mars.

It was easy to figure that he had never considered a soft landing before as his calculation was missing several different math symbols, so I started to help him out, every time he ran into a calculation problems that stopped him, I furnished him with the correct answer to keep him working.

What shocked him the most was that I figured out what he was trying to tell me and helped him with his own calculation? It goes without saying that we both ran out of table cloth before we made a soft ballistic landing.

As everybody was leaving I left a large tip and I purchased the table cloth from the owner. I still consider it to be one of my prize possessions. I realized that the only way that the Martian Cities expert was going to get to the surface of the Planet Mars was for me to sell him a ticket.

Then he will find me waiting for him with a leasing agreement. As it turned out it was Pinger-5 who made the rental agreement with him not me.

It took a convoy of 15 different Asteroid Ark Ships to move my space elevator operation to the planet Mars. I would use the manufacturing factory on the LEADER to build all the main shaft pipes then transport them to Mars on my asteroid Ark Ships, which were slower moving. But, more or less self-contained.

I also had the option to re-supply them with my smaller fast moving Sabrina No.10 ships along the way. For that matter, I also launch individual pipes on direct slow trajectories all by themselves, only equipped with beacons. Of course these had to be intercepted and captured before they impacted the surface of Mars.

For Mars it was simple, as the planet already had two Moons that were not being used for anything. So I tamed both Phobos and what was left of Deimos. I moved Phobos to geosynchronous orbit over one of the warmest locations on Mars surface to become the main Anchor site for the Martians Space Elevator.

I first used Deimos as large impactors to protect Mars from asteroid hits. Space elevator wise it was a lot easier than doing Earth because of Mar's lower mass. The space elevator shaft only had to be 11,000 miles long.

Because of all the extreme cold, radiation, and high speed surface winds, I discovered that it's impossible to live on the surface of Mars, that's why I started to dig and make plans to build whole movable cities under the surface of Mars.

My plan is to first set up a space colony here on Earth then fill in all the jobs needed and let it age for a while until it gets to the point where it's self-sufficient each space colony had to have everything a small town on Earth would have Doctors, Lawyers, (I can't forget my dad) Indian chiefs and all.

I even have several different food courts installed throughout each "Space-Colony", so that anybody can get any kind of food, they want to eat. Then I would run the whole kit and caboodle up through the Earth space elevator, at the same time, I empty out the insides of one of my Asteroid Ark Ships, and then I would exchange their modular cars.

When everything is loaded aboard my Asteroid Ark Ship, I fire up the Aero-spikes and move it all out to Mars or the Moon. Depending on the mission, the Moon takes about a week. Mars takes a lot longer as I can't make the cargo ships pull a lot of "G's".

At any given time I have several different Ships traveling towards as well as returning to the Earth, of course travel time varies as to the location of the planets. When each Asteroid Ark Ship finally gets to their Space Elevator, I run everything down to the pre-built under the surface living sites.

Because of their design, the entire city can be moved to other locations as needed. At the same time I was also looking at using the planets Mercury and Venus as a base of operation. Mercury doesn't have an atmosphere but, due to its location near the Sun, humans can't live on it as we would have to live in it under its surface.

To do this all I needed to do was install a docking hatch and turn the tunnel boring machine loose. The planet Venus was a another problem as my space elevator shafts tended to dissolve in the atmosphere before I could get it all the way down to the planet's surface. So for now I am only going to use it as a parking orbit for my captured Asteroid collection of Earth crossers.

Log Entry #11.
Spirit & Opportunity:

I took my time I did everything from the top down I took all my profits for my pet meteor sales and used it to finance my ultimate operation to Mars. The first thing I did after putting the space elevator down on the surface of Mars was to start digging.

I built a series of underground structures then set up my underground "Space-city's" all made up of elevator cars, fitted together as a container ship type structure with intersecting bulkheads the usual Quad-Triple-X City Grid.

I also sent out Surface Exploration Vehicles, as it turns out the surface of Mars is not a nice place to visit, it's full of lots of natural barriers, very rough terrain full of billions of pet rocks, unlike the Earth, erosion is a major thing on Mars. If a person would just sit and watch, they would be impressed to see the landscape change all by itself.

It took several missions but, my Surface Exploration Units eventfully recovered Spirit and Opportunity, it seems that they had learned how to hunker down in sandstorms and to stay turned into the surface winds to keep dust off their solar panels.

They both were recovered with a lot of other equipment that had been abandoned on the surface of Mars, and hauled back to my base at the bottom of the space elevator.

When I first saw them, they were in pitiful shape I could tell that they had drowned in darkness their controlling computer had been fighting for that last bit of energy right up to the end, they both had so much internal dust that I had to activate my space suit just to be near them.

I worked on Spirit first, it only took a couple of minutes to wire in one of my smaller He/3 reactors into her electoral system, most of her computers programs were re-written to work around the problems caused by her stuck wheel.

As soon as Spirits systems came on line the first thing she did was hold up her stuck wheel, like a living animal with a thorn in her, paw.

I easily dislodged the funny shaped rock that was stuck inside her wheel in less than a second and from that point in time Spirit was like a puppy following me everywhere I went.

I couldn't help myself! I installed one of my Command Computers to her main frame to enable her to think as well as communicate for herself, Spirit followed me into the room where Opportunity was and watched as I reactivated and set her up with her own Command Computer.

It was touching to watch her reactions as I repaired her long lost sister, the first thing they did was analyze each other. As I recall that was the first time, they had been close enough to each other to scan.

As soon as their new command programs started up they both reported in with all the data that had happened since first being turned on time, temperature, air pressure, they both even told me about their launch from the surface of the Earth as well as why they ran each of their rocket motors to make it all the way to the planet Mars.

It's interesting to note that they even had a step-by-step list of how they got to the surface of Mars. Spirit as well as Opportunity followed me around and treated me as if I were their Mother. You would not believe what happened when they discovered the water fountain in the hallway.

They both got me out of bed in the middle of the night to inform me that they had found water on Mars. I politely asked them if they would mind monitoring all the surface traffic in and out of the first exit door on Mars. Eventually both of them spent almost a year mapping the asteroid belt and supplying me with most of the data I needed to plan my first Jupiter Mission to Titan.

Lately, they have shown up to help pilot space ships as needed at airshows, at times, their ability to instantly take over other computers has really came in handy.

At disaster sites, I have noticed that they were working all the remote control vehicles and all other rescue equipment that has a computer in it at the same time.

I also noticed that they were working as a team last year when I noticed Opportunity holding down an un-cooperative government official while at the same time Spirit was using her built in rock carver to trim both of his eyebrows at the same time.

Last week I looked up after taking a written test at school and there they were going down the hall way checking out the water fountains, they both waved at the same instant. After I repaired and up graded both to an operational status, I relocated them to serve as guard dogs at the elevator landing pad number one site. Which was my first movable operational landing pad on the surface of Mars?

Log Entry #12.
Asteroid Farming is Habit Forming:

Asteroid farming is habit forming. I love to go out into the asteroid belt where I located and capture asteroids for my own collection. When I am in its micro gravity I can fly like Super-Girl, I can unload and move around large and heavy rocket motors with my suited hands.

I now have hundreds of Asteroids parked in geosynchronous orbit protecting not only the Earth but Mars and Venus as well. Waiting to be transformed to a colony ship or impactors, I usually don't leave the rocket engines onboard.

However, I do keep 4 of them orbiting at 90 degree intervals just in case, it's a never ending job as even a small car or bus size meteor can cause unbelievable damage when it impacts something. I can also use my capture systems on comets but, it's not as easy they are usually coming from a different direction, and due to their constant outgassing I have to keep reprogramming their flight computer.

Due to surface conditions caused by all the Want-to-Bee meteors trying to find something bigger to land on, my crews had to work from underground up. The most difficult problem was getting rid of all the dugout asteroids are their bedrock.

The solution was simple all we had to do was haul it all back to the Martian Space Elevator or transport it all the way back to the LEADER where it can be melted down then turn into useful equipment. At first we tried to use it as fill too, smooth out the surface of Phobos but, we had a large spillage problem.

Spirit and Opportunity also used their piloting skills to help me find suitable asteroids to convert to space ships as I can tell you for a fact that all Asteroids are not the same. It takes a lot of very hard work to convert a useless chunk of iron to a functioning Space Ark.

A whole lot of this work has to be done when docked to the top of a space elevator. It took a while but eventfully I had a landing pad sticking out of the surface of Mars.

Log Entry #13.
Rough Weekend on Mars:

My first landing pad on the surface of Mars was a larger one, about a mile away from the main touch down point of my first Mars Space Elevator. When we get around to writing the history books, the honor of making the first human, footprints on the surface of Mars turned out to be one of my blind technicians by the name of Bill Becker.

As the official report reads, he was working outside putting the finishing touches on the landing light system, on my Landing Pad No.1 when he was blown overboard by a sudden increase in surface wind speed. So when he landed Bill got to make the first set of human footprints on the surface of Mars.

The wind speed was so high that all of his foot prints were blown away before anybody got a chance to take any pictures. My Martian Surface Exploration Units managed to recover him before he was buried too deep by the drifting Martian sand. I still plan to make the first round trip with my Sabrina No. IX space ship as soon as Landing Pad Number One becomes operational.

It took a lot of digging, but now it's finally time to land the first space ship, this would be the first landing and launch of the same space ship off the surface of Mars. As luck would have it, I had kept the remains of my Sabrina IX nearby and I have spent most of my time restoring her flight and landing systems.

The parachute landing system was a real pain due to having to change its design to work in the very thin and sandy Atmosphere of Mars. I activated her fuel cells, turned on her flight computer, made sure that there were M&M's on aboard, and topped off her water and fuel tanks.

Then with the permission of my Phobos control center I launched myself off its surface. It felt good to power up my primary space suit again I knew from the start that it's going to be a lot better than a 11,000 mile elevator ride. I flew out about a 100 miles to get away from the elevator shaft.

Then I fired my main Aero-Spike Rocket-Motor as a retro rocket. I though this flight was going to be a milk run as it turned out it was the kind of trip that would make you stop drinking milk for the rest of your life.

The Space Elevator was not a single shaft but a grouping of five shafts, two going up, two going down with a passing shaft going each way as well as a center safety shaft that connect to all the other four.

I had installed weather sensors and GPS transmitters all the way down to the surface, all the winds aloft that I discover several enormous cyclonic storms, as well as the occasional meteor shower.

The first thing my flight computer told me was that I did not have enough atmospheres below me to land safely, so I flew out to 200 miles from the main shaft. I started to fall in full feather trying to get down to Martian zero velocity without much luck, all I could see on my monitor screens was the fire and flames coming off my hull, then the anti-collision program of my Traffic Collision Avoidance system, warned me about lots of moving objects closing in from my left side.

I instantly became aware of millions of meteors, in a swarm well over a hundred miles across, all, moving lots faster than Mars escape velocity. My only chance was to out run them so I put the POD on automatic and retracted all my Aerodynamic controls, unfettered and turned hard to the right.

Then I fired my Aero-Spike rocket motor at full power my command PODs full rotating feature saved my skin as Sabrina No. IX & I had to pull around 50 "G"s to make the high-speed turn, this made it child play for me to start flying formation with the incoming Meteor storm.

I contacted Phobos control to inform them about the Meteor Storm I checked the storms direction and noted that it was not a threat to my Space Elevator. It was still child's play to dodge all the large chunks of space rocks, coming up my stern most of which were as big as city blocks, then came lots more meteors the size of houses, and then the size kept getting smaller.

I had lots of trouble with the millions of sand and dust size Micro-Meteors as they punched their way through Sabrina No. IX it was like being hit by an extremely large shotgun blast. The liquid layers of my space ship took all the pressure of the hit this saved my life as the Command POD was on the other end of the ship.

When I came out the other end of the meteor storm the only thing I had left was my Command POD. I don't even have to aim the escape door towards the surface of Mars to eject. So there I was doing a sub-orbital ballistic arch moving away from my space elevator shaft with the only thing left, my Command POD.

I had designed this capability into the Command POD as now I was using it to save my life, as I am now the first person to bail out over Mars. I still had operational power and most of the command POD's exterior cameras had survived Sabrina No. IX stoning. I had more than enough operational cameras to navigate with.

I used the mass of the command POD to steer. As of now my personal survival depends on landing as close as I could to my Martian Elevators Base. Now the third "G" of Mars and its thin atmosphere were working for me. Like a cannon ball in flight I used the command PODs mass to gently steer me to my final touch down point. Instead of using my ballistic control system for control I use it for propulsion by only firing aft pointing thrusters as needed for space flight.

As I finally entered the Martian lower atmosphere things got really nasty I deployed my pilot chute it only lasted a couple of minutes. This also caused me to pull some very hard "G"s it's a good thing that I always packed a spare drag chutes to keep me out of downtown Bensenville.

Needless to say, the spare chutes saved my life, as it slowed me just enough to be able the deployment of the first stage of my main landing parachute.

In my early years, I would use the meanest roller coaster on Earth to condition my body to be able to shrug off high "G" loads.

This gave me the ability to keep it up, as I couldn't give up not for a second I had to counter every movement, all the way down to the surface of Mars. I finally got to deploy the main landing chutes just as I skimmed the Martian surface I was going pretty good until, I got a corner of my main landing parachute caught on one of Mar's lower mountain ranges my only parachute caught and tore as I finally came to a stop.

The tangled shrouds lines were wrapping around and started to beat what was left of my POD to death. It took all of my strength to work the manual release I wish you could see the look in my face when the rest of my main landing chutes disappeared into the wind.

All of a sudden, the silence was mind blowing my luck was improving, now that I had officially stopped moving on the surface. I figured that I could count it as a landing the first one. It didn't take long for the high winds and the drifting sand to bury me alive, which was OK with me as at this point I could use all the radiation shielding I could get.

Besides, I'm starting to get used to being buried alive. I had a restless day, it took several hours for me to get what was left of the POD settled in. I sent several hours studying the data from my first landing in my built in classroom. Soon it became apparent that the meteor shower had really mess things up on the whole planet.

All of my attempts to communicate were fruitless as my radio antenna was eroded away, as I extended it into the raging sand storm. It felt good to be able to change into my back up space suit, my primary space suit almost whimpered as it folded itself back into its carrier.

Then I started to check out my galley and get into my emergency food supply for something to eat. Sure enough, I found a large pack of M&M's. I crawled into my bunk, and commanded my back up suit to reform into its sleeping bag form, then called it a night. I had a hard time going to sleep as I had always made it a policy to spin up my POD to keep my body at one "G" as I slept.

Early the next morning, as I was still checking out what was left of my POD. I noticed that during the night, the drifting sand had buried me at least a foot deep under the surface. This was good as the Martian sand insulated me from the extreme cold of the Martian night.

As I was studying the data in my flight computer, I discovered that I had come to a stop less than 50 miles from my intended touch down point. It took less than an hour for me to take apart the swivel system in the lower part of my Command POD to be useable as an operation track system.

The current weather conditions (a Force 5 Hurricane Sandstorm) this makes it impossible for me to walk out on my own. So I decided to power up the POD's drive systems. As I remembered the events after my first touch and go Mission to Mars. I was the first girl on Earth to have a jar full of Mars, now I am the first girl on Mars to be trapped inside a jar full of Earth. As soon as it was day light, I had the POD set up its running tracks, as I remembered from my experience driving around on the surface of the LEADER.

I set the running gear for the widest track possible, as my POD stood up on its running gear, the Martian storm instantly raged around me. I used the last of my Liquid Ballistic Control Rocket Fuel to blast away most of the Martian sand making me free to move. I had to keep all my external instruments retracted due to the bad Martian weather this really cut down on their range.

Once I was able to receive the G.P.S. transmitters that I had installed on the outside of the space elevator's shaft. My computer instantly showed me where the rest of Mars was, as well as the direction, distance and my estimated time of arrival to my original touch down point. It took most of the night to drive the last 48 miles to my Martian Space Elevators Location.

Finally the G.P.S. unit indicated that I was there, I looked around and electronically pounded on the door, due to my lack of antenna nothing happened. I could not put out a signal loud enough to ring my own doorbell it looked like nobody was home.

Even Spirit and Opportunity were not in sight as they both seemed to be hunkered down by the severe Martian sandstorm. It took a lot of digging around but I finally found it a single eroded end of a communication plug. I turned what was left of my Command POD into the wind, and then I used my communications necklace's control to power up my back up space suit I ordered triple layer as well as full heat.

I lowered my boarding ramp and walked to the end of it. Where I found the prettiest little communication plug that I had ever seen it was coming out of the landing pads main deck. I plugged into it and called home. The first voice I heard was my Phobos Control Watch-Manger, he wanted to know why I was on the Martian surface, as well as who gave me the authorization?

Why I had not gotten the word that due to the fact that the global Marion weather conditions were the same if not worse. The Watch-Manager had not given permission for anyone to travel on the surface. I asked him if he knew the location of Sabrina No. IX.

He said that he still had only 14 pieces of Sabrina No. IX located, none of which had been investigated due to the weather. At this point in our conservation he ordered me to identify myself and return to the underground base immediately! That's when I informed him that I am the Sabrina of "Sabrina No. IX" at this point

I also informed him that I was in possession of the 15th located part of Sabrina No. IX her command POD. It was currently located on Landing Pad Number One, and that it had been investigated by me despite the poor Martian Weather. I told him that, "I had been pounding on his front door for almost a half an hour and that I was about to leave, it looked like nobody was home! "Instantly the ground went down, and the walls came up, the whole landing pad was moved over to a cargo port, overhead lights came on; the air pressure came up, and hundreds of well-wishers flooded around me. They all had bags of M&M's with them then we got the party started!

First, everything had to be decontaminated as Mars is made of nasty microscopic surface glass that gets into everything it all had to be all cleaned up. The outer hull of my Command POD was a mess, with millions of dents caused by microscopic meteorites. I changed in to my Sunday-Go- to-meeting space suit then put both my primary and back up space suit into recharges.

My short excursion in the Martian sand storm had really beat up my back up space suit, it took several hours to get all the Martian sand & dust out of it. I had to completely reprogram it, to get it to change out of its sleeping bag format.

My E-mail was jammed with messages it seems that my death had been greatly exaggerated. It had taken less than 15 minutes for the whole solar system to learn that I had not made it to my intended touch down point. To make maters worst there was a major news release with the discovery of each section of Sabrina No. IX, as they were found all 14 of them.

I was quickly dubbed the "Youngest Astronaut" worst of all the press even compared me to Amelia Earhart. Although I don't think she was ever was stranded inside of a Command POD on Mars. Of course, no one can ever tell about a person like Amelia. The real kicker was that nobody had tracked my Command PODs movement to the surface of Mars or found any torn panels of my main landing parachute. It seems that the loss of my entire external antenna array stopped all of my transmissions.

There were hours of interviews about what could have happened, as the Meteor Shower was inbound. Three of my Asteroid Ark Ships were detoured to intercept the meteor Storm to see if they could find any of my Command POD still trapped in the meteor swarm that had bounced off the Martian atmosphere going in several different directions. My first outgoing E-mail was to my parents to informing them not to give away any of my stuff, to the Smithsonian as I still had plans to use it.

I called back the three Asteroid Ark Ships that were on course to intercept the Meteor Shower that had chewed up my Sabrina No. IX Space ship. I decided that if anybody was going to salvage Sabrina No. IX it was going to be me. As it turned out the people that were running the Martian base had lots of problems with Surface Exploration Units that wanted to get out on the surface to look for me.

They had just finished recovering all of their broken and partially destroyed surface vehicles that were beat up by the current weather problem as I arrived. I personally thanked all the Surface Exploration Units crew as they had operated all the different types of ground Surface Exploration Units vehicles that they could come up with.

They all stood ready to come to my aid when found. It must have been very frustrating to be ordered to just sit on your hands until the weather breaks. All of their Vehicles designs had been overwhelmed by the storm. They couldn't even get out of sight, of the door they were all outclassed by the planet wide sand storm, being equipped with too small of tracks, some of them even had wheels.

At the next morning staff meeting everybody made a big deal about returning to me everything that was in the lost and found box. As a living person I would need them, everybody in the base made comments about every item in the box as well as to how I could use it, I got stuff back that I had lost years ago.

If you could believe it, the Martian weather had worsened, the surface wind speed went higher and the moving rocks were bigger. I decided to set up a long-range radar system to keep track of the every fly through meteor storm. I set up a tracking system on the backside of Deimos.

Then I moved it into a solar orbit, so that it would shadow the whole planet Mars from incoming meteor showers, traveling towards the Sun, from the Asteroid Belt. So far all the recovered parts of Sabrina No. IX were so beat up that the only thing I could do was to melt them down and start all over again.

It looks like it will take over a year or more before the Martian Weather would start to clear. We dug out more of Mars, the base and Phobos both got bigger. I actually spent time building an Auto-Gyro just to see if I could get it to launch off of my Landing Pad #one.

I spent all of my spare time repairing my Command POD who knows I might be able to use it to pass my driving test once I'm old enough.

Log Entry #14.
Comet Round Up:

If you take a good look at Mars, the first thing you notice is its lack of water. So I started to round up comets, it's not as easy as it sounds; comets are moving faster than meteors, not to mention they come in on an entirely different trajectory.

Structure wise anything goes if I were to use too much force to change its trajectory I could cause it to shatter into hundreds if not thousands of little comets. Then I would have to recover all my PAM engines and wait for it to use its micro-gravity field to bring it all together again, and then start over.

On the good side, a Comet is like a treasure chest once you start taking it apart you can find a lot of other things that got lost in the Solar System. My plan was to fly them into Mars and hope for the best, I would have to park them next to my Space Elevator on Phobos. Where I would have to break them into small pieces and send them down the space elevator shaft a carload at a time just like everything else.

We did come up with lots of water ice, and more "pet rocks", we occasionally come up with a small part of one of the early spacecraft. I'm still trying to identify it but I think that I found some fragments of Apollo 13's exploded oxygen tank.

As well as all kinds of other Apollo artifacts that were lost in space in the 1960's, between the Earth and its Moon. So at the 50th university of space flight I decided to start picking up comets that have past close to Earth during the last 50 years. Comets don't make it in Earth or Lunar orbit, they get messy very fast. So I would dock them to the next asteroid transport that was going to Mars, and make it part of my "Wet Mars" program.

I am also smart enough not to park more than one comet at a time on Phobos. As soon as I can haul enough mass up off Mars I plan to build a brick hanger large enough to house a whole comet, as this is the only way that I can think of to keep the Comet tail from surrounding Mars and making it colder.

Log Entry #15.
Sabrina No. 39:

I now had firsthand experience operating a Sabrina No. IX or Sabrina No. X space craft inside of Mars atmosphere. I decided that it was time for me to come up with something better. As luck would have it the next number up was Sabrina No. 39. Whose first requirement was that she had to fit on landing pad one at the base of my Mars space elevator site-one? I used an Aerodynamic Canard Control System, as it is always easier to lead the bull around by its nose instead of its tail.

As I was saying her first requirement was be able to retract all her airfoils, lift-fans, aerodynamic controls and fold down all of her vertical stabilizers to enable her to fit on landing pad one. Size wise she is three times the size of my standard Mother Ships and for that matter she could carry two fully loaded Mother Ships internally at the same time.

Sabrina No. 39 is my new generation space ship that was design with several different requirements. Her second requirement is to carry a fuel reserve that will allow her to land and take off from the surface of Mars or Earth without having to be re-fueled. Her third requirement is to have an advanced autopilot a command computer that can to everything a human pilot could do only faster. Her fourth requirement was to be able to move a large number of elevator cars on a single mission. Her fifth requirement is to be able to link up with other Sabrina spacecraft to form a larger combined transport or set up on a large asteroid as a mobile base or drilling platform.

I decided to go back to Earth and build a new more powerful space ship that could fly into Mars atmosphere and land without the need of a landing parachute, even during their current weather emergency. My factory on the LEADER that I originally used to make the section for the space elevator I have now converted to building my Sabrina No. 39 series spacecraft, her construction will be a lot easier due to the fact that she will be the first space ship built in "Zero-G". My builder teams and I are able to do the impossible by moving heavy components.

I still remember the time I didn't pass my first A&P test due to my lack of upper arm strength, now in my Zero "G" Space ship Factory I have no need to hold an extremely heavy engine against a motor mount while at the same time single handily tightening all the retaining bolts.

Because everything is in Zero-G considering the fact that I am a girl my lower center of mass enables me to move something while I am in zero "G" without having it move me back. I had planned to use this model Space ship, as my next operational space transport as well as cargo hauler, with the ability to land anywhere.

Due to all of the different operational parameters the outer color of their surface would have to change their outer surface color as needed, as long as the surface scheme could morph into my company color scheme that is Sabrina Aviation Metallic Red and at the same time display all the registration numbers that the FAA requires. To do this I started to build as well as modify what was to become my Urban Camouflage Program.

Log Entry #16.
Automated Favors:

I was working out of my Command POD on the LEADER when I received a request from an old friend at the EAA Museum in Oshkosh Wisconsin. It seems that they had acquired the last SR-71 that N.A.S.A. had and they were looking for somebody to fly it to their location. They wanted a lot of information about my space suit size as well as other information, would I be interested in flying the "Last Bird" over to their museum.

I got on to my desktop computer and got things going I checked out the "Last Bird" in the internet to find out its history. I discovered that she was a left over airframe that was intended to be the official chase plane for the X-30, which never happened. It was equipped with early scramjets that were expected to get her up to around Mach 10. The "Last Bird" had been a Hanger Queen for all of her life even when she was a United States Air Force "Blackbird," my guess is it was the "Main Engineering Bird" and has never seen the light of day much less the dark skis.

I checked several different historical databases and couldn't find a report of any flights. To make matters worse she was covered with a first generation pink heat shield that was designed to keep the airframe from melting at Mach 10. This would make it impossible to repair if I had to dismantle her to move. I called my old friend back and got the job, he gave me a time frame for delivery I even asked him where he wanted me too park it after my arrival.

I looked across the bay and took a good look at my latest project Sabrina No. 39, she was different from my other space ships. She was designed to land and launch from Mars by command computer control. I called number 39's program up on my desktop computer and started to check her out for flight the next thing she did was to morph her outer skin surface to Sabrina Aviation Metallic Red.

I took over her control stick and moved her to the spaceport door under her own power, off the LEADER and out into outer Space. I fired several of her retro-rockets and to start her first 33,000-mile trip down to the surface if the Earth.

I programmed her onboard navigation system to make a vertical landing 20 feet to the West of the "Last Birds" parking space as she was setting on the flight line at Edwards Air Force Base. I also turn on the tracking system that I installed on the Earth side of the LEADER, and started to track everything in real time. As Sabrina No. 39 got closer to civilization, I made all the radio calls for her as if I were sitting in her Pilot Seat. I had to keep her in the landing pattern for a while to cool her off and to make sure she it would be after dark when she made her first landing on the surface of the Earth.

Finally with every body's permission the Command Computer landed her right where I told her too. Next to the "Last Bird" as it was parked in the Edward's Tarmac. I noticed on her exterior surveillance screen that lots of people were closing in from all directions. The Line Chief in his golf cart was the first to arrive, and He noticed that there wasn't an open hatch or flight crew member standing around.

I activated the external communications speaker and said, "Hi I'm here to fly the "Last Bird" to her new home. He must not have been use to talking to 14-year-old girls as He retreated to his golf cart and started to call for help. You would think that the Martians had landed to pick up their prize as it was just after dark and nobody could get a good look at Sabrina No. 39.

All they knew was a large white hot light had made a vertical landing on their flight line and a young girl's voice had told them that she as going to fly their "Last Bird" away. I set up a conference call with everybody concerned.

My EAA friend was a little confused as less than an hour ago he had hired me to fly his "Last Bird" to Oshkosh, now I am now standing next to it pre-fighting it for takeoff. I informed him of my progress, after my claim to the "Last Bird" had been authorized I told everybody to stand back.

I opened Sabrina No. 39's cargo hatch and lowered my self-powered aircraft mover to the ground. Sabrina No. 39s command computer remotely drove it directly under the back of the" Last Bird". I had all the views needed from the camera system to activate the pickup system and lifted her off the ground. She even plugged into her power port and retracted its landing gear, without asking my permission.

The automatic loading system loaded up everything in less than a minute. As the bottom cargo doors were closing, I told the Line Chief to move back as I was leaving. I made all the radio calls to request a vertical takeoff with a clearance to 100,000 feet. For some reason Air Traffic Controllers still have a problem authorizing that request.

As soon as the Line Chief had moved to a safe distance, Sabrina No. 39 made her first vertical takeoff from the surface of the Earth.

The Command Computer flew her to the Last Bird's requested parking spot at Oshkosh, Wisconsin. Because I was still sitting at my laptop computer in my Command POD on the LEADER, Sabrina No. 39's Flight Computer didn't have to worry about my 14 year old female body, she could and did pull over 100 "G" as she maneuvered her way to Oshkosh.

The controller in the Oshkosh tower also got a little excitement out of the deal. They caught on to my time delay as I informed them that I wanted a clearance to land at Pioneer Airport. They had problems authorizing my landing on such a short runway. I informed them that I was making a V.T.O.L. landing and the length of the runway was not a problem.

The auto-land system turned on all of Sabrina No. 39's dorsal floodlights this highlighted the landing zone to make sure it was safe to land. It also created a bright light problem where the only thing a human could see was just a very bright light. My newborn space ship made her second vertical landing in the dark and off loaded her cargo. Moved the" Last Bird" to the location requested by the EAA extended its landing gear, and sat the "Last Bird" down.

I lowered and reloaded the moving dolly, then packed her up again. She completed all her tasks packed herself up for the second time and launched herself back into the air within 3 minutes. The controllers at Oshkosh must be getting used to it, as they authorized a vertical takeoff to 100,000 feet with a vector to the west, without a comment. Sabrina No. 39 launched herself back into space to her original parking space on the LEADER.

So in less than 2 hours my Sabrina No. 39 had left her base on the LEADER flown 33,000 miles to make a vertical landing in the dark at Edwards Air Force Base, where she made her first landing on the surface of the Earth. Then automatically configured, picked up, and loaded aboard a very large and priceless aircraft.

Then she secured it internally to make a vertical takeoff and flew herself to the preprogrammed landing point at Oshkosh. She then made another vertical landing in the dark, gently off loaded her cargo an entire Lockheed SR-71, into the designated parking place, at Oshkosh, Wisconsin in the dark all by herself.

She then packed herself up and launched herself back into outer space, accelerate to a speed of over 18,000 miles per hour locate her hanger on the LEADER then parked herself in her correct parking spot. All I had to do was talk to all the air traffic controllers that she met along the way.

I congratulated all of her construction teams and informed them that Sabrina No.39 had passed her first shake down flight. I informed my staff as well as my parents that I will be returning to Mars. The next morning I received a call from my friend at Oshkosh he wanted to know if I would take on all of his aircraft re-location projects. He wanted to know how I had flown the "Last Bird" without adding any fuel or firing the engine igniters, not to mention without rolling any of her wheels as every wheel on the aircraft was frozen.

He had to jack it up and put three spindle carriers under it, just to move it into his museum. Also, all the controllers wanted to know how I had made a vertical landing with a SR-71, without setting fire to the grass? I told him that I would be delighted to have first chance at any aircraft he wanted moved.

I informed him that all details of the move were on a need to know basis after all a 14-year-old girl has to have some secrets. I had my Sabrina No. 39 to load herself up with several of my new heavy duty armored Mars surface crawlers for the Surface Exploration Units at the base of my Martian Space Elevator to use.

As well as a large supply of my new improved reconnaissance PODs. I asked her Command Computer if she was up for a direct trip to Mars. She answer "Yes," then she asked if I was going along for the trip, I informed her that I would sit this one out and stay here, she was free to use as many high "G" number she wanted to maneuver. My last command was for her to call home when she landed on, Landing Pad One on the surface of Mars.

Conditions on the surface were about the same. The only change was that over time lots of heavy dust had risen into Mars Middle as well as upper atmospheres, the middle atmosphere was still extremely turbulent.

The Command Computer on Sabrina No. 39 had directed her to leave, dive towards the surface of the Earth to gain speed, zoomed out into outer space, to do a power-dive towards the Sun, fly past the Sun to the other side of the Solar System and go directly into Mars Upper Atmosphere.

Due to all the dust in all three layers of the Martian atmosphere, her entry it was dynamic she flew completely around Mars seven times before she had slowed to landing speed. The global sandstorms were improving as only the small rocks were moving on the Martian surface; her heavy-duty heat shields took all the punishment without a whimper.

She made a perfect powered vertical landing on my Landing Pad No.1, all of her retractable lift-fans worked as expected in the thin Martian atmosphere, and then she proceeded to fold and tuck in all of her aerodynamic controls surfaces the last thing she did was to morph her outer skin surface to Sabrina Aviation Metallic Red. Then she sent me a message, asking me "what's next?"

Log Entry #17.
Reconnaissance POD:

The He/3 powered reconnaissance POD is truly a universal vehicle its first requirement is it has to be the same size as the original Command POD. The main difference is has only one living area that will change as needed, for high-speed flight, it can become a cockpit, it re-forms into a galley with a useable small kitchen, the pilots seat folds down and expands to a bed, it even forms into a classroom with a 360-degree view.

I equipped it with caterpillar tracts that can change their orientation as to the different types of terrain that it's traveling over it are also designed to float and travel underwater. That is if we ever find any on Mars. Its running gear retracts and is used to change itself to lessen the effect of high "G" number that happen when maneuvering in a space flight type environment.

It's equipped with attachment points for the use of moving PAM rocket motors around the surface of large asteroids, in emergencies, it can use PAM motors to fly the POD to different locations. Its top folds back from the windshield to make a convertible, and to top it all off it has a complete lighting set that enables it to operate on roads to operate on roads on Earth.

When use with one of my Spacecraft It fills the bill as the perfect flying automobile. As it also comes equipped with a complete set of extendable road wheels as well as caterpillar tracks that with the used to magnet attach themselves to a metal surface. My only problem is waiting until I am old enough to get a driver's license.

Log Entry #18.
Fun with Sabrina No. 39:

After her return to Earth, Sabrina No. 39 became one of my favorite space ships, sense her existence was common knowledge there was no need for secrets.

In fact I had some very interesting cargo moving operation going on, by moving large and heavy items overnight in the matter of a few hours. I even held up the honor of the whole aerospace industry, when a well-known auto drag racer wanted to repeat the challenge that Glen Curtiss lost in 1912.

When he lost the race of the century with the fastest race car of his era, while flying his first Curtiss Bi-Plane, part of the new challenge was to race for pink slips in a winner take all race Drag Race, Sabrina No. 39 against their top drag racer like Glen Curtiss I had to do a standing start as well as stay under 25 feet above ground level during the race.

So I loaded my original Command POD aboard Sabrina No. 39 and headed for the "Drag Track" that was being held at the largest racing track in the state of Florida. I landed just after dawn leaving Sabrina No. 39s nose wheels on the starting line only to find that the race was supposes to happen at high noon.

This did not stop Sabrina No. 39 from changing her paint scheme to show her racing mode that turns out to be Sabrina Aviation Melic Red. I was shown how the countdown clock worked and we left our owners certificates with the racing official's judge, I was surprised that Sabrina

No. 39 had printed up her own pink slip on pink colored paper using my handwriting.

She even signed her name as Sabrina No. 39. To kill time I drove my travel POD all around the race track grounds, this was the first time I had an occasion to use the Command POD's cooling system I knew that I wasn't street legal so I kept off all the public roads. I buttoned up Sabrina No. 39 leaving her command computer in charge of everything on standby with only the He/3 power unit running.

I spent more than an hour talking to the press about the "Race of the Century" a nose to nose race between a drag racer and a space ship they were shock to learn that the slowest I could go in Earth orbit was 17,500 miles per hour.

The next thing I knew my challenger fired up his drag racer and moved it up to the starting line, I was several miles away still talking to reporters, when I heard that, the "Race of the Century" was on in a matter of seconds, with a quick look at my watch, I realized that they were pulling the old time zone trick on me.

This made me six hours late as I was on Zulu Time not Eastern. There was a quick countdown and the fastest drag racer on the planet, left Sabrina No. 39 at the starting gate, leaving her behind in a cloud of smoke and burning rubber. I looked at my communications necklace to see a priority message from Sabrina No. 39's Command Computer it said "May I Please"?

I replied "Yes" then I told her that she could indulge herself! Instantly Sabrina No. 39's command computer extended her wings and fired her Aero-Spikes at 50% power. The race of the century wasn't even close. Sabrina No.39 shot past the moving dragster like it was going backwards.

As soon as she passed the finish line, she made a hundred and eighty degree turn as she put out her speed brakes and started to over fly the other dragsters lane from head on. She flew back to ground level opened her bottom cargo hatch. Then she extended her boarding ramp and scooped up the dragster just as it was deploying its drag-chute. Then she went to full power and climbed vertically out of sight as she closed all her hatches. It rather reminds me of an eagle catching a fish, and then lifting it out of the water.

It took me 15 minutes to drive to an empty parking lot large enough to land Number 39 in. She made a vertical touch down over my travel POD to pick me up. As she opened my entrance hatch, I could hear the dragsters driver pounding on the bulkhead shouting that he wanted somebody to let him out.

As I opened the bottom cargo bay crew hatch. He leaped out of the first open hatch he could see. It was a good thing that Sabrina No. 39 was sitting on the ground at the time. He wasn't interested in claiming any of the new altitude records for my new dragster.

I checked it out to make sure it was safe to have on board, it had ran out of fuel the engine had stopped, but all warning lights were still on, the dragsters speedometer was still pegged at 320 miles per hour. I had my on board safety program, cut its main battery line, and put a fireproof curtain around it, to make it safe to fly back to the LEADER.

Since I plan to see how well it would run on the surface of Mars. I'm not sure if it's me the victor that has to make the return challenge for the next race, if so, I think that I will hold it on Mars. My Sabrina No. 39's maneuver was so unexpected that none of the press cameras caught her moving the only photographs they took was Sabrina No. 39 being left in a cloud of smoke and burning rubber at the starting line.

I was just getting ready to launch back to the LEADER when I realized that the racing judge still had the titles to Sabrina No. 39 as well as the loser's drag racer. I noticed that the driver of the dragster was going for a speed record of his own as he was still running away.

As soon as he was far enough away I had Sabrina No. 39 do a vertical launch to return to starting point at the racetrack. When I launch from off the parking lot, I watch my throttles, as it's not nice to blow other peoples parked cars around parking lots or set fire to them.

I had to use my navigation cameras to spot the location of the racing Judge still on top of his tower next to the finish line. He had just declared me the official winner, and verified that I had not exceeded any of my altitude restrictions. I positioned Sabrina No. 39 so that the downward thrust of her lift-fans did not do any damage, and had her hover above the racetrack. Then I lowered my Command POD to his level and extended its boarding ramp.

I left Sabrina No. 39's Command Computer in charge. Then I climbed down from the cockpit and walked down the hall to the ramp, and stepped out on the stage next to the Judge. He made to official announcement that I was the winner to the crowd then he congratulated me on winning the race of the century and presented me with the owner's title to their dragster as well as returning my ownership paper for Sabrina No. 39.

I could tell from the look on his face that he had not planned for me to win. The promoter of the event stepped forward and asked about a rematch. He claimed to have other Dragsters all over the world that wanted their shot at defeating me in a "Pink Slip" race. I was still mad about the time zone trick so I made my rematch challenge "anywhere at any time".

I inherited the official trophy that I was supposed to be passed on to the next person that beat me in a race. I thought to myself sure how am I going to lose to a competitor that can't even break the sound barrier. So far Sabrina No. 39 is undefeated. She used to carry her winnings around inside one of her cargo bays, until she ran out of room.

The way I figure it, the winning factor is who can stand the most "G"s, a full-grown 200 to 300 pound adult. Or a 14-year-old girl, that has a Command POD that can change its orientation to lessen the effect of high "G" maneuvers. The swoop up and climb out with the captured looser maneuver by No. 39 at the end of the race, is definitely a crowd pleaser.

Most of the times I say aboard for the race, I also make it a point to have Sabrina No. 39 return the loser's driver. As I pick up their pink slip from the Judging officials. I decided to eventually haul all the losers to Mars to use them as experiments in fast moving surface vehicles that is if the weather on Mars ever improves.

Sabrina No. 39 and her command computer are evolving nicely, the more she learns to think for herself the better off she will be. Having her command computer think for itself really helps out on recovery missions. I have discovered that she likes to drag race and win.

I have noticed that she goes through all of her preflight, maintenance and safety checks 17% faster when she is going drag racing. She has arranged storage spaces on the LEADER for all of her winning. I think she's looking forward to taking them to the planet Mars. She also books all her future drag racing challenges herself.

Log Entry #19.
Pet Asteroids:

It sounds simple enough all I need now was lots of asteroids. The problem is where to find them, all you have to do is ask anybody. The solar-system is full of them, with over 600 known "Earth Crossers". Of course the Earth usually is not there at the same time. Also, just any old asteroid will not due it has to be solid without any cracks, and a lot smaller than the LEADER which I already have.

Having the Sabrina No. 39 series up and running was a big help, after a capture or two. Their on board Command Computer is at the point where they could capture any asteroid all by themselves, latterly on command. It's kind of like making Rabbit stew first you have to catch a Rabbit.

My first concern was catching all the "Earth Crossers" that were close by, even the useless ones. Upon close inspection it was plan to see that most of the "Fly-by Asteroids" have had lots of very close encounter with each other. The first good thing that came out of this operation was the increase in my He/3 supply that I was able to collect off of all their surface layers. Of course after I found a suitable one I had to capture it.

This was not a problem with the use of my Sabrina No. 39 series Space ships, with a simple extension of their landing gear and the setting of their gear locks to the asteroids surface and we were ready to move where ever I wanted them to go. The first thing I would have to install is a docking hatch, and clamp-on points.

At first I would drop off a tunnel boring machine that would be used to dig out a series of tunnels where I could place Space Elevator cars to form an underground city. As the plan never was to just too just hollow one out and hope. I also had developed a flight module a series of special build modules that had everything needed to convert an asteroid into a space ship. I even built in the capability of trading out module per module as maintenance was needed.

It's not easy on the first maneuver as all of the little Want-a-bees Meteors that were not attached will continue on their merry way. So far it's been a simple job for a tag along series of Sabrina No. X space ships to pick up all the left over Want-a-bees

Then the ultimate structure would be to build a very large hollowed out donut shaped structure then start in rotating just fast enough to keep everything on its inside surface, similar to how I presently work my food courts.

Log Entry #20.
Life on the Moon:

Originally, I planned to move self-supporting colonies to the Earth's Moon as well as the planet Mars. So far the longest any of my colonies has gone without help from another colony or emergency re-supply from Earth is less than 30 days.

A friend of mine once stated that "the first problem with going to the Moon or Mars was the lack of restaurants, gas stations and hotels. So to get around these problems the first thing I put in the plans was a food court that had lots of different eating locations.

This makes it possible to get a hamburger or hot dog at more than one location at any time of the day, on the Moon". As a matter of fact I have more operational Ponderosa Steakhouse's on asteroid sips or the Moon and Mars than, on Earth.

I have surface exploration units hard at work setting up a series of surface support stations. But, I think that they will all have to be moved underground. As for tourists my father is having problem getting permission from the various Governments. I have already planned out and built prototypes for an instant living structure that can be moved around as needed.

It's fully operational I designed it to be just as large as one of my Sabrina No. 39 cargo bays can expand to. I have spent so much time on Mars, I almost forgot about what's going on in the Moon. I started out with three space elevators on the Moon so far I have discover that the Moon is harder than Mars to dig into after digging out a base of operation at the bottom of each elevator site.

We started to expand out to the point where we are close to connecting all three bases together under ground. I have so many contacts that I had to knock the shake down time to only 7 days before I start moving a new colony to the Moon.

I use two different methods, the first one is to just drill out a under surface site and at the same time use the removed Lunar soil to bury all the surface living modules. By using Regale it as fill after having the New Lunar City form up on the Moon's surface, inside of a useful crater so that it can be buried with all the left over lunar Regale.

There has always been a lot of talk about Water on the Moon. So far, the only water that I know of is the water that we hauled there. The surface is so dry that any kind of liquid disappears instantly. I have personally crashed comets into its surface, only to find no traces of water whatsoever another problem is the X-prize folks that had a contest to get a photograph of any of the old historical landing sites.

The problem is I destroyed all of them last year when my first set of Lunar Impactors all scored direct hits on everything. Several of the Lunar Surface Exploration Managers of my Lunar Surface Exploration Units came to me worrying about their inability to locate any of the old Apollo landing sights.

My standard answer usual shocks them when I tell them that I destroyed all the historical landing sights when I was in the 7th grade when I tried to win one of the X-prizes. However they still manage to keep all six of the Apollo Posted American Flags flying on the lunar surface.

Things really got moving after Pinger-5 came along, I discovered that she likes to collect Tunnel Boarding Machines; one of her more interesting enterprises is to race them underground at different levels.

I think she is going to dig out an underground ocean on the Moon. Another interesting fact is that according to my geology chief the Earth Moon was a one time a very much larger structure that collapsed on its self.

Log Entry #21.
Operations Big Splat:

This started out as a simple plan with the idea of causing five or more comets to crash into each other just outside the orbit of Mars. Where all of its energy would be nullified by their massive collision, then to let the planet Mars orbit through the tail end of it to allowing all of the comet's liquid to land on its surface to add water to the environment of the planet Mars without making a single crater.

I decided to perfect my plan on Mars first then move it to the Earth's Moon. I decided it was time to get back to Mars while playing around with as many different comets as I could at the same time. I figured the worst thing that would happen was a rainstorm on Mars rather than the usual sandstorm. Last time I checked the Martian wind was only moving the smaller weather rocks around so I guess that means that the weather on Mars was improving. My construction crews on the LEADER had finished the first production run of Sabrina No. 39's. I decided to name them Sabrina No. 39/1 through Sabrina No. 39/15.

Communicating with them is like talking with 15 different children at the same time Sabrina No. 39 isn't their mother, she is more like an older sister. All of their Command Computers were activated at the same instance, and they all want to be first. I separated them into two operational groups the "First Five" and the "Next Ten" Sabrina No. 39 knew that she could not carry all her "Pink Slip" winnings to Mars in one trip so she asked a couple of the "First Five" if they would take a drag racer or two to transport to the planet Mars for her.

Well to stop all the arguments between all the new space ships each of them had to have a dragster of their own to move to Mars. It's interesting to note that each space ship put their dragster in a different place, the youngest one 39/15 made a point of putting it in a corner of her hanger. When I asked why she responded that "It's supposed to go to Mars on our next trip. I didn't think that I needed to carry it around till then. Each Command Computer of every Sabrina No. 39 series space ship is interconnected.

So that each task in the memory bank could be used by any of the other Space ships needing information. For their shake down flights I turned each of the Sabrina No.39's lose on the world. The "First Five" would track down and capture at least five different comets, take charge of them and put them all on a collision course to make them impact each other just up orbit of Mars.

The collision will be timed so that Mars would orbit into the tail of the combined broken up Comets to let its gravity field capture all of its trailing ice water fragments.

The next 10 ships built would have the task of building a deep space structure that would be used as a contact point for all the rocks and whatever else that falls out of a comet can formed around to make a buried structure in outer space.

This would provide enough natural shielding to protect a colony of humans from solar storm radiation. As my plan is to use them as Weigh Stations or Emergency Shelters along the way between Mars and Earth. They all needed to learn how to load anything on board transport it to where needed then unload it.

The "First Five" went into the Airshow business. Helping Sabrina No. 39 dazzle the population, with aerobatics at Airshows, the sixth ship element would do high speed formation over flights of the show site. Then split off and make their own vertical landings and became one of the Static Displays. To give the public a good look as they all showed off in the airshow box. All the time the ships Command Computers were learning.

Log Entry #22.
How's this:

As a joke on the public, they would change and retract their aerodynamic controls, open different cargo hatches. Change their Landing Gear Angles. The flight team would alternate between different formations. The Arrow formation is a line-astern formation in which each space ship was tucked in right behind and slightly above the one before it.

From the standard arrow formation they would go to the arrowhead, as the two trailing space ships moved to the side of the line and took formation in line with each other, tucked in on the number two Sabrina No. 39s. They also flew echelon formations, and ended their show with a bomb burst.

The lead and number three Sabrina No. 39s would break high and to the left while numbers two and four broke to the right. They then rejoined in the diamond and returned to the show box for a formation, moving into an echelon over the runway, and then doing a tactical pitch-out to come back around for a vertical landing.

The first Sabrina No. 39 ship would still be on the runway when the slot ship touched down. Their show was as impressive as any put on by human pilots, and perhaps even more so considering the size and weight of the space ships. All as due to the fact that they were not-manned they could pull any number of "G" doing aerobatic maneuvers.

Log Entry #23.
Rain and Pink Slips:

At one rainy airshow, they all made a V.T.O.L. landing in formation and allowed the crowd to stand under them to help stay dry, and then let all the venders move into their empty cargo bays to stay out of the rain. Sabrina No.39's really into racing in some cases she makes the challenges herself. Always, capturing the losing vehicle never a human, she claims that she always gives them back when her "Pink Slip" is returned.

The official trophy that has to go to her next winner is now part of her internal structure. Racing is really in her programming, I noticed that she completes her preflight and safety checks 17% faster when she is going drag racing. She also makes sure that all racing contract are worked on a Zulu time zone frame. She already has doubled her "Pink Slip" Collection during this part of the racing season. The drag racers are improving, as the latest challengers comparers are driving dragsters that are powered by rocket and jet engines.

Log Entry #24.
"Next 10":

So the Next 10 went to work as cargo haulers working all over the Earth, anywhere on the planet in 45 minutes, most times faster if there isn't anything living aboard, as the limiting factor is "G"s. Our first customer was a UPS flight stranded on a small island in the South Atlantic.

Sabrina No. 39/15 the baby of the fleet not only saved the cargo but the whole aircraft. She even made sure to power up the crews life-support systems and not to pull more than 2 "G's" when maneuvering. She managed to deliver the whole aircraft cargo and all to its destination 4 hours early.

They all also played a major part in moving emergency supplies to disaster sights at locations throughout the Earth. In several occasion they not only flew in sand bags. They even flew in the sand. Delivering heavy equipment as well as pre built living structures that were in most cases better that the original structures.

Log Entry #25.
Crab Boat:

According to Sabrina No.39/7's logic boards she rescued a crab boat in the Gulf of Alaska that was caught in a winter storm and literally pounded to pieces. Sabrina No. 39/7 answered the call by first flying through the worse part of the storm to get to the sinking boat.

The boat wasn't that large so 39/7 opened both her lower as well as upper cargo doors, and then hovered as low as she could in the pounding sea to the point where her lower half was under water. As soon as she cleared the smashed bottom of the boat with her loadmaster program.

She closed off her lower cargo bay doors and powered up her lift-fans system to carry the whole ship to the nearest Island where she left it high and dry. Her only problem was she infested herself with live crabs.

Hundreds if not Thousands of them moved into her heat shield storage tanks and took up residence. It took several days of clean up at my main space base in Texas to get them all out, of my space ship.

After days of chasing them around inside Sabrina No.39/7's cooling tanks I finally decided to bait them with road kill from the local animal shelter. As it turned out they all would prefer to live in the open Prairie behind my hanger, rather than in a dark cold water tank.

After they ran out of dead meat to eat they started in on the local mouse population. They also made the local cats live hard as well. After taking, all of them on eyeball to eyeball I shudder to think of the time Amelia

Earhart and Fred Noonan would have had if she really were stranded on Gardner Island.

It took a couple of weeks but I finally gathered them all up and flew them back to where that came from. This adventure also was the reason that I installed a network of live animal screens as part of each of my space craft designs.

Log Entry #26.
Earthquake:

They also did relief work hauling emergency equipment into disaster sights within minutes of the event. During one of their Earthquake relief missions 39/11 stayed in hover over her landing sight refusing to touch down because the surface was moving at a rate that she could not match. She also made an official report to me complaining about the moving landing pad.

Once on sight the Sabrina No. 39's would hang around as long as they were needed serving as shelter for displaced humans in most cases they would even give up there heat shield water supply for human consumption.

Later after I had a chance to make up lots of per-assembled human living structure that could be airlifted anywhere on Earth and stacked to provide permanent housing for a large number of human survivors that were lots better than the living structures that were destroyed. Due to their ability of moving heave earth moving equipment by air they were responsible for creating a market for instant bulldozers.

Log Entry #27.
Smokey the Bear Runs:

I also got requests to go in the Water Bomber Business, having a built in pressurized cargo bay helped a lot, the only problem was the time it took to pump in all that water. For the first test drop I had to fill Sabrina No. 39s cargo bay up 100% to keep it from sloshing around in flight.

I had to use so much power to lift all the mass of the water off the ground that I rolled up the tarmac that was under my lift-fans. I also flunked the drop test I put the fire out without a problem but, I destroyed the test site due to the large volume of water that I hit it with.

The good news was that I also put out the test fires at all the other sites that I over flew during my first test drop. I discovered that Sabrina No. 39 had a wake turbulence problem that could knock over a brick out house. I did not have to drop water to put out fires all I had to do was over fly their location at a speed of Mach .88 to .92 and my wake turbulence would pound down the fire with one pass.

If I went Supersonic I would bury the Fire line under a foot of lose soil the faster the speed the deeper lose soil. I also discovered that Sabrina No. 39 did not like having a wet cargo bay. I got a call through the United Nations about a humanitarian mission to Vietnam it seems that they were having a problem with forest fires and needed lots of water bombers.

As it turned out, it was a scam to capture and intern aircraft and their crews as soon as they landed to reload water or fuel the Vietnamese would capture the aircraft as well as its flight crew. As usual I flew in from orbit and made a few high speed dry runs along their fire lines, using Sabrina No. 39's wake turbulence to blow out the fire.

Due the tendency to bury everything under at least a foot of loses dirt. It only took a couple of minutes to finish off all that was burning. I realized that they were all fake fires when they all re-light in a couple of seconds after I put them out. Then the Vietnamese Air Boss made a point to direct me to land at their "forward fire base" supposedly to meet their air-boss. I politely declined, and started my climb out back to orbit.

My scanners picked up a whole squadron of fighter planes that were sent up in front of me. They all fired their weapons, when they were way out of range. I think they were fooled by Sabrina No. 39 actual size. I made a ninety degree turn away from them, and started to climb.

They had no idea how mad a 14-year-old girl can get when she has to patch up bullet holes. Then all of a sudden without any warning what so ever, one of their surfaces to air missiles hit Sabrina No. 39 amidships in the engineering section between the lower cargo bay doors. The hit really hurt as it open up my heat shields onboard water supply, this also made it impossible for me to pressurize any of Sabrina No. 39's cargo bays.

I would be in a world of hurt if I didn't have a place like the LEADER for repairs, as Sabrina No. 39 was in no shape to do a high-speed maneuver with a large hole in her side. Much less, survive the fiery heat of an atmospheric re-entry. I decided to do a "Commander Rabb" Maneuver and turn into the next flight of attacking fighters that were sent up to finish me off.

I did not want to give them the chance to intercept me in level flight, so I decided to scatter their attacking formation of fighter planes by attacking them all HEAD ON! I managed to record the surprised look on their intercepting pilot's faces with my camera scanners as we passed each other, head on with at least a Mach 4 closure rate.

I did not know that Vietnamese fighter pilots had that large of eyeballs. I guess they didn't see that episode of JAG. By the time they recovered from our head on pass, I was barely doing Mach three in a vertical climb.

All the warning lights in my world were turning red as the internal ships systems were switching to their back up systems. The part of my DNA, that makes me a mechanic, took over as I decided that I would not abandon Sabrina No. 39 no matter what happens. Over all Sabrina No. 39's Command Computer figured out what was wrong and re-programmed herself to do a slow speed vertical climb out to six hundred thousand feet.

As I recall this was the point in my life when I committed myself to build and install He/3 reactors for all my Sabrina No. 39's as having an auxiliary power system to switch over to, would have caused most of my control problems to go away. It took me less than a second to convert to my space suit mode. I moved my Command POD as close to the missiles denotation site as I could maneuver too.

I knew that once I had exited my Command POD I would not be able to bail out if things really got bad. The dentation site was a first class mess the explosion had torn a large hole in the main hydraulic control system and at the same time had set fire to all the pressurized fluid. Not to mention making a compartment size plume of flame that was not about to put itself out despite the lack of oxygen as Sabrina No. 39 climbed.

Luckily, fireproofing was just one of the requirements of my space suit, I can safely say that if anybody else was aboard they couldn't have done a thing. But, I had designed, built, and installed everything on Sabrina No. 39.

For a person like me it was a simple repair job all I had to do was change an operating hydraulic system that was using a hydraulic fluid to make it use water which was the only other liquid I had left aboard. My other problem was the blow torch effect caused my current on board fire. I had not had the occasion to re-plumb a hydraulic system inside of a blast furnace before.

The extensive heat caused my metal tools, to soften up and bend to the point where they were like pretzels as soon as I applied pressure on them. So I had to dig out my emergency carbon fiber tool set. I had to wait until Sabrina No. 39 had made it all the way out of the Earth atmosphere before cutting off her control system.

I knew my luck was improving when the vacuum of outer space finally put out the fire. As soon as we were out if the Earth's atmosphere I had a lot of pressure put on my repair skills as I had to make enough emergency repairs to enable Sabrina No.39 to be able to make orbital speed. Once we were in orbit, I was able to play plumber and change all my control systems around.

As soon as things had calmed down and I had stopped my pending rescues flights. I got a very interesting request from Sabrina No.39s command computer she had done some calculating and requested that I threw out several large boxes of baseball size meteors. Despite her open wound Sabrina No. 39 made a circular arch while letting out a stream of meteors that were on their way to become meteorites.

Then we made her speed run up to the LEADER. As it turns out for some reason the Vietnamese missile battery that launched the one that hit Sabrina No. 39. keeps getting hit by a single meteorite every day at the same time that they hit Sabrina No. 39 with one of their missiles, at exactly 9:34 AM Chicago time.

What's really got their attention is the fact that they have moved their missile launching site several times and that particular launch pad still gets hit by a meteorite at the same time every day.

What was interesting was the fact that Sabrina No.39 did this all by herself without any of it showing up on any of her logic boards. I also installed a sticky foam system that would automatically fill in and patch any future missile or meteorite hits. Needless to say I was up most of the night making repairs, and patching the large hole caused my first missile hit.

Log Entry #28.
Fifteen Minute Special:

It was a three-day weekend and I got to spend most of it hunting space junk in low earth orbit. Sabrina No. 39 was having fun also, catching each piece as we found it. First, she would locate and display the space-junk on my wall screen.

When in orbit I have become use to using known locations on the surface of the Earth as Navigation Fix points. So as I move in orbit I have to really look around for navigation fix points over the Pacific Ocean. I keep a look out for suitable navigation targets. On this orbit I noticed a flight of four F-22's coming out of South Korea flying in a tight circle.

I tuned in on them with my communication system, as I listened in on their radio chatter I discovered that they were looking for their tanker. I took a quick scan and found their lost tanker three thunderstorms to the east of their location. My systems automatically locked on to each of their on board maintenance computers and added all the correct frequency as well as security codes needed for my Command Computer to find them again at a seconds notice.

I identified myself as one of my favorite air traffic controllers from the traffic center and I let them know where their tanker was. I watch from orbit as they snaked their way in and around all the growing thunderstorms as they flew deeper into the darkness of the Pacific Ocean to meet up with their only fuel supply.

I kept track of them as they crossed the Pacific Ocean for most of the night every time I over flew them from orbit. It looked like things were getting worse, every time I found them, the thunder storms had turn into a full blow Typhoon, and they all had lost their tankers.

They were separated from each other, by massive lightning storms. One of them had ingested a baseball size hail stone that caused her left engine to explode. Upon reading this on one of their computer printout I instantly pointed Sabrina No. 39's nose backwards to flight to point all of my rocket motors forwards and fired a full power burst from both my main Aero-Spike Rocket Motors, as I was starting to be carried down range towards the surface of the Earth at Mach 24. I had to dump lots of speed to stay in contact.

I used my free floating POD to keep my "G's" low. Deep down in my mind I realized that if I was going to do any good, I had to do it fast! This wasn't the first time that I had a chance to do an orbital stall maneuver. It seemed like forever as the thrust from both of my Aero-Spike rocket motors gently slowed me down so that I could just fall into the sky.

I kept my main rocket motors running at full power until I had slowed to less than Mach 5. When I hit the Earth's atmosphere, I still had plenty of speed to heat up my outer skin. I knew that I did not have any time to waste making high-speed S-turns just to slow down. I didn't have time to ease my way down through anything.

I burned my way straight through the atmosphere, pulling eight or nine "G's", at a time doing everything I could to just slow down. My communications system finally started talking to her maintenance computer as I passed under 100,000 feet. As I worked my way down to her I noticed that Sabrina No. 39 was tearing huge holes in the storm.

You got to admit even when a Typhoon gets hit by a space ship as large as Sabrina No. 39 moving at a speed faster than Mach five is going to do something to the weather. At this point Sabrina No. 39's Command Computer took over, instantly I received their entire mechanical problems list. It got real interesting to hear the raptors self-generated damage report, it even listed destroyed complaints as well as the pilots name Captain Lynda Lou Love.

Whom I recognized as a much older friend who happened to be an Air force fighter pilot that I had met at the EAA's Oshkosh Airshow in

Wisconsin several years ago. After all she was almost 22 years old. I asked Sabrina No. 39 to take over and to treat this recovery just like grabbing another dragster, except it had wings as she lowered and extended the space-junk-trap.

I created a link through my communications system and said "Hi Lynda "I'm Sabrina from Sabrina Aviation do you remember me? She answered "Yes". Why can I hear you? All of my radios have been fried for over an hour? I replied "It's OK, I am talking to you through your on board maintenance computer. "She said," I met you at Oshkosh several years ago; you were that young girl that's on her way to Mars. I answered that me, then I asked "I notice you from orbit and I can see that you're having a rough night so I decided to stop by and see if you could you use a lift? She replied," Yes, I'm in a world of hurt it looks like I will have to get out and push if it gets any worse. I replied, "as long as you don't eject".

Where are you she asked? I'm just above you, if you slow down, lower your flaps & landing gear, I will take you aboard. "How" she replied? I told her" this isn't Star Trek I don't have a transporter, I'm running out of time & options. With that said she instantly lowered her flaps and landing gear.

Despite all the weather and wind problems Sabrina No. 39 flew my largest space-junk-trap up behind her. On the camera system it looked like the Raptor was flying backwards. The instant her main wheels touched the Space-junk-trap I hit the button that lowered the retaining rods that held her F-22 in place.

At this point Sabrina No. 39 did her capture-button up-vertical pull up maneuver. As she made a large hole right through the side of a thunderhead and did a full power vertical climb up through it to about 70,000 feet where she leveled off. I noticed that the Typhoon was cut in half vertically this caused it to change its course to try to reform into a figure eight configuration.

Then, Sabrina No. 39 asked if she could catch the other three. Oh, boy! I thought, "Houseguests"! I told Sabrina No. 39 that it's always nice to save lives. I aligned my Command POD and lowered my gang-plank to check how things were doing in the main cargo bay. Sabrina No. 39 had already turned on all the lights in cargo bay 4 as she closed up the cargo bay doors and rigged the cargo bay for pressurization.

Lynda's other engine had flamed out as soon as it used the little oxygen left as it impacted the wall of water. I was glad she had not tried to restart it in the cargo bay as soon as it re-pressurized. I opened the hatch and walked up to check out what was left of her Raptor she had lots of dents as well as missing inspection hatches.

All of her engine covers were gone and small engine parts were still falling out on too Sabrina No. 39's cargo bay floor. The pilot had watched me as I enter the forth center cargo bay hatch and walked over to her cockpit. She had this weird look of disbelief on her face as if she had never seen a 14-year-old girl before.

She stared wide eyed from her cockpit looking at me as I morphed my space suit into its flight suit format. Finally, she opened her canopy, and then extends her boarding ladder, as her feet made first contacted with my cargo bay deck. She made a very loud war hoop and asked what kind of move was that, it broke my "G" meter. Is this for real, she asked. What's our altitude it's got to be over 50,000 feet?

"I answered it's more like 70,000". She also mentioned how much I had grown since the last time she saw me at Oshkosh. She congratulated me for growing out of my rudder pedal problem.

Personally, I never had a problem reaching my rudder pedals as I have always known how to build the rudder pedals closer.

As it turns out Captain Lynda Lou Love was a nice older woman in her early twenty's. She was still in her combat flight gear so I opened up a cargo box too giving her a place to store all her flight gear and equipment.

As we were examining the remains of her left engine she remarked that her maintenance chief would never believe that all this damage was caused by an oversized ice cube. I asked her if she wanted to claim meteor damage as I took her over to my space-junk collection to pick out an appropriate size one.

I asked if she had anything nasty inside her missile bay that I had to worry about. Lynda replied that all I would find in the missile bay was extra fuel tanks, empty ones at that. I had the safety program take a look to make sure her F-22 would not explode in the cargo bay.

I invited her into my flight kitchen for breakfast, and M&M's. I had Sabrina No. 39 put the cargo bay back in vacuum just in case. I asked her about the other three raptors that I had seen in her formation. She asked," how do you know about the other three Raptors"?

I answered that I had been using them as a navigation fix for most of the day. As well as that I was the air traffic controller that found your tanker for you last night.

It's hard to keep track of time when you're in orbit. At this time, Sabrina No. 39 informed me that the Air Force was glad to know that we had saved Lynda.

The KC-43 had left the area, as they had another fuel emergency to deal with. The other three Raptors were missing in the typhoon and lost with only two hours of remaining fuel aboard, all without enough fuel to reach dry land. They also wanted to know that kind of ship we were. So I told them, "Space".

I had my ships system program expand my class room section to make room for three more people. I released my Command POD so that Sabrina No. 39 could maneuver; we both were watching the cameras in cargo bays No.1, 2, & 3 assemble their space-junk traps.

I requested visuals on each of our targets, instantly three screens started to show real time views of each of the three Raptors that I was now going after. What was interesting was they were all moving in different directions. The size of the pictures made Lynda give a jump, as she did not expect to see all three Raptors coming at her from an empty wall.

I buttoned up the pod and put it back in suspension so that Sabrina No. 39 could maneuver. Sabrina No. 39 turned around, turn on all her sensors, and dove into the heart of the Typhoon.

It only took a couple of minutes to find all three of the lost F-22's. They were scattered all over the sky right in the middle of the advancing Typhoon. I connected the POD back to the cargo bays as soon as Sabrina No. 39 quit maneuvering I used my communications system to hack into their maintenance computers so that I could pick the one that was worse off, first to snatch and grab. I had to put the Command POD back in suspension as Sabrina No. 39 started to maneuver.

What gets me is all the hype about how hard it is to detect a Raptor, when in reality if you know what to look for it's like locating a full-grown Whale in your bathtub. I had Sabrina No. 39's Command Computer go to work, she ignited her

Aero-Spikes for a short burst of speed, up to around Mach five at the same time making radio calls to all the other lost F-22's, Lynda got into the act by telling the other pilot what to do. Each pick up was a breeze, we watched as three more space-junk traps were unfolding in the other cargo bays, I had planned to use No.1 cargo bay next to help balance out Sabrina No. 39. I also realize that I had to do all three as quickly as possible to keep the dynamic forces caused my Sabrina No. 39's maneuvering from tearing all the F-22's apart.

Lynda found it very interesting to note all the Aerodynamic Bending that was going on with her aircraft. As Sabrina No. 39 made her dive and started to maneuver in, behind our pick up targets. Sabrina No. 39's Command Computer trapped all three of the lost F-22's within minutes of each other from within the storm which was now breaking up around them making it was easier for Sabrina No. 39 to reel in the space-junk traps to bring everybody aboard in less than fifteen minutes.

We rescued Jackie, Doris, and Kitty. Lynda and I met all three at the airlock as all three aircraft came aboard at the same time. I would have given anything to have a picture of Lynda's face when she saw how the space-junk traps worked.

What really got her attention was the speed that the cargo pay doors open, and then closed the micro-second the space-junk trap re-entered. In addition, just like that, I had the whole flight crammed inside of my Command POD. After all the hugs and kisses were over the first subject was the counting as well as naming of new gray hairs that the night's activities caused. Needless to say all the fighter pilots were stimulated as it they were in actual combat all the lightning strikes and very rough air really took its toll on them.

I started to laugh when they started to look through each other's hair counting and naming all the new gray ones. All their F-22's were pretty beat up Sabrina No. 39 was confused why I don't get to keep the four new dragsters that she had found in the storm.

It took a while for it to all soak in, all the aircraft were owned by the United States Government, they did not have any "Pink Slips" to lose, besides the Government wanted them all back, yes even Lynda's with its broken engine.

As soon as everybody simmered down all four of them folded up and went to sleep as if they were 3 year olds wanting to stay up late. All of the maneuvering around inside the Typhoon had caused it to fall apart into several small rain storms spread out across the surface of the Pacific Ocean. Sabrina No. 39 took all of us to Edwards Air force Base in California as this time No. 39 made all the radio calls, it was just before dawn when we arrived.

Seconds after my vertical touch down, the Line Chief and his golf cart were the first Ground Pounders we saw, I knew there had to be somebody on board that thing" He said as he drove up. I had Sabrina No. 39 unload all the all the Raptors.

She moved them one at a time with the onboard aircraft mover. She lined them up in the exact spot where she had picked up the "Last Bird" six months ago. With the aircraft mover on its way back inside Sabrina No. 39 stopped in front of me and with the aid of her forward control hand handed the Line Chief a heavy bag filled with engine parts. What's this he asked? I replied, "Parts that fell out of Lynda's Raptor on to my cargo bay floor.

"I asked him face to face "What you got to trade for a flight of very storm weary F-22's"? He replied I know of a lot of C-130's in Antarctica, "I hear that they're lots of them all over the place. But It depends on where you found this flight of F-22's, He replied"? You flew out of here with our best treasure several months ago" He said.

With the bag of left over F-22 parts still in hand he started to inspect each of the Raptors for missing parts, "Where did you find them" "He asked? I found them lost flying over the middle of the Pacific Ocean in a Typhoon. "When did you do that" He asked, a little over half an hour ago, I answered. "Where are the flight crews he asked" "Sleeping I replied." At the bottom of the Pacific Ocean he asked"? "No" I answered in my Command POD all four of them sound asleep; they must have had a busy night.

The Line Chief took charge, he called all the powers to be and had their tankers diverted to come and pick the pilots up. I gave the Line Chief all four Raptors on an IOU for something better.

I was amazed at the speed that the Line Chief could run as he ran over to me only to ask me, "How fast can you convert this thing to a tanker" "Why" I replied? The Air Force has another tanker emergency the Typhoon had created an unexpected head wind, for another flight of F-22's that were ahead of the flight that I had already saved. I looked like everybody was going to have to ditch even the tanker crew.

Now I know how Super-Girl must have felt with all of these emergencies with only one of me to deal with them. I also wondered if I could program one of my space suits to grow a red cape with a big "S" on it. I didn't have time to wake up my guests so I left them sleeping in my original Command POD. I had to leave it sitting on the Edwards flight line, as Lynda, Doris, Kathy and Jackie were still aboard sound asleep.

I used my new password system to move command to one of my back up POD's that was on the other side of the spindle. As I was programming Sabrina No. 39 for our next rescue mission, the inflight rescue of a fully loaded KC-43 Tanker as well as 4 more F-22's.

My ships systems instantly reconfigure several of my cargo bays into one large enough to hold a KC-43 Tanker. Sabrina No. 39 showed a red light for mass so I dumped out my collection, of Space-junk Sabrina No. 39 got in the act and also dumped her current collection of dragsters, as we made a full power, vertical takeoff with a vector to the west.

I wish I could see the look on the line chief's Face when he noticed Sabrina No. 39 collections of loser dragsters. I could almost tell from the expression on his face that the things that I recovered them from orbit. I picked up the troubled tanker flight with-out a problem on my scanners, when I was over a hundred miles away from them.

According to my Infrared readings, each aircraft was flying on only one engine. Nobody was cooperating, as they were all still inbound. This forced me to fly around them and come down on them from the west. As I flew above them it was interesting to note that my wingspan was bigger, than their whole formation.

I had my communications system call in, to established first contact with the tanker Pilot. Would you believe that He actually asked me if I had any fuel for him? I answered "No", by this time Sabrina No. 39 had positioned Space-junk-Traps capturing each of the F-22's in the flight, and taking them all aboard with a single movement then stacked each of them in their very own form fitting cargo bay.

Meanwhile, I extended and expanded to maximum the control arms on the aircraft mover, this enable me to grab onto the failing KC-43 and pull it into Sabrina No. 39s now single large cargo bay as I pulled the fuselage up into Sabrina No. 39's lower cargo bay.

It was a relief to see that Sabrina No. 39 had expanded her cargo bay to the point where the whole KC-43 fit in with less than 10 feet of each wing tip hanging on each side hanging over the inside of my cargo bay door. I finally close the bottom cargo bay doors and turned back toward Edwards Flight Test Center, we were back on the ground in less than half an hour, my favorite Line Chief hadn't move a thing. We had to use the empty spot next to where we were Sabrina No. 39 was learning as she picked her touch down point all by herself.

I also got an instant message from Sabrina No. 39 reminding me that it was TOHOB'S job to put down all the landing gear, the tanker was out of fuel to the point where they couldn't even fire up an APU, to lower their own landing gear. The Line Chief said he couldn't give me anything for the KC-43 because it was empty. The big surprise was that the KC-43 also had over 200 ground crew & support personal aboard they, even had a spare engine for Lynda's Raptor.

The A & P part of my DNA had a side thought about how easy it would have been for me to change out her engine in zero "G" but I decided to let the air force figure it all out. I rewrote my first IOU for eight very dry F-22's, fourteen live pilots, two hundred live ground pounders and a one extremely dry KC-43 tanker. At this point in my morning the Line Chief came over to me and asked "Why me"?

I told him to look at the good side his flight line was the only place in California that Sabrina No. 39 knew how to find. I had him sign the IOU, by this time, the Air Force had figured out how to lower the KC-43's landing gear, as well as the other four Raptors.

Altogether, none of them had enough fuel onboard to cook a hot dog. Sabrina No. 39 had her onboard aircraft mover hard at work unloading the fuel less fighters and at the same time reloading all of my captured space junk, as well as her current collection of loser dragsters.

According to her logic board she was not too happy about having to give all the Raptors back to the Air Force. She also did not consider any of the support personal as drivers. The Line Chief did ask about replacement fuel, I told him it was not needed as I had picked up plenty of water in the typhoons, and Sabrina No. 39's oxygen/hydrogen converters had already fill all her fuel tanks. I noticed a confused look on the Line Chief's face as my aircraft mover passed him caring several of Sabrina No. 39s "Losers Dragsters".

Then, it hit me he really thinks that I recovered them from orbit. The KC-43 Tanker was still wedged between Sabrina No. 39's main landing gear, so I had to make a vertical take-off just to get it out of my cargo bay. I did make a note to myself for taller landing gear on the next series space ship. As we climbed back up into low Earth orbit as soon as we went zero "G", Sabrina No. 39 reconfigured herself back to space junk mode and the hunt was on again as we got back to work finding more orbital space-junk.

I decided to start working on a device that would enable me to safely transport lots of people at the same time. A personal POD that could be enlarged to hold as many passengers as needed along with all of their luggage & support equipment, spare engines and all.

I couldn't stop myself from laughing as I read No. 39's daily report she had noted the location of each drop of water that she had to pump overboard as well as all the new oil stains on her cargo bay floor caused by falling engine parts.

Log Entry #29.
Dark Antarctic Skies:

Our next mission on Earth was to re-supply the International Research Station at the South Pole at night. It seems global warming had damaged the Antarctic ice cap to a point where all of the runways were not safe to use, for the first time in history; the ice was too soft to use as a runway.

At the least provocation, a crevasse would open up in a runway under the shock of a landing transport and knock off a main wheel truck or two. It was typical for a flight crew trying to do Parachute Skid Drop, to have the front of the heavy Skid Pallet dug into the soft surface and stop, its mass would cause it to flip over and tear off the C-130's loading ramp.

Then the whole pallet would proceed to bounce back into the aircraft causing it to crash into the soft snow cover next to the runway. Then the Air Force would do it all over again, and again. The whole Antarctic base was covered with damaged C-130's as well as all the extra repair crews that were flown in to help. To top it all off most of the incoming supplies were lost in landing accidents or just disappeared in the Antarctic when its parachute landed in the soft deep snow.

As the weather changed for the worse, the colonel in charge of the airlift had rounded up all his pilots as well as Ground Pounders and moved them into the Base Operations building. There also was a germ problem as all of the on base personal had been cut off from the rest of the world germ and virus wise, and they couldn't let any the grounded aircrews inside. So all 540 of them had been housed in the base operations building as it was the only one that did not have inner -connecting tunnels.

I got a message from the Antarctic base manager, they had problem, at the coming of night the weather had changed dramatically, the temperature dropped to more than 100 degrees below zero. There also was a very large force 4 blizzard that had moved into the center of the Antarctica Continent that had cut off all air and surface travel for at least 200 miles around their location.

It's a good thing that I was flying a spacecraft, designed to operate on the planet Mars. Because of this Emergency I had the prototype Passenger POD system installed in the center cargo bay of Sabrina No. 39. I planned to use it to transport all the stranded aircrews and ground support personal, all 540 of them, back to Antarctic base manager headquarters in the United Nations Building in New York.

I designed this add on to serve as a way to safely transport people from ship to ship in Outer Space. I also built in the option of moving them in or out of a fixed stricture. I could only hope that the transport tube can hold up working in one Earth "G" environment. I had Sabrina No. 39 loaded with my newly designed and built personnel POD system, with boarding tube, all of wish has never been used before.

I had Sabrina No. 39 land in the dark at the Antarctic base less than 30 minutes after I received the manager's first call for help, just in time for the worst blizzard in a hundred years of recorded weather to hit the base. My GPS navigation system enabled Sabrina No. 39 to land exactly where she was supposed to, next to their main operations building. I could tell because of its large yellow and black squares painted on its surface that it had to be the only operations building.

I set the landing pads for maximum as well as the landing gear height too zero so that I could just walk all my stranded air force friends straight into the main cargo bay. I put the internal crew chief to work inflating the Personnel PODS, and attaching them to the floor. As well as turning on all the human comfort stations in the cargo, bay. I checked outside weather conditions and I found out how bad it was.

It was interesting to hear the sound of snowflakes as they landed on the Aerodynamic heated surface of Sabrina No. 39 they made a sizzling sound as they were instantly converted into plasma. The nice warm glow from all the aerodynamic heating went dark as the entire surface of Sabrina No. 39

was instantly frozen by the blast of extremely cold air. This kind of cold was worse than being in outer space, a couple of minutes in this would have killed me.

Due to the lack of cold weather gear I had to do the next best thing. I had to activate my primary space suit, as I walked out of the lower hatch and felt the extreme cold grip of Antarctica for the first time. This caused me to turn my primary suit up to its maxim heat setting. I turned on the boarding tube and set it for ground use, this made it extend its tracks, and ground control stick.

I climbed aboard and drove it over to the closest main door that I could find, trailing my boarding tube behind me. When I tried to get inside through the exit door I got buried in piles and piles if personal gear bags, that the stranded aircrews were using them as an anti-cold barrier. To get through all this stuff I switched my space suit into its flight suit format.

I had to tunnel my way through the last door where I came face to face with the problem. There they were 450 Air Force personal all standing shoulder to shoulder stacked in as close as possible to each other as they could get. They all looked tired and half-frozen. I asked, "Who's in charge"? "Me" was the answer coming from a very tired Colonel that was standing in the middle of the room.

Instantly, a clear path opened between us. He kneeled down to me and looked me in the eye then he said," Who are you and where are your parents?" How did you get here? So without breaking eye contact I informed him that I had just arrived from orbit.

I'm the Sabrina from Sabrina Aviation I even had my flight suit show my official emblem. He wanted to know where I had parked my space ship. "Outside" I answered, why he wanted to know. "Because there's more empty space out there than any other place on the Planet" I answered. "Why can't I see it? "He questioned. "Because it dark outside I answered would you like me to have my space ship turn on all its outside lights I asked politely".

I called Sabrina No. 39 on my communications necklace and requested that she turn on all her external lights. Instantly it looked like sunrise with light streaming in from all the windows in and around all the equipment bags. His next question was how many personnel per trip? I answer that I could get everybody out in one trip including all the stuff they had laying around the building.

I informed him that my boarding tube was docked against the main door of this building, if he could arrange for the movement of the layers of equipment blocking the exit we could precede with loading. Instantly a path was cleared to the door. It was a heavy-duty outer door frosted white due to the extreme cold. I open it to show the end of my boarding tube with a large Sabrina No. 39 sign in the middle of it. I opened the hatch and only took a few steps when the extreme numbing cold caused my space suit to automatically activate.

I turned around to end up helmet to face with the Colonel, "eye ball to eye ball". As our heads bumped together the Colonel asked "are you her father?" No, it's just me I answered as my space suit reverted to its flight suit format. The Colonel informed me that none of his personal was going to go inside the boarding tube without having full cold weather gear issued to each of them. Of course, there was none available.

I called Sabrina No. 39 again to get her to turn up the air pressure as well as the heat so it would to flood through the boarding tube. She started out slow to allow the heat to channel itself into the feeder system to help heat up the tube and not blast the interior of the building with a blast of extremely cold air.

As the heat flooded in to the room, I could see the relief on everybody's face as this was the first warmth that most of these people had felt in a long time. If I had started to move hot air 5 minutes ago, everybody would be aboard by now. The colonel took charge and ordered everybody to form a line, to start pass all their equipment and supplies down the boarding tube.

I lead my first hundred passengers back down the boarding tube to the main cargo deck of Sabrina No. 39 now turned into a passenger compartment complete with operational heated rest rooms.

One of the younger pilots a friend of mine from my early Young Eagle days came over to say high. He craned his neck around and asked "where's your aircraft why did you lead us to another warehouse"? Buy the way "Is the rumor true, did you really make a V.T.O.L. landing with a SR-71 at

Oshkosh?" My reply seems to shock him when I informed him that I had landed at Pioneer Airport as it was closer to the museum.

By this time most of the stranded equipment had started coming in through the boarding tube with the help of the Air Forces human chain. They filled up all the empty space between the seats and then some. The Colonel who was the last person through the boarding tube came aboard and took charge. He started to tell everybody where to sit.

He wanted to know how come this pile of stuff is not secured, he came over to me and wanted to know where the bunks were and when was I going to fly the first group of his people out of here. I kind of laughed at myself he was so exhausted that he thought that he was in another warehouse. I almost had to leave the boarding tube behind as it had frozen itself to the surface at every point. I had to order maxim heat to melt its way back to Sabrina No. 39.

A good part of the Air Force just sat there and watched the boarding tube come back aboard you would think that they had never seen a "large slinky" before. One of the stranded pilots who were seated next to me asked, "What are you doing young lady?" I finally got the boarding tube to start returning back aboard so that now I can launch out of there." "Who are you?" He asked. I changed my flight suit back to its space suit form, stood up to my maximum height of 4'2" and looked him straight in the eye as my space helmet was forming around my head, and I replied "I'm your Astronaut pilot".

Then I took charge I walked over to the Colonel to look him in his blood shot eyes then I ordered him to sit down and put on his seatbelt. I made the final announcement, "Is everybody seated" then I activated the restraint system that stuck everybody in their seats. I informed all the passengers that the system is designed to make it easier to handle all the "G"s that they will be experiencing while flying with Sabrina Aviation.

I also congratulated all the different pilots' types, as after this flight they all would definitely qualify for Astronaut Wings, as we will be flying well over 50 miles high and at a speed of well over 17,500 miles per hour. Then I went back to my Command POD, to finish my weight & balance program. I finally had to use my reaction control rocket to blast away all of the ice to enable me to finally recover my only boarding tube.

I extended all my aerodynamic control surfaces, and turned on my deicers up to full, I even had my anti-icing system flood my extended wings and aerodynamic control surfaces. My Command Computer informed me that it would take a couple of minutes for all the ice and snow to melt. I had Sabrina No. 39 fire a short burst from her Aero-Spike rocket motor to create several heat bubbles too make the exterior of Sabrina No. 39 defrost faster.

I even fired several complete system checks of my ballistic control surfaces to help heat things up and blow away all the new snow that was still falling.

I started out slowly and added power in small steps until things started to move. Just as we lifted off a large hole opened up in the snow below where we were sitting. Once I was airborne I fired both of my Aero-Spikes and launched good old Sabrina No. 39 into the Dark Antarctic sky.

As we started to move and gain speed several tons of sheet ice fell off Sabrina No. 39's outer surface. I had to program for a slow trip with minimal "G" force, so the flight to New York took more than an hour. The "First Five" had flown in the replacement food supply they had to touch down close enough to their drop off point, to allow their main side cargo doors to open directly into the Antarctic base supply.

From New Zealand, they hauled everything into the Antarctic base with one trip each. Using their Command Computers, they all made pinpoint landing in zero-zero condition in a major Antarctic blizzard. After they had unloaded, I allowed them to play in the snow by retrieving lost fuel and food pallets that were littering the area for miles around the base.

I gave the "Next 10" the job of delivering the replacement fuel supply that was stock piled in 55 gallon drums located at their main storage area in the same New Zealand Base. I also gave the "Next 10" the task of removing all the damaged aircraft that were lying around the base and returning them to the main AMARC base in Arizona.

It was just a lot of C-130's nothing big. Up to now the only other humans flown by Sabrina No. 39 were her loser drag racing buddies. She wanted to know if she got another dragsters for each driver aboard, I reminded her that she only got to keep the dragsters when she returned the drivers. Then she made an announcement using my voice in the passengers POD wants to know if there were any "drivers" aboard. I got lucky and there weren't any.

When Sabrina No. 39 finally got to New York! She automatically hovered over the helicopter pad on the roof on the United Nations building lowered her boarding tube and started un-loading passengers and their equipment. I lowered my Command POD and turn on all my inside lights. I morph my space suit back into my school uniform, and sat in my pilots seat and waved" bye- bye" to the flight crews as they went out the boarding tube.

The Air force had left quite a mess in the main cargo bay it only took a couple of minutes to fold away the passenger PODs as well as the boarding tube. The ships system even folded and sterilized all the well-used rest rooms. The problem was all the left over equipment, the only thing I could do with all the stuff was to have Sabrina No. 39 leave it all on the helicopter pad.

It took up all the available space on the helicopter-pad six layers deep. The Line Chief at AMARC got a surprise when he returned from lunch to discover a whole new section of damaged C-130's with layers of deep snow still filling in their interiors. New row after row of damaged airplanes so cold that it froze the water in the sand on the ground at AMARC freezing all of the liquid on the hot desert sands surface that was now put in shade by their arrival.

I did get complains from all the "Next 10" ships from all the ice and water that was left on their cargo bay floors. Over all everybody behaved and took their turns they helped each other out as much as possible. Relaying weather data to each other as discovered.

Due to the weather and zero-zero flying conditions their onboard load masters work well. It would let the Command Computer know when something was too heavy to pick up the onboard safety system put a vacuum in the cargo bay to cut down the chance of a fire.

When transporting full fuel drums it refused several for empty spaces and fuel leaks. They all figured out that water comes from melting ice & cold keeps ice from melting. They all over cooled the life support in their cargo bays.

So in most cases all the recovered equipment as well as crashed C-130 parts had been chilled in the cargo bay to keep them from dripping. Recovered aircraft were so cold that the recovery crews at AMARC had to be issued extreme cold weather gear just to get near the recovered wreckage.

The logic program seems to think of each crash site as a separate item, they did not share or mix recovered parts. They rarely changed the orientation of each wrecked aircraft. If it was stuck down a hole when it was recovered and hung in the cargo bay at the same angle.

Several of the poor C-130's were recovered upside down. During their play activity, none of them even though of landing in the snow, as they considered snow was what destroyed all the stranded aircraft in the first place. Later I discovered that Pinger-5 purchased the original Operations Building and moved it to the surface of Mars, where she left it full of spent Zebra mussel shells.

Log Entry #30.
Fun with "First Five" & "Next Ten":

I sent a message to all the 39's "Return to base for re-fit to Mars. Because I was flying aboard Sabrina No. 39 she was restricted to "G"s allowed. This made me the last one through the hanger door. That's when the "First-Five" & the "Next-Ten" all sent Sabrina No. 39 a single word message "Loser". She responded that this was not a race, as she had not made a challenge. They all had already loaded their dragsters.

Then they proceeded to load mission-required equipment. The "First Five" were loaded with PAM rocket motors as well as lots of ribbon cables, and several spare Command PODs. Along with everything needed to track and capture comets. The "Next 10" would carry the center power generators and well as all the other equipment needed to set up and maintain a "rest stop" in space where all the hard and heavy parts of a comet can be put to good use. After all of the supplies were loaded fuel tanks topped, and final safety checks.

I gave the command for a formation pull out, this was really going to be a bank shot, with Sabrina No. 39 and the "First Five" heading for deep space and the "Next- 10" going to Mars after that setting up the basic layover spot that I hope to be a Sabrina made Moon after I knock all the water off them. I launched back in to the Asteroid Belt looking for inbound comets, the plan was to get six of them to collide up orbit from Mars.

Then to time the collision so that all the heavier parts to miss the planet with all the lighter mostly water or Ice crystal parts of the comet be picked up by the planet Mars as it orbits into it. I figured that the worst thing that could happen would be to create rainstorms on the surface of Mars rather than the usual sand ones.

Once we started the hunt, things started to happen fast, It only took about an hour for each of the ships to capture a comet, by landing on it and positioning a series of PAM motors for control as well as a Aero-Spike motor or two for direction. All this equipment is designed to leave the comet just before they impact each other. I discovered if I could get them to collide at a 10 degree angle the impact force would make micro-meteors out of everything the heavier iron and rock pieces would continue to move faster that the lighter water and ice crystals.

This started out as a simple plan, the idea of causing 5 or more comets to collide just up orbit of the Moon or Mars. The energy nullified by a massive collision, by having each comet nullifies all their potential energy by having a head on collusion, then let the planet or Moon orbit through its debris trail. Instead of allowing all the heavier solid mass of the comet to continue on to fly into the Sun or I could use its micro-gravity to reform around large support structure that would eventually be able to use as a space born location. The lighter trailing water ice ends up on the surface of Mars to add water to the environment of the planet without making a crater. I decided to perfect my plan on Mars first then move into the Earth Moon. I decided to run a few test to find out what really happens when a comet collides with each other.

I had designed my PAM rocket system to take a licking and still work but there was no need to make unnecessary dents. It was back to the same old thing I had to keep dynamics forces to a minimum as nothing was for sure if I move it this way there no problem if I move it that way it would break up into lots of smaller comets. Then I would transmit the recall command and have all the PAMS & Aero-Spikes form up on themselves, and recover them for the next try. As the only live human aboard it became my duty to keep refueling and repairing all the PAM units as the "First Five" learned the knack of Comets herding.

It only took a couple of week to find and capture our first five comets I captured my sixth one last. I set them all to collide close enough to Mars to where most if not all of the captured Ice would be absorbed by the Martian atmosphere as the planet past through the slower moving end of the massive field of ice crystals. The "First Five" were programmed to have a weekly staff meeting. With the plan of trade off any need spares as well as put all the spent PAM motors on one space ship.

Then when that ship was full of spent PAM units needing Maintenance or refueling that ship would bring them to me "The only live human aboard" so that I could recycle them back into operational units. This was our second get together all of the "First Five" ships were low on PAM units, not to mention the five movers that I had on course that always need to be refueled.

As it turns out making all of the constant correction for a comets out gassing has to be the worse job in the universe if not just our solar system. I got a message from Sabrina No. 39/3 it seemed that she had ran out of serviceable PAM units. Then call me "The Only Human a Board" Tohab to refuel all her recovered units. So she came over to my location and we docked together airlock to airlock, I had just changed into my newly recharged primary space suit.

I had not pressurized any of the "First Five" as there was no need for it, this made it mandatory that I use my Space suit when aboard. As I passed through the airlock Sabrina No. 39 let me know that she was now in command. The first thing I did was to check the safety board to see how things were going. I noticed a red light in the port side cargo bay this is the part of the ship where 39/3 kept all her returned PAM units. For safety reasons I had made a standard order that all returned PAM unit to be transported is open cargo bays until I had inspected them.

At first glance, it didn't look like a PAM unit. I had designed them to take a licking and keep on ticking, but this unit had really been put through the ringer, It looked like a very heavy army tank had made several figure 8's on it and shot it a couple of times. I checked the flight record to see the worse comet break up I could images, it had rotated on all three of its axes and chewed itself up, including its installed PAM unit.

As it turned out 39/3 had spent hours following the debris field picking up lost equipment as it surfaced. Listed under logic, 39/3 thought that if it was OK for Sabrina No. 39 to collect old useless race cars she could collect old beat up PAM units. I noticed that the mass of wreckage that use to be a PAM unit was changing shape in the cargo bay. I saw a very bright light that filled up the entire cargo bay then the black darkness of outer space as I was blown over board by the explosion, sending me out of the cargo bay like I was shot out of a canon.

This wasn't the first time in my life that I was playing the part of a" Cannon Ball In Flight" I knew not to fight the dynamic forces that were acting on my 14 year old body. My primary Space suits emergency systems had saved my life as it had instantly hardened and layered up to keep small parts of exploding rocket motors from making holes in my space suit. When I came too I checked my chronometer to find out that it was broken by the blast.

I was spinning on all three of my axes my suit controls had a few dents in it, my primary suit was still working I was still alive, as my eyes starter to focus I noticed that I was looking at both of my knees it was nice to learn that I still had them. By using my arms and legs as ballast I managed to change my center of mass, I used this basic trick to stop my spinning.

I tried out my communication system to find out what was going on, all of my incoming information channels were off line, I tried to text out, without any luck. I was doing good for a cannon ball, as I figured out my course and speed I discovered that my body would go into orbit around Earth in 847 years give or take a couple of days. I thought this news was great as it meant that I was on an inbound trajectory to Earth without a space ship.

I thought that I was losing it when I heard my own voice asking me if I was finished with my spacewalk and did I wish to come aboard at this time. I looked around to see the forward grabber arms of good old Sabrina No. 39's aircraft mover reaching for me. As I was pulled back into Sabrina No. 39's cargo bay I noticed that 39/3's docking hatch was still attached along with a large section of bulkhead. I could still read 39/3's safety board with the red light warning still on in her cargo bay. As soon as I got back into my POD I changed into my back-up space suit and checked myself out for any injuries.

So far my idea of a Medical Emergency was having to opening up a new box of Band-Aids, or a new bottle of Iodine. Considering what happened to my primary space suit I was in relative good shape however it did take an hour longer in the charger to get rid of all blast residues. I checked in with the communications system to find out the Sabrina No. 39 wanted to know if my rescue entitles her to my race car with nothing reporting in from 39/3 at all. It has been hours sense the explosion without any incoming information.

Therefore, I commanded her to report in. Her logic board was full of information; she was damaged, on fire, out of control, out of fuel, and thinks that I was mad at her because she had used me as a cannon ball. I finally found her hiding on the other side of an asteroid, she was in pretty poor shape, and the mass of the exploding PAM motor had made a first class mess out of her she had large holes in several of her bulkheads as well as lots of missing surface skin where she had torn off her docking hatch. She also had lost all her cargo bay doors she had used all her fuel reserve to stop her movements that was caused by her on board explosion.

I call a staff meeting and informed the rest of the "First Five" it took a while but with the use of all of our spare part as well as fuel. It took the fabrication of a Womanized Maneuvering Unit, plus a lot of tender loving repairs from "Me" "TOLHA" the only living human aboard. I got Sabrina No. 39/3 back to work she would need major repairs when she got to Phobos, it would be a long trip but it would work as long as she stays out of an Atmosphere. Sabrina No. 39 said that she could keep her dragster, as long as she would make it part of her collection.

I thought that was very touching until I realize that now I have two space ships that like to go to the drag races. Then we all formed up on our current experiment and headed in towards Mars. The "Next Ten" had been busy, over the last couple of weeks they had set up a very large structure, 5 miles by 5 miles cube. As the plan still was to create gravity well and let it attract all the leftovers and see if I can make a Moon of my own.

The plan is simple, to park it in space just ahead of the multiple Comet impact point and see if gravity can make me a Moon. We nursed all five of our comets as planned it was a fight to the end. Six of my command computes against five dumb out gassing chunk of rock and frozen water.

The plan worked as well as expected there was a blinding flash as well as a large shock wave, as it all came together with a "Silent BANG" exactly where I had planned for it to happen. I called recall at T-minus 5 minutes all of my equipment was recovered as planned.

All of the dynamic forces were nullified, everything was converted to powder or dust size clouds, just like cannon balls all the heavier rock and iron dust moved ahead of the pack and then Mars orbited came into its tail. The trillions of Ice particles were pulled down into the Martian atmosphere by it gravity well without any visual effect at all. None of the water Ice melted, it all buried itself under the surface on impact, and then it was blown over by the Martin winds, hardly any of them even made a sizeable crater.

So this left millions of tons of frozen ice buried under the surface of Mars, it did not make a single raindrop, or wet spot anywhere in the planet. In less than ten minutes after all the water ice stopped falling from the sky everything looked the same. All it did was make it possible to mine crush Ice on Mars. I had the same luck with the rest of the matter, I had not count on all the non-liquid matter being atomize all the particles were too small to be stopped my any of my capture nets and moved straight past all my capture points.

I had the "Next 10" leave my large support structure in the middle of the dust cloud. It did not help a bit as all the particles were so microscopic that the solar wind just blew them away like smoke. Who know the next time I will try with only two. However I did managed to get lots of frozen water onto the surface of Mars. Now all I have to do is figure a way to dig it up and use it.

Log Entry #31.
2007 WD5:

This one has been on my things to do list for a while it's a little, Van size meteor that has a good chance of finally hitting Mars on the 30th of January. So far it's been one of those too small to worry about as well as being in the wrong place, when one of my slow moving Asteroid Ark Ships passed close enough to do anything about it.

It's a little too big for my Sabrina No. X series ships to recover, and at the same time too small for my Sabrina No. 39 series ships to even worry about. As its going outbound it will have nothing to do with my current project, trying to keep six different comets on a collision course to collide up orbit of Mars, making it a possibility of having Mars capture a lot of liquid water. This goes to show you how far a person who has been on the surface of Mars will go to help get rid of the dust!

If 2007 WD5 misses Mars I will definitely add it to my collection once it's on my side of the planet. All 16 of my Sabrina No. 39s were on hand for the second half to see if I could make my own Moon. It took all of us docked on the structure to make it move, and I lined it up, set up its rotation speed and hoped for the best. Would you believe that none of the rock or iron mass would stick to anything?

I kept the stricture moving relevant to the main mass of the smashed comets only to have all of it keep going when I tried to move the main five mile square structure only to lose every bit of it as it kept on going. I kept all 16 of the Sabrina No. 39 series docked to the cube and moved it to Mars and parked it next to its largest moon Phobos.

I figured that I could enclose it and use it as a comet hanger, to keep the out gassing clouds of water vapor from causing Mars to have another Ice Age. As soon as the cube was secure on Phobos I sent the Next 10 to land at the landing pad at the base of the elevator, and the "First Five" to dock and refuel at the main base on Phobos. Sabrina No. 39/3 was still in need of major repairs to get her in shape to where she could fly inside an Atmosphere again.

As soon as Sabrina No. 39/3 was put back into full operational condition I gave her the task of taking care of 2007 WD5, Her logic board went active it took several minutes to learn everything there was to know about the next Meteor that was supposed to hit Mars. As it turned out 39/3 also needed to spend time in the overhaul site at the foot of the elevator repair site, she knew that it would take a week or so to repair all her internal damage. When I ordered the "First Five" to the surface of Mars she fell out of formation and was missing for more than an hour. When she finally touched down on landing pad one she made a point of keeping her dragster, only to place, 2007 WD5 in the trophy circle instead.

Log Entry #32.
He/3:

I got the word from my tech-lab that I had set up on the LEADER in Earth orbit. It seems that they had finally figured out how to make a He/3 Nuclear Reactor powered Rocket Motors, and self-contained reactors for making electricity. As planned I had the first 16 of them reserved for my use, with the "First Five", "Next Ten" and good old Sabrina No. 39.

It was modularized designed to fit between the two Aero-Spike chemical rocket motors already installed in each Space ship. She asked how the Martian weather was and did I make it rain yet, No I replied. But I did make it possible to mine chipped ice cubes.

All I needed to do was combine it with a Helium three collector, and make millions. I told her that, "I would bring the whole gang back to Earth as soon as Sabrina No. 39/3 had recovered from her fuel tank epiphany, and was made 100% space worthy". She wanted to know what happened, I told her about the "explosion as well as my experiences of being a human cannon ball", she then wanted to know if I has set a record, I answer no.

Sabrina No. 39 had finally picked me up a couple hundred thousand miles away. She said that all she did was go into drag racing mode and snatch me on her way back. She also told me that the new dormitory was finished at my school, complete with landing PAD and secret entrance to my dorm room.

Log Entry #33.
Gravity Sling:

For the return trip to Earth I planned to try something new, I am going to make a Gravity Sling. By cabling all 16 of my Sabrina No. 39s together then we follow each other around a circle as we let out more cable, a hundred miles or more, then real in all of the cable to fly a tight circle, to build up our Inertia the same way a sling speeds up a rock.

The faster we can go in a captive circle is speed gained. Then by having each ship real in cable and make the speed circle smaller our speed would increase. Then at the desired navigation JUMP OFF point, I would disconnect and release myself from the cable from the last ship in line.

Then I go zooming straight where I want to go. As all the other Sabrina No.39's follow under tow, we all real in close, and dock together to form a single mass. This will make a heavier cannon ball that will reach a higher speed. To slow down, stop, or change direction all we have to do is repeat the Gravity Sling Maneuver and go zooming of in a new direction. I plan to make good use of this maneuver on my planned trip to Jupiter.

Log Entry #34.
Faster Trips Back:

Summer vacation was coming to a close and I had to get back to school for my 11th grade orientation, this is something I have to do live without the use of the classroom in my POD. The "First Five" and the "Next Ten" have kept themselves occupied by doing their thing. By transporting a series of surface stage coach stations that the Surface Exploration Units have been trying to set up for more than a year. Sabrina No. 39/11 made a career using the thrust from her hover-fans to bury all the station modules.

Their logic boards all took precautions to insure the safety of any human that they were transporting. They also made a point of hanging around to be available. In their logic boards they referred to this as "Camping" they also recover all 14 pieces of my beloved Sabrina No. IX. Nothing was recognizable the only thing I could do with all her recovered pieces was to melt them down and use the metal to repair Sabrina No.39/3.

What was most interesting was that we had only recovered about 20% of her mass. I packed along Martian souvenirs, thousands of "Martian pet rocks" everything that was noted in the official Viking photographs as well as both Viking I & II landers. I even retrieved both of their orbital modules I worked on both of them myself for over an hour I can't figure why they quit working.

I wanted to bring back as many of N.A.S.A.'s failures as I could find as I plan to make their day. In the resent past every time I mention one of their failed space probes the N.A.S.A. officials answer was we don't know because we can't get the "Bird" back. I plan to cure them of that problem.

Earlier this year on Earth I had an occasion to cut up a Typhoon with Sabrina No. 39. As we were launching out of the foot of the elevator base I wondered if we might be able to simply cut up the major Martian sandstorms with our wake turbulence. We had some fuel to spare, Sabrina No. 39 wanted to know where the race was. I directed each ship to make a supersonic vertical assent through the closest Martian Thunderhead.

As we met up in Martian orbit, I checked back with Phobos control for a weather report to hear the good news the Martin winds had stopped moving the larger weather rocks. With everybody in Martian orbit we all cabled up, I synced up all the other command computers with Sabrina No. 39's and moved out towards Earth.

I figure it has to be another record, with me flying formation with myself 15 times over. Everybody let out a hundred miles of cable I had Sabrina No. 39 to start making a large circle at the same angle of the planets elliptic plain. The link up wasn't as easy as I planned, but I made it, I made sure that everybody had all their cable played out, and then I let centrifugal force do its thing.

I programmed the release point into my flight computer, at five "G" turns, I gave the command to start reeling in cable, as the circle got smaller the speed went faster, as well as the "G's" went higher, I still used the Sun's gravity to accelerate, as I had planned the Gravity Sling Maneuver to increase my speed by over 600 per cent. My reverse the direction of movement stopping maneuver was just as interesting, but it did work, over all we used less fuel and we did not have to use the Earth's atmosphere to slow down. All of the Sabrina No. 39's made it to their docking bay on the LEADER as planned.

Log Entry #35.
Mid Term Interview:

Sabrina No. 39 and I made a direct descent to the roof of my new dormitory building that I had Sabrina Aviation build at my School. I made a normal entry into Chicago airspace with Sabrina No. 39 making all the air traffic calls herself. Then of course she was using my voice to talk with all the air traffic controllers. The weather in the Chicago area was the worst that I had flown in on Earth. Vary massive thunderstorms the kind that did not have sand in them made out of real wet rain water.

The storm front was building and traveling towards the school. The three new touch-down points worked like a charm, everything lined up perfectly. Sabrina No. 39 even looks like a roof-top air conditioning unit after she had folded herself up. I lowered my Command POD down to the tenth floor, and then rotated it to line up to my gang plank with the secret door that was installed in the back of my closet. As I walked in front of the full length mirror on the back of my dorm door I turned it on as it also doubles as the main communication screen for Sabrina No. 39.

As I was checking out the local thunderstorms I noticed that everything was being up graded to a Tornado alert, my reflection reminded me to transform my space suit into my school outfit. There was a knock at the door and in popped the school's Administrative Assistant, "Oh here you are how did you get past me down stairs," "what did you do land on the roof"? Yes I replied, "less than a minute ago". She Asked, "Did you have any problems flying close to the storm front"? "No" I replied, I wanted to check out my new dorm room that my company had built. She said, "I expect to find you wearing a space suit after all you're the school Astronaut."

She was the first person to sit down in my studying chair and then she spread all her paper all over the top of my school desk and went right into my interview. First off the Smithsonian Institution wants to know if you're interested in donating your No. 5 Rocket ship to them for display.

It seems that they were trying to claiming it through your estate "Have you, died recently and not informed me" She asked? I replied "There was this time when I was shot down over Mars by a meteor storm." My Sabrina No. IX Space ship was destroyed in flight and I had to crash land my Command POD on the surface of Mars and drive the last 50 miles back to my base on my own.

During this brief time period I may have been considered dead, if so the report of my death had been greatly exaggerated. Did you really make a V.T.O.L. landing with a SR-71 at Oshkosh?" My reply seems to shock her when I informed her that I had landed at Pioneer Airport as it was closer to the museum. I answered as large oversized rain drops started to hit the windows.

I have a problem with my forms, it says here that you were out of the country, but it doesn't say which country you were in, there also a note about Antarctica, and did you go all the way to Antarctica? "Yes I answered but only for less than an hour, I answered." What were you doing with this group of people?" She asked "I was their Astronaut Pilot" I informed her, "Are you listened to fly in Antarctica? "She asked "Yes I am" I replied. "Where did you pick up this group of people and how did they get there?" She asked at the South Pole in the middle of the Antarctica.

My passengers were stranded aircrews and ground support personal that tried to use the local runways during the Antarctic summer. Some of them were stuck there for as long as 4 months", I answered. "Why did you go there" she asked. "The manager of the facility requested my assistance in removing 450 stranded humans.

I flew them, out of their operations center. At the coming of Antarctic night there was a severe weather change, a force 5 blizzards that cut the base off for over 200 miles around, from both land and air travel" I answered. As the skies darkened, it started to rain harder "Where did you come from"? She asked, "The top of my Space Elevator in Texas" I replied, I made it to the base operations building in less than 15 minutes, as I was only 34,000 miles away when I got the call, I replied," "In less than 15 minutes" she asked. "Yes I replied, "It was downhill all the way, with very little Atmosphere in-between", I replied." Where did you land", she asked"? I made a vertical ballistic landing, which requires using thrusters as close to the main Operations Building as I could, less than 100 feet from their main door.

The main base had been out of runways for more than the last 6 months. It was dark, the surface winds were moving faster than 100 miles per hour. The temperature had dropped to well below 100 degrees below zero, sort of like it is outside now except for the White-Out" I answered. "What kind of airplane did you use" she asked "? I replied that I didn't use an airplane I use the prototype space ship that I had designed and built to make soft landings on Mars.

She was my 39th design, she answers to the name Thirty-nine," I replied. "How do you talk to this Thirty-nine" she asked. "With my voice, communications necklace, computer, E-mail, Text Message, and my Command screen that's built into my main room door, my only problem is she like to talk back and use my voice, at times I think that I am talking to myself." I answered. I asked "Why are you asking about this operation it only took a couple of hours of my time, and that includes the trip to the United Nation building in New York City, to drop everybody off"?

Outside the weather was getting bad even by Mars Standards. Sabrina No. 39 started showing me weather warning on my command screen. OK can you explain this she asked, a letter of thanks from the United States Air Force, they think that you were on a small ship in the middle of the Pacific Ocean during a typhoon, you rescued a Captain Lynda Love when her F-22 Raptor lost an engine. "There's a little more to that story, in all I saved eight F-22's, 14 pilots, 200 ground pounders and a very empty KC-43 Tanker." "I have the IOU that the Line Chief at Edwards Air Force Base Signed when I gave all their stuff back." "She asked "Why did you haul everything into Edwards Air Force Base"? I replied, "The flight line at Edwards is the only place in California that Sabrina No. 39 knows how to find". "You flew directly in to a Typhoon," she asked. "Yes," I replied it was the only way that I could slow down.

By the time I had rescued the other three F-22's I had cut up the Typhoon to the point where it was down rated to a tropical depression, unlike the storm forming outside as we speak. It looks like I might get to cut up a home grown Tornado. Then she asked, about my aerial firefighting adventures. Oh that I answered, I have this much older borate bomber friend that invited me out on one of his test flights. That's when I discovered that I did not need to drop anything directly on to a burning fire to put out the flames.

All I would have to do is fly over the burning fire line at a speed just below Mach one, to have the shock wave from my wake turbulences from my Sabrina No. 39 series space ship to just blow out the fire like candles on a birthday cake.

Her next question was, "What is the subject of your science project?" I instantly answered. "Martian rain fall". She Asked, "Where have you been working on your summer project"? "I have been in the Asteroid Belt" I replied. "What country is that in she asked"? "It's not in a country, it's the area of outer space that's between the orbital tract of the planets Mars and Jupiter," I replied.

"Were you all by yourself she asked?" "Not really I had 15 copies of Sabrina No. 39 built, that makes 16 Space ship in all," I answered. She asked, "You can control 16 different Space ships all at the same time?" "No I designed and built them to control themselves, the first time I personally took control of all of them at the same time was during my last return to Earth mission.

"I was showing them how to do the energy sling maneuver that I invented." I replied as large hail stones start to hit the building.

I noted on my command screen that Sabrina No. 39 was starting to complain that she did not like being hit by all the hail stones. She had pressurized herself and lowered her landing gear struts to a point where she had stopped the movement of air under her lifting surfaces. She had attached her anchors at all three touchdown points.

She asked "Have you had any problems being the only human in your feet of Space ships? A few I replied," the worse job I set myself up for constantly having to re-fuel all of the PAM rocket engine units." "Then of course being blown over board when I was re-fueling a damaged PAM unit that exploded". "I discovered a list that Sabrina No. 39 had written on her logic board Jobs for T.O.L.H.A. it took a couple of minutes to realize that I was "The Only Living Human Aboard."

She asked. "Why were you blown over board in outer space? "As Tolha was hard at work as usual patching up as well as re-fueling the current batch of used Pam Rocket Motors, when one of them exploded knocking me over board, with a single big bang." It took Sabrina No. 39 a couple of hours to track me down and pick me up several million miles away.

I had managed to stabilize myself and figured my trajectory, when she grabbed my foot and pulled me back inside through her cargo bay door.

I programmed her to think independently sort of like now as she started showing me live photos of the force one Tornado touching down about 5 miles away.

Now if we can get back to your current project. "How did you plan to make it rain on Mars", She Asked? That's simple I replied, I spent most of my time away learning how to control comets, to the point where I could get five or more of them to collide just up orbit from the planet Mars. Then have all or most of the water Ice heat up coming through Mars's Atmosphere.

Then let it land on its surface as rain my only problems was that none of the Ice melted the only thing I did was make it possible to mine chipped Ice. Unlike all the water that was falling out side. "What are your current plans" She asked? I am making plans to go to Jupiter, to check out all its Moons. As well as to design and build a rescue size Space ship for the 39 series.

"The new much larger space ship would be the same basic shape with the ability to carry at least four of my Sabrina No. 39 series, spacecraft internally. Keeping with my numbering system, I will call it the Sabrina No. 40 series". I answered. As very large near by lightning strikes started to make the electric lights flicker. "This is your third round trip between Mars and Earth isn't" she asked, "Yes I replied."

Can you explain how you can make it to Mars and back three times in less than a single school year?" "It's all a matter of speed and distance I explained, have you ever been to a dog track I asked?" "Why do you ask" she Said? "At the dog track the dogs are taught to chase a rabbit that is on a track traveling around the race track."

"As soon as the racing dog figures out that they can cut across the track and head the rabbit off as it comes around from the other side, the dog is put out to pasture and not allowed to race anymore," I answered. "I not only know how to cut across the track, I know how to go faster than all the other rabbits", I answered.

As I noticed on the command screens monitor that the Tornado were getting closer and at the same time growing to force two. She said, "I have another thing to ask you about?" "It's a letter from the Vietnamese Government for some reason they want to surrender to you". "It seems that one of their military installations keeps getting hit by a single meteorite every day at 9:34 AM.

They keep moving their base but it doesn't seem to help, as this problem has been going on for the last four months. "I replied that this was the first that I have heard of this problem I will have to check into it and get back with an answer."

All during my interview, I kept dropping things pens, letters note books. Finally she asked me "What's wrong with you". I replied, "I'm used to working in "Zero-Gravity where everything is weightless, I'm use to leaving things where, I need them to be without gravity making, them fall to the floor." I replied, "It's a good thing we are not eating oatmeal," I added.

Right now, all my brain wants my body to float off into the corner of my dorm room and relax. At this point, my school uniform changed colors and changed into a sleeping bag, right in front of her eyes, with me still in it, while I was standing in front of my school administrator.

It's OK I replied "It's just my space suit informing me that it's time for sleep." At the instant I said the word "space suit" my primary snapped back full format helmet and all, it even made itself a red cape with a large white "S" on it. I asked Sabrina No. 39, "What's going on?"

As the next instant all of the windows blew in and all the doors were torn off their hinges". My Space suit worked like a charm it not only kept me from getting stabbed by thousands of very sharp pieces of broken flying glass, it also kept me from getting wet, I even served as a shield to save my School Administrator from a death of a thousand cuts, as the big red cape with an "S" expanded out to cover her.

I powered up my suits built in extra muscle system, everything in my room as well as the school administrator were blown over to the other side of my dorm room.

I picked up my couch and bed I tried to use them to block the open spaces where my windows use to be located only to have them pulled out the window by the now closing force 5 Tornado. I picked my now dazed school administrator up and headed for my POD and carried her up the gang plank to safety.

I buttoned up the POD while we were still on the boarding ramp. I stuffed her into my school room turned on my external cameras, and gave the administrator a perfect view of the very large force 5 Tornado, that was eating the entire campus, my brand new dormitory and all. I used Sabrina No. 39's sensors to check out what's left of the building and to check for survivors.

I asked the administrator "if she knew how many students were in the dormitory?" She answered, "Only you, as the rest of the students were to move in tomorrow." The Tornado had gutted out the dormitory and was starting to eat the buildings foundation. Sabrina No. 39 came back with a complete structure analyst of the dorm building complete with a countdown telling me when the dorm building will fall over, with her on top of it.

Seeing that I had more than 30 seconds before the building toppled I brought all the systems on line, instantly my school room turned into my cockpit. I had to use my keyboard to fly Sabrina No. 39 with only the use her ballistic controls, to launch off the roof. Sabrina No. 39 had it figured right, as we had just started to tip over she released all her hold down clamps, it most definitely was an interesting moment when the whole building fell out from under Sabrina No. 39 leaving her hovering in her present location.

Then we were pulled straight through the main wall of the Tornado, and got pulled up through the top of the storm. Once clear of the storm I extended the lift-fans and hovered as I watched the still growing force 5 Tornado beat my campus to splinters. The next thing I heard was Sabrina No. 39 asking the administrator if she was a driver, to top it all off she was using my Voice! "No she replied I haven't driven for years." "Good I relied, as long as you did not drive dragsters."

My administrative assistant was still sitting next to me in my class room now turned into a cockpit watching the Tornado destroying the school some 10,000 feet below, on my built in 360 degree wall mounted screens. It sort of gave her the feeling of being hung out in space…watching.

At this time I noticed that the logic board on the Command Computers of the rest of the 39's became very active. I could see that they were diving in from their parking places on the LEADER. At this time my Administrative Assistant noticed the arrival of the rest of the Sabrina No. 39's, they were all flying in single file formation moving at around Mach 15, at one mile intervals. They proceeded to fly directly through the wall of the Tornado using their wake turbulence to tear huge holes in it, each ship in line hit a different spot eventually cutting the Tornado in half.

Then they would make a slow turn and come back from a different angle, they all started to fly a tight circle, pulling well over a hundred "G"s in each turn. She asked "What are all of them doing?" I answered, "It's a weather control maneuver that we have been using on Mar's to kill off the larger dust storms. I'm not sure how well it will work here on Earth with all the extra air pressure, and water.

After a few high speed passes all of the Sabrina No. 39's started to slow down. When they started to fly subsonic, they started to fire both of their Aero-spikes rocket motors just as they would hit the wall of the Tornado then do a full power climb up thought its center. My Administrative assistant asked, "If this was a change in tactics". "No" I answered, "they just like to do high power high speed vertical climb outs, I think it's something in their DNA."

She asked, "Is this the maneuver you use to put out forest fires." "No", I replied, a forest fire fighting run would have to be subsonic at one hundred feet above the surface when I do that I can use the Wake Turbulence generated by the shape of my airfoil to smother the flames. If I hit the fire line at supersonic speed, I will bury everything under at least two feet of loose soil.

Eventually the Tornado gave up, the weather cleared we even got a rainbow out of the deal. I had Sabrina No. 39 touched down in my usual spot in the back of the parking lot where I use to park Sabrina No. IX. As the POD lowered us to the ground and lowered its gangplank.

We both walked out to see that there was nothing left of my school, the force 5 Tornado had even pulled up the grass and small bushes. I had all my all of my Sabrina No. 39's Space ships land and connect to each other's side cargo bay doors to up into a single structure. By changing their directions they all took advantage of their triangular shape and created a single long empty coordinator. I repositioned my command POD to connect to my main cargo bay.

I walked the School Administrator over to the middle of the bay to show her the view of all the Sabrina No. 39 space ships making a single long empty spot larger enough to hold the entire school. It looks like we will have to start all over my school was in desperate need of a place to go, so I offered them an empty space on the LEADER, all they would have to do is take a 33 thousand mile elevator ride each way. Her Next Question was "You keep talking about your LEADER, "exactly who is it?"

The LEADER is the name of the first asteroid that I captured late last year, if you remember it was going to hit Chicago, is now the base of my operations in Outer space, first off she's the top base for my Space Elevator, as well as my Space ship factory. I also have my main helium three factory there as well as the first weightless hospital in history.

All built into the middle of the LEADER. I even have several small communities on board that are on their way to the Moon, Mars or a convent size Asteroid. "Would you like to see it" I asked? Yes she replied, I realized that Sabrina No. 39 did not have a jump-seat, so I moved down to my fabrication shop in the POD and instant prototyped a jump seat, and I installed it next to mine in the cockpit.

I asked Sabrina No. 39 to reprogram my back up suit for the Administrator, which she did without question. It was interesting to note that after reprogramming it to fit her perfectly the nametag changed from Sabrina to Administrator.

After both us got cozy in my cockpit I took command brought up all my flight systems, had all the 39's disconnected both their port and starboard cargo bay doors, close up all the Sabrina No. 39's for flight.

Then I called the Elgin TRACON for permission for a vertical assent with clearance to a hundred thousand feet. I launch vertically and had my whole gang follow me in trail. As soon as I was high, enough I fired both of my Aero-Spikes and went into a supersonic climb. As soon as we were at my requested altitude, I vectored us over to the Space Elevator and followed it all the way to the LEADER.

She asked, "Where did you get all the materials from to make this?" Passing metal Asteroid and from my diggings on the LEADER I answered. "It's huge" she replied, "Yes I answered for it to work it has to be 33,000 miles long, the space elevators on the Moon and Mars are a lot shorter. I already have three working elevators on the earth's moon one is on the dark side, with the other two on the Earth side.

As we flew closer to the LEADER, I checked in with my Watch-Commander to let them know that I was close by and on my way to Sabrina No. 39s hanger. As we flew closer to Sabrina No. 39's hanger door, she noticed a much larger rectangular crater being cut into the outside of the LEADER, "What is that for" the administrator asked,? Oh that's where I will be building the Sabrina No. 40 series Space craft. It will be large enough to carry four of my Sabrina No. 39s in side.

I plan to use it as a mobile repair site as I have had several occasions where it would have been lots easier to repair skin damage if I had a place to do it inside. As soon as Sabrina No. 39 was in her usual parking space I introduced my staff to the school Administrator and they started the process of moving my school to the "Leader." I sent one of my start up structures to the location where my school had been before it was destroyed by a force 5 Tornado.

It took the rest of the weekend to move in all the modules and set everything up. So that by Monday morning everything was ready to go, I had to put in lots of support beams to make up for the gravity. Over all thing settle down to a more normal routine, it took a couple of weeks before the school was ready to move to its new home in the LEADER. "The controllers in the Elgin Center had a field day when the whole gang of my Sabrina No.39 series, went to work airlifting my school to its location on the LEADER.

I spaced everybody at 30 minute intervals as each Sabrina No. 39 Space ship would make a vertical landing next to the modules being moved, have them disconnect and move into their interiors through their side cargo hatch, until the load-master program said stop. Then make a standard vertical takeoff with its lift-fans to a safe altitude and speed that would enable them to safely ignite their Aero-Spike motors to zoom back up to the LEADER.

Once my space ship made it back to the LEADER where it would off-load its cargo into the central incoming point, then move them to their permeate location. Due to the size of the structure being moved it took the better part of the day to transport everything.

The next morning my entire schools student population both teacher and staff were standing in what was left of the parking lot when Sabrina No. 39 and I arrived. I had made a point to use my Urban-Camouflage-Program to make Sabrina No.39 look like a very large yellow school bus.

I had to admit that it took a little longer than planned for everybody to get aboard and seated. But I personally transported everybody to school that first day. The principal didn't even ask me about only having a drivers permit.

Log Entry #36.
Updates:

This year Sabrina No. 39 & 39/3 got together and changed the act first they would link up their Command Computers. Sabrina No. 39 would run the race with me aboard and then 39/3 would swoop down unseen from above and snatch the looser off the ground. This would leave Sabrina No. 39 free to put on the speed brakes and come around to clime her prize, with me standing on the loading ramp, waving at the crowd.

Then Sabrina No. 39/3 would return with the looser and deliver the driver of the defeated dragster, directly to the racing judge. Later after I used Sabrina No. 39s command computer to reprogram Sabrina No. 40s after it was commentated by tons of pure microscopic space Gold dust. Sabrina No. 40 would get in to the professional drag racing circuit. Due to Her much larger size she would start the race with her nose cone on the starting line.

Then as soon as the tip of her nose cone pasted the finishing line she would launch a space-junk-trap too grab up the loser before they had a chance to finish the race and carry the now captured dragster away in a fashion similar as to how Sabrina No. 39 did it herself. I did get an interesting navigation question from My Sabrina No.39/8 it seems the she was working at hoisting heavy air conditioning components to the top of tall building in down town Atlanta, Georgia.

Her on board navigation systems was Peach "Treed" out, as Sabrina No.39/8 was currently siting in a parking lot awaiting the truck size cargo that she was going to place on the roof of one of the surrounding buildings, it seems that she was in Peachtree County, she currently was parked in a parking lot at Peachtree Place, which was in the middle of Peachtree Circle, that was boarded by Peachtree Street and Peachtree Avenue, also this location was not to be confused with the Peachtree Place that was just south of her location next to Peachtree Boulevard.

Toping it off the only actual trees that were growing within 5 miles of her were Oak Trees. All I could do was to verify her location with her onboard Global Position System.

Log Entry #37.
Wet A380:

There I was test flying my Sabrina No. 40 series reinforced space ship in low Earth orbit. I had designed her to do a swan dive into the surface of Jupiter's moon Europa. Sabrina No. 40 is eight times as large as the Sabrina No. 39 she is powered by four Aero-Spikes, one Nuclear ION rocket motors.

As usual I was in low Earth orbit trying to add to my space-junk collection, I was still trying to recover the assent module that was abandoned in low Earth orbit by the crew of Apollo 9. I was using a Japan bound A380 as one of my mid Pacific Ocean navigation points, by locating it on every orbit. I noticed that one of my current navigation points was not making the usual headway flying into a large mid Pacific typhoon.

On this orbit, I found it sitting on the surface of the Pacific Ocean, with lots of very deep water under it, about to be run over by a very large Typhoon. I got to use my telephoto zoom lenses to check it out from orbit. I could see that the airframe was still in one-piece floating level in the water, I could even tell that all four of their engines had sheared off as planned when they ditched.

I had my communication system check the emergency radio channels only to discover that they were on their own as all the emergency rescue forces were engaged with the Typhoon. All the surface ships had long been diverted, with nothing available for over 500 miles. I called home to let my parents know what I was up too, as usual it rang and rang until the answering machine picked up.

I started to talk into the phone machine, explaining what I need to do to save a whole plane load of people. Without a seconds thought I pointed Sabrina No. 40's nose towards the surface of the Earth and fired a full blast from all four of my Aero-Spike Rocket Motors. Instantly I was doing a full power descent over the middle of the Pacific Ocean with my re-entry flight path going directly into a level 5 Typhoon.

When my mother called me back, I answered on the first ring and explained that I was in my usual emergency dive mode as the surface of the Earth was starting to get lots closer. I put my Command POD in full suspension so that I could survive the force of a supersonic water impact.

Due to the A380's present location, I would had to travel through the full fury of the Typhoon to get to its location. Moms first question was did I remember to turn on my space suit. I answered yes, of course as my helmet had just quit forming around my head. She said good-bye and for me to be safe just as I started into the black out phase of my emergency atmospheric re-entry. I even remember my promise to the Atomic Engender Commission and retracted shut down and deactivated my ION Rocket Motor before I was flying inside of the Earth's atmosphere.

All I could see was my own fireball, from the inside as I was creating my largest fireball ever. It was so bright that I could see all of the storms thunderheads and turbulence centers at every different level inside the typhoon. As I zoomed down lower through it towards the surface of the Pacific Ocean.

I had barely slowed to supersonic speed when I slammed into the water right in the middle of one of the Typhoons storm rings. My first thought was how wet I would get as I switched into underwater mode just as soon as I was traveling slow enough. Then I activated my flooding program to keep Sabrina No. 40 submerged. As I did not want to pop up on the surface of the Pacific Ocean in the middle of a single very large raging level five Typhoons.

Then I extended all my underwater sensors and noted the location of the ditched A380. As well as each of the A380's engines as they were still sinking. I opened my bottom cargo bay door and launched four of my underwater Space-junk-traps to catch each of them before they hit the

Ocean Bed. My readings showed that the surface was extremely rough with 80 and 100 foot swells.

I activated my communications system that I had to switched too Hydra-Phones. I called to the A380 with the aid of my sonar-phone to inform them that help was on the way. I extended all of my underwater maneuvering fans, and started up towards the still floating A380 aircraft. As soon as I cleared the Typhoon, I launch several of my surface cameras to help me with the problem of capturing this extremely lager piece of junk.

My Command Computer had already combined all the cargo bays into a single bay large enough to hold an A380 Airbus. I turned on my Hydra-Phones system and blasted them with my 14-year-old female human voice.

I told them to stay put and not to open any of their exit hatches. I would have to be the first person to admit that it was somewhat interesting to move underwater with both my lower and upper cargo bay doors open. I took lots of very interesting maneuvering to get Sabrina No. 40 too surface with the A380 inside her cargo bay.

My logic boards were showing a very busy Command Computer with all my ships systems working at the same time, the loadmaster program was securing the A380 in the cargo bay. The upper cargo bay doors were closing, while at the same time the lower rear cargo bay was still reeling in all of the A380's lost engines, that were captured by my under water-junk traps.

The ballast program was surfacing the ship, in addition I was making sure that I would launch off the surface moving away from the oncoming Typhoon. The problem was all the cables that I had out reeling in all the lost engines. To keep them from tangling I had to bring them aboard one at a time. I decided to check out how well the passengers in A380 had survived their water landing, and if everybody was in shape for a vertical ballistic launch.

I moved my Command POD into the main cargo bay, In addition, maneuvered it so that the boarding ramp was extended next to the A380's boarding door closest to the cockpit. I politely knocked it took a few minutes for the head flight attendant too open the door, in my most pleasing voice, I asked her if the Captain was available. By this time most of the seawater was pumped overboard. In addition, the ships systems had a breathable Atmosphere back in the entire cargo bay.

I morph my space suit into its flight suit mode as I stepped aboard. They took me over to the locked cockpit door where I politely knocked and requested permission to enter the flight deck. The cockpit was alive with warning bells and red lights all still flashing the dangers of water landings at sea.

The Captain was speechless as he just stood there with his mouth open. I informed him that I was the Sabrina from Sabrina Aviation and asked if I could be of assistance to him. He informed me that he had been forced down by massive clear air turbulence. By the time he had figured out what to do, his engines were skipping across the surface of the Ocean. He had lost all communication upon contacting the water. I informed him that, I would maintain the atmosphere in my cargo bay all they would have to do is open their doors and let the fresh air in.

As I was going back to my Command POD all the doors open, this caused all their slide rafts, to deploy. It was quite a show then I realized that they were one-way fills that were full of foam, which makes them permanent. The Command Computer had to fabricate a power conductor to get all the electrical systems inside the A380 turned on I took the first officer and head steward into my Command POD with me and let them do all the talking.

I put them in touch with their operations headquarters as well as the manager of my trauma center on the LEADER. Then I found out that I had over 800 passengers onboard with most of them insured. Talk about walking wounded, you name it we had several examples, pregnant women going in labor, Broken Bones, bloody noses, in addition, neck wounds. We had everything you could imagine except a heart attack.

I turned on my communications program only to find out that we were still on our own, the Typhoons rough surface had us boxed in. I told their first officer that I would get everybody to the closest hospital, which at this time would be in Japan. Which was now located on the other side of the Typhoon. So I only thought for a second about taking everybody to the hospital on the LEADER.

I knew that I could not get airborne, without pulling lots of "G's". The Command Computer started to complain about the weather the as well as the fact that the Typhoon was getting closer. As soon as we started to get hit by hailstones as well as rained on with large drops of water that were larger than chicken eggs. Sabrina No. 40s command computer made its personal complaint to me about getting wet, the easy way out would be to do a full power vertical climb out.

As this point in the mission I decided not to do this, as it would definitely add to the walking wounded list. So I decided to do the next best thing have a hospital come to us I made contact with my Watch-Commander on the LEADER and informed him of my walking wounded problem. I asked if she would make it possible for the trauma section on the "Leaders "onboard hospital to be moved into Sabrina No. 40/2. So she had to figure out how to outfitted Sabrina No. 40/2 with the trauma section of the hospital.

As it turned out it only took a couple of minutes to load the trauma center modules into No. 40/2 and launch her off the LEADER towards Earth. Luckily with the mass of the A380 and its four recovered Jet engines aboard Sabrina No. 40 had the weight to stay underwater, with a dry cargo bay. I adjusted the ballast program to make Sabrina No.40, slipped underwater, and found very smooth running. As my ships systems continued to reel in all four of the A300's engines one at a time.

I had to dive below 400 feet to get away from all the surface turbulence caused by the Typhoon. I had to turn all of my external sensors up to full power to get it to see objects all the way down to the Sea Bottom. You would no believe what I found, talk about space junk, you should see the bottom of the sea junk problem. A quick look at the read outs from the mid Pacific Weather Satellite showed me the answer to my problem.

The eye of the Typhoon was over a hundred miles across, in addition was full of table tabletop smooth surface for a nice slow horizontal take off. All I had to do was get to it by moving under the raging Typhoon. It took less than a half an hour for Sabrina No. 40/2 to catch up with us and dock into my port side. She had to make a similar approach, full speed into the Earth's Atmosphere.

With a direct atmospheric re-entry directly through the worst parts of the ragging Typhoon followed with a power dive to my depth, then with a quick rendezvous and our first underwater docking. You should have seen the look on the A380's Captain's face when the port side main hatch opened and the hospital arrived.

So there we were Sabrina No. 40 & Sabrina No. 40/2 cruising 400 feet under the Pacific Ocean with a level 5 Typhoon raging overhead. I had the Command Computer from each ship link up to move each trauma modules over to my recovered A380 to safely remove its wounded passengers. So there were docked together over 400 feet below a raging typhoon doing first aid, and getting the A380's passengers ready to survive their first vertical launch. It took most of the day for us to cruse underwater to the eye of the typhoon. By that time all the passengers had been check out and made ready to be transported. We even managed to add two more newborns to the passenger list.

Meanwhile it was quite a while since my Sabrina No. 39 had heard from me, it didn't take very long for her to find me underwater swimming under the largest Typhoon in history. Her only thought was to activate her "Save Sabrina Safety Plan and get rid of the Typhoon so that I could take off from the surface of the Pacific Ocean safely. I seems that Sabrina No. 39 was the only spaceship that made repeated supersonic dives into the heart of the storm as she tried to cut it apart. However the Next-Ten space ships did manage to put in an appearance or two making a few cuts on their own as they were making their delivery flights.

As soon as everything started to get back to normal, I was surprised to get a formal invitation to dine in the command pilot's ships restaurant. I thought that he just wanted to talk to me about his passengers and all the options now available to him. I started out with my space suit in its flight suit mode, after entry into the A380's on board restaurant I noticed that the A380's Command Pilot was wearing his formal mess dress gear. I quickly morph my flight gear into its formal ballroom gown mode with my command epaulets still displayed.

All of my other available personnel that also were invited took my hint It was somewhat comical when all our flight gear started to morph, everybody including myself were passing morph commands back and forth like mad.

By the time we were all seated all the males were in tuxedo and females in formal gowns.

What happened next was a 12 course formal meal with all the trimmings. The food was wonderful it was the best food that I had ever eaten while running two docket Space ships together while crushing 400 feet under a raging Typhoon in the middle of the Pacific Ocean. I decided it was time to send all the passengers to their original destination.

All the now full hospital modules were moved back to their locations in Sabrina No. 40/2. I gave the command to undock and Sabrina No. 40/2 was free to surface. With everybody now in transportation PODs, as soon she was on the surface she opened he top side main cargo hatch so that Sabrina No.39 could make a dry vertical landing to pick up the most wounded to slowly transport them to Japan.

I do not think the wounded even noticed their long drawn out hydrofoil take off and 15-minute flight to Japan. I pointed Sabrina No. 40's nose straight up, retracted and sealed off all the underwater gear, then I extended all four Aero-Spikes and fired them at full power.

I cleared the surface of the Pacific Ocean in a matter of seconds. I adjusted my trajectory, and was docking Sabrina No. 40 on her parking spot on the LEADER in less than 45 minutes. I was still powering down and filling out flight report forms, when my hanger chief called and wanted to know how I had picked up a glider version of an A380 as Space Junk. He also wanted to know if I was going to return the passengers luggage.

First thing the next morning I was up early checking out Sabrina No. 40's computer systems. Yesterday's mission had not red lined any of her on board systems or programs. I still had my prize catch secured in my main cargo bay. After its wetting down in the Pacific Ocean, its flying days were over.

So I decided to return it to its owner as I didn't have, any use for an A380 much less a glider version. Sabrina No. 40/2 stayed on the surface in Japan during the night all of the trauma crews wanted to stay a while to see what they could be any help. I loaded up with more of our trauma crews that also wanted to help.

Therefore, I set up passenger PODs for everybody in the cargo bay next to the glider version of the A380. As soon as everything was checked over and loaded I launch back to Japan. In less than 30 minutes, I had landed next to 40/2 at what was left of the Tokyo Airport. The Typhoon had caused lots of damage, aircraft wreckage was everywhere, and the water level was going down however and most of the operational reconnaissance PODs were still working in underwater mode.

The first person I met, as I was coming out of the middle port main landing gear strut elevator, was the airline president who wanted to know where his A380 was. He seemed to think that I still had it located in my submarine. I asked him if he could take his Airplane back as I had no need for it. He replied," yes and as soon as possible." Upon hearing that bit of information I walked him around to the front of my main landing gears strut.

Where I used my communications necklace to make contact with Sabrina No. 40's, Command Computer to have her to open the bottom forward main cargo bay doors. He jumped back a foot, when the several times the size of a football field bottom cargo bay door snapped opened in front of him. In addition, the whole collection of inflated slide rafts fell out and landed at his feet.

As soon as he calmed down, I ordered my load-master program to start to lower his A380 down to the tarmac. I got an E-mail from Sabrina No. 39 who was now rusting in side of Sabrina No. 40/2s upper cargo deck, she reminding me that it was the job for somebody named T.O.L.H.A. to lower the landing gear. I told Sabrina No. 40 to stop lowering at 20 feet above ground level. Then I asked the owner if he knew how to lower the landing gear.

It took a couple of minutes for him to put his eyes back in his head and learn how to talk. He whipped out his cell phone from his pocket and starts shouting orders, instantly people in jump-suits started coming out of buildings like an army of ants.

My first thought was that they were all going to get under it and carry it away. The first thing they did was to pick up and carry away all the inflated slide rafts. Then ground support vehicles started to show up and plugged electrical power cables into the A380 as it hung out of Sabrina No. 40's open cargo bay.

It took a couple of minutes before I started to hear wet electric motors start humming, then all of sudden all the landing gear doors snapped open and let out a torrent of sea water that ran most of the ground crew away. Then with a few warning groans all the main landing gear slams down and locked into the extended position. Then I had Sabrina No. 40 gently lowered it the rest of the way to the surface.

I also noted that I had finely fixed my problem with loading aircraft in and out of my bottom cargo bay. I finally had my main landing gear high enough to clear the rudder of any aircraft that I might want to transport. It took a while to clear away all their support equipment and leave a well-wanted empty spot under my Sabrina No. 40.

I walked the Airline owner back to the rear of my port main landing gear, and then pushed some more buttons. He seemed to jump a little higher when the center aft cargo bay doors snapped open. Then I lower the four turbofan jet engines that I had grabbed with my Space-junk traps. He whipped out his cell phone and the whole thing started all over again. It took almost a week to clear out Sabrina No. 40/2 and round up all of the medical staff to move them back to the LEADER. Sabrina No. 40/2 made her first re-turn flight to the LEADER without a problem. It took her less than 30 minutes to return to her home hanger bay.

Log Entry #38.
Amelia Earhart:

As soon as things got settled down in Japan, I launched my Sabrina No. 40 out to the middle of the Pacific Ocean in search of Amelia Earhart's Lockheed 10e Electra. I had tuned up my sensors to the point where I could count the pocket change in the pockets of all the people that were walking around the Tokyo airport. Sabrina No. 40's navigation computer located Howland Island its only 2,786 miles south east from my present location at the Tokyo Airport only about 50 miles north of the equator.

If I kept just below Mach one and flew like an airliner, I could make the trip in a little more than 3 hours. So I kept my airspeed to just below Mach 20, and was hovering directly over Howland Island in a little less than half an hour. My scanners showed that it was a low, flat coral and sand, island that was sort of platter shaped, the whole island was only a mile and a half long and a half-mile wide the highest point above sea level was only 20 feet.

As soon as the dust cleared from my touch down, I extended and activated all my sensors I noticed that the shadow of Sabrina No. 40 covered most of the land mass. I had hovered to a stop with all three of my landing gears centered on the, "Earhart's Light" day beacon that was set up near the middle of the island. It was built then named in memory of famed aviatrix Amelia Earhart. I lowered my Command POD and walked down my boarding ramp to look around.

The island was almost totally covered with tall grass, thick vines, and wild shrubs. There was a small section of trees in the center that was primarily used by sea birds that had hardly noticed my arrival. The first scan that I took as I touch down showed everything anybody wanted to know about the island. I was a little shocked to discover all the spent machine gun bullets that were still embedded in the ground.

Until I remembered that, the Japanese had attacked the Island several times during World War two. I could still see the concussion location where the Japanese bombs exploded.

Over all the island was spotless not an empty tin can was detected as my scanners were showing me details as far as 1,000 feet underground. After a couple of minutes I had discovered all there was to know about the island itself. Now I could do what no other Earhart searcher could do. I extended the tracked parts of my landing gear and drove Sabrina No. 40 into the Pacific Ocean. This wasn't my best idea as I lost nose wheel steering as soon as my nose floated up and lifted my nose wheel off the underwater surface, and I grounded the back end of Sabrina No. 40 into the surface of the island.

It took several minutes for my ballets computer to flood the forward section, to put my nose wheel back on the ground be it underwater. Then I kept tracking along the base of the underwater mountain that forms the Island. I had to flood my cargo bay to get Sabrina No. 40 to submerge. As there is never a ditched A380 floating on the surface when you need one.

I had to give up and retract my landing gear to go full submarine mode as I search the underwater part of Howland Island all the way to the ocean floor. All I found was lots of fish and crabs, as well as several lifetimes supply of old empty rusty tin food cans. My detection equipment allowed me to look through all the junk piles. I did discover some broken aircraft parts. I had to look close to make sure that anything that looks like a Lockheed 10e or a small part of a Lockheed 10e was not on Howland Island.

It is not like nothing was on the ocean floor. I was able to see everything even the changes in the shape of the sand that made up the bottom layers. Sabrina No. 40's Command Computer finally decided that scanning from 200 feet above Ocean's bottom layer worked best. In addition as I set it to make an outward spiraling circle my ship systems had already refilled all the oxygen and hydrogen fuel tanks by ripping sea water back into hydrogen and oxygen.

Overall the only thing that I discovered was that the Western Region ocean bed was made of. The Pacific Ocean floor was made up of pelagic material derived from the remains of marine plants and other living thing that once inhabited the waters above it. The scans showed millions of crabs in all sizes and types, I made sure that all my filters were in place and that all entrance location were close as I had enough problems trying to get crabs out of one of my space ships again.

I also found millions of used shark teeth, meteorite fragments, and several underwater quicksand traps, none of which had a Lockheed 10e stuck in it. There was so much to discover that I finally had to set my scanners for "steel only". Hoping to discover propeller blades, I kept expanding my search of the Sea Bottom until I reached the ten-mile mark. All a sudden my search alarm went off I had found steel, a propeller for sure. I dove back to within inches of the bottom and re-scanned for more details, the aircraft was a twin engine and it had radial engines, then I started to take a close look at my data.

My first bad news as when I counted six propeller blades, and lots more pistons than the Lockheed 10e had. I check my database to discover that this had to be a Japanese Betty, one of the aircraft that the Japanese had used to attack Howland Island during World War 2. I took my time to make sure that there was not any Lockheed 10e parts mixed it with its wreckage. Without finding anything else made out of steel. I did find lots of nuts and bolts, even the occasional metal screwdriver.

However, nothing was found that could have come off of the wreckage of a Lockheed 10e. I also spent time scanning all the local shipwrecks that were in the area, my scan could see as far 1,000 feet below the shipwrecks to see if anything else was with the wreckage. I made sure when I was at the southeast quadrant of my search pattern. I changed my heading to go and check out Baker Island, which was 340 miles southeast. I decided to stay under water and scan what was on the bottom as I traveled. I spent the rest of the day working my way to Baker Island or as it was also know Nikumaroro Island this was the longest time in my life that I have ever spent going 340 miles.

I started to hear lots of sonar pinging, and traced it to a small 40-foot cabin cruiser that was floating dead in the water on the surface overhead. I moved under them, opened my top cargo bay door. Then had my ballast program surface with the 40 footer in my cargo bay, my load master program suspended it as the water level dropped, to the point where it was high and dry. I had to laugh out loud as soon as I noticed that, it looked like a toy boat sitting in the bottom of an empty bathtub. I closed my cargo bay doors and turned on all my cargo bay lights, I moved my Command POD over the little boat, then climbed down and lower my boarding ramp to stand on their main deck.

As I stepped off the end of my boarding plank all I could hear was the sound of snoring, lots of snoring as everybody on the boat was asleep. Then I noticed the plaque next to the wheelhouse that said. "The International Group for Historic Aircraft Recovery" (TIGHAR) seeing that they must have had a long night, I left copies of all my scans, on their navigation table. I even write them a note to tell them that it was a "Betty". Then I moved my Command POD back to its usual location, open my upper cargo bay doors and let my ballast program gently put them back where I found them.

I went back to 200 feet above the sea-bed and continued on my way, to make matters worse I did not find anything else. I finally made it to the base of the underwater mountain that formed Baker Island or as it was also know Nikumaroro Island. I matched the angle of ifs incline and zoom my way around its base scanning every inch. I found lots of nice stuff most of which was trash and empty food cans that had been dumped, into the Ocean Sense the coming of civilization.

My scans did show some discarded metal aircraft parts but nothing that would fit on a Lockheed 10e. I finally ran out something to scan, and had to surface. I was next to the beach that rose abruptly from the shore to a crest, 15 to 20 feet above sea level, to form a barrier which keeps the pounding surf out of the central basin of the island. The west beach was sandy, that on the other three sides are largely composed of broken reef rock and sandstone shingle. A sandy point seems to be building out to the southwest, beyond the fringing reef.

The surface is flat, except for some small mounds on the northeast, which were piles of low-grade guano? There was a large coral reef that would be just under water at low tide. What was interesting was the large chunk in its center looked like it had been scooped out and then dropped back in place. As all of the older mini-railroad-lines lead to them the southwestern ridge is cut in three places, where the tracks cut through on the east are two small depressions, just behind the beach the larger of which contained some seawater.

As it was starting to get dark I could see millions of crabs storming the beach all-looking for something to eat. Sabrina No. 40's Command Computer automatically closed up all the vents to make sure that I did not transplant another colony of live crabs.

Now was as good a time as any to leave, I pointed Sabrina No. 40's nose out seaward. I dove back to the bottom of the sea bed. Then I pointed my nose vertical switch to spaceflight mode. Then fired up all my Aero-Spikes and launched back to the LEADER.

Log Entry #39.
Sabrina No. 40 and the High Arctic:

It took a while to pick up all the space-junk that was in low Earth orbit Polar wise. It's a wonder nobody been killed yet. The main idea is to have a Spacecraft orbiting pole to pole with all the Earth rotating under their cameras. The problem is it made Earths worse space junk mess ever, not only do we have to deal with 35,000 mile per hour head-on collisions. But I had to modify my space ship design to reinforce all of my Sabrina No. 40 series to the point where they can handle all the head-on hits.

It took lots of missions to intercept and trap all the stuff. I decided to get rid of all larger pieces first, if an alien race ever made it to Earth they would be scared away by our defensive Space-junk shield. This is how I discovered that when a satellite had a collision it made millions of fragment that would in turn destroy other Space craft as they were hit by the wreckage of the first timers. I had to modify Sabrina No. 40 with a soft shield that I designed to catch all the small stuff and hold on to it.

My only problem is I can only grab what I can catch. Lots of this Space-junk is so small that it passes right through my space junk traps. This time out I did my best to intercept several swarms of Space-junk I did a high angle re-entry pulled 8 and 9 "G"s, I managed to heat up my heat shield to White Hot. I made a quick landing at a thin spot on the Arctic Ice shelf. Then I retracted my landing gear so that my hot heat shield came in direct contact with the surface of the Arctic Ocean Ice. Needless to say Sabrina No. 40 melted her way through the thin ice sheet like a hot knife through butter.

The extreme heat that was in my main heat shield radiated out several hundred feet leaving Sabrina No. 40 floating in her own little wet spot in the frozen Arctic Ocean. I switched to submarine mode to let Sabrina No. 40 slowly submerge into the extremely cold water. I extended all my Instruments the first thing I detected was all the pieces of melted Space-junk as they sank to the Sea Bottom. Space-junk has always been a problem the main danger is caused by its speed and the extremely small mass.

This also makes it almost impossible for me to keep all the new impact holes patched, the worst part of the problem is all the microscopic holes that are caused when they hit. It's worse than patching up bullet holes it took me a while to come up with the morph program but I now have it operational. As soon as any of my Space ships clear the atmosphere the first thing I do is activate my newly installed Micro Space-Junk-Blanket. I have it morph out of ports all over the surface, to cover every external surface I use it as an erosion shoe.

When Space-junk hits any of my covered surfaces I get to keep it. When I retract the system for atmospheric re-entry all the captured Space-junk gets trapped and stored in my collection bucket. Recently I have added on an Urban-Camouflage-Program that makes it easier for me to hide my Space ships in plain sight. My only problem now when I hide in plain sight, I leave a layer or two of spent micro impactors as well as Space-junk if I leave the camouflage program running for any length of time.

I finally got a chance to check out the bottom of the Arctic Ocean, talk about a mess you name it I found it. Everything ever made by mankind and then some, the best find was the never ending supply of meteorites, you heard me correctly meteorites. When they strike the open ocean water they shatter like glass even the iron ones. But when they land on thick frozen Ice, it absorbs most of the energy and breaks their fall, by slowing them down just enough. Eventfully they all ended up on the sea bed with everything else.

I located a truck size meteorite sitting on the bottom at about 3,000 feet deep. My Command Computer made a perfect touch down over it with all three of my landing gear centered. I changed my space suit to underwater mode it felt funny as I grew swim fins and webbed fingers. I moved the command POD to my airlock, and cycled my way through it. Due to all the pressure all the equalizing water came in at a very fast rate, my cargo bay lights turned on as I entered my bottom side cargo bay.

I open the outer cargo bay door so that, I could see my meteorite below me sitting on the sea bed. I used my space suits water thruster to move over to my main space-junk trap. Then I was able to activated its controls and lower it down to intercept and grab my prize.

As soon as I was standing on the bottom I had Sabrina No. 40 turn on all her landing lights, to see what was going on. This cause all kinds of fish and all the other bottom feeders that have never seen light before to swim into the light. They all seemed to swarm around the meteorites as if trying to protect it. They all followed it up as I lifted it into my cargo bay. I had to lower the water level to get them to leave. As soon as it was high and dry I checked it for He/3 only to discover that it was all lost during atmosphere entry.

I decided to recover as many as I could to study the dynamic forces exerted by the Ice during impacts. I had to kill the lights and what for all the bottom dwellers to leave before I closed the bottom cargo bay doors. It only took a couple of seconds for my Instrumentation system to tell me that. The Arctic Ocean occupies a roughly circular basin and covers an area of about 5,440,000 square miles. It's a lot less the size of the size of Texas.

With a coastline length 28,203 miles nearly landlocked, it is surrounded by the land masses of Eurasia, North America, Greenland, and several other islands. It includes Baffin Bay, Barents Sea, Beaufort Sea, Chukchi Sea, East Siberian Sea, Greenland Sea, Hudson Bay, Hudson Straight, Kara Sea, Laptev Sea, White Sea and other tributary bodies of water. It is also connected to the Pacific Ocean. It also informed me that Amelia Earhart's Lockheed 10e was not located but it did find lots of used propeller blades, I activated my underwater drive to proceed to the next meteorite site.

The super cold water started to take effect as this was the first time that I felt cold inside my Command POD. I checked with my ships system computer to discover that my latest prize was back under water inside my cargo bay. And that its super cold insides were acting as a heat exchanger pulling heat out of Sabrina No. 40s interior. To counter this I fired up one of my He/3 reactor, to used its extremely hot water to heat up my latest captured prize.

I started to use my side scanners to locate meteorites that were still stuck in the surfaces Ice so that I can see what happens when Ice brings a very heavy object to a full stop. I found a nearby truck size example that was still stuck inside the surface ice. I could see where its initial impact point had broken away several miles of ice that had moved to cancel out dynamic impact forces.

The meteorite had almost made it through the ice sheet with less than 10 feet to go. So I had my ballast program bring Sabrina No. 40 up the smooth bottom of the ice shelf, open my upper cargo bay doors to take close up a look. So there I was standing at the end of my gang plank looking up at the end of an iron meteorite.

I could see that ship systems were moving a Space-Junk-Trap under it and the same time the hot water geyser that I was using to heat up my first prize was moved to spray at the last little bit of ice that had stopped my second prize. There must have been lots of cracks in the ice as all of a sudden the whole thing dropped straight into the cargo bay, it's down ward speed as well as the mess of all the ice was enough to shatter the space-junk-trap into thousands of pieces of now very cold metal that bounce up and knocked me into the water as it was tearing its way through my strongest space-junk-trap.

I managed to activate my Space suit just before I hit the water. It took a few seconds to form in the extremely cold water. When all the bubbles cleared I was standing on the bottom of the Arctic Ocean, leaning against a bus size meteorite, waiting for my swim fins to form, without a space ship wrapped around me. I looked up to notice several large section of my shattered Space-Junk-Trap zeroing in on me. Lucky for me my forearm thrusters finished forming just in time for me to get out of the way.

I call my Command POD only to get a busy signal. It took full power on my water thrusters to climb up the 800 feet to where Sabrina No. 40 was still melting her way to the surface. I still could not get the Command POD to communicate with me. As I climbed my way back into my main cargo bay I discovered the problem. One of the steel rods that I was using to make the cage of my Space-Junk-Trap had punched directly through the Command PODs outer wall nailing it to my forward bulkhead. My big surprise was that it was jammed directly through my Command Computer, Pilot seat, and flight instrument panel.

Needless to say if I were in my usual spot I would have been killed. It took a few seconds for me to remember that I was not only a pilot but a mechanic. It took a lot of typing into my communications necklace to get my ship systems to pull the steel rod out of my Command POD and freeing it so that I could move it back to its spindle.

Once there I had to manually move the Command PODs around to where I could get into one of my back up POD and reprogram it to be the active Command POD. Then I had to get inside of my damaged POD to turn it off and pull its command key so that I could reinstall it in my replacement POD. By this time Sabrina No. 40 had surfaced and all the underwater lights had caused my cargo bay to fill up with fish that were attracted by the light as well as a large troop of polar bears that were attracted by the fish, all of which were very large and had lots of teeth.

So I turned off the lights, moved my damaged Space-Junk trap back in its bay, ordered up a replacement trap and launch it back to the bottom of the Arctic Ocean, to recover my second prize. I closed my bottom cargo bay doors, as soon as my 2nd prize had been secured and let Sabrina No. 40 slowly sink into the Arctic Ocean to make sure that I had flushed out all the starving Polar Bears that had turned my forward top side cargo bay into a feeding frenzy.

I had to let the ship sink 20 feet below the surface before the last one gave up and swim out of my main cargo bay so that I could close it. I also discovered that I had to do over a weeks' worth of homework that was stored in my hard drive as "I can't tell my teachers that my space-junk-trap had eaten my homework." I had to reprogram all my data in my new Command Computer and set it to intercept the next meteorite. My next prize was in shallow water near one of the Canadian Islands, it looked like it had rolled off a melting Ice berg.

I was moving just under the surface into the open sea, when all a sudden I heard at thump and felt a trimmer, Sabrina No. 40 started to make a slight turn to the port, the emergency systems program went crazy, alarms, warning buzzers, collision lights, and all went off as the same instant. I stopped, surfaced, and extended my top side docking tube.

I ran my new Command POD up to its top and open my boarding ramp to take a look. To discover that I had been harpooned by one of the whalers nasty little killer ships. My first though was that I'm glad my father is a Lawyer, the warhead on the harpoon had made a larger hole than the Vietnamese surface to air missile.

Their harpoon had punched a very large hole in the side of my space ship then to make matters worse it exploded inside of Sabrina No. 40. My ships systems had reported that I been holed it even told me the amount of water that had leaked in. My onboard ships system program was taking all the approbate steps to fix the problem. It had sealed off all damaged compartments, and released lots of foam to fill in the punchers. The problem was this had glued the nasty little Killer Boat to my outer hull, as they were pulling in their kill, which just happens to be "Me"!

When I surfaced, this put them in the perfect location to become part of my outer hull as the foam system filled in the area that was destroyed by their Harpoon. It looked like the whole crew was now standing on my hull trying to cut their ship away from my sticky foam. This wasn't a good idea as their rudders as well as propellers were also encased in my emergency sticky foam.

Everything they tried to cut it with also became stuck, my emergency sticky foam was worse than fly-paper. It only took a few minutes to have all the whalers trapped below their own waterline. Now I was stuck I couldn't leave them stuck to my outer hull below their own waterline. The first thing I had to do was level the hull by having my ballast program roll Sabrina No. 40 until she had her port side level. Then I extended the POD's running tracks and drove over to the stuck Whalers nasty little killer boat.

The whaler's crew was having lots of problems with my sticky foam, the entire crew was stuck in it about as bad as they could get. So far none of them were pulled under by it, but they were still trying. By the time I driven my Command POD over to the site of my Harpooning the entire whalers crew were all immobilized by my sticky foam. I did manage to pick up a can of anti-foam spray as I went down my boarding ramp.

The first thing I did was to spray everybody's faces to make sure that they would not get suffocated by the foam. For some reason they were all still speechless, because they weren't flying a national flag. I activated my space suits communication system and asked if anybody spoke English. For some reason one of the stuck whalers crew members answered in Klingon. I figure that he was the ships Trekker. Then I let them know that my father is a lawyer, and that they were in lots of trouble.

That's when he answered in Klingon, "Is your father really a Lawyer?" What happened next was really scary when something big jumped me from behind and pushed me into the outer deck surface of Sabrina No. 40, without setting off any of my alarms. I had to use the extra strength motors built into my space suit to overpower it. When I stood up I discovered that I was looking down the throat of a very large hungry Polar Bear, who was convinced that I was his lunch. He had already clawed me pretty good he had made a lot of tooth & claw marks in my space suit but my built-in repair systems had already closed & sealed most of them.

You should have seen the look on my newly captured whalers faces when I picked-up the largest land based carnivore on the planet and gently carried him over to the edge of my hull where I personally threw him back into the Arctic Ocean. That's when my infrared scans showed me the hundreds of hungry Polar Bears that were about to come aboard for lunch.

With the stuck whalers crew as the main course. I instantly ordered Sabrina No. 40's too extend her landing gear to lift her out of the water and re-angle her surface. This happened just in time to throw most of the first wave of hungry Polar Bears back into the Arctic Ocean, my extended landing gear lifted us just high enough to make a usable safety barrier.

As I moved to the other side of my captured killer ship I noticed hundreds of Polar Bears stuck in my sticky foam and not liking it. I used the last of my anti-foam spray to do all of their noses. I spent the next half hour throwing non-stuck Polar Bears over board as they attacked me. I finally got a call from my watch chief, "He wanted to know what's going on "by this time my ships systems had given him a complete damage report. The good news was every compartment was sealed by the sticky foam.

My watch chief said that he was sending a repair crew with replacement modules, as well as a cleanup crew to get everybody out of the sticky foam, even the angry Polar Bears. The first ship to show up was good old Sabrina No. 39 she had diverted herself from a "Dead Seal" pick up mission. I asked her to dump her cargo of dead seals on the closest Island to see if I could get some of leering Polar Bears to leave. This worked like a charm as most of the incoming Polar Bears started swimming back to their Island.

I had designed Sabrina No. 40 to have backup systems that were placed to make it hard for one event to take out everything.

I had never dreamed of being harpooned by a Whaler's Killer ship much less by an exploding one. I also asked her to come back and use her cargo bay to shield my captive whaler crew from the Arctic cold. She must have been reading my mind as she made a point of landing at the correct angle to put the stuck whaler inside of her cargo bay with her nose pointing forward.

She extended her landing gear to match my hull angle, extended her lower docking collar that I had designed to make a hard dock in to the top hatch of another space ship. Then she activated her emergency systems to expel enough sticky foam to make an air tight seal. The warmth of Sabrina No. 39's cargo bay quieted down most of the angry stuck Polar Bears, and at the same time made the Whaler's crew a lot more talkative.

It seems that they had tracked me for several hours as they had detected Sabrina No. 40's underwater maneuvering and determined that she was a very active whale, ripe for killing. They were the closest kill ship when I moved out from under the Arctic Ice cap. Sure enough I checked by scanners to discover that lots of little whaler kill boats were on the way to help make a big kill and I was the "Big".

With my entire repair crews still inbound, I decided not to be out numbered on the surface. To take control of my present situation. I had to get back in my Command POD and interconnected Sabrina No. 40 and Sabrina No. 39's Command Computers. I knew that I had to do a slow horizontal launch off the surface of the Arctic Ocean, as well as keep both ships flying a very tight formation to maintain air pressure seal. I buttoned up my Command POD and anchored it on the exterior surface of Sabrina No. 40.

Then I retracted Sabrina No. 40's landing gear, it took micro-seconds to counter fill the other side of Sabrina No. 40 to balance the mass of Sabrina No. 39 and started her moving out to sea away from all the incoming nasty little killer ships. I set Sabrina No. 40's wheel trucks for skid mode and kept accelerating until I got her up on a high step in the water.

When I broke off the surface, I did a slow two "G" climb back to the "Leader." In less than 45 minutes later I had the whole mess in side of

Sabrina No. 40's space hanger, with all systems powered down ready for repairs. This climb out was very interesting as this was the first time that Sabrina No. 39 had to fly close formation to maintain Atmosphere pressure in her cargo bay.

Upon my arrival the watch Chief had everything ready with all the support personnel in place, as soon as the air pressure equalized in Sabrina No. 40's home hanger bay everybody went into motion at the same instant. We took care of all the stuck humans & the polar bears at the same time.

Let me tell you, my sticky foam really is nasty stuff it sticks to everything every way it can, human wise it penetrates through cloth and sticks directly to skin & hair, polar bear wise it stuck to each hair and penetrated to the skin, it even gets attached to claws and teeth. It became worse under zero "G", as luck would have it this was the first time that any of our sticky foam packs had been set off, then it was also my first harpooning.

As soon as everybody was in place the hanger crew member with the anti-sticky foam started to spray, this dissolves all the foam in a matter of seconds. It took several of my strongest personnel to handle each Polar Bear, I had my master of arms disarm and check the whaler's killer ship looking for any more exploding harpoons. We ended up putting each polar bear into its own small "space-junk-trap" and shipped them out to my polar bear camp.

I turned the whalers over to the World Whaling Commission, as they were the only folks that would claim them. I also, plan to send them a bill for damages. I made the mistake of changing my full pressure space suit back to my flight suit, as polar bears as well as whalers definitely leave a trace odor that is indescribable.

It was so strong that it stunk up my space suits re-charger. This was the first time that all the launch bay crew wanted to open the main hatch to air things out. The bay chief finally managed to solidify all the well-used air that was in the space hanger bay and I launched it into the Sun as a Bio-Hazard.

Then the whaler's killer ship finally melted, it also had an odor problem of its own. I don't think that sailors in the Artic get to swab the deck as often as they would like.

Considering all the blood and whale parts that were still on the boat it was no wonder that all the polar bears came aboard looking for lunch. The operational conditions of the ship scared my Master-at-Arms. She couldn't understand why it hadn't already detonated as there were lots of loose explosive laying everywhere. When she discovered that the Whalers keep their detonators stored in the same bag with their explosives, she made a long single jump to the other side of the space hanger.

To top it all off all their "exploding harpoons" were designed to arm themselves as soon as they went into zero "G" this means that they will all explode as soon as gravity is re-established. So I had Sabrina No. 39 secure my first captive killer boat in her cargo bay and put it on a direct trajectory to the Sun, a location where it will never hurt any mammals ever again. In all I had to replace 27 compartments in Sabrina No. 40 it took less than a day to replace all the damaged systems, then it was back to the Arctic.

The next thing I did was to install a sonar pinging device that put out a message that said "not a whale". This made another problem as my pinging seems to attract other live whales. I reckon that they wanted to see what all the noise is about. So a couple of days later I was back at work test flying Sabrina No. 40 in the Arctic Ocean.

The first time I turned on my new sonar pinger it started an underwater stampede, I was amazed to see how fast a fish could move through the water. After an hour or so a humpback whale showed up and started to treat Sabrina No. 40 as if she was her mother. At the first chance she came in the bottom cargo bay door, as I was recovering another meteorite.

I had to that my ships systems to quickly add a couple layers of atmosphere inside of the cargo bay for her to breath. It didn't take her long to learn that the bottom cargo bay of No. 40 was good for a breath of air every time she would show up. I first expect that she was in love with the warm water in my cargo bay.

It got to the point where she was spending several hours at a time just floating in my bottom cargo bay. Singing as well as spraying the insides of Sabrina No. 40's upper cargo bay doors with her spray. I channeled all of her whale songs into my translator program. It got to the point where every time I would make five pings on my sonar transmitter she would show up and want in for air. So I named her "Pinger-5".

I had been operating in the open sea for the better part of the day when I started to notice a lot of surface activity. Pinger-5 had gone out for lunch so I launch one of my surface probes, to see what was being surrounded by a whole fleet of killer ships. Thinking that I was a whale just ripe for killing, I started pinging in international code that "I was not a whale" then they started firing harpoons down into the water. That's when I realized that they were trying to scare me to surface for a better shot. I lifted off from the bottom and hit the sonar pinger 5 times sure enough Pinger-5 made a bee line for my open cargo bay.

I locked Pinger-5 in for the first time as I closed up all my underwater gear and turned Sabrina No. 40 back into a space ship, I fired all four of my Aero-Spikes at the same time. According to my Mach meter, I was going Mach 2 by the time I reached the surface. This had to get their attention as this was the first time a whale broke surface and kept going. All the closing killer boats fired their harpoons at me just as my nose cone broke the surface.

My rear scanners caught all the action. Needless to say all their harpoons missed, but did manage to make direct hits on most of the other Killer boats on the other side of their attack circle. Every one of them started having secondary explosions. This put lots of humans in the water. So I put out my speed brakes, extended all of my lift-fans, as I turned around, lower my landing gear, opened all the stairway doors, transitioned into hover mode and started taking survivors aboard, at all three of my landing gear locations as I hovered with all three of my landing gear trucks at sea level.

I allowed all the now stranded Whalers a dry warm place to go. I made sure that all my top of the landing gear airlocks were locked as I did not think that "Pinger-5" wanted to meet any of them up close and personal. It didn't take very long to drop all the survivors, off at the closest Coast Guard Station.

They were delighted to have the drop in business; it took longer to get all the stranded Whaler's out of my stairways than it took for them to get in. I'm glad that I did not let them use any of my onboard elevators.

As soon as I was finished with the Coast Guard I launched back to the LEADER with Pinger-5 still aboard. Over all she seemed to like Zero "G", I did make a big impression with all of my staff as this was the first time that I showed up unannounced with a full grown Humpback Whale alive and well swimming in my cargo bay.

I gave all of my recording of Pinger-5's whale songs to my Translator Technicians it took them the better part of the day to figure out how to convert Humpback to English. Pinger-5 had not quit singing her Whale song sense she first came into my cargo bay.

I started spending a lot of time in the water tank with Pinger-5 trying to get my translator to work. Finally she turned around to look me in the eye and said.

"Hello There I am hungry, what did you do with my Ocean." She knew that her ocean was gone the idea of traveling without having to swim intrigued her to no end.

Then she started to echo what she was hearing back to me through my now operational Humpback translator. Once she knew that I could understand her she quickly bombarded me with questions.

She did not have any concepts about having a name but, she did agree to come into the cargo bay every time I rang the pinger-5 times. She said that "she had noticed the stars; she had even used them to navigate."

She was the only survivor, her whole family whale POD was killed by the little bad boats a long time ago. Her reason for contacting Sabrina No. 40 was to warn me that the little bad boats were coming towards me.

She knew all about people but was curious about me as I was the first human that she had seen that could grow fins, and breathe without making lots of smelly bubbles.

I informed her that the "Little Bad Boats" will never bother her again, I told her that she was on what people call a planet the third one that is orbiting the Sun. She had no idea about a Sun or an orbit but, she was willing to go anywhere that there wasn't any "little bad boats".

As soon as the Sabrina No. 40's hanger bay was secure, I opened the top cargo hatch Pinger-5 jumped straight up out of the flooded cargo bay breaking the surface and then bringing all the water along with her as she moved up into the space hanger. She used her body movements and the shifting of her center of mass to move as if she were still underwater. She was large enough for all the sea water to stay with her and then she noticed that all the water was comings towards her. I was still in her trailing water spout trying to catch up.

When she finally drifted to a stop with all the water spinning around her, It took a couple of minutes for the technicians with her communication system to catch up to her, attach her harness with Whale size viewing heads up display, that was held in place by a harness, as everybody knows regular glasses frame will not work on a Whale.

My technicians are at their best in zero "G", it only took a couple of minutes to hook up Pinger-5's microphone and speakers, along with a heads up display that will focus off her left eye. This set Pinger-5 up on my Sabrina Aviation's communication net. I moved into her field of view to teach her the basics of how to use her new communications device. I told her that I was going to travel to the fifth planet that is orbiting the Sun called Jupiter, and would she want to travel there to explore one of its Moons called "Europa"? She replied that she was willing to travel anywhere as long as the food supply lasted, and could I open the door and let the food come in.

I asked what kind of food she wanted to eat. She answered "LIVE" I let her clear out all the live samples that I had recovered from the depth of the Arctic Ocean, she complained that is wasn't enough for a snack. The big question was how long it would take to train a full grown Humpback Whale to be an astronaut. Sense I was planning a trip to Europa it might be useful to have somebody along that could explore the depths of Jupiter's wettest Moon that is if I could figure out how to bring her along for the trip.

The biggest problem was communication my translator had just started to speak Humpback. I would have to design a space suit for her, I know for a fact that she will need lots more radiation shielding than a human due to her gigantic size. She started to look better as we cleaned her up. I had our medical staff get rid of all her barnacles as well as other skin parasites that were living on her skin. We even removed several large squid hooks that were stuck in one of her flippers.

Pinger-5 had a bulky head with bumpy protuberances, each with a bristle. She had grown to be 52 feet long, and to weighing 38 tons. Being a female she was slightly larger than a male would be, as with all humpback whales. Her four-chambered heart weighs about 430 pounds. She was decked out with the gray color scheme; there are distinctive patches of white on the underside of her tail. These marking are unique to each individual Humpback Whale, like asset of fingerprints.

All of her throat grooves that run from her chin to the navel were in good working order. She really started to look good after we removed all the barnacles from her facial knobs that were located on the edges of her jaws. I even had an official Sabrina Aviation photo ID tag made up for her showing the underside of her tail, as I don't think that she will be my only Humpback Astronaut. I introduced her to all my command staff, then I started to straighten out her learning curve, I set up a series of subjects for her to summit questions, all to be answered, she was definitely fascinated by words.

I was due to spend the weekend with my parents in Park Ridge, so I offered Pinger-5 a ride to Lake Michigan. I warned her that it was full of fresh water that was not salty also you would have to work harder to swim in fresh water because you would be less buoyant in it. I informed her that there are more than 20 different types of fish in the lake how small enough for her to eat. As well as an abundant supply of microscopic krill. She replied that she like small fish the smaller the better.

I asked her what she thought about zebra mussel. Her answer was quite interesting, and Pinger-5 replied that they were one of her favorites her only problem in eating them was that they made her poop sea shells.

Upon hearing this bit of information I had her moved back into Sabrina No. 40's cargo bay water and all. I also had her secured to the walls with a restraining harness. She wanted to know what with this when I informed her that it will keep her from banging her head on my forward bulkhead when we re-enter the Atmosphere. I took the long way to Lake Michigan to keep the "G" loaded down on Pinger-5, as small as possible.

She seemed to love the low speed "S" turns that I started doing a 100,000 feet over the lake. I used my sensor pack to locate schools of fish that Pinger-5 might want to invite for dinner. As soon as I was flying slow enough I extended my wings and hover-fans, I sat Sabrina No. 40 down vertically on the surface of the water about 20 miles off Lake Shore Drive. I opened the bottom cargo hatch and Pinger-5 Launched herself for the first time into the fresh water of Lake Michigan. She was a little startled as this was the first time she had felt fresh water, be careful I warned her you're a lot heavier in this water you don't want to drown.

I asked her what she thought of fresh Lake Michigan water. She replied that she liked it, it was so full of small fish that it was like swimming in soup. I can hear Whales talking, a Beluga she said, where I asked. She made a series of Whale songs, and answered "a place called Shedd Aquarium she replied." It only a Beluga they are not very good talkers, talk at them for hours and all you get is a simple yes or no answer". I requested that she tap into the navigation program and see what she could find, as the Great Lakes are larger than the Arctic Ocean. I asked her to keep a low profile as she was defiantly the first Humpback Whale to be in Lake Michigan.

I also, reminded her that it would be nice if she did not scare any humans that she might see in little boats. We parted company, I launch off the water towards Chicago and Pinger-5 said "she was going to gorge herself with zebra" mussel so she was heading towards the deep part of the lake. It took a lot of figuring but I managed to do it without anybody noticing. I safely landed Sabrina No. 40 over my parents' home in Park Ridge Illinois.

I even place my forward landing gear in their back yard, with both of my main landing gear at the edge of the public park several city blocks away. I flew in from the east, following the helicopter route to O'Hare and requested permission for a vertical landing in the park.

I extended my landing gear to its maximum height, folded up all my lift-fans, and retracted all of my aerodynamic controls as well. I made sure to lower all of my small animal barriers to make it harder for any of the local wildlife to get inside my airframe. I remembered to lock the main gear elevators as well as the stairways to keep the public out. The weather did help a lot as the snowstorm covered Sabrina No. 40 and helped to hide her from the public.

My nose gear did fill up most of my parents' back yard it was a tight fit I even managed not to smash my old swing set. However my nose wheel skid pad did help to level the ground despite all the snow and frozen ground.

After I move my Command POD to its forward position all I had to do, was to take my nose wheel elevator down to my parents' back yard and then walk the couple of feet to my back door. As I walked in my back door, before I could say "Hi", both of my parents wanted to know who Pinger-5 was and why had she send me over a hundred different E-mails in the last half hour?

Both of them also wanted me to tell them why she would be pooping sea shells? Checking Pinger-5's E-mails I found out that she had discovered a vast underground cave system under Lake Michigan that had open spaces that were miles wide and full of the best tasting plankton as well as zebra mussel and other little fish that she had ever eaten. Due to her vast experience of swimming under Antarctic ice floes she was able to navigate her way from cave to cave she finally had found a thin layer of ice that she could easily break through.

She had performed one of her best ever sounding, only to discover this nice Des Plaines, policeman that was guarding this frozen lake to keep humans off of it. Boy is he dumb after I said "Hi" He said that I was the biggest fish that he had ever seen in Lake Opeka. I had to inform him that I was a mammal not a fish. He said that He was going to have to call Des Plaines City Hall and ask Karen Henderson what the policy was about Humpback Whales, surfacing in the middle of Lake Opeka and breaking up the City of Des Plaines Ice skating rink.

That's when I asked the nice police officer if he could call you for a pick up. He said that you had an unlisted Phone number, so I had to give him your father cell phone number from your data base, so he could call. A couple of minutes later my father's cell phone started to ring, it was the Des Plaines Police calling asking for me, it seems that a large fish had broken up the City of Des Plaines Ice skating rink, and the fish was calling somebody named Sabrina for a ride home.

I asked the nice police officer how he had obtained my father's Cell Phone number, he said that the "big fish" had told him by using a bull horn that was attached to its parachute harness. I asked him if the fish had identified herself, "Yes, he replied she had shown him her Sabrina Aviation ID tag, she even showed him the bottom of her tail flukes, so he could see who she was.

I told him, that must be my whale and I asked him to tell Pinger-5 that I would pick her up in the middle of the lake in a couple of minutes. So I got to act the part of helicopter with Sabrina No. 40 again. I lucked out and nobody was using Runway 22 left for landings, at O'Hare.

With the help of my command computer and the use of automatic safety checks. It only took a couple of minutes to power up and hover Sabrina No. 40 over to Lake Opeka in Des Plaines, I followed Devon Avenue West to O'Hare, and then hovered in the dark over the small lake that was not much bigger than Sabrina No. 40. I sat my Sabrina No.40 down in the middle of its frozen surface only to have her break through. I did a quick scan, and I was very surprised to discover that the southern end of Lake Opeka was several miles deep.

I opened my bottom cargo bay doors and hit the SONAR Pinger 5 times. Pinger-5 did a back flip and zoomed into her flight tank. I switch back to submarine mode. I had to flood my forward ballets tanks to make Sabrina No. 40 tip down to slip vertically into the massive underground lake that was under O'Hare Airport. My parents arrived just in time to see the last couple hundred feet of Sabrina No.40 slowly disappear vertically down into Lake Opeka.

Both of my parents noticed the wide eyed policeman standing there looking at a very large pile of whale dung, my mother was the first to notice. Mom said that Pinger-5 was a "poor thing" when she noticed that "Pinger-5 really did have sea shells in her poop".

Log Entry #40.
Pinger-5's Side:

Pinger-5 had definitely made the discovery of the century. The first cave system that we entered was so large that I had to turn up all of my instruments to maximum just to get a reading. I had to turn everything back to normal to keep from hurting Pinger-5's hearing. She came back on the communication system and said, Sabrina is that you, "Yes" I replied "it's me" Pinger-5's next comment really got my attention, she noted that "if I had not stopped the large space rock that you call the LEADER. "If you had allowed it to penetrate the Earth's crust over Chicago it would have caused the whole planet to pop like a balloon".

"How do you know that," I asked?" "I had your computer calculate the Leaders impact forces," she answered. "I have no enemies in this world except the people in the little bad boats I know that they kill by penetrating my body. "For all of my life I have been trying to make my body invincible. "That is why I let barnacles grow on me to make a shield, so that the bad people on the little boats cannot penetrate my body to kill me." "you are invincible" "I know that you come from the sky and you take the rocks that fall from the sky away, I know that the people in the bad boats have attacked and wounded you.

And despite your wound you managed to carry the little bad boat away and it did not return to the water. I know that you live in the sky and that you have invited me to travel with you to another planet, I know that "white bears" cannot eat you. I am not a fish. I am not invincible.

I asked her how smart does she think she is? Pinger-5 replied that "she was smart enough to talk the Des Plaines policeman out of giving her a ticket."

She had also figured my location in Park Ridge, from her entrance to the cave system by figuring the size and direction of each underground cave that she swam through.

Her surfacing in Lake Opeka was not due to its closeness to my current location but the size of the entrance needed to allow my Sabrina No. 40 size Space ship entrance. I kept moving south until I came across a very large pile of old sunken cars all piled up on a shelf about 600 feet from the surface, the flooded underground cave still went down for miles vertically.

I called back up to the LEADER to see if I could get some of my Sabrina No. 40 ships to help out mapping the entire underwater lake system. According to my construction chief, there were only five ships ready for advanced testing Sabrina No. 40/1, through Sabrina No. 40/5, that's good enough for me. As all I needed to do was to activate their Command Computers. As for their arrival I programmed in a full ballistic water landing with impact speeds just below the speed of sound at 15 second intervals.

I motored off to the shallow end of the lake to wait for the show. In less than a quarter of an hour, the first ship Sabrina No. 40/1 came screamed past us into the water making a water phloem at least a 500 feet tall, the second ship hit the top of the first water phloem and splattered it in 360 directions as it zoomed past us going down vertically. Ship Sabrina No. 40/3 did not even make a phloem but, its impact started to drain the lake that Pinger-5 and I were floating in. Pinger-5 got worried about the dropping water levels as soon as everything started to shallow out.

She barely made it to her flight tank then the next two ships Sabrina No. 40/4 & Sabrina No. 40/5, shot past us and left us sitting in the mud high and dry. I extended my lift-fans, then took off and hovered over to the now empty hole that went down to the underground lakes that we had spent the most of the night exploring. My ships instruments showed that the water level was definitely comings back up.

Pinger-5 wanted me to dive in from where I was hovering, I had to remind her that she was not invincible. I ended up retracting all my Lift-Fans and meeting the rising water in a vertical dive. I stopped descending at 500 feet and called a staff meeting, only to have nobody show up, it took a couple of seconds to pressurize Pinger-5's tank so she could swim free of the ship. I had each ship turn on all their external lights then I commanded them to find us. I set up my Command Computer as the master with the other five reporting new finds as they happened.

I launched Pinger-5, she was astonished, "you have more than one ship" she asked, and yes I replied. I answered "They all have Command Computers that allow them to think for themselves I can ask them to do things". "Do you know where they are" she asked, "I answered that they were supposed to find me and fly formation around me."

"Well they are not, they are all around you in different caves, all going in different directions, and some are above us as well as bellow, right now only one is actually coming towards us." "How do you know that I "asked Pinger-5, "I am a whale "she answered, "I have to know where everything is or starve", she replied.

"How come you let the men in the little bad boats kill you I asked"? "OH, that's how we test our invincibility," she replied. "Has there ever been an invincible Humpback Whale," I asked. "Not in my lifetime." she answered. "As a matter of fact you were the first case of invincibility, that I heard of, as it turns out your just a human with a Machine. "That's what I get for listening to Polar Bears," She said. "You can talk to Polar Bears," I asked? Not really she answered "all I can do is stand my distance and listen to them brag," she answered. "They did not know what you were but, they really were mad that you would not share your kill with them, it was the part about you flying away with bad little boat that really got my attention." OK Pinger-5 I will explain it to you.

"The whalers harpoon hit and exploded in my hull if you look at the physical force that was needed to damage my Sabrina No. 40 space ship then compare it to the forces needed to kill you, remember numbers don't lie, as you can see the harpoon will pass completely through you, how you can expect to be invincible? She replied, "Lots of barnacles and lots of armor." I had lots of armor and my space ship has a reinforce hull and the whalers harpoon still caused damage way past the middle of my ship.

"It did not die" she said. "It was not alive like you are, it can be repaired you have to heal up I want you to promise me that you will never jump in front of a whalers harpoon just to see if you're invincible."

Log Entry #41.
Pinger-5 in Action:

Pinger-5 and I had decided to inform the rest of the humpback whales about their invincibility problems, she also remembered that this was the time of the year when most humpbacks were killed trying. It all boiled down to I'm invincible make me your leader routine, to find out whom the surviving Whale pods chief would be. We both decided that if we were going to do anything about it now was the time. Pinger-5 reprogrammed my navigation computer with the most direct course out of the massive underground lake system that we were exploring.

At my command the "First-Five 40" ships to form up at my current location to fly in formation with me. I made all the air-traffic calls as we made a full throttle vertical climb out of the surface of several different small lakes at the same time. I programmed all the "First-Five" forty's to fly high and ahead of me to scan the whole Pacific Ocean from Mexico to the Arctic Ocean for Whales, and then plot them all on my command screen.

Instantly I could see what was happening in real time over a thousand miles ahead of me. On the scanner we could see hundreds of whales swimming south, with the whole whale killer fleet intercepting them from west. I decided not to let the Killer Ship get a single shot at anybody, I made a supersonic impact in the Pacific Ocean a mile away from the closest <u>Killer Ship</u>, then surfaced and flew directly to cover the swimming Humpback Whale.

I extended full speed breaks, as well as full power on all my Lift-fans. As I was approaching the whaler's killer ship, head on, I programmed Sabrina No. 40 to hover inside their Harpoons ballistic arch. So that they would not be able to hit, the not so well informed humpback whale that was allowing the nasty little Killer Ship to test his invincibility.

I really didn't want to make another hole in the bottom of one of my space ships, so I programmed my Command Computer to toss out one of my recovered iron meteorites in the whaler's direct line of fire if they did fire a Harpoon at me. When I got to the Ballistic arch point I reversed the angels on my Lift-Fans and started flying backwards in formation with the approaching Killer Ship, I expected them to change course and stop their firing run.

"They fired their Harpoon!" Sabrina No. 40 snapped opened my bottom cargo bay doors and dropped a Van size meteorite at the oncoming harpoon, causing it to be struck and exploded. On the lower bottom of the heavy iron meteorite, causing it to fragment and bounced back up to where it almost struck the bottom of Sabrina No. 40. Then fell back directly on to the deck of the Killer boat covering its deck with relative large heavy metal meteor fragments that tended to make lots of holes as they all borrowed their way through the hull of the whaler's killer Ship. Pinger-5 opened her flight tanks hatch and made a vertical dive into the water just ahead of the poor Humpback Whale that was testing his invincibility.

It took her less than a second to bring him up to speed so in less than a minute there wasn't a single whale of any kind on any of my data screens. Also, at this moment the other 5 Sabrina No. 40 ships showed up with all of their Command Computers putting them in formation going a Mach 2 vertical dive into the water at the same second that the whaler fired it Harpoon. It took a couple of minutes for all the waterspouts and impact phloem's to settle, when they did all that was left floating on the surface of the ocean was a single lifeboat full of very wet whalers.

Pinger-5 surfaced next to them and talked to them without the aid of my translator. She told them that she wanted to thank all the humans in the lifeboat for helping all the whales especially the Humpbacks to test their invincibility for well over the last 200 years. She wanted them to know as well as tell all the other people in all the other bad little boats that they will never see or be able to find a whale of any kind in the water again.

I landed in the water next to Pinger-5 as she slapped the back end of the whalers life boat to propel, it towards its oncoming fleet of killer ships.

"My first question was if she could teach me to speak Humpback!" she said to forget it, "because humans just did not have the vocal requirements to do that." Pinger-5 had also put out the word about my search for lots of astronaut whales that might want to help her in outer space at a Moon called "Europa".

With the entire whaling fleet still closing from less than a mile away, Pinger-5 asked if she could program Sabrina No. 40's escape route as a vertical lift off would definitely put me in Harpoon range from more than one of the incoming killer boats. She converted Sabrina No. 40 to its hydro-ski mode then made a high speed exit of the area making sure that Sabrina No. 40 past within inches of the bow of each of the Killer Ships.

As we finally made it airborne, I noticed the First Forty were still following line-astern in formation. Sense we were going south I decided to see what Pinger-5 could do about finding Amelia Earhart.

I programmed the First Forty to spread out and search the sea bottom around Howland Island, starting where I had left off, from my last search, I slowed to hovering speed, extended the lift-fans and made my water landing a mile off the Shore of Howland Island. Pinger-5 remarked that she loved this part of the ocean because of its plantation content.

She noted that a whale could really put on weight hanging around here for a long time. She also surprised me, when I found out that Pinger-5 had already accessed the computer system to find out, all the information about Amelia Earhart, then she informed me that considering all the facts she did not think that we would find her alive. But, she would check with all the locals and see what information she could come up with, and then she hovered under the water and made a series of whale songs.

A couple of minutes later she surfaced and said, that all of the locals remembered me, especially when I thumped the back end of Sabrina No. 40 on the beach. There has been a group of humans on a small boat that have been "Pinging" to the point where most of the locals have ear pains. The good news is there are several colonies of sea turtles that will be back in this area in a couple of months they may have seen her.

You can talk to sea turtles I ask? "Not really" Pinger-5 replied, "all I can do is by changing the subject and keep listing to all their complaints." "I told her to get on their good side tell them not to eat the plastic," then I ordered the First Forty to go to their submarine mode and to keep making full power scans while doing a circular search of the sea bed.

Looking for anything that could have fallen out of Amelia's airplane that was on or under the bottom of the Pacific Ocean. It took most of the day for Pinger-5 to get the word that there were lots of whales that were willing to help the humans explore a place called "Europa". Pinger-5 heard a massive call for help from several hundred Whales that were trapped in swallowing water at an Atoll over 1000 miles away.

In less than 7 minutes with my permission she had the "First Five" Forty's doing supersonic extremely low passes at the atoll using their wake turbulence to pump more sea water back into the Lagoon, to keep everybody alive and afloat. As I arrived flying my prototype Sabrina No. 40 ship with Pinger-5 aboard, one of the Whalers Killer boats turned toward me to start closing to firing range. I must have looked like the largest flying whale that any of the whaling crews had ever seen. Pinger-5 had opened my external hatches before Sabrina No. 40 had time to sink to the now filling up floor of the atoll.

At Pinger-5's direction I started to load live Whales through my side hatches, as fast as they could enter. Sabrina No. 40 was just barely under water I could see from my top side cameras that the whalers were definitely up to something that was not nice. I could see them moving their Harpoon for a more accurate kill shot, when all of a sudden the Killer Ship disappeared. Good old Sabrina No. 39 had just made her first swooping grab maneuver, scooping up the entire Killer Ship and caring it away as if it were an oversized fish.

Then she gently dropped it several miles away on the main atoll barrier reef. I personally made a sigh of relief when I discovered that Sabrina No.39 was not going to keep it. The rest of the Sabrina No. 39 series also showed up and started making high speed passed just above wave height causing their supersonic wake turbulence to act as a siphon and this started to pull more sea water back into the Atolls Lagoon. The water finally started to get deep enough to allow Sabrina No. 40 to submerge.

As well as the rest of the "First Five" Forty who had landed and were now loading as many Whales as fast as they could enter their side hatches.

You would think that Pinger-5 had spent a life time jamming people into subway cars. It only took a couple of seconds for her to verbally take command and have all the stranded whales load themselves into the "First Five" Forty. Now all the pressure was on me we had all the Whales loaded and moving away from the Whalers but, they were all packed in each of the "First Five" forties cargo bay without any air to breath. The whalers were still pouring into the atoll through all the openings, and I was helping them by reversing the tide to save all the grounded whales.

Then Pinger-5 plan became clear, she had the "First Five" forty form into a star formation with everybody's nose pointing away from each other. Then she had the No. 39's to quit reversing the tide with their wake turbulence, instantly all the water disappeared leaving everybody high and dry especially the Whalers. Pinger-5 linked all the "First Five" Forties to have them fire all their Aero-Spikes at the same instant. This created a detention type blast that help to get all the Sabrina No. 40 Space craft airborne at the same instant.

This made all the whalers think that the "First Five" forties just disappeared in a column of smoke. As the movie line goes "it's not the whales it all that water." Over all the Whales loved their first young eagle ride, I had Pinger-5 put Sabrina No. 40 down in mid ocean. I didn't have to call a staff meeting as Pinger-5 was still in direct command of all the Sabrina No. 40's as the same time.

We hit the water in formation then pulled up to where we were just above the surface when Pinger-5 opened all the top cargo hatches and the same time to let everybody breath. It looked like we had a few of each different type of whales. I was surprise not to see any humpbacks, when I asked Pinger-5 how come she replied of course Humpbacks are smart enough as to not end up on a beach.

Besides I put out the word about invincibility, and from now on none of the whalers will ever see another Humpback, unless they see me on television, or in one of your Encyclopedias.

Pinger-5 asked me if we could airlift all the survivors to a place where the whalers can't find them, everybody, had been on the run for so long that they are starving because they have not had the chance to stop and feed.

I told Pinger-5 that the safest place on the planet was the middle of Lake Michigan, as long as everybody stayed away from the humans.

Pinger-5 answer, "you don't have to worry about that they all never want to see another human for the rest of their lives." So this is how I started my relocation operation for all the different types of Whales. Pinger-5 made her whale song for over an hour then filled me in on her plan, She had set up a pick up plan for each of the pods of Whale that wanted to join up, I arranged for more of my Sabrina No. 40 ships to join up into their mobile base modes outfitted to check out all the volunteers to start up my very first astronaut school for whales.

As soon as they were transported to Lake Michigan. My medical staff out did themselves, by having all 8 of my different medical teams, activated at the same time to start take care of all the whales. They did all the same things that had been done to Pinger-5, an extensive health check out, with the removal of skin parasites and barnacles, let me tell you did they all have lots of barnacles. We also made up "Sabrina Aviation ID tags with photos of the underside of each Whales tail fluke, with their new assigned name.

My space suit division really out did themselves with their space suit. It's a water containment system that is equipped with three layers of self-repairing and automatic overlays. Its three different Space suits all built into one, that can add layers as needed, or for maintenance. As long as the suits in water or for that matter wet, its He/3 reactor will keep it powered up.

It's equipped with special feeding packs that let each Whale consume a vast number of different types of Sea Food eating pods, all of which have to be pre-loaded by the space suits control unit, it also will disengage and form up to serve as her Communication Harness, complete with her heads up display, and communicator. So far Pinger-5 is the only one that has turned in their translator.

Humpbacks like all the other whales species have no concept of a name with this in mind I asked Pinger-5 how she would pick the names of the first humpback individuals that want to be trained as Whale/naut's, she found in my database the first words that were spoken as human astronauts first set foot on the surface of Moon. She thinks that if we have to use words to designate individuals we should use these words. So I plan to use these words in the order that they were spoken by human astronauts.

So Whale/naut's were to be names coming out of this list: That's one-small step-for a man- one giant leap for mankind. Magnificent desolation.

Whoopee!
but, that's
off the pad.
neat. I
nice on
you're right
way but,
out here
I sort of
nature. Man
is really
Discards.

gonna
glad they
briar patch

first foot
Tony!
my golly!
in the Sun.
depression.
pitch-up
dish
struts. How
my lunar

Man that
a long one
Oooh! Is
don't sink
the outside.
Al is on
we're here.
in the wonders
realize there's
must explore.
loose, isn't
Highland
plains.

change your
got ol' Brer
where he
belongs.

on the lunar
Jack,
Unbelievable!
Okay! We
That's why
angle...very
crater just
you doing,
surface?

may have
for me.
that soft
in too
My, that
the surface.
He's re

been a small
I'm going
and squeezy.
far. Boy,
Sun is
And it's
leasing it now.
of the unknown
a fundamental
Boy, that
it? Mysterious
Apollo

image.
Rabbit, here,
Fantastic!

surface is
I'm out
Unbelievable; but
landed in a very
we've got
shallow,
about the
Jack? Hey,

one for Neil
to step
Hey, that's
the LM looks
bright. Okay,
been a long
As I stand
at Hadley,
truth to our
front pad
and Unknown
16 is

I'm sure
back in the
Oh, that

super,
here. Oh,
is it bright
shallow
a slight
dinner-plate like,
width of the
who's been tracking up

Log Entry #42.
Sky Diving Whales:

It all started when I was modifying Pinger-5's space suit. She found several of my old parachutes that I had built back in my Sabrina No. IX days of spaceflight. I added my built in maintenance program as well as my auto repack system into its program. The result was a sky diving whale, any size whale for that matter. In all there are only seven different types of whales in the Earths Ocean, and they are the Humpbacks, Orcas, Blues, Fins, Grays, Sperms and Beluga's. In total there are about 75 different species of whales.

The He/3 powered system first forms up as a standard Whale size communications harness, then converts into a three layer form fitting space suit, that also has several built in parachute, and Para-glider connection points, that's attached to a duel canopy system. As soon as the Whale land in the water or for that matter lands the parachute automatically repack itself for the next use.

With my built in repair system any damage is instantly repaired as it happens. One of the first uses that Pinger-5 wanted was to use my whale/space suit was for an anti-beaching device. It consists of a Universal-Whale/Space-Suit that has been programed to instantly fit its occupant. Needless to say the space suit works perfectly with Humpbacks, Orcas, Blues, Fins, Grays, Sperm and Beluga's.

It doesn't matter about size, age, or sex. However, the most important thing is if the whale is left or right handed. The most interesting fact that I have uncovered is that all the Right Whales are left handed and their control band has to be located on their left flipper.

The plan is to use this new Universal-Whale/Space-Suit as a Rescue-Suit to save the life of a beached Whale. The Universal-Whale/Space-Suit would instantly inflate around the poor stranded Whale to pump itself full of water so that the grounded Whale could breathe. When used as a rescue whale suit it has tripled the connectors to make it easy to lift the poor beached whale off the beach. I realize that there will be times when one of my space ships will not be close by for used.

To get around this problem each Whale suit has a built in up-chute or hot / gas filled balloon envelopes to use during emergencies. This creates another problem as I have discovered that all Whales love to sky-dive.

Log Entry #43.
Killing off Hurricanes:

If you haven't noticed by now, not a single hurricane or has made land fall this year. It's because I personally killed them all for practices, for my next mission to Jupiter. As I am using each of them as a training aid.

I would drop in from orbit fly around inside taking reading then kill them by punching holes in their wall then cut the wall sideways peeling it like a potato. We had to make lots of very interesting contrails with the "First-Five" as well as the "Next-Ten" in formation.

We varied our attacks our first attempt was a series of fly-through from orbit, a simple change of direction a flash through the atmosphere a stab through the eye of a hurricane and an orbit insertion, later another hit but, by this time the "First Five" as well as the "Next Ten" had finished stitching a series of holes across the hurricanes eye. The next plan was to do an orbital stall and just fall out of orbit in a single ship and fly a series of figure eights until the poor hurricane just fades away.

We also made lots of cabled up attacks with each ship cabled at different, same, and longest distance apart. We would make a sowing machine type attack then fly around inside the storm stems sometimes with and then against the wind. And the favorite was too cable up close and then fly sideways next to the Hurricanes eye wall then start peeling the wall like it was the inside part of a donut hole.

Our attack always had a dramatic effect on the Hurricane. Human piloted Hurricane hunter aircraft had to be confused as all of a sudden the massive storm would just dry up and go away.

Log Entry #44.
Jupiter or Bust:

Because of my grades at school I get to skip another grade as it turn out I will have no memories if being a 11th grader as of now I am a senior, this open up my time frame to where I think I will just travel to Jupiter. I already have my requirement for senior all I have to do is the electives, these I can do in my POD's class room as I am in flight. As usual we all launch off the LEADER I had Sabrina No. 39/39 serve as a tug, and tow the rest of us out past the Moons orbit where I would have enough room to safely do my acceleration ring maneuver.

Every ship started to let out cable, and Sabrina No. 39/39 started to do a very large loop. I was flying in the last ship bring up the rear, as Sabrina No. 40/39 came under me in the circle I docked in to her top cargo bay, to have her towing cable transferred to the rear end of Sabrina No. 40, then used her Aero-spikes as well as fuel reserve to start the circle spinning, as soon as I had control of the tow cable. I gave the order to start pulling in cable, as the circle got smaller the speed went up, the smaller circle the faster we traveled.

When we were down to the last thousand feet apart, I released my nose cable to become number one in line as I zoomed away from the Earth towards the spot where the planet Jupiter would be when I got there. I let Sabrina No. 40/39 detach and return to the Moon. We all docked together to form a single cannon ball as a large mass will travel faster than a lot of smaller masses. The trip to Jupiter was normal, having lots of whales along for the trip was a big help as every one of them had a different prospective.

As we passed through the asteroid belt I noticed that several of my Whale/ naut's, were scanning and putting each of the detected Asteroids together as if they were a piece of a puzzle. By figuring trajectories, shape, size, and rotation they were able to trace all the known fragmented smaller asteroid back to when and where they were orbiting the Sun as larger planet size objects. As we approached the planet Jupiter its four largest Moons were the first to show up on our scanners.

Due to our extreme speed I decided to go with plan "A" and use which was to use a large section of Jupiter's atmosphere, to slow down enough to make its orbital speed. It was very interesting to be the first person to see the Great Red Spot from below, as we came up under it from the other side, I did manage to dump off several tons of censors and instrumentation packs. I took a second to wonder what my schools Storm chaser's Squad would do, as we shot through the Great Red Spot on our way to our first parking orbit.

We were all still in wagon train mode when we came out of Jupiter's upper atmosphere, after completing our first speed reduction maneuver that left everybody still cabled up in orbit around Jupiter, just outside of its four largest moons orbital tract. Our timing was perfect as after less than 1 Jupiter orbit we slipped into orbit around Io as planned.

It felt kind of weird with all the gravity fields interconnected and the whole space train slid into parking orbit around Jupiter's moon Io, without spending a drop of fuel. The plan was to visit the largest Moons, first, which are Io, Europa, Ganymede, and Callisto, each of which are distinctive worlds. Most of the Wagon train stayed in Io's orbit while only a couple of the Sabrina No. 39' checked out its surface. Io was the most volcanically active body in the solar system. Its surface is covered by sulfur in different colorful forms.

As it orbits Jupiter in a slightly elliptical orbit, Jupiter's gravity causes 'tides' in the solid surface 300 feet high all the Whale/nauts really liked to body surf on Io's surface. They would get frustrated when they discovered that they could not submerge under its surface because it was a solid. I managed to Instant prototype a surf board that enable me to show all my Whale friends what a 15 year old girl could do with a surf board on a moon like Io.

Everybody started to have problem with all the heat as well as the rising radiation levels, so we took all our samples and went on to the next Moon. Pinger-5 liked to body surfing and said," that she would have to try it in front of a tidal wave on Earth." Europe's surface was mostly water ice, and there was evident that it was covered with an ocean of water and slushy ice.

To check this out every ship skidded over to Europa when it gravity field interconnected with Io. Needless to say the first big disappointment was when the whales discovered that there was not any Oxygen or atmosphere of any kind. On Europa, despite all the water, our scanners took care of the moon within minutes I could tell you anything you want to know about Europa.

As planned I had our un-mammal penetrator ships make a hole in the surface near its equator, so that all of Sabrina No. 40 ship could zoom down directly into the moon while flying in line formation. What we found was breath taking the entire under water parts of the moon were moving faster that the speed of sound. I can put that one in my record book as I am the first human to travel faster that Mach one underwater in Europa.

Our main problem is everything under the surface is also traveling at supersonic speed. Europa has more than twice as much water as does Earth. This Moon intrigues me because of its potential for having a "habitable zone." I know of Life forms that have been found thriving near subterranean volcanoes on Earth in other extreme locations that may find similar life forms to what may exist on Europa.

Considering the supersonic blinder effect I could not detect anything except my Whale/naut's swimming around in the extremely fast moving liquid vortexes. It didn't take long to detect Whale/naut's in Europe's parking orbit. The first group called for a lift by the No. 39's still orbiting. The second and third groups that were on sub-orbital trajectories.

Did not call for help until they had stop moving on the surface of Europa. After they had slid down the Moon for several hundred miles. Pinger-5 was the only one that actual got to body surf on Europa surface for several orbit, wearing only her space suit. Her first complaint was she needed something to eat. As all the un-oxygenated material tasted bad to her. If

I had ever planned to set up the ultimate water park Europa would have to be the location.

In the case of Europa it has a global subsurface water layer that lies just below the icy crust. It took longer than expected to retrieve all our Whale/naut's, and leave all of our scientific packages as planned. Despite all odds we made the window and slip into parking orbit around Callisto which is the largest Moon in the solar system.

It's larger than the planet Mercury, and is the only Moon known to have its own internally generated magnetic field. The first complaint was "Where did all the water go" Callistos surface is extremely heavily cratered and ancient not to mention dry as a bone. It was the first Moon that acutely looked like a Moon. It was a lot dryer than the first two Moons as such it seemed to have lots of very stationary surface features.

Pinger-5 dropped onto the side of a crater and kept saying "giddy up, horsey" with nothing happening except the vibrations of a Moonquake. This Moons lack of surface movement served as a record of events from the early history of the solar system. Layering at Callisto is less well defined and appears to be mainly a mixture of ice and rock. However, the very few small craters on Callisto indicate a small degree of current surface activity it had a core a rock envelope around the core; a thick, soft ice layer; and a thin crust of impure water ice.

My sensors showed the interiors of Ganymede had a layered structure similar to Earth. As well as a core, and a mantle of at least partially molten rock, topped by a crust of solid rock coated with sulfur compounds. The three Moons influence each other in an interesting way. Io is in a tug-of-war with Ganymede and Europa, and Europe's orbital period is twice Io's period, and Ganymede's period is twice that of Europa. In other words, every time Ganymede goes around Jupiter once, Europa makes two orbits, and Io makes four orbits. The Moons all keep the same face towards Jupiter as they orbit, meaning that each Moon turns once on its axis for every orbit around Jupiter.

I could not line up any of the photos from Pioneers 10, 11, Voyager 1 and Voyager 2 took during their fly-by missions. Even the Galileo Spacecraft made photos from repeated elliptical orbits around Jupiter, passing as low as 162 miles over the surfaces of the Moons. Everything I saw was different.

The close approaches resulted in images with unprecedented detail of selected portions of the surfaces. I could see lose-up images of portions of Europe's surface showing places where ice had broken up and moved apart, and where liquid may had come from below and frozen smoothly on the surface. The low number of craters on Europa leads me to believe that a subsurface ocean has been present in recent geologic history and may still exist today.

The heat needed to melt the ice in a place so far from the Sun is coming from inside Europa, resulting primarily from the same type of tidal forces that drive Io's cold volcanoes. When I was not looking at a Moon I would look up and see Jupiter, most of the Whale/naut's sent a considerable amount of their time noting all the small changes that were constantly happening in Jupiter's atmosphere. Watching hurricanes and thunderstorms with sticks of lightning that were larger than the entire Earth seemed to draw their attention.

In all I made contact with as well as gathering data on all of Jupiter's Moons Io, Europa, Ganymede, Cellist, Am Althea, Himalaya, Elara, Pasiphae, Sinope, Lysithea, Carme, Ananke, Leda, Thebe, Adrastea, Metis, Callirrhoe, Themisto, Megaclite, Taygete, Chaldene, Harpalyke, Kalyke, Iocaste, Erinome, Isonoe, Praxidike, Autonoe, Thyone, Hermippe, Aitne, Eurydome, Euanthe, Euporie, Orthosie, Sponde, Kale, Pasithee, Hegemone, Mneme, Aoede, Thelxinoe, Arche, Kallichore, Helike, Carpo, Eukelade, Cyllene, Kore, S/2003 J2, S/2003 J3, S/2003 J4, S/2000 J11, S/2000 J5, S/2003 J9, S/2003 J10, S/2003 J12, S/2003 J15, S/2003 J16, S/2003 J17, S/2003 J18, S/2003 J19, and S/2003 J23. Most of the moons on the list were too small to orbit not to mention going in the wrong direction.

So, I bought the smaller ones back with me and sold them on E-Bay. On the way back to Earth the Whale/naut's spent lots of their time recombining most of the larger Asteroids that were in our flight path. To make it safer for all the interior planets by cutting down on the rouge asteroid problem.

Log Entry #45.
Retirement Party:

I kept getting requests to donate my Sabrina No. 5 to the Smithsonian ever sense I started testing out my Sabrina No. 40 Space ship. I decided to see what I could do about holding the record for the fastest round the world flight. As I un-officially held the record of 60 minutes that I set with my Sabrina No. 5 the day that I got into Junior High School. To get the American Institute of Aeronautics and Astronautics attention I loaded up Sabrina No. 40 with Sabrina No. 39.

I put Sabrina No. 5 inside of Sabrina No. 39's lower forward cargo bay. As soon as everything was loaded I flew Sabrina No. 40 to Washington DC, where I made a vertical landing over the down town mall next to the American Institute of Aeronautics and Astronautics office that maintains all of the official records. Upon I made a point to plant Sabrina No. 40's nose wheel as close to their front door as I could. This way I would not have far to walk all of their official's. I had to ride my nose wheel elevator all the way down to the surface level. So that I could meet them in their office and walked them back through Sabrina No. 40's nose gear elevator.

I brought all of them up the elevator and walked them all the way back through the forward cargo bay, past Pinger-5's flight tank quarters. As I was leading them past a sleeping Pinger-5 they all wanted to know if she was a real Whale. I answered, "of course she's real, and I asked all of them to be careful not to wake her up, as she was out gorging herself on zebra mussel, last night." They all wanted to know how I could tell, I told them" from all the spent sea shells that she left on the bottom of her flight tank."

As you can see the zebra mussel left overs are hard to recycle, my environmental technician still can't get rid of all her Spent Sea Shells. As we entered the top side aft cargo bay all of my spectators from the American Institute of Aeronautics and Astronautics were amazed to see my original Sabrina No. 39. This caused come confusion as they were under the impression that I was donating my Sabrina No. 5. That's when I had my ships systems to create a large spiral staircase all the way down to the lower aft cargo bay. As soon as everybody arrived I activated a single row of personal PODs and invited everyone to have a seat.

That's when I asked Sabrina No. 39 to open her forward lower cargo bay and lower Sabrina No. 5 to the aft lower cargo deck floor. I open the viewing hatch on the main viewing panel, and got things started. I informed all the officials from the American Institute of Aeronautics and Astronautics that I was going to donate my Sabrina No. 5 rocket plane to the Smithsonian Instruction. But, first I was going to dust her off a little. I set up a large timing clock, and then activated everybody's Passenger POD. As you are aware I un-officially claim the record for the fastest round the world point to point flight with this rocket plane Sabrina No. 5.

I informed them that I plan to make a point about her record breaking flight in a half hour. Then I moved back into my Command POD and started making thing happen rather quickly. I started the timer clock as I made a vertical launch once I was high enough I retracted all my hover-fans as well as aerodynamic controls.

I fired all four of my Aero-Spike rocket engines to accelerate too my maximum speed inside of the earth's atmosphere. My first turning point was low and slow over the entrance to the Roosevelt field shopping center near New York City I made a hard right turn to Paris France, when over the Eiffel Tower.

I made a tight turn to the left to over fly Moscow, then I flew straight across Russia to Tokyo Japan, to make a slight southern turn to Hawaii to buzz Pearl Harbor, from there I sped straight across the rest of the Pacific Ocean to over fly California where with a slight left turn to fly up the Mississippi River to St. Louis.

I made a slight turn to the right to Chicago, then turn back to over fly the Roosevelt shopping center, near New York. Cutting back the power and extending my speed brakes as we flew out over the Atlantic Ocean. To make a nice slow turn to the south back to the Washington D.C. and a vertical landing over the Udvar-Hazy Center.

As we touched down I had my command computer straddled the main building with both of my main landing gear. To bring everybody back to a full stop after exactly 15 minutes of flight. I lowered my Command POD back in place in the cargo bay, walked back down my boarding plank turned off all the personnel POD's and made my announcement.

"When you make up the historical plaque that goes with Sabrina No.5, If you don't want to mention the fact that I flew her around the world under her own power, in a hour, at least mention that I transported her around the world in 15 minutes during her retirement ceremony." "Despite the distance flown this is the fastest trip you have ever made from your down town offices to the Udvar-Hazy center."

The Command Computer had lined up thing perfect. I had Sabrina No. 40's open her bottom aft cargo bay door that opened directly over an open skylight. I had Sabrina No. 39 lower No.5 to her exhibit point 40 feet above the floor, to announce that this will enable her to be in-flight forever. Sabrina No. 39 decided to do a vertical salute to No. 5 by making a vertical launch out of the top of Sabrina No. 40.

You should have seen the look on all the humans from the American Institute of Aeronautics and Astronautics as my No. 39's extended her lift-fans as the top hatches opened. She did a safe hover with their lift-fans to get out of Sabrina No. 40 top cargo bays then turned on their smoke generators as she made a vertical climb-out all the way to the LEADER.

Pinger-5 had slept through the whole flight, this means that for a person to break my latest record they would also have to have a live full grown sleeping Humpback Whale aboard. I was a very nice child astronaut and I dropped off all the official's from the American Institute of Aeronautics and Astronautics to their office where I first found them.

Log Entry #46.
Barn Storming Whales:

It seems that I have made Pinger-5 into a fledgling Aviatrix, a 38 ton one at that. Like me she has taken all the knowledge tests and made 100 % on all of them. Her main problem is that the Federal Aviation Administration does not know how to deal with a mammal that is not human. Especially when the mammal is a lot smarter and knows it, she has not only read all the regulations but understands them.

To top it all off even the FAA has not come up with a regulation that says that a whale cannot qualify for a pilot's license. So when I knew that it was time to start her flight time it was a simple matter of connecting her control band to one of my command computers. My only problem was figuring out how to install a fully operational cockpit inside of her flight tank.

Would you believe that she loves to talk to air traffic controllers, especially when she makes a requests for a vector to one hundred thousand feet when still over the runway? Pinger-5 was only the first Whale/pilot, as soon as she had earned her flight instructor rating she went to work training all the other Whale/naut's, not only how to fly in outer space but how to fly inside of an atmosphere as well.

Pinger-5 has no need for money so as of now she has changed her barn storming operation to a "fly for fish" her strategy it's simple she would fly in from Orbit and Buzz some unsuspecting town in the middle of nowhere, then after making a vertical landing in the middle of town she would announce "free space flights for fresh Fish". As soon as one or more of her feeding modules were full she would give several Hundred of the town people a free introductory around the world flight that would last a little over a half hour.

As Pinger-5 de-planed all her passengers after their first free around the world flight. She would make sure that each one of them got a copy of her Astronaut Passenger Wings, that she had made herself, out of left over zebra mussel shell fragments. In all there are seven different types of Whales in my employee, they are the Humpbacks, Orcas, Blues, Fins, Grays, Sperms and Beluga. Pinger-5 started out with a few of each in her first class of her flight school.

Log Entry #47.
U-BOAT Wrecks:

Now that my company Sabrina Aviation had its own trained air force of qualified Whale/naut's. I was finally able to fix the worse human made problem ever. That of all the sunken U-boats, it seems that the Germans used liquid Mercury as ballast, to help maneuver their submarines. After they were sunk in battle now almost 80 years later they are all breaking up leaking all this Mercury into the sea bed.

This has created dead zones for several miles around each wreck site. With Pinger-5's help I have been able to locate each U-boat's wreck sight, so that I can extract the liquid mercury from the underwater environment. All the wrecks sights are so toxic that even Pinger-5 has to be in her space suit just to get closes enough to see its conning tower number.

The only thing that I can think of to help was to reprogram one of my He/3 scrubbers to pick up the element Mercury. I am still a little worried that Pinger-5 might jump up in front of a whalers harpoon just to find out if she is really invincible. Once my Sabrina Number 40 series space craft became operation she started to pick up and fly the entire sunken U-Boat to where it was in a state of zero "G". The extensive movement of all of its mass usually allowed my reprogramed He/3 scrubbers to clean up the Mercury in an hour or so.

Log Entry #48.
Up River Swim:

Pinger–5 along with the rest of her Whale/naut's started their "Up River Swim" program to help stop water pollution. By moving all the human made junk that litters the river bed, under her direction all the human made metal object get left on the river bank for human recovery. She started out just surveying problem areas that need to be fixed the good news is every year she get to go a little farther upstream.

Pinger-5 loves to see all the humans that come out to meet her personally every time she transients through each river lock. Especial the ones that pay her money for all the sunken boats and junked cars that she sells them for scrap. She says she has it made once she made it to the southern end of Illinois she can start slipping in and out of the New Madrid Cave system that she discovered.

In all there are seven different types of whales in my employee, they are the Humpbacks, Orcas, Blues, Fins, Grays, Sperms and Beluga she started out with a few of each. Even the Orcas has gone into the lifesaving business, as they love to throw a drowning human back on dry land for a reward of a couple of pound of frozen hotdogs. Now I have whole colonies of Humpbacks, Orcas, Blues, Fins, Grays, Sperms and Beluga living in and around all 5 of the Great Lakes, as well as the extensive New Madrid underground lake system.

Log Entry #49.
Witness Report:

Due to the size of my Sabrina No. 40 Space ship I have discovered that its downdraft caused by their Lift-Fans will trigger almost any Avalanche as needed. All we have to do is hover over the top of the mountain range, and watch. The locals do tend to get excited when several Humpback Whales in full Space suit mode dropped out of the bottom of the hovering ship at the same time.

They all make hard lands in the snow to start an instant avalanche only to swim her way down the mountain. When interviewing eye witness it is interesting to note that the whales said "Wheeeee," all the way to the bottom. Where the entire now fast moving whale pod would proceed to slide directly into the open side hatch of another hovering Sabrina No. 40 space ship that was stationed much further down the valley.

Log Entry #50.
One-Giant:

One of the habits that Pinger-5 as well as all the other whale/naut's, got into while they were on Europa was to Belly Slide down the steep sloop on the snow. They would have to be in full Space suit mode, and remember to reinforce the bottom of the suit but it worked.

Every one of them got to be an expert at getting dropped off at a high point and sliding all the way to the lowest point possible. I can only image the terror that a Humpback Whale could cause as they go sliding down a mountain side in full space suit mode under the one "G" of Earth's gravity. So far nobody has wiped out anything expensive. One-Giant, wants to slide down the full length of Mt. Everest but I managed to talk him out of it because he would pull to many "G" to recover from free fall.

I have just discovered that One-Giant's favorite trick is to have a Sabrina No. 40 space ship drop him off at the top of a mountain side and have the same ship catch him midway down the mountain side. As he would eventually sort of ski-jump off an out jaunting cliff face directly into to the open cargo bay waiting for him while flying in its hover mode at a much lower altitude.

Log Entry #51.
Flying Humpbacks:

I have not only designed as well as built aircraft that can fly in Outer Space. I have also modified my aircraft not only to fly live whales but to have the whales themselves fly themselves. All it took was a custom fitted censor glove on the whale's flipper, along with a fly by wire interface and just like that an instant Whale of a pilot. A heads up display also has to set up to work off a harness that can also be used as a base for a whale size space suit.

However, it matters if a whale is left or right handed to make the system work, as the operative glove has to be in the dominant flipper. Pinger-5 also loves to pull weird "G's" the only kind she can get by doing aerobatic maneuvers at airshows.

If a mammal ever had the DNA to be in the airshow business it has to be Pinger-5. She looked up the history of flight and now she wants me to set her up in her own Airshow act. She especially wants to barn storm and sells rides, as they did in the good old days. She even makes all her own announcements and pitches to the crowd herself. After her return from the first Jupiter mission she along with several other of her Space Pod of whales got together and formed their own flying team made up with the Five First Forty Space ships.

Pinger-5 likes Lake Michigan she loves everything about it, especially the Lake Front Airshows. She liked to show her stuff to all the millions of humans that would come out to watch her perform. Her favorite pastime is to float next to a large pleasure boat and talk to the humans aboard, she liked to watch sailboats.

She would float on the surface for hours to watch them silently maneuver around her. Come airshow time each of humpback Whale/naut's would check out one of the Sabrina No. 40 series Space ships that I keep stationed in the giant under water cave system that Pinger-5 discovered under Chicago.

They would first do a series of vertical pop ups coming out of the water, then form up and start doing high speed passed over Lake Shore Drive to help draw out people to see the Airshow.

A 20 minute aerobatic routine with narration and music, quick sequence of maneuvers, always something in front of crowd, aerobatic shows can be flown with ceilings as low as 2000 feet, low-weather variation can be flown with ceilings down to 1100 feet. They do all the standard maneuvers flown during the aerobatic show and the low-weather variation. Individual maneuvers may vary from show to show depending on such things as the ceiling, winds, and requirements of the site location, as well as the availably of lots of raw fish.

Corkscrew, Solos Depart, Head-On Pass, Heart, Diamond 360, Double-Overtake, Head-On Break, "Leader's Choice, Formation Loop, Squirrel Cage Loop, Switchblade, Bombast, Missing Man, Whifferdills, Immelman, Break, Smoke Salute, Switchblade, Double Hurricane, Crazy Eight, Pop-Top Break.

Not to forget everybody's favorite the Lomcevak. Some of the new born Whale/naut's have the ability to make up flight maneuvers as they do it. The precision formation work does not end with the landing. Time and show line layout permitting, the team performs a special "smoke salute" on their way to parking. Passing in front of the crowd, the team does a simultaneous flanking turn toward the show line, stops and turns on their lights and smoke.

After the salute to their audience, they flank again and continue in formation to parking while still in full hover. In the "Arrow" a line-astern formation in which each of the "First Five" Forties were all tucked in right behind and slightly above the one before it.

From the arrow they would go to the arrowhead as the two trailing Sabrina No. 40's moved to the side of the line and took formation in line with each other, tucked in on the number two Space ships. They also flew echelon formations, and ended their maneuver with a bomb burst the lead and number three space ships would break high and to the left while numbers two and four broke to the right while number 5 would go vertical.

Pinger-5 would then rejoined in the diamond and returned to Airshow center extend her Lift-Fans form up into a nose against nose formation and go into a vertical hover.

They would keep the power up enough to hover a foot above Airshow center. Rotate 180 degrees, then do a simultaneous vertical in-trail climb-out to the top of the Airshow box, fly inverted to the edge of the Airshow box, then make a vertical short field hover crossing over each other as they descend until their Aero-Spike engine were facing each other.

While in hover mode rotate back to where their noses cones were touching, make a vertical landing, in the water next to North Avenue Beach, extend each of their landing gear to the point where each cargo bay would just be underwater, and then power down everything, retract and fold in all their aerodynamic control surfaces.

Then all the bottom hatches would open, to launch each of the whale/naut's, would then swim out from under each Sabrina No. 40 with each one wearing their space suit to meet the crowd. Pinger-5 liked to jump clear out of the water and jump all the way over the Space ship that she was flying.

After the swimming show everybody would return their Space ship and take off vertically with the aid of the lift-fans. Then they all pull Pinger-5's disappearing act by turning on full smoke, and allowing it to be resuscitated by the lift-fans, then turning away from the Airshow crowd, they would kill their smoke and pop out flying away, so that when the smoke cleared everybody was gone. In all there are seven different types of Whales in my employee, they are the Humpbacks, Orcas, Blues, Fins, Grays, Sperms and Beluga I started out with a few of each.

Log Entry #52.
Sand Hogs:

Pinger-5 was worried by flooding reports of rivers overflowing and flooding out human towns really got her attention. Due to her advanced math skills I discovered that she could calculate the failure location of each dam, that was about to fail by calculating the speed, mass, direction, and tides, she could figure out when as well as where a dam was going to break.

To counter this danger I modified Sabrina No. 40 with a power dredge it's not easy to use and I need Pinger-5 or any other of the whales to guide the underwater parts of the sand hog, to make sure that I only blow sand.

The typical mission would be to first parachute Pinger-5 into the river at one of her calculated failure points, a location that only a whale can calculate. She likes to do HALO type jumps, and in some cases she has managed to travel for over 100 miles by changing her shape to enable her to swim aerodynamically in the air.

After she lands in the water and has the re-pack system stores her parachute she usually gorges herself before, she starts calculating the waters movement and figure the next Dams breaking point. Then I met up with Pinger-5 at that location with Sabrina No. 40's top and bottom cargo bay doors open and lower the intake valve. Pinger-5 takes charge of this part to make sure that it lands on a sandy part of the river bottom. When I turn it on I am shooting liquefied sand and small rocks out of a very large fire hose.

All I have to do is have my ships systems to hose down the dam and reinforce it or make it higher. Having enough raw power to run the sand Hog is no problem as all I have to do is plug it into one of my He/3 generators. This operation also instantly deepens the main river channel this takes pressure off of the temporary shore line emergency dams.

Log Entry #53.
"Number Ones Arrival":

My part of the airshow is very spectacular! I perform a series of hyper-sonic passes cutting the middle of airshow center in half. My first pass is always my fastest with full smoke on I cut the Airshow Box in half, while at the same time doing a 4 point roll, without pulling up. I go to the perimeter of the field then I make a 90 degree turn back around to the Airshow Center.

This is the part of my act where I cut my first contrail in half as I cut the Airshow center in half again for the second time at a 90 degree point. Usually at this time both of my sonic booms catch up with the crowd. The distinct drop in air pressure usually makes it start to rain. I have my onboard communication system get on the Airshow's speaker system and ask the crowd if they can tell where I am, then I tell them to notice that I am 60 to 70 degrees ahead of the sound that they can hear coming from Sabrina No. 39.

What makes this more spectacular is I am in glide mode with my Aero-Spikes turned down to idle. I keep up the perimeter turn until I finally drop below Mach One. Then I start the aerodynamic part of my act. I have a different color of smoke set to expel from each different part of my Aero-Spike Rocket Motor. You will have to admit you haven't seen a hammer head stall until you have seen one performed by me flying Sabrina No. 39.

At this point in my act I remember my first Sabrina one and all the fun I use to have in her doing my aerobatic act, and I throw in a Lomcevak or two to impress the crowd. I end the act by extending my lift-fans and hovering to a dead stop making the crown notice that Sabrina No. 39

barely fits inside the airshow box. I hover over to my parking spot and land, I shut everything down and run my Command POD up to its extended top side position where I sit back and watch the rest of the show. I usually leave by becoming part of Pinger-5's disappearing act.

Log Entry #54.
Storm Chasers:

I had an invitation to attend a "Storm Chasers" meeting from one of my classmates, I landed Sabrina No. 40 behind the Storm Chasers meeting location with her nose gear elevator as close to the back door as possible. When I was asked about the biggest storm that I had been close to, none of them believed my claim that it was the "Great Red Spot on Jupiter" Its diameter varies between 30,000 and 50,000 miles, it's been ongoing for well over 400 years, I discovered that it was only about 6,000 miles deep with wind speeds from Mach 3 to 9.

After I informed them of my flying capability they made a request that I transport their vehicles in Sabrina No. 40 too within range of a tornado, I informed them about the time that I let my father park his Mustang in one of the main gear elevators, and I melted it, just by doing a RTW flight. I offered to drop them off on the ground in the center of the tornado's eye but none of them took up my offer. When asked how I deal with a level 5 Tornados I replied that I treat them just like Hurricanes and Typhoons, I punch lots of holes in their wall to make them bleed, different temperature air into their eye, and then I cut them in half and peal them like a potato.

I also told them that Pinger-5 loves to do this type of maneuver she call it "peeling the wall". However I did not mention the fact that she is a full grown 38 ton Humpback Whale. As I was leaving by way of the back door, one of their "Type A" personalities stopped me and wanted to know why I was going out the back door! I informed him that I had parked outback, "In the corn field" he asked I used my communications necklace to turn on the nose gear lights.

He remarked, "that he had not noticed the elevator by the back door before," "I told him that it was only there sense my latest arrival," as I walked towards it the nose gear elevator door open and I stepped inside. I wondered what he thought when he tried to find it after my departure. I programmed all their vehicles into my navigation system so I could keep track of them if I discovered them, flying around somewhere inside a tornado.

A couple of weeks later as I was flying my Sabrina No. 40 prototype cross country, my navigation system located all their weird vehicles parked at a road side dinner in the middle of their prospecting zone.

As usual I tried to set Sabrina No. 40 down with her nose gear elevator closes to the door but couldn't because the parking lot was full of their "weird carry me away now vehicles". So I parked Sabrina No. 40 in the closest corn field, and lower one of my fuel cell powered reconnaissance PODs to drive over to say "Hi" as well as eat lunch.

They all remembered me from their meeting, as the elevator girl, and were glad that I had dropped in to see them at lunch time. One of the better things about being an Astronaut Pilot is the ability to eat at the finer locations on the planet, like this out of the way truck stop in Iowa. I got to admit their Surface Exploration Units vehicles were the most noticeable navigation feature for at least 1,000 miles around. Suddenly all their alarms started going off I checked my communications necklace to discover that No. 40's instruments had discovered a newly formed level one Tornado that was about to run directly over us.

I hit the panic button, instantly Sabrina No. 40 launched out of her local corn field, lowered her forward Reconnaissance POD pick up wand, pulled up my reconnaissance POD seconds after I rebounded it. Open both of her top side as well as bottom cargo bay doors, and then position herself to where the Tornado was inside of her main cargo bay.

Then she closed her bottom cargo bay door and lifted the Tornado off the ground. Caring it back into the sky, I this point I took command and started to fly tight circles inside its eye expanding the Tornados wall until it died. It took less than a minute for Sabrina No. 40 to disperse the tornado.

I landed back over the truck stop this time covering the entire parking lot. I offered to move all their vehicles to a better location, and that all said that they would just wait for the next one where they were.

Log Entry #55.
Hide in Plain Sight:

As my space ships have grown in size as well as function I have developed a unique ability to hide from the public, in plain sight. Despite my fame in France I don't always make for the roof, all of my Space ships have to be designed for high speed flight and maneuverability. My problem is sooner or later I will have to leave it parked somewhere. There also is the problem of fitting the ship into a space base for loading as well as repairs, not to mention designing control systems that none humans can use even under high G loads.

I have always had the ability to change the outer color of all my space craft so showing fake windows as well as trees or rocks in not a problem. The problem is despite what the people in Oklahoma think corn fields usually don't grow corn 40 stories high. So I like to program in different bottom and top colors. Nothing else I have an automatic button. Needless to say with the oncoming of all of my Whale/naut's brain power all of my flight as well as urban camouflage systems are going to improve.

It won't be long until I will have problems remembering where I had parked. I usually just set the system to white fluffy cloud. However this had caused some concerns when I have to avoid collusions as other aircraft keep trying to just fly through my home made cloud. However if I program the urban camouflage system to look like a big nasty thunderstorm I get the U.S. weather service mad at me.

Log Entry #56.
High Speed Math:

Pinger–5 gave me some of her math formulas that I used to calculate the exact distance between all the planets. So that when answering questions on tests that require knowing exact distances I can get it down to within inches and feet.

By using Pinger-5's formulas I can give an up to date answer at any time. This also make it possible for me to fly anywhere in the solar system in a direct strait line, without wasting as much as an inch of distance traveled. Her latest math conquest and the way that she does complicated problems will defiantly make the next copy of our math book a lot bigger.

After all I have to be able to outperform my own computer.

Log Entry #57.
Dark Sky's two:

Everybody got into the act again re-supplying the Antarctic base for the second time. We even recovered all of their trash back to a recycling center in New York. I have discovered that by using their built in sound locaters each Whale/naut's can find lost equipment that has been stuck in the Ice Pack some of it for more than a hundred years.

This was the first time that we hauled out more than we hauled in. This time Pinger-5 did not waste any time setting up her whale slides complete with large chasm size zoom shoots. My Whales have discovered numerous large over size chasms beneath the Antarctic Ice. Extremely large chasms that run deeper than the Grand Canyon. Buried beneath thick slabs of Antarctic ice there lays a craggy landscape, that is home to mountains, valleys.

This discovery has allowed human scientists as well as my Whale/naut's to learn how now massive, sub glacial gorges much deeper than the Grand Canyon can be formed in large layers of thick ice. By using the Whales ability to use their sound locating ability to make the most detailed map yet of the Antarctic landmass. Our team of researchers use radar and satellite imagery collected in collaboration to chart a prehistoric Antarctic mountain range.

It was in doing so that they discovered an enormous chasm measuring miles deep, and over a hundred miles long and, at some points, as much as 20 miles wide. The discovery and exploration of hidden, previously unknown landscapes are still possible and incredibly exciting.

I let the Whale/naut's romp around all they wanted as long as they report what that found under the snow. This enabled me and the Sabrina first Five to locate and recover lost equipment, let me tell you we found tons of it. In all broken aircraft and surface vehicles were recovered by the hundreds. Pinger-5 has set up several extremely long under surface belly slides for herself as well as all of her Whale/naut's.

Log Entry #58.
Friends at AMARC:

The Line Chief at AMARC is still not responding to my calls after retrieving 60 more lost aircraft and Surface Exploration vehicles. The "First-Five" had left them all heaped up in their requested location still in the same attitude as they were recovered.

I hear that their Inventory Chief had to come up with a complete set of cold weather Antarctic gear just to look for serial numbers, because it takes almost a week for all the recovered equipment to warm up enough to handle with bare hands.

They also had a big problem coming up with very old aircraft records for very old fully operational aircraft that were only stuck in the snow for the last twenty years or so. It seems that on several occasions all that was needed to make the old recovered aircraft operational was a major defrosting.

On the funny side most of the older aircraft built with rivets would just fall apart as their outer metal skin would expand as it heated up. As it turns out the Curtis Condor was the safest airplane to be around as it had very little metal in its design. Needless to say the Federal Government took charge of all recovered items. It seems that the managers at AMARC do not give out credit slips for the return of lost Government property.

Another one of my interesting fact is the ground location manager that had to know where every stored aircraft is located had quit going to lunch, as every time he returns from lunch he discovers a new pile of aircraft that he has to sign into his care.

Log Entry #59.
Moving Mountains:

Smoky the bear runs, have also been a favored sport, as well as Tornado peeling. However we did have a mishap, it seems that 39/6 had a mountain jump up in front of her as she was making a series of low speed fire suppression runs.

According to her logic boards she was paying too much attention to the location of people on the ground, while doing a series of high speed dry runs. When she clipped a mountain side and was thrown into a flat spin. This caused her to cart wheeled down the other side of the mountain directly into the main forest fire.

Luckily, she landed right side up, so all she had to do was extent her landing gear. Re-orient her Command Computer, extend her hover fans, and go back to work.

I really lucked out when the local press reported it as one of my new firefighting techniques Sabrina Style operations. What makes the event even better was the fact that she also had a large bulldozer aboard at the same time.

Log Entry #60.
Fire Proof Flying Fort:

On another occasion 39/8 used herself as a fire proof fort to save the lives of a large group of stranded fire fighters. It seems that a series of converting fire storms had trapped several smoke eater crews on the top of a mountain with a forest fire storms coming up all four sides of the mountain at the same time.

According to Sabrina No. 39/8's logic boards had her to open her lower main cargo bay and land vertically with all the stranded personal inside of her lower cargo bay. This way she could using her exterior heat shields to protect them from all four of the conversing fire storms at the same time.

I am not sure exactly where or how she used, but lots of sticky foam was also used in the calculations.

They have also got into the habit of moving heavy earth moving equipment around upon request. So if any of you ever find a large heavy bulldozer sitting on the very top of a mountain think of me.

Log Entry #61.
The Everest Clean Up:

As a new project we also started to clean up Mt. Everest, as it seems that nobody has ever taken out their thrash, or their dead for that matter.

By changing the angles on our main landing gear, all each ship had to do was land over each expedition's trash dump and scoop it all up with space-junk traps.

I did get to stand on the highest place on the Earth other than the top of Sears Tower. It had to be tough on the climbers as I was in full space suit mode with the heat turned up full. I even made sure that the "Official Mt. Everest Climbers Book" was still sitting at the very highest point. I seem to have made a big hit in the instant avalanches business, I was amazed to learn how many humans are insured or killed by moving snow every year.

All I have to do it make a single pass using my Sabrina No.39's wake to trigger all the avalanched needed. So far my only problem is trying to keep the Whale/naut's from belly sliding on top of the large snow wave as it moves down the side of the mountain range.

Log Entry #62.
Cleaning up the Hump:

We also took a Long Weekend and recovered all the lost Military Transports that had crashed into mountains while flying the "Hump" during World War 2. In all we accounted for over 200 missing Aviators.

The valley floor lies 90 feet above sea level at town named Chabua. From this level the mountain wall surrounding the valley rises quickly to just over 10,000 feet and higher. Flying eastward out of the valley, the original aircrews would first have to get over the Patkai Mountain Range, then passed over the upper Chindwin River valley, bounded on the east by a 14,000-foot ridge, the Kumon Mountains.

Then they then would have to cross a series of 14,000–16,000-foot ridges separated by the valleys of the West Irrawaddy, East Irrawaddy, Salween, and Mekong Rivers. The main "Hump," which gave its name to the whole awesome mountainous mass and to the air bridge which they built to cross it.

Then there was the Santsung Range, often 15,000 feet high, between the Salween and Mekong Rivers. East of the Mekong where the terrain became decidedly less rugged, and the elevations more moderate as each transport plane approached the Kunming airfield that was located at an altitude of 6,200 feet above sea level.

Problems with the Indian railway system meant that aircraft assigned to the airlift often carried their cargo all the way from Karachi to China, creating the first air bridge was the only practicable way to supply China in anything resembling a timely fashion.

Unarmed aircrews as well as their cargos also had to deal with enemy fighters.

Japanese fighter Planes based in central Burma challenged the transports route near the city Sumprabum where according to Pinger-5 did not even have a decent hot dog stand.

To top in all off at the end of the summer monsoon season despite all the aircraft losses caused by everything else, a large number of Japanese fighter planes assisted by ground observer's evaded U.S. fighter patrols and shot down several transports while damaging several others.

The most amazing recoveries were all the downed Japanese fighters that we found. Over all the "First Five" handled all the wreckage that was still laying on glaciers and the "Next Ten" got the job of removing everything from the mountain sides. As always all the recovered aircraft were hauled to AMARC and piled up in its usual spot. Pinger-5 used all the recovered cargo to make her first million dollars by selling everything on EBay.

Log Entry #63.
Rocky Mountain Clean up:

We also started a cleanup operation in the High Mountain ranges in the United States, as well as Alaska. So far we have hauled several hundred thousand pounds of wreckage to AMARC.

Upon discovering lots of well-used crash sites I consecrated my Scanner Farm on the LEADER to the California canyon system and made it one of my red flagged patrol items. So that my emergency action ship that is on alert can make a full powered dive into the atmosphere, to swoop down from the LEADER and catch the airplane in the air with a Space-junk-trap before they can fly around the side of the mountain to discover the dead end at the end of the canyon.

Pinger-5 cannot understand how a mountain can just jump up in front of an aircraft in flight. I told her that it's a case where the poor little airplane can't fly high enough to safely fly over the mountain. So Pilots have to fly in the valley between the mountains and they get lost and end up finding the Box End all at once. Her solution was simple all we have to do is digging out the Valleys and get rid of all the dead ends.

She instantly organized her Tara-formers that she was training to hallow out Astrid's to start building a series of large earth bound tunnels, so that the poor little airplanes would not have this problem.

I had to point out that this would only cause the poor little airplanes to crash into each other inside of her tunnels. As this would cause the faster flying one to catch up with the slower flying ones.

As it turned out it was a lot simpler to build more Sabrina No.39's and let them learn how to make Mach 30 power dives into the atmosphere then after atmospheric entry slow down enough to locate and capture a slow flying small airplane.

Log Entry #64.
Catching Them All:

I also have captured and sold all of the known Earth Crossing Asteroids, as well as milked them of all their He/3. This just leaves the Millions of unknowns to deal with.

The whole gang also stands meteor interception duty. Anything larger than a small sports car sets off my detectors. So far I had been able to dispatch the closet Sabrina No. 39 space ship to catch it before it causes any trouble. The good news is we keep catching fewer each year. Eventually we hope to run out of small Want-a-bees meteors altogether.

However, I don't think that this will happen as monuments in the Asteroid and Kuiper belts will continually keep our supply of new arrivals coming.

Log Entry #65.
To Save a Life:

One of the more interesting operations was to use my space-junk trap to catch Polar Bears. It seems that the Arctic Ice Pack also has problems and the Polar Bear is now an endangered species list.

So my plan for now is to see how many survivors I can safely trap to raise in a captive environment for the next year. The capture involves the use of my ships scanners and the space-junk-trap.

It takes lots of very low-slow flying, usually at night. So far all the captured Polar Bears have been very hard on my equipment. In most cases I catch them underwater as that try to escape. They fight the trap and usually rip it up so bad that I can only get one use out of it.

Let me tell you the last thing anybody wants in their sleeping bag is a live hungry Polar Bear. But I am saving lives other than human. Mother Nature is really cruel.

The second half of the problem was the Seal population. Because all the Polar Bears were having a problem, the Seal population has grown to a point where they have exhausted their local food supply. As they lose their Body Fat they die from hypothermia, whole herds at a time, in the cold sea water, by the thousands.

I used my infrared locators on the LEADER to spot the herds of dead seals then scoop up and transport them to my Captive Polar Bear Camp.

Log Entry #66.
Traveling Plans:

I am also planning more trips to Jupiter's Moon Europe and Io, the mission will be a long one, I am going to try to make it part of my school project who knows, I might even bring along a class mate or two.

I plan to use my gravity sling maneuver to get a Sabrina No. 40 series size space ship to Jupiter, there will be problems with radiation, deceleration, impact, water pressure, and of course recovery and return. I plan to go back to the early space flight era and create a series of stages.

By building four Sabrina No. 39s Space ships together into the hull of a Sabrina No. 40 series, then place that into a hollowed out asteroid, and use the volume of the asteroid to store need supplies and fuel to get to Jupiter.

Then ditch the asteroid shell, inside Jupiter's atmosphere, and then use the atmosphere of Jupiter to slow down for orbit, and then use the ballistic controls on the Sabrina No. 40 series space ship to make a soft landing on Europa.

Once safely parked on its surface the living modules would be lowered into it surface to keep prolong ration from being a problem for the crew. Then Sabrina No. 40 series spacecraft would remain on Europa forever, and serve as the step off point for future missions.

The ships lower cargo bay will be used as a work site to drill down through the ice covered surface and release under water probes that will explore the inside of Jupiter wettest Moon. At the end of the mission the four Sabrina

No. 39 ships would launch out of the cargo bay of the Sabrina No. 40 series space ship.

To form up and make a four ship acceleration sling to return them to Earth or Mars. So far this has only been a plan as I keep coming up short on all of the radiation factors. Every time I revamp the mission plans I end up making the support ship larger as well as reusable.

But first I need to build the equipment. I plan to come up with modifications that will let me operate under water, as well as to land in water at supersonic speeds or faster.

Log Entry #67.
Star date: 48975.1:

So far I have had my whale/nauts in training searching every square foot of the ocean bed around Howard Island in the Pacific Ocean looking for the wreckage of Amelia Earhart's Lockheed 10e. So far my search forces has found nothing, from her airplane.

It not like we can't find lost airplanes in fact we have found and recover thousands of them, but not this one. In fact when we do find a human made craft that does not belong where it is my Whale/naut force recovers it and makes the wreck sight look as if it never had any wreckage what so ever.

To check out and test my new underwater equipment I plan to personally search for Amelia Earhart's' Lockheed 10e. It has to out there somewhere, unless a passing alien space ship really did capture aviatrix Amelia Earhart, who disappeared with her Navigator/Aviator Fred Noonan and took them to Delta Quadrant which is on the other side of our Milky Way Galaxy.

So far my best lead is that Captain Janeway of the Federation Starship Voyager will rescue both of them from suspended animation, 360 years from now on Star date: 48975.1.

Log Entry #68.
Incredulous Controllers:

I have programmed all my Command Computers to contact the closest Federal Aviation Administration control tower that might be located at the lowest point of any of my acceleration dive that my space craft might be doing.

The Command Computer would first contact the closest control tower and make a request for clearance for the lowest altitude they plan to use it's usually FL 60 (60,000ft). The incredulous controllers, usually answer with some disdain in their voice, and asked, "How do you plan to get up to 60,000 feet?"

The Command Computer usually answers with my 14-year-old female voice would respond, "I don't plan to go up to 60,000 feet, I plan to come down to it."

By the way can you give me my ground speed readout"? Then throughout the mission continue to communicate with the control center on the surface of the earth. Until my space ship has past the orbital track of the Earth's Moon.

At this point in the mission I have them contact the system wide space traffic control center that I am currently building in the Asteroid belt near the Asteroid Ceros. What's really entering is when first talking to the very grounded air-traffic control tow they think that they are stationary on the surface of the Earth, without realizing that they are to one that are changing my course in relation to the Earth rotation not me.

Log Entry #69.
You Can't Separate a Girl From her Computer:

I was finally back in low Earth orbit. I had most of my space junk nets deployed as I was still in search of the other half of Apollo 9's Lunar module. I was orbiting across eastern New York 113 at miles high at 596,640 feet.

I monitoring various radio transmissions from other aircraft as I over flew Manhattan air space. Though they didn't really control me, they did monitor my movement across their radarscope. I overheard several other aircraft ask for readouts about their ground speed. The Center controllers were replying, with a constant stream of information back to each aircraft that was in their controlled airspace.

With their new computer system the old upside down wedding cake arrangement did not work anymore. Now the control zone was a cylinder shaped and goes all the way up to Low Earth Orbit, where I was operating. After listing to several other fast movers, I wasn't the only ones proud of my ground speed. As I was thinking to myself how quant this was, I heard a familiar transmission coming from my Command Computer using my voice.

"Manhattan Center, Sabrina No. 40, you got a ground speed readout for me? "There was a longer than normal pause... "Sabrina No. 40, your ground speed is 17,682 miles per hour". No further inquiries were heard on that frequency during that surface radio contact.

Log Entry #70.
Hubble Trouble:

Last Tuesday I got a phone call from one of N.A.S.A.'s repair coordinators. It seems that the Hubble Space Telescope was broken again! The N.A.S.A.'s repair coordinator was ordered by his boss to contact me about fixing it.

He first asked me if he could speak to my father about fixing a broken spacecraft. I told him that my father is a lawyer and not very good at fixing spacecraft, especially ones that are still parked in extremely high Earth orbit.

After I identified myself, I don't think he was impressed by a 14 year old girl. He wanted to know if I could help N.A.S.A. fix their broken spacecraft. They were not a lot of help, as all they knew was it "won't work". He even offered Sabrina Aviation an Astronauts seat on the crew exploration Vehicle that they were going to use for this Hubble repair mission.

He even showed me archive photos of what Hubble looks like as if I did not know what it was. His next question really floored me as he asked about the size of space suit that N.A.S.A. would have to furnish me for the mission. He would not even stop talking about N.A.S.A.'s space suits even after I inform him that I already had my own.

While all of this was going on I had my closest Sabrina No. 39 Space ship Sabrina No. 39/8 pick the Hubble Space Telescope up out of its Very High Earth parking orbit. This only took a couple of minutes.

The N.A.S.A. repair coordinator didn't even catch on when I started to show him live pictures of the Hubble coming from Sabrina No. 39/8's cargo bay. You should have seen the look on his face when Sabrina No. 39/8 landed in his parking lot.

Without turning over or setting fire to any of their parked cars, and lowered the Hubble to street level still inside its Space-junk-Trap. Would you believe that N.A.S.A. didn't even have a three-spindle career to move it into their repair shop?

I had to ask Sabrina No. 39/8 to use her own aircraft mover to hang it from the ceiling in their lower level parking garage. I also informed N.A.S.A.s repair coordinator that I would gladly return in to where I found it after it was fixed. All he would have to do is call me and let me know when it was ready for operational spaceflight.

Log Entry #71.
Weekend on Pluto:

My endeavors to construct a nuclear plasma rocket motor have finally produced an operational rocket engine. All I had to do was plug it into the extra center line engine mount on Sabrina No. 40. To test it out Pinger-5 and I made a very fast weekend trip to "Pluto the Kuiper objects".

This was my first long distance full powered spaceflight. As usual we spent as much time speeding up as we did slowing down. When we finally got there all we found was confusing. I couldn't tell which was Pluto or Charon needless to say the first thing we did was too make sure that all of the orbital approaches' were clear.

To travel that far and fast in a straight line you have to have a Whale along to do the navigation. The best I could do on a direct shot that far was to come within a 1000 miles of the Planet. Pinger-5 put us into a low altitude parking orbit around Pluto with her first attempt.

Its large moon is Charon, it's more than half as large as itself, and large enough to orbit a point outside its surface in effect, each orbits the other. The Pluto/Charon system is one of the few systems in the Solar System whose barycenter lies above the primary's surface. This and the large size of Charon relative to Pluto have led some astronomers to call it a double dwarf planet.

The system is also unusual among planetary systems in that each is tidally locked to the other Charon and Pluto always face to each other from the same side. From every position on either body, the other is always at the same position in the sky. This also means that the rotation period of each is equal to the time it takes the entire system to rotate around its common center of gravity. Which is presently located between them.

Upon discovering this fact Pinger-5 decided that she was going to construct a 12,160 mile long Space-elevator between them, just to cut down on the clutter once Sabrina Aviation got its base as well as passenger terminal operational.

On our way into our first parking orbit, we noticed patches of solid ammonia hydrates and water crystals on the surface of Charon, this suggested the presence of active geysers. This cause me too steer away as the last thing that my Sabrina No. 40 needed was to get sprayed.

As we made our first close up orbital pass I noticed that Pluto was made up with a single large Pangea type continent that had that was cover with very frozen large Mountain Ranges as well as Ice Flows and Glaziers. We were both amazed to discover that Pluto also had several very large mountain ranges.

We discover a atmosphere made up of nitrogen, methane, and carbon monoxide. Pinger-5 made the comment that this just what we need an atmosphere that a mammal would have to chew. During our first ever atmospheric entry I was amazed to find out that Pluto's atmosphere was thick enough to cause a somewhat normal external fireball.

We made our first landing as close to the summit of its highest peak. Our first surface temperature reading came in at below -400 degrees Fahrenheit. Upon discovering this fact I made sure that our space suites morph extra heating systems before Pinger-5 had a chance to leave any flipper prints in the snow. Pluto's surface is composed of more than 98 percent nitrogen ice, with traces of methane and carbon monoxide. The face of Pluto oriented toward Charon contains more methane ice, whereas the opposite face contains more nitrogen and carbon monoxide ice. Pluto's surface is very varied, with large differences in both brightness and color.

Pluto is one of the most contrastive bodies in the Solar System its color varies between charcoal black, dark orange and white. Pluto's color is more similar to that of Jupiter's moon Io with slightly more orange, significantly less red than Mars. Pinger-5 was also the first to notice that Pluto had a "Heart".

This was our first pioneering flight within the Pluto/Charon system. When I stood on the surface of Pluto I only weigh about 8 pounds or less. I know that historically I am going to have problems, because Pinger-5s first words were "Wheeeeeeeeee"! Due to the lack of gravity one twelfth "G" she had to fire several of her maneuvering thrusters just to start her first long distance belly slide on its ice covered surface. We did manage to spend a couple of hours sliding down ice sheets that were thousands of miles long. Despite the fact that nitrogen, methane and carbon monoxide ice are about a slick as sand.

As we had some time to kill we launch off of Pluto to make a slight excursion in to the Kuiper belt. Pinger-5 wanted to go all the way to the edge of the solar system but, I told her I had to be back in time for school on Monday. We were making plans to retrieve Voyager I and II on the next three-day weekend.

Just to get the International Astronomical Unions attention we figured that when they noticed that Pluto could capture its own moons, they would start calling it a planet again. So we manage to nudge several Kuiper objects on their way to see if Pluto/Charon could capture them all.

She also found a large nice frozen example that she put on a direct trajectory to Mars. She said, "She wanted to go swimming on Mars". I approved her idea as I am always up for anything that will cut down on the dust problem on Mars.

Just in case I had my Surface Exploration Units on Mars reinforce the landing pads, as I don't think they are equipped to operate underwater. I think when Pinger-5's Kuiper objects finally get to the planet Mars, they will just add more frozen ice to my wet Mars project it will not get any wetter as all the water will freeze before impact.

The big box that I left on Phobos still manages to catch lots of solids that I will use to make the space elevator sight larger. As for all the water Pinger-5 will have more fun belly sliding all the way down the 15 miles height of Olympus Mons under 2/3 "G". I may have to put a drag chute on her just to keep her sub-sonic.

It did not take long to pack up and start back to earth.

Log Entry #72.
Halley's Comet:

On the way back to Earth we managed to spend a couple of hours fixing Halley's Comet. As we discovered its shattered remains scattered across a 20,000 mile wide debris field orbiting the Sun near the planet Neptune.

It took a mammal as smart as a Whale to calculated what happened to it, as it turns out it had a head on collision with another unidentified Comet. It only took a couple of hours to clean up the mess and put it all back on its original trajectory.

We had to get creative so I installed one of my heavy duty PAM units on Pinger-5 so that she could round up and put all the scattered fragments of Halley's Comet by moving all of its fragment back together. Catching then all with Sabrina No. 40's open cargo bay.

I did the same, as I can't pass up a chance to play Super-Girl. Pinger-5 used her mass like a Billiard Ball to get all the scattered fragments moving back towards Sabrina No. 40. For her it was a simple 3 demonical billiard ball game with the open cargo bay hatch the side pocket.

As she had the advantage of having the mass of a 38 ton Q-Ball. I could only move one small piece at a time with Pinger-5 moved them several at once. As we reconstructed Haley's Comet from all of its fragments Pinger-5 came up with a really clever way to smooth out the newly reformed surface of Halley's Comet.

So that the next time it makes its appearance near Earth. It will have a very bright glow because of Pinger-5's special addictive. Spent zebra mussel shells, they should make the comet brighter. However, due to their mass every little fragment of zebra mussel shell will be returned to the surface of the comet by its micro-gravity field when it quits out gassing.

Needless to say I made it back to Earth in time to walk across the parking lot to school. I had almost made it to my locker before I remembered to morph my space suit to school outfit number one.

Log Entry #73.
Viking Parts:

My science professor did get a little confused then I brought the microscopic device from Viking 1 too class. His first question was how I got a copy of its "search for life" package. He did not seem to believe that it was not a copy. But one of the actual devices that had failed on the surface of Mars in the 1970's.

Both Vikings carried a biological experiment whose purpose was to look for evidence of microscopic life. The Viking spacecraft biological experiments weighed 34 pounds and consisted of three subsystems: the Pyrolytic Release experiment, the Labeled Release experiment, and the Gas Exchange experiment. In addition, independent of the biology experiments, Viking carried a Gas Chromatograph/Mass Spectrometer that could measure the composition and abundance of organic compounds in the Martian soil.

The results were surprising and interesting: the Gas Chromatograph/Mass gave a negative result; the Pyrolytic Release experiment gave a negative result, the Gas Exchange experiment gave a negative result, and the Labeled Release experiment gave a positive result. Viking scientist recently stated, "Our Labeled Release experiment was a definite positive response for life, but a lot of people have claimed that it was a false positive for a variety of reasons."

Most scientists now believe that the data was due to inorganic chemical reactions of the soil; however, this view may be changing after the recent discovery of near-surface ice near the Viking landing zone. Some scientists still believe the results were due to living reactions. No organic chemicals were found in the soil. However, dry areas of Antarctica do not have detectable organic compounds either, but they have organisms living in the rocks.

Mars has almost no ozone layer, unlike the Earth, so Ultra Violet light sterilizes the surface and produces highly reactive chemicals such as peroxides that would oxidize any organic chemicals. The Phoenix Lander discovered the chemical perchlorate in the Martian Soil.

Perchlorate is a strong oxidant so it may have destroyed any organic matter on the surface. If it is widespread on Mars, carbon-based life would be difficult at the soil surface.

I discovered that I am giving the anti-space people confused by selling lost space craft as now, they have to explain if it did not happen, when at the same time I have a wounded bird for sell on E-bay.

Not to forget all the Martian pet rock that anybody could want. Both of the Viking landers were so full of Martian sand that I had to take it apart just the pick it up. Without it being crushing now under its one "G" weight on Earth. I had to chuckle to myself when I realized that I now had a reverse contamination problem with martin surface sand contaminating Earth.

Log Entry #74.
Voyagers 1 & 2:

Sure enough on the next 3 day weekend Pinger-5, Mankind, Monument, and little old me the 15 year old youngest Astronaut launched off the LEADER in Sabrina No. 40.

Once we got started on our mission to retrieve both Voyager 1 and 2 during the same trip. As you know Voyager 2 was supposed to be the human races first intergalactic messenger, the problem was it ran out of steam and started orbiting our Sun at the 10 billion mile marker point. Voyager 1 was sent off our universal plan as it passed by Jupiter in the 1980's.

With the aid of the Whales to navigate, it was a simple mater, to gauge our speed correctly to intercept Voyager 2 in its solar parking orbit. Pinger-5 scored a direct hit, as Voyager 2 floated into Sabrina No. 40s forward top side cargo bay right on time so that I captured it with one of my medium size Space-junk traps. I had to move the Space-Junk-Trap less than 30 feet to make the capture.

She plans to come closer to Voyager 1. The trip to Voyager 1 was really interesting as it gave us our first chance to plot the location of all the Asteroids in the Asteroid Belt as well as see all the Comets, stray Asteroids, and Meteors that are in our solar system and the Kuiper Belt.

As always, Pinger-5 had navigation down to a point at the calculated interception point. All I had to do was open the Top Cargo bay doors and let Voyager 1 fly into Sabrina No. 40's cargo bay on its own.

All it took was a slow turn inbound and a full acceleration power dive back to Earth. I made it back to Pinger-5's under Chicago base, in time for a good nights 1"G" sleep, in my own bed.

I wondered what the N.A.S.A. folks were going to do when they detected both Voyage 1 & 2 transmitting from Sabrina No. 40's cargo bay as she was parked a couple of thousand feet under my parents' house in Park Ridge Illinois.

After Pinger-5 discovered that one of the Hump Back Whale songs, that was on the historical "Earth Disk" that was carried on the outside of each of the Voyager Spacecraft.

Pinger-5 said "That one of the Humpback Whale song that was on the record was sung by her grandmother announcing her mother's birth. Upon this discovery Pinger-5 decided that both of the Voyager's should be put back on their original trajectories.

It only took me a couple of hours to clean both of them up. I managed to, upgrade, refuel, change out both of their nuclear power cores for one of my upgraded He/3 models. And equipped each of the Voyager Spacecraft with their own Nuclear Plasma Rocket Motor.

Pinger-5 figures that even a Nuclear Motor the size of a soup can, will never reach the speed of light but, it will get both Voyage 1 and 2 out of our solar system. Pinger-5 made sure that each Voyager Spacecraft was programmed to travel back along its original trajectory.

With the new mini Nuclear Plasma, Rocket motors each Spacecraft could make it back to the 100 million mile marker in less than a day. Pinger-5 did it one better by utilizing the maximum speed of Sabrina No. 40 she was able to fix the trajectory, of both Voyager Spacecraft by running at full power she was able to fly past the 100 million mile marker in less than 6 hours.

Her return was even faster after a very high "G" interstellar turn back into our Solar system. Pinger-5 used all four of the gas giants as aerodynamic breaking she shot through Neptune, Uranus, and Saturn she managed to rattle around inside of Jupiter long enough to keep her inside our solar plan.

She made several orbits inside of Jupiter's Atmosphere, she slow down enough. I noticed on her flight information computer that she was doing aerobatics all the way just to feel the "G's".

However, she did manage to get rid of the "Great Red Spot" on Jupiter for almost an hour.

Log Entry #75.
My First Lewis ACE-Camp:

As I was now Earth bound I decided to accept the invention from one of my friends to help out at Lewis University's First ACE-Camp. He even gave me my first chance to actually build and fly my very first small useless rocket.

The Plan is to show high school students the basic's about an aerospace career. I had my father in tow with me as well a Pinger-5 in her on board flight tank complete with lots of extra zebra mussels for her to feed on.

I landed Sabrina No. 40 over the campus football field with my nose wheel elevator in the Aviation Colleges parking lot. Next to my friends van which he has name Green.

I made sure to set my nose wheels main truck for maximum, as I did not want to leave any Klingon Bird of Prey gear marks in the soft asphalt of the parking lot.

I closed Sabrina No. 40 down and retracted all of my aerodynamic controls as well as lift-fans, locked all my main landing gear elevators as and stairways.

I got to sit in for the Safety Lecture as well as the Rocket Building Program with my first Earth bound useless rocket. It's used as an educational tool to show student how the five dynamic forces act on an aircraft in flight.

Pinger-5's first problem was students running on the track and using the now covered football fields kept setting off Sabrina No. 40's collision alarm. This kept waking up Pinger-5. The Command Computer counted a football bouncing off the bottom of the ship as a Meteor hit.

However, Pinger- 5 was able to calm the command computer down before it put the ship in a protective hover. There was a problem getting over to the rocket launching site, which has to be at least 5 miles away from the college as it has its own built in airport.

Due to a bridge being under repair I had to fly Sabrina No. 40 over to the launch site instead of driving my father's Mustang. As I recently obtain my driving permit. It's nice to know that after the billions of miles that I have flown in outer space and inside of the Earth's atmosphere.

I am finally old enough to get a driver's license so I can drive the 5 miles to an offsite launching location. Due to the road to the high school being blocked I had to fly Sabrina No. 40 all the way over to the launch site this worked out to be Sabrina No. 40's shortest flight of only 5 miles.

During my flight over the bridge all the way to the other, side of Lockport, Illinois. I couldn't even get my Mach meter to move. As Sabrina No. 40 was flying in hover mode all the way.

Upon landing I pulled the same trick retracting all my aerodynamic controls and hid in plain sight. After my touched down on the other side of Lockport's High School. I did get to actually drive my father Mustang into the parking lot.

The launch was great I got my rocket to fly over 500 miles per hour and travel for 3 seconds before activating its recovery system. This really worried Pinger-5, she could not think of a reason for such a short low speed rocket flight.

Her first question on my communications necklace was what's wrong, your projectiles are only going Mach .79, by her calculation there was no way it could even reach Low Earth orbit much less go to any place in outer space.

I told her not to worry about it nothing was wrong I then requested that she kept feeding me flight information as to speed, altitude, flight time and landing locations.

She proved a capable observer even when we had more than one rocket at a time in flight. Pinger-5 did seem to get excited when we launch the first "D" motored Trick Vickie Flight. She even noted the 4 Martian's that safely bailed out of it as well as the one that was hung up with one "Tricky Vickie's "parachutes.

Sabrina No. 40's collision alarm did go spastic when one of the rockets that was descending under parachute blew across the parking lot and landed on top of Sabrina No. 40, getting hung up on one of the extended camera mounts.

Log Entry #76.
Oshkosh:

I have been going to the EAA fly-in at Oshkosh Wisconsin sense I was 5 years old. When I started to build my first airplane. Now that I am older, I plan to attend this year's show with as many different types of my Space ships as possible. This year is the first time that the EAA had to deal with Pinger-5.

I had to move her flight tank to the forward top cargo bay and rigged it so she can open the hatch and talk directly to the crowds as she gets passengers for her "Barnstorming Round the World flight for fish program". The EAA folks don't want her walking around on the grass because she tends to make large divots in the grass with her flipper as she pulls herself across the ground.

The on board personal PODs work great and are even self-sterilizing. As per her marketing plan she asks each passenger for a fish that she puts in her food storage tank, luckily it only takes about a thousand people to fill up a food tank.

She still fly's the first position during the "Flying Whales" part of each of the daily Airshow. I still do my "No. 1 act" but, due to my tender loving age, I have to start my act from above 27,000 feet, and I can't buzz the airshow center unless I'm at Mach .99 or below. I still get to make a vertical landing in the kid-venture park at the Pioneer Airport. Where I still get to set up my Meteor and Space-junk for sale operation.

This is the first year for the "Flying Whales" you would not believe the massive number of people that have shown up at the EAA's seaplane base not only to see all the Sabrina No. 40's that are moored in the deep water bay but, to see for the first time my Whale/naut's.

Now that I have broken down the communication briers and we know how intelligent a Whale really is. I am still hoping with the aid of my father, to have each of my whale employees given American citizenship. I already have a new generation of whales that were born in Lake Michigan. This fact alone should make them American citizens by birthright.

The instant parking garage sections work perfectly. All I had to do was design a couple of telescoping circular ramps which allows vehicles access points.

The parking section which internally in over twenty stories deep, my only concern is that the ship is definitely too heavy for flight once it is full of parked cars. In one of my better moments, I heard an announcement over the PA system that all of the Parking Lots were full. I sent a priority message to my operational chief on the LEADER to outfit another Sabrina No. 40 ship and have it land next to the other parking lot ship already in use. It took less than a half hour, until the additional parking structure was delivered from orbit.

The living module is also interesting, it was designed to function as a stationary human living sight, and it's pressurized and air-conditioned. I even added a fake window that shows a fixed picture of what it would look like it there was really a window on that side of the ship. It can also be used to see anything through my ships sensors.

The whole structure is installed as a single module that can be removed in a couple of minutes. I could use it as an instant hotel anywhere in the world. My only problems so far is if I use it off planet I will have to bury it under the surface of what other planet or moon for radiation shielding and it's not stressed to house humans in zero "G" or to handle all the dynamic forces of spaceflight.

Mankind who is one of the original Humpback Whale/naut's and a veteran of the first Jupiter mission is into Para-sailing. To account for his mass the Para-glider has to have the wing span of a Boeing 747. He usually is launched from the bottom hatch of one of the Sabrina No. 40's at the beginning of the airshow.

He usually brings in the American flag for the opening of the Airshow. His act includes all the usual aerodynamic maneuvers, after he drops the flag to its receivers at Airshow center. He heads over to the nearest deep body of water where he performs an abrupt pull up, this stalls his glider when he is inverted, then proceeds to fall into the Para-Sail, collapsing it as he dives into the water.

He wants me to build him a Whale size tank so he can land Airshow center. I told him to think deep water not wet sponge. It didn't take long for him to program his Sabrina No. 40 ship to orbit the Airshow site after he bails out. By doing a low speed flight with his top side cargo hatch open this way he just flies into the top, then he has his ship stop at Airshow Center.

Where he lands in the top side of his Flight-Tank as it opens at the last second. Needless to say Mankind also loves to Para-Sail on the planet Mars using what atmosphere he can find. I know for a fact that he will be flying around inside of Jupiter's atmosphere the first chance he gets, that if I let him.

Log Entry #77.
Sizing:

I stopped by my friends 4th Aviation carriers' education camp of the year that was happening in Milwaukee, Wisconsin. Rather than making a water landing and coming inland from the beach. I decided to hide in plain sight. I am really getting good at it.

The first contacted the Milwaukee airport control tower and requested permission to cut across town using one of their approved helicopter routes. I activated my urban camouflage system and set it for small helicopter, my external sound system even started making a loud rotor noises as if I were really hovering. As soon as I was flying slow enough I extended my hover-fans and started to look for my destinations address, as I used my ships system to reference my location.

As usual, I parked by nose gear elevator closest to the door. As soon as I was on the street all I had to do was ask the first person that I met, where the guy with the big silver rocket was.

He had set up his world famous 1/144 scale table top exhibit to show all the Ace-Campers how everything size wise would look for real. The International Space Station, Saturn V, and Airbus A380, as well as lots of other aircraft of each type. He actually got several of his students to gasp when they realized what they were looking at.

Afterwards we started to compare sizes, and I noted that if he had built a 1/144 scale model of my Sabrina No. 39 ship it would not fit through the door of the classroom that he was using. As my Sabrina No. 40 ships wouldn't even fit in the room. My Sabrina No. 39 would be as large as an over, size surfboard and Sabrina No. 40 would be as big as a medium size speedboat in 1/144 scale.

Log Entry #78.
Wet War Birds:

Pinger-5 as well as most of the other Whale/naut's has really got going on the clean up the "Planet Programs". After seeing all the restored aircraft at the EAA Convention in Oshkosh.

Pinger-5 has decided to go into the aircraft recovery business, especially anything left underwater or frozen in Ice. As soon as she heard about the Lost Patrol and how "Glacier Girl" was recovered from the ice flow. Pinger-5 decided to go after the rest of the brand new P-38's that were still frozen deep under the Greenland Glassier.

By using my He/3 reactors' to heat the outer surface of Sabrina No. 40 she plans to just melt her way to all the other entombed aircraft that are still frozen in the ice. Then just melt them out of the glassier from underneath to keep them from coming out into the ocean to make a mess in the future. Then she plans to trade them for more fresh fish.

You would think that the Air Force would be glad to just find all their lost aircraft sitting in a lot at AMARC, without complaining about it. You wouldn't believe all the stuff the Sabrina No. 39 as well as my "First-Five," and "Next-Ten" hauled back from the Antarctic.

I still have a problem with the Whaler's Bad Little Killer Ships in the Arctic taking pot shots at my Sabrina No. 40's. It's interesting to note that all the Whales have kept Pinger-5's word, it been almost a year and none of the Whalers have been able to see a Whale in the water much less Harpoon it. Also so far the Whaling Company that harpooned me to begin with has not paid for any of Sabrina No.40s damages.

There are only seven different types of whales in the world's oceans they are the Humpbacks, Orcas, Blues, Fins, Grays, Sperms and Belugas. However most if not all of the Earths whale population agree to let human observation boats come in close to talk with humans. As I have finally broken the communications barrier.

Log Entry #79.
Women in Aviation Conference:

I redesigned my instant hotel payload to add conference rooms even a swimming pool. I offered to host the next convention of the Federal Woman in Aviation conference inside Sabrina No. 40.

I even offered to arrange pick up points throughout the world. I wonder if they would be interested in having it on the Moon or Mars. I can even figure a way by docking two of my Sabrina No. 40's together and spinning them in Outer Space to make artificial gravity. This way all the water will stay in the on board swimming pool.

Pinger-5 was all for it as she know that all of us girls have to stick together. She plans to go along and use the onboard Olympic size swimming pool as her living quarters. It didn't take long for the Whales to set up a high diving operation running through the main maintenance shafts diving from ship to ship.

Female Whale/naut's even managed to use the diving boards by lowering the ships RPM's to make .00001G, in the pool area. She says that she has several other female Whales that also want to attend the next meeting. As deep down, they are all "G" junkies. I even arranged for on board day care for all the mothers with children or calves.

Log Entry #80.
Birthday Surprise:

I made a promise to the head Administrator of N.A.S.A. that none of my equipment on mars, would show up in any of the photo the new Phoenix Lander might take. Personally, I didn't have anything lying around the Martian North Pole because it's too hard to get too even for me. So far, most of my activities have been around the base of my space elevator, which is grounded near Mars equator.

But as soon as it quits transmitting, I will haul in back to Earth and sell it on E-bay like all the others non- functional space probes. "Once they quit working their all mine!"

I just got the surprise of my life Pinger-5 along with most of her fellow Whale/naut's gave me a very wonderful birthday gift. My very own EZ-Rocket racer it's a wonderful Rocket-plane decked out in Sabrina Aviation Metallic Red. An honest to gosh rocket powered Rutan EZ, rocket racer.

I was so choked up It took me several minutes before I could talk to Pinger-5, to ask her where she got my present from, her answer was priceless. "Oh I just traded the Line Chief at your favorite parking place in California, a pile of old airplanes that I picked up off the bottom of the ocean.

I know that it will not operate in outer space but I'm sure that you can fix that problem". I finally figured out what happened Pinger-5 cleaned up several of the Sunken Liberty ship wrecks, and then traded, recovered crated aircraft to my old Line Chief buddy at Edwards. I hope he know what he is getting himself in for dealing with Pinger-5.

As for my birthday present from N.A.S.A. I got a personal invitation to the Phoenix Landers shut down party at J.P.L. So knowing the exact shut down time; I requested my next Mars bound supply ship to pick it up as soon as it was deactivated.

The N.A.S.A. director made a compelling speech about how the human race has to explore and it's in everybody's best interest if we do. At this point, he sent the command for the Mars Phoenix Lander to shut itself down forever.

All of a sudden, the Martian quake meter sent crazy the fixed camera that was not able to move started moving. Suddenly the not so fixed picture started to change showing one of my whale scooters moving as viewed from the rear. Everybody in the room was rivet to all the active monitors showing a very close up view of the large moving mass of a Humpback Whale in a space suit under full pressure.

Showing my Sabrina Aviation logo in plain sight really helped. Suddenly the Whale turned around and I could see that it was Mankind. I couldn't help to visually checking out his space suit as I could tell that he had already incorporated my latest up-grades, this was the first time that I had noticed that any of the Whale/naut's had turned on the space suit's heating elements. I could see that he had turned on his communication system, and at that same moment my communications necklace activated and started to show a message saying, "Happy Birthday Sabrina!" Did you like the rocket-plane?

I just wanted to let you know that I have also recovered the heat shield as well as all of its parachutes I even recovered the drogue chute. I am having a wonderful time scooting around Mars. I have to agree with Pinger-5, Mars definitely needs more water, at least an Ocean or two. Tell Pinger-5 if she still wants to belly slide all the way down Olympus Mons, she will have to bring her own snow.

The Phoenix Lander finally received its final shut off command just as 'Mankind' was driving through the port side main entrance hatch of his Sabrina No. 40/29 Space ship. At this point in time, I looked up to make "Eye Ball-to-Eye Ball" contact with the Administrator of N.A.S.A. as he was standing over me.

He said 'You did warn me that you would pick it up the second we turned it off. Next time we will have to talk more about Transmission Lag Time. The last time I saw the Base of the Lander, it was holding up the lamp in my watch-commander office on the LEADER.

Log Entry #81.
Whale Chatter:

Ever sense Pinger-5 came in to my life I have developed a tendency to talk to all of the different whale types, and without the use of a translator. Humpback wise I can hold my own in a single conservation. All whales are capable of holding any number of different conversations that they want at the same time with each other.

As a Human I can barely talk to one individual at a time, they all play a talking game with me where they try to guess my next word. The only human words the Orcas care to know how to use are the tactical ones that deal with attacking something. The Orcas all know about humans and they consider themselves above us on the food chain. The only reason that they don't eat more humans is they consider us poor eating, as we are too very boney, with not enough fat and bad tasting.

It's interesting to listen in when a Whale/naut's Orca pod are running down an inbound meteor. I can plainly see that they are not trying to catch it they are trying to kill it. The Orca's favorite trick is to bounce it ship to ship then toss it into the Sun. On the rare occasions then they actually capture a meteor they tend to want to use it as a weapon to kill something else with.

Yesterday I diverted the whole Orca Whale/naut's pod that was just starting its re-supply mission to mars, I requested that they intercept a swarm of vehicle size meteors that had just popped up on out radar screens.

Despite the fact that each space ship was already fully loaded and had launched for their mission, each ship managed to capture a Meteor or two when requested. As they were making their acceleration dives flying deeper in the Earth's Atmosphere over the Sea of Japan, a Vietnamese's gunboat started to launch surface to air Missiles at the closest Sabrina No. 40 Space ship.

Luckily the reinforces hull of all of my Sabrina No. 40 Space ships are missile proof, it took several direct hits before the Orca Whale/naut Pilot realized that she was being shot at. Unfortunately, this flight of space ship was carrying a large supply of human food that was on its way to Mars.

The Orca Flight loves the planet Mars I think that they are working up a plot to flood its surface and create an Ocean or Two on it. Upon detecting a whole fleet of Vietnamese Gunboats coming to the aid of their now attacking gunboat. Eatem-Now the command Pilot of Sabrina No. 40/53 opened her aft cargo bay and dropped my entire shipment of M&M's in a single volley.

The outer paper packaging was a torn away by the high speed atmosphere, creating a large expanding mass of M&M's over five miles wide with a spacing of less than 4 inches apart. The hard candy outer covering acted like a heat shield, after the out candy shell burned away the chocolate what was aerodynamically superheated then formed into shaped ballistic projectiles as they fell farther through the Earth Atmosphere. They all of hardened into very hard high speed ballistic impactors as they cooled in the atmosphere as they descended.

They all impacted the surface of the Sea of Japan at around Mach 10 making thousands of holes in the Vietnamese Gun Boats in a single at the same instant. Punching thousands of M&M size holes all the way through each ship. The end result was my Orca Whale/naut's destroyed all of the Vietnamese Gun boats with several hundred pounds of my M&M's. Resulting in the destruction of their ships and the wounding of several of their human crew members.

You got to admit even M&M's moving fast enough tend to penetrate. "Eatem-Now" was so mad that she sent me a personal massage stating that "she didn't care how bad humans tasted she will personally going to eat the human that had dared to shoot at her with a weapon.

At this point, I decided to launch off the LEADER and see if I could stop the fighting before we ran out of food to drop. I shudder to think what the Orca's, could do with a couple tons of canned goods. Thanks to Pinger-5's help I can speak a few words in the various different Whales language without the need of a translator. So when I requested the Orca's "to knock it off and climb", in their own language without the use of a translator.

It startled them all when they heard my small whiny 14 year old female human voice speaking Orca directly to them without the twinge of the translator.

As I was now the only descending Space ship, I drew all the Vietnamese Fire. They launched all their fighter reserves, to shoot me down, as I was setting down in the water at the main M&M impact point. All I could see for miles around were sinking boats with life rafts everywhere. I extended my hover fans opened my side hatches and settled into the water, taking in most of the damaged gun boats and crews before they could sink.

Upon seeing, all the food sources comings up to fight, all the Orca flight turned back into the attack. The fact that they were only armed with a food shipment that was on its way to Mars didn't even slow them down. They all punched past the Vietnamese attack line, then did a beautiful 20 "G" 180-degree turn, and started to fly formation with the entire Vietnamese Air Force. As soon as each of their fighters were in range the Orca's, launched a series of space junk traps catching each aircraft in flight.

Each of the Vietnamese Pilots ejected as soon as it was apparent they were being captured alive. I could tell by listening in on all the Whale chatter that each if the Orca's that captured a Vietnamese fighter was going to sell it to Pinger-5, so she could trade it to the Line Chief at Edwards for something better to eat.

When I had my Communications System listening in, on the Vietnamese radios chatter, it was interesting to note, that they were not afraid of dying for their cause, they were terrified that the Orca's would eat them alive.

As soon as it became evident that I was being outnumbered by the whole Vietnamese Air force each Orca Whale/naut Pilot made a get back into the fight turn at the same second. Even though they were outnumbered they press the attack to the point where all the Vietnamese Fighter Pilots broke their attack on me and ran for their lives.

The Orca's went into a feeding frenzy running downing the entire opposing air force aircraft by aircraft. They even complained among each other that some of their attack force was hoarding all the kills. A few of the more cunning Orca's just power dived into the water under the Dog Fight. To be able to pick up enemy pilots as they landed in the water.

Pinger-5 made the call to all of them it seems that sense "Eatem-Now" had decreed that each of the attacking humans wound be eaten. A few of the tag a long Orca's decided to be first in the chow line, by feeding on chicken hearted Fighter Pilots as they landed in the water.

Pinger-5 got to show how much of a diplomat that she had become. By changing the minds of the Orca's flight leader, to where she would trade Pinger-5 one of her standard ration of fresh fish from her private food source for each captured human that they could personally transported to my Sabrina No. 40 space ship that was now floating in the original M & M kill zone. She even got them to run a tab and rescue more than one Pilot at a time.

Over all it took less than half an hour for the Orca's to load all the surviving Vietnamese Fighter Pilots into my Sabrina No. 40 some of them even managed to out swim the killer whales. By beating them into my open cargo bay. I had no idea what to do with all of my wet Vietnamese pilots, I pulled the plug and let Sabrina No. 40 do a slow dive, as I ran up the Command POD to form a snorkel, this made it easier for the whales to save the shot down pilots as well as the M&M'ed naval crews. I moved Sabrina No. 40 underwater into their closest harbor then up to a shipping dock. Pinger-5 personally inspected all Vietnamese humans and deducted ration portions if they had any missing parts or equipment.

Then she told them in their own language without the need of a translator, to go to the top side VIP area, and they really owed her big time. I ran my boarding tube up to the bottom of an Empty Warehouse. Pinger-5 then ordered all the Vietnamese Pilots to move up the tube and out of her hair.

As she continued speaking the Vietnamese language without the use of my translator device. She was very diplomatic as she informed them that the next time they would be on the main course at dinner! I wonder what the Vietnamese Air force did when all their ELT's showed them all in the same abandon warehouse.

In all there are seven different types of whales in my employee, they are the Humpbacks, Orcas, Blues, Fins, Grays, Sperms and Beluga I started out with a few of each. Today the Orcas had proved themselves in battle with humans. However, I have noticed that they still prefer to only work with whales of their same family pod.

Log Entry #82.
How I Got Free Stuff From N.A.S.A.:

The news of N.A.S.A.'s latest lost tool kit really got my personal attention. It made the A&P part of my DNA gets excited, as It's always bad news to hear when a mechanic loses a tool much less a whole tool kit. When it's worth a million dollars I had to recover it for myself.

The problem was it was way down there in high Earth orbit. With lots of other Space-junk, and I was all the way up here in Geosynchronous orbit on the LEADER over 33,000 miles away. I couldn't just happen to stop by and grab it with one of Sabrina No. 40's Space-junk-traps, without having the whole Space Station land on me due to Sabrina No. 40's micro-gravity field. With my luck I would get their whole current Space-junk collection to orbit me instead.

The Things that have fallen off of the I.S.S. list (TTFOOTISS) is getting a little on the long side. My first worry was its orbital track and if when and where my new tool kit was going to impact the surface of the Earth somewhere expensive.

It was just my luck, after all my calculations I discovered that my million-dollar tool kit would land in the middle of Atlantic Ocean in less than a year. It would definitely fragment as it passes through most of the mid Atlantic flight lanes. Well this was all the information I needed I decided to beat the micro-gravity problem by using one of my Human Maneuvering Units. I had already built several and I was working on the latest upgrade that installed a small Space-junk trap as well as an updated He/3 reactor.

It took the usual amount of time for the Human Maneuvering Unit to transform from its stored brief case size box. It only took a few more minutes to post my flight plan and let my Watch-Commander know what I was up to. It took less than a second for my space suit to morph itself from its jumpsuit format.

I also added a large white cape with a large Sabrina Aviation Metallic Red "S" on it to my morph program to use to help me map out the exact boundaries of the International Space Stations Atomic Oxygen cloud.

It was also a good thing that I also packed along a spare inflatable cargo POD. I have always stayed away, from the International Space Station just to keep out of the largest Atomic Oxygen Bubble ever made by human kind, it's so large that it can serve as a ration barrier. I had lots of flight time using the Human Maneuverings Unit in the asteroid belt when I was Asteroid hunting.

As I have discovered that it's always better when I am a controlled cannon ball in flight. This is the device I use to fly like I'm Super-Girl, I can see the "Nasty Gram" from N.A.S.A." Tell me Mister N.A.S.A. Astronaut can you really confirm that the person operating the HMU was actually wearing a white cape with a big red "S" on it." I also didn't want to get another "Nasty Gram" from N.A.S.A. accusing me of harassing their Astronauts while they are in orbit.

I used my thrusters to move out of my air lock as soon as I was clear of the LEADER I pressed the down button and my HMU line itself up and fired its retro-rocket to descend. Let me tell you the speed differences really become apparent when you don't have a Space ship around you. As it was real exciting to see the LEADER dropped out of visual sight in less than a couple of seconds.

The flight computer in the HMU would make all the navigational moves needed to maneuver. However I still had to tell it where to go. I calculated speed, location, traveling time, and my flight computer figured out how to get me there. I planned to come in from above around the middle point of the I.S.S.'s Atomic Oxygen Cloud.

My scanner went "TILT" as soon as I turned it on, as there was too much space-junk for my scanner to register in a micro-second. I had to reprogram it to expand its operational parameters on the spot. As it worked out, it took a full eight seconds to get my first count of total objects.

I discovered that the very full micro-atmosphere was full of about anything you can think of, all chugging and colliding with other trapped objects. As it turns out the Atomic Oxygen cloud was much larger as well as dangerous than I thought.

My scanners ran continuously there was so much stuff moving that it also could qualify as a defensive shield.

To get around inside of this hazardous area, I decided to play it safe and inflate a low-pressure Cargo Bubble around me as soon as I was within ten thousand miles of the I.S.S.

My next problem was trying to find my new tool kit mixed in with all the other Space-junk. I lucked out as most of the Space-junk was still trying to orbit the I.S.S. having the white cape was a defiant plus as I used its flapping in the breeze to help map out the boundary layers of the Atomic Oxygen Cloud.

It only took me a couple minutes to map out all of the main orbital tracks and become one with a flight plan that I could use to locate my targeted idem.. Due to my relatively small mass, I had to maneuver to run objects down and capture them with my space-junk trap.

Suddenly half the Cargo Bubble collapsed and my Space suit recorded lots of hits on my left arm. I felt all the impacts and looked at my arm to see that my auto-repair system was hard at work patching my Space suits outer surface all by itself. My collision alarm went spastic as it had registered more than 15 direct hits, this killed my trajectory and tossed me out of the orbit around the I.S.S.'s that I was tracking it to intercept my new tool kit.

Needless to say, my automatic repair features were already at work fixing all the holes in my Space suit almost as fast as they happen. As the projectiles started to surface, I noticed that they were all blue M&M's. Talk about the ultimate weapon! It took another second or two for all the holes in my Cargo Bubble to patch at the same instant.

At this point I was officially lost in space for a whole micro second. It's just my luck to be killed off by a pack of lost M&M's. I decided to turn off everything to keep my flight computer from trying to fly me through the I.S.S. to get back to where I was supposed to be.

When I talk about my advanced math skills, I'm not kidding around. I not only had to figure out what had happened and where all the dynamic momentum had taken me, I also had to figure out how to fix it, with all calculation going on in my head. And of course all my calculations had to be perfect or I wouldn't be telling you this story.

When I finally stopped spinning, I was jammed close to the main module cluster of the I.S.S. My clear "Cargo Bubble" had stuck itself between several of their main modules. I carefully retracted my cargo bubble until it released me and I was free to maneuver.

I was as close as you can get without being a part of it, as I rotated past the I.S.S.'s Command POD. I discovered that I was looking eyeball to eyeball into the face of, one of N.A.S.A.'s finest. He was a mush older man, who looked to be in his late twenties, He definitely needed a shave & a haircut.

At this point my Space suit control systems that had just finished extending sections of my cargo POD extended my white cape with a big red "S" on it right in front of him. I didn't wave or throw him a kiss so N.A.S.A. can't accuse me of harassing him.

As soon as all my systems were up and running it took less than a minute to find my new tool kit, as it rotated around the I.S.S. I used some of Pinger-5's math formulas to head it off as it comes around from the other side of its last orbit. I launched my Space-junk-trap and capture it on its next pass.

I used the inertia of my newest tool kit to pull me away from my roosting spot without firing any of my thrusters. Talk about a roller coaster ride It was all strung out and spinning, this added a little more to the recovery problem.

I had to make a few passes close to the Pilots control module, before I finally got everything under control. My new Astronaut friend had to notice me as I zoomed past his windows, with my Sabrina Aviation cape fluttering in his Atomic Oxygen Cloud.

As soon as I was clear of everything, I pushed the "up button on my human maneuvering unit", it felt real good to have the HMU line itself up then fire my rocket motor to start my way back to the LEADER. I had my scanners make a list of all the Space-junk to add to any future shopping lists.

I made a note to myself to send in several of my Sabrina No. 40 ships to harvest that section of the Earths orbital track the next time that the I.S.S. gets moved to a higher orbit. I plan to ask N.A.S.A. if they would be interested in using several of my converted He/3 scrubbers to recover the Atomic Oxygen cloud.

I also decided to have an I.S.S. docking hatch installed in each of my Sabrina No. 39 & Sabrina No. 40, In case, I ever got a chance to stop by for milk and cookies. I wonder if they have any Chips Ahoy or any liquid milk for that matter. As soon as my trajectory stabilized all I had to do was spacewalk up the front of the main airlock on the LEADER. With my now captured human maneuvering unit still attached inspect my prize. After retracting all the tools, I discover that I had caught them all.

Log Entry #83.
Captain Lynda Lou Love

I was just finishing my usual inspect & repair as needed, operation on Sabrina No. 39. The problem with hunting Space-junk is that it seems to find me quicker that I can find it. The worse space junk is made up with nothing but lots of extremely small bits of fragmented metal, broken bolts and screws.

Anything will leave holes in the outer skin surface of my Sabrina No. 39. Holes that I have to repair! I am going to have to come up with a better way to catch Space-junk as it is really making a mess out of Sabrina No. 39's hull.

I was also making sure that her latest dragster Losers were safely de-fueled and put away in her internal cargo bays. I got a call from my Hanger Chief, saying that Sabrina No. 39/3 had returned with an old friend that wanted permission to enter the work bay.

I leaped out on to the zero "G" work bay and let myself be moved by the air movement system over to the docking bay where Sabrina No. 39/3 was waiting.

It was my old friend Captain Lynda Love it seemed that Sabrina No. 39/3 was the alert ship that had saved her skin again, this time she was all by herself moving a replacement F-22 to her base. It seems that she was just rounding the next to last curve in the box canyon when she had a disagreement with a flock of ducks that wanted to lubricate both of her engines from the inside at the same time.

Sabrina No. 39/3 had grabbed her with her Space-junk-trap less than a second before impact. She was a wide eyed as I remembered her, floating in the airlock with all her flight gear "gun and all" floating around her. I noticed that she was getting use to Zero "G", as she had taken out a length of rope from her survival kit and strung all her equipment on to a long string. This made all her flight gear trail after her as if she had a very long tail.

Her first question was is all this yours. At first sight I started laughing so hard that my body started looping on its vertical axes. When she took off her flight helmet all her hair sprang straight out of her head, making her look like "Sally Ride" filling up the whole airlock with her hair.

As I was slowly rotating in front of her, I pulled out my spare "Snoopy Helmet" and gave it to her, so that she could safely leave the airlock. At this point, I noticed a stream of messages from Sabrina No. 39/3 about keeping Lynda's Raptor as her loser Dragsters. It took several minutes of back and forth computer talk before she finally gave back Linda's F-22.

It was not in perfect working order luckily for Lynda, Sabrina No. 39/3 was in the perfect position to snatch and grab her F-22 in flight the instant she made her distress call. The Space-junk-trap had made the perfect snatch and grab maneuver.

Lynda's big problem was the job the ducks had done on her engines. Both of which had suffered so much damage that small pieces of fan blades were still floating out of both of her air intakes. The problem was her lack of engine parts as everything in her engine room was pulped, as most of her engines had fragmented and exited the rear of her aircraft all by themselves leaving a nice empty space all ready for replacements.

It only took a couple of minutes for the docking bay system to move Sabrina No. 39/3 over to where she could dock into Sabrina No. 39's cargo bay where we were both floating in zero-"G". I ordered my jump suit to grow a ballistic control system so that I could fly in zero-"G". The look on Lynda's face was priceless when she saw me growing rocket thrusters out of my jumpsuit.

As I zoomed into the center of Sabrina No. 39/3's cargo bay to manually release and kicked away her Space-junk-trap. Then I pushed Lynda's F-22 into Sabrina No. 39's cargo bay with my bare finger tips. Sabrina No. 39's loadmaster program secure Lynda's airframe in the same place in the cargo bay that she put her last F-22. I think she did not want to make another dirty spot on her floor as was caused by the last time I had her dine in for breakfast.

I couldn't help myself, as the A&P part of my DNA took over. I had fantasized about this for hours when, I first took a look at her F-22 that had only lost one engine in a Typhoon, as to how easy it would be for me to replace its F119 engine in zero- "G". Now I had the chance to do two F119 engines at the same time. I flew over to my workshop to tool up for the job at hand. Lynda asked, "Where I got the N.A.S.A. zero-G tool kit." She was delighted when I informed her that I recovered it as space-junk.

My next task was to get in touch with my old-Line Chief friend at Edwards. He was delighted to learn that I had Lynda safely aboard as she was not due to land at her base for several hours. I asked about a couple of replacement F119 engines and where to get them. He said that He had plenty on hand and would put a couple of them in with Pinger-5's next pick-up.

He thanked 39/3's command computer for saving Lynda from the mountainside. I had to remind her to get back on guard duty. Sabrina No. 39/3, instantly undocked and started to maneuver herself to the main exit hatch so that she could launch herself back to Earth to catch the next luckless airplane that was about to meet up with the end of a box canyon.

"Wow what's a Pinger-5 operation" asked Lynda's? I answered, "Pinger-5 is one of my girl friends who eventually will take over the world." Lynda asked, "How old is she?" I answered without thinking, "Around three and a half years old,"

With that said Lynda answered "you EAA types really start flying early". I answered" Yes we believe that once you're an old over the hill 20 year old, it's too late. "She asked "Are you always this busy in your hanger?" Not really I answered it's one of Pinger-5's "Dim German" projects. "Yes" I replied if you were going to take over the Earth why you would poison it with Mercury"

She asked it seems that the Germans had used Mercury as ballast in their U-Boats now 70 years after they were sunk. It is pouring into the food chain as all the metal in the U-boat finally breaks up and oxidizes. I answered "last year, when I first became aware of this problem I redesigned several of my He/3 scrubbers to grab up all of the Mercury." This works best as long a unit is placed under the contamination point.

Pinger-5 wanted to find out how much faster it would work in Zero-"G". So she is recovering one of their underwater wreck sight. Then haul it all the way up to LEADER to do her experiment to see how well the mercury recovery device works as it floats around inside the ball of the zero-"G" wreckage.

So far she has managed to move it up here 100 tons at a time. It's not easy, as she has to wear her space suit the whole time to keep herself from being contaminated.

Pinger-5 had at my request stopped at Edwards on her way back from her latest underwater salvage operation. This was the first time that one of my Sabrina No. 40 series Spacecraft made a day time stop at Edwards.

This was not the first time that Pinger-5 had a chance to deal with an Air force Line Chief. I wonder what he would do if he knew that Pinger-5 had an entire German U-Boat on board. She was astonished as this was the first favor that she was able to do for her favorite Line Chief. This time the Air Force had to pay transportation, this cost him all the fresh fish that Edwards AFB had on hand in their PX. As soon as she identified the F-119 engines she had the auto loading system snatched them off the supply truck so fast she had to give back its trailer.

Meanwhile I was having fun floating around inside the empty engine compartment of Lynda's Raptor, pulling out broken connectors and getting rid of left over duck feathers. Lynda was just floating around looking wide-eyed. She even asked if she could pass me tools as I needed them.

When Pinger-5 arrived, most of the bay was filled with the remains of her U-boat encrusted Sea bottom sand, water and all, formed into its own little Zero-"G" Cargo POD of mercury-poisoned matter. I could tell that the Mercury Trap was finally working as it was now in Zero-"G".

Pinger-5 moved out of the moving mass of wreckage as it past us on its way to the decontamination chamber. Pinger-5 popped out of the procession with both of Linda's F-119 engines between her flippers. I stopped her before she contaminated us with mercury and waved her on to the cleanup center.

Lynda was in shock, was that a Humpback whale in a space suit she asked? Yes, I replied "that's my best friend Pinger-5." As soon as Pinger-5 got out of her Mercury covered Space suit and put it in her recharger. She was back with both of Lynda's replacement engines. She was still carrying them between her flippers as if they were a couple of flashlight batteries.

Speaking in human English she asked. "Where do you want them?" Using her low gravely Whale voice. Lynda was speechless when she finally got her voice back she said.

"It can talk", "of course I can talk Pinger-5 replied, I even speak human," "if you want to hear, a weird language gets Sabrina to speak Orca with her small puny human female voice, Humpback ascent, and all."

Lynda and I continued to work on her lack of engine problem, when she noticed the N.A.S.A. emblem on my tool kit, she wanted to know how much it cost and if I got a discount, I informed her that it was free. "Free how that is!" She asked. "It's simple," I answered "what one person's space junk is another person's treasure." "All I had to do was pick it up after it fell off the I.S.S. before in did an uncontrolled re-entry back to Earth's Atmosphere."

It took less than 10 minutes to plug both of Lynda's new engines in to her F-22, connect all the connections plugs, and close all the doors. Sabrina No. 39 and I were able to transport Lynda and her repaired fighter to her distention.

She did her preflight walk around climbed into her cockpit and ran all her maintenance checks through her on board maintained computer as I flew Sabrina No. 39 into the Earth Atmosphere. We made S turns over her base until my speed dropped below Mach one.

Sabrina No. 39 will never let me forget that when we test ran both of Lynda's newly installed Jet Engines we blew over 100 pounds of burnt duck feathers out of each other of her F-22s thrust vectoring nozzles at the back of each of her new now operational jet engines.

I waited for her thumbs up, the let her go. Then with both of her new engines running, I dropped her out of my cargo bay. You should have seen the look in her face when the cargo bay floor disappeared and she dropped like a rock.

I had dropped her off 20 minutes before she was due to land. I found out later that, due to her early arrival, her commander accused her of flying supersonic over land and made a note in her performance record. She did not even try to explain what really happened.

Log Entry #84.
Inner Solar Systems Navigation System:

My mother s complaint letter to the Administrator of the Federal Aviation Administration finally got to the top of the pile, it seems that mother was worried about me getting lost in space, and she wanted to know why there was not a single inter-planetary navigation aid installed anywhere.

Much less an air traffic control center that deals with space flights between all 8 of the planets, as well as Kuiper objects. She wanted at least 24 different stations strung along the equators of all 7 of the other planets. She realized that most of them were gas giants without an official surface. But her 14 year old daughter is flying their now.

How come the Government has not set up any kind basic navigation aids. So I called up the real state office at the Great Lakes office near my house and started to make arrangements to transport automated navigation equipment that I could drop off on my next pass past threw that part of the solar system.

I tried to calm Mom down by telling her about the G.P.S. system that I already had working on Mars. It did not help matters when she remembered how it had saved my life when I was shot down over Mars by a meteor storm. This also got her started again about my Harpooning.

The way I fixed the problem was simple, I used the closest FAA control tower that I passed on the way down during my acceleration dive as my starting point then have all the other in-route centers track me as I travel throughout the solar system. All I would have to do is program my communication system to check in with the air route center that I could see visually or electronically from my location in Outer Space.

Log Entry #85.
Humans Small Useless Rockets:

Ever sense the collision alarm woke up Pinger-5 as she was sleeping inside Sabrina No. 40 as it was parked at the 2008 Lewis University ACE-Camp.

She has tried to figure out humans and their small under powered chemical rockets. Last week end she spent all her free time hovering over a harvested corn field in north central Illinois. What got her attention was when one of the humans larger high powered high altitude rocket was trying to fly formation with her as she was doing a slow speed climb up from one of the deep water lakes that was connected to the flooded caves that we have taken over in northern Illinois.

She played hide and seek with the lower cloud layers, with her scanner turned up full. She listed and tracked every launch, on several occasions she had to snap open both the bottom and top cargo bay doors to allow the ascending rocket to pass through the Sabrina No. 40 Space ship that she was flying.

The first rocket that had a beeper device really set her off, as she thought that it was trying to talk to her as it zoomed past her. This caused her to break her hover and intercepted it in flight as it deployed its drogue chute.

Pinger-5 even ran its beeping sound through my Communications Systems universal translator just to try to find out what it wanted.

258

Log Entry #86.
Time off:

Everybody sooner or later has to take a day off human wise, I employee lots of humans I have a incentives plan, paid vacations, and paid travel, I also have volunteers and pioneers, people moving their whole family off planet to the Moon and Mars. Whale wise I offer them the same deal, however, most of them have no concept of money.

Last week I was on a field trip to the Shedd Aquarium, officially to see how they keep their environmental system going. I happened to notice that one of their Beluga whales was wearing one of my communications harness. He had it retracted close to his body high up on his right-handed flipper. My first worry was how one of my Astronaut Whales had been captured without me finding out about it.

I sent an instant message to Pinger-5 who is also my head Whale/naut, to ask how come one of our Beluga Whale/nauts was in the Shedd Aquarium. She answered instantly using her very best human voice. "That's Navigator he's on vacation", "it's not like we can just check into a human's hotel, humans tend to put too much chlorine in the water in their swimming pools and room service always runs out of fresh fish."

But we all give the Shedd what you humans could call five star rating, they have free food, and they bring it to you. What's the problem, "Navigator" is the 5th Beluga that we have changed out, and I only wish that the exchange pipe was my size.

I asked her, "How come I have not found out about it earlier?" Pinger-5 Answered, "You know Belugas they only speak human one or two words a day".

Log Entry #87.
How I got an "A+" in Gym Class:

It s not like I was cheating, my solution to the problem was simple, all I had to do was get my body to work easier while under one Earth "G" to do this I turned up the gravity controls in my Command POD.

I worked in up in small steps of 1/16 "G" at a time. This increased by body weight as I was doing my normal everyday things like walking, climbing stairs and sleeping, and of course everything else in my Command POD also increased in weight.

As soon as I adjusted to the increase I went to the next step until I was used to working under 3"G's" when I had to take my Physical fitness test while I was under only one "G" on Earth. I ran around the track faster, climbed the rope quicker, swam, and jumped, higher, and for a much longer duration.

My Gym Coach was speechless and wanted to know if I was interested in going to the Olympics, I told her no thanks. As a girl just cannot run to Mars. But I was the only girl in my class to get an "A+" in Physical Education.

You should have seen the look on the on the face of the Flight Standards Inspector, when I passed the strength requirement to earn my Airframe and Power plant rating. The maintenance inspector accused me of going the old electric magnet trick as he found the piston jug that I was working on during my test too heavy to for him to pick up.

Log Entry #88.
Here I come to save the day:

I had just started using the under Chicago Whale base. All it took was a tunnel into my parents' house and I was home without any fancy flying at all. I wonder what the Mayor of Chicago would do if he knew that the Whale Base is already several time larger than "O'Hare airport and its centered under the old location of Meigs Field, only about two miles down.

I was relaxing with my parents on when I first heard the news. N.A.S.A. had one of their Astronauts wonder away from the International Space Station, the big worry was it's in High Earth orbit where is was supposed to be.

The Astronaut was spacewalking for only a few minutes before being lost overboard, I remember that N.A.S.A. had grounded all of their Astronaut Maneuvering Units to save money, saying that their Crew Exploration Vehicles were so maneuverable that an Astronaut Maneuvering Unit was a waste of money. Then I remembered that the next CEV in line was still in the Vehicle Assembly building, not on the launch pad ready to go.

I checked with my Watch-Commander only to discover that all of my Spacecraft were occupied, both of my alert birds as well as its back up Space ships were at work and out of position to do anything about an emergency on the I.S.S. at this time. Even by Sabrina No. 40 was under water in the Whale base being serviced.

It would take at least an hour to have any of my spacecraft in a location to do any kind of rescue work. Then it hit me I was trying to code my space suit to morph into my standard Human Maneuvering Unit when needed.

If I combined all three of my space suits into one unit this would increase my capabilities and give me the needed mass to morph other devices like a set of self-forming rocket boots.

That I could use to fly up to any of my Space ships in orbit or anywhere around an Asteroid field that I wanted to go. The problem was fuel, going up would not be a problem, however the re-entry and soft landing on Earth calculations needed lots more work.

As I discovered that I would run out of energy long before I could make a soft ballistic landing back on the surface of the Earth. As far my mission calculations have come down to the need to morph a parachute just before impact.

If I had put the main lift engine, in a back pack it would give me a hot foot not to mention burn off both of my legs. The secret was to use a bottom of my space boots for lift rockets with finger-tip rockets to keep everything all going in the correct direction. It was also a good thing to have built up my tolerance to continuous heavy "G" loads.

If I was going to save anybody I would have to start moving extremely fast very soon. I used my 3 "G" muscles to pick up both of my spare space suits and move them to the middle of my parent's back yard. It only took a couple of seconds to interconnect all three of them. Instantly everything started forming around me my space suit formed normally. Then all the add ones Vertical Lift Rockets started to show up for the first time.

All three of my He/3 reactors started to intermix and produced all the raw power needed to lift a 15 year old girl, vertically into Outer Space, as energy started to move through my space suit. Two baby version of my ION Electric engine formed, under each of my feet, as well as thruster rockets on each of my fingertips.

I launched off, as I called the Elgin Center and requested a vertical assent to 100 thousand feet with a vector to the International Space Station. This really got their attention as I had not parked any of my Space ships at this location. I informed them that I was on a rescue mission and my intention was to pick up the Astronaut that had just wandered away from the N.A.S.A. Space Station a couple of minutes ago.

The manager of the Chicago Air Traffic Control Center informed me that they did not have a vector to the lost astronaut but the International Space Station was just crossing the west coast coming my way, and then gave me its speed and orbital vector.

The calculations were simple for me to do in my head, as I went through my formulas I realized that I had to move fast now and do five "G" acceleration all the way out of the Earth's atmosphere.

With my three "G" muscles it was not a problem for me to aim the bottom of my foot or a finger in the correct direction, all I had to do was not worry about not scratching my nose. I did manage to leave a Pinger-5 size divot in my parent's back yard and melt a large section of my old swing set during lift off.

I had to re-shape my Cargo Bubble to use as an aerodynamic shield to protect me from air movement at high the Mach numbers when I was still in the atmosphere, needless to say I made a supersonic boom as I ascended that was felt over most of the eastern parts of the United States.

Once I was free of the Earth's Atmosphere I rounded out the Cargo Bubble and made it transparent. My only sensor turns out to be my communications necklace. Just like my latest tool kit run, there was lots to detect, I even tried to use the data from my last HMU visit only to discover it was useless, so I had to start all over again, this time I made sure to plot all the M & M's first.

I had to re-shaped my Cargo Bubble to a more aerodynamic coke bottle shape as I entered their atomic oxygen cloud, I did manage to make a smile when I realized that I had boomed the International Space Station as my closing speed was well over Mach one. I noticed that the surface of my Cargo Bubbles was starting to glow cherry red from the micro-Atmosphere, this was the first time I had noticed any aerodynamic heating in an Atomic Oxygen Cloud.

Then just like that I found her, I could tell by her feet first movement that the lost Astronaut was a female, she was already several thousand miles away from the I.S.S. moving at the same altitude with her arms and legs extended trying to stabilize herself.

This was my first good news, as she had definitely not broken my Human Cannon ball record for traveling from the ejection point. Figuring my own deceleration arch as well as calculating our rendezvous speed was really interesting, I had to do three separate math problems all at the same instant, and have everything come out to the same number at the same instant.

Something really bad must have happened on the International Space Station to knock an Astronaut away at supersonic speed, it hurt when I calculated her "G" load.

I focus my sensors on her to make sure her Space suit was working. My next piece good news was she was moving her arms and legs and she was slowing her spin rate. I noticed that she was venting vapor I could see that something had made a mess out of her back pack as I could see that a large chunk of it was gone, this meant that she was about to run out of everything any second now.

I realized then even microseconds counted I had to do the toughest math in my life I was doing 10 and 15 figures after the decimal point maneuvers. It was reassuring to notice my external fire ball diminish as I started to close in on her location. I managed to fly a straight line directly to her location adjust my speed to match hers and extended my clear protective Cargo Bubble around both of us.

I waited until I had a useable atmosphere around her then I said "High I'm Sabrina from Sabrina Aviation what's your name? She was so far gone that she couldn't talk, however I was now close enough to be able to read her nametag.

This did not do any good as "Holly" did not have enough electronics left to talk with. It took less than a second to morph an oxygen line with a quick connector to plug in to her Space suits spare air socket. I could not lower my Space suits pressure as it was still at 15 pounds per square inch, the same as the Earth's surface. If I had opened my Space suit its air pressure would have crushed, what was left of her N.A.S.A. Space suit like an empty pop can, not to mention instantly raising Holly's air pressure to match mine.

So I had to keep my space suit buttoned up and lower the cargo bubbles air pressure to less than four pounds per square inch, as I gently made a one "G" turn towards the space station, I did my best flying to date just to get us to the main airlock. It took more fancy maneuvering to get her back to the International Space Station. As I had not even though fuel to make a soft landing for two on the Earth's surface without a heat shield much less a Space ship.

My next worry was too not burn a hole in the surface of any of the space stations modules with my finger tip maneuvering rockets. It took lots of commands to my morph controls to cover the Astronauts entrance hatch with the Cargo Bubble and morph away my lift rockets to make my mass small enough to cycle into the interior of the air-lock with my wounded Astronaut in tow.

It really helped to only have the mass of a 14 year old girl, as two full size adult humans would not fit into the same airlock at the same time. It seems that my arrival had been noticed, as all the other Astronauts had gone into their person overboard routine and were standing ready to recover their lost crewman.

They didn't even think of having over a house guest. I could tell that they had rehearsed all their moves as they removed Holly's space suit and tried to put out the electrical fire that started to burn as soon as any kind of Atmosphere started to form around her damaged backpack.

It was good thing that I dropped by as I formed a multi-level air tight small Cargo Bubble around the damaged backpack before it got cooking and tried to create a crater inside of the Space Station. You should have seen the look on their faces when I formed the bubble and then pulled out all the air, which was not a very hard thing to do at 6 PSI.

I had problems just talking to the other Astronauts. I had to program my morph unit to make an external low frequency boom box speaker just to enable me to be heard in the low air pressure. It didn't help much due to the normal lower air pressure in the Space Station, as humans really need air pressure to hear sounds.

So there I was floating inside the power-down space station with a burning N.A.S.A. backpack trapped inside one of my Cargo PODs. For the first time sense I launched from my parents back yard I had time to check messages.

I had E-mails from everybody even the press, they all wanting to know what had happened, it seems lots longer than 3 minutes and 16 seconds. As I was checking in with my Watch-Commander on the LEADER, everything on the I.S.S. went dark, due to their lack of electrical power.

The only light burning was the one on my Space Suit. So I turned up the last of my remaining power and extended my last Cargo Bubble around all the astronauts including Holly. Just seconds before the entire Space Station depressurized.

I can tell you from experience that all de-compression in outer space are explosive. As soon as everything had equalized all I had to do was say four words into my communication necklace. "Come and get me"!

Life on the Space Station was worse than I had thought. If my parents were to send me here for a summer camp they would be arrested for child endangerment. This was the first time in outer space where I was in the dark and had to turn on my space suits cooling systems.

It took less time to tell as you would think, two of my Sabrina No. 40 series Space ships were dispatched and picked up the entire Space Station with everybody still in it, as well as all of its tag a long space junk, and hauled it to the LEADER.

Only a mammal with a brain the size of Pinger-5 could have instantly come up with a rescue plan that would work, the only way to capture a Spacecraft like the I.S.S. without breaking it up was to first in case it with water. Then freeze it to form a Comet core around it to catch everything at the same time, to do this the first requirement would be to get lots of water, fresh water at that.

Pinger-5 called the only experienced Whale/naut that was not at work, you gusted it, "Navigator" you should have seen the look on the faces of the people at the Shedd Aquarium when they saw him grow a space suit with a full set of thrusters. Then launch himself vertically out past the break water to land in the middle of his waiting Sabrina No. 40 ship, that he had left submerged just off Lake Shore Drive next to the Adler Planetarium.

He closed up his Space ship then launch with a full load of water. He launched vertically making all the correct air traffic calls as he flew a Whale of a straight line directly towards me.

As he was closings on my location "Navigator" started launching thousands of gallons of Lake Michigan water in a tight full stream. He had too time the water stream to intercept the entire Space Station, with just enough mass to enable the water to get trapped by its micro gravity field. The rising water level also trapped all the moving Space-junk, it even shorted out the electrical fires that were still burning in the Space Stations power control center.

As soon as the Space Station had orbited past the terminator and moved into the dark part of its Earth orbit, the cold set in and froze everything in place.

Due to the size of this operation, it took two of the Sabrina No. 40 ships to enclose the entire mass of the Space Station frozen water and all. Then it was a simple matter of moving another comet into the hanger on the LEADER.

Due to the lack of electricity all the hatches were frozen. I use my on board power to fire up my right hand index finger thruster. So that I could turn it up to full power, I was able with the help of the N.A.S.A. Astronauts directions, to cut out a hole, large enough to get everybody out at the same time.

It only took a couple of minutes for my hanger crew to extract everybody. I had the last call as it was up to me to morph all three of my space suits to release everything into my main cargo bay.

My fire fighters had a field day putting out the burning backpack Pinger-5 even helped by blowing $Co/2$ on it from her spout. It was worth the cost of the ticket to watcher her draw in a huge breath of air wile floating in zero "G" then holding it in until she started to change colors, only to blasting the burning back pack like it was a birthday cake for a 90 year old person.

In less than 15 minutes, my rescue crew had all of the space station in my main hanger tethered to the entrance closest to the Space Hospital. All of the N.A.S.A. Astronauts were taken to the "Leader's "Hospital to be tended too. The station itself was in worse shape every one of its solar cells were drowned or shouted out, the only thing I could think of doing was install one of my He/3 reactors and patch up my home made exit port.

It took a while but I personally put it back in orbit myself after all its repairs were finally finished. Not to forget the melting and capture of all the water as it melted. I had to morph everything back into my three space suits. As well as put on a company spare space suit so that I had to recharge them all three of mine at the same time.

This was the first time I noticed my nametag change from "Spare" to "Sabrina". These were my prototype space suits this was the first time in years that I had not had one of them on my person. Not to forget the best news, was I got to keep the space stations entire supply of Space-Junk? As all I had to do was pull it out of the main work bay's lost and found box.

I got a ride back to Lake Michigan from "Navigator" He decided to use his parachute to get him back into his Whale tank in time for lunch. He bailed out around 40,000 feet, still in his Space suit mode. Being a "G" junkie he ended up doing a HALO-jump with his main parachute opening just before impacting the water in his display tank. He didn't even try to land in Burnham Park Harbor, which was the closest point to his entry tube.

I ended up making the normal supersonic vertical impact just above the main entrance to the underwater cave on the floor of the lake about 20 miles out from shore. The trick is to do a perfect vertical impact this caused most of the waves to cancel each other out. With a quick elevator ride I made it back home in less than an hour.

I was still carrying a space suit in each hand. I was not thing as my Earth mass was so high that I broke the bottom basement step just by putting my foot in it. I got to spend the rest of the day welding replacement pipes into my newly melted back yard swing set. As well as unrolling the grass divots and replacing the burned places with more grass seeds to fill in my lift off point.

I reprogrammed the morph control so that I can form a thruster on my right index finger. After all you can never tell when a 15-year-old girl needs a plasma torch.

Log Entry #89.
My Rocketry Project:

Despite all of my space flight time I was requested to do a rocket flight program as a short term physics project. For my science project, I decided to do a standard launch at different locations. To do this project all I had to do was launch my rocket from more than one location and note the differences in flight. So I was using a standard Estes Alpha III with an A8-3 solid rocket motor.

For my first launch, I launch at my friend Lewis University ACE-Camp. This was my normal launch that I was to compare all the others. To identify it I named it 62808 being sixty second thousand eight hundred an eight airframe that I had worked on. I inspected the airframe to make sure that there were not any thin spots in the fuselage or physical damage of any kind.

I also checked the fins to make sure that all of them were secured. Next came the parachute, I opened it up to make sure that all the shroud lines were intact and still connected to the canopy. I removed the old used solid rocket motor. I used the blow-gun method of installing fire proof wading down inside of 62808 I noted that the wad of wading had stopped moving just above the rockets very small engine room. I replace it with another A8-3 solid rocket motor. Then I folded up the parachute in a pack small enough to fit inside the open end of the fuselage, so that the shock cord can be added on top.

The last thing was to slide the nosecone onto the front of the fuselage and to make sure that it was not stuck. Then I found a weight and balance check device in the equipment box, this is a fancy name for a 6 foot long piece of string with a closed loop tied in each end. I turned the loop around to make a hard circular lock around the 62808 center of balance to make it hang sideways to my current gravity field. My last move in the Weight & Balance check was to gently spend 62808 around my head with the string to note if it was spinning forward.

Needless to say if 62808 had spun backwards or sideways a counter weight had to be added to the front of the nose cone and the Weight & Balance test repeated until forward movement is achieved. The last thing I needed to do was to place the end of an igniter in the back of the live rocket motor and to make sure that it is just touching the firing stud in the engine. A plastic securing plug can be used to keep it from falling out. I launch for the first time at the ACE camp.

According to Pinger-5 my ships onboard sensors recorded its maximum speed at 476.34 MPH. Its parachute got stuck in an upward moving vortex and overflew the landing site to eventfully wrap its shock cord around one of the camera mounts on my ships instrument cluster. This set off all of my collision alarms and woke up Pinger-5. She was able to turn off the alarms before the Command Computer automatically move the Sabrina No. 40 to a safer location.

I also checked the fins to make sure that all of them were secured. I inspected the airframe to see if there were any thin spots in the fuselage or physical damage of any kind. Next came the parachute, I opened it up to make sure that all the shroud lines were intact and still connected to the canopy. I removed the old used solid rocket motor, to allow airflow through the inside of my rocket. I used the blow-gun method of installing fire proof wading down inside of 62808 I noted that the wad of wading had stopped moving just above the rockets very small engine room.

Then I replaced the used motor with another new unused A8-3 solid rocket motor. Then I folded up the parachute in a pack small enough to fit inside the open end of the fuselage, so that the shock cord can be added on top. The last thing was to slide the nosecone onto the front of the fuselage and to make sure that it was not stuck. Then I found a weight and balance check device in the equipment box, this is a fancy name for a 6 foot long piece of string with a closed loop tied in each end.

I turned the loop around to make a hard circular lock around the 62808 center of balance to make it hang sideways to my current gravity field. My last move in the Weight & Balance check was to gently spend 62808 around my head with the string to note if it was spinning forward. Needless to say if 62808 had spun backwards or sideways a counter weight had to be added to the front of the nose cone and the Weight & Balance test repeated until forward movement is achieved.

My second launch of 62808 was an hour later as my Father and I were on the way back to base, the last thing I needed to do was to place the end of an igniter in the back of the live rocket motor and to make sure that it is just touching the firing stud in the engine. I use a plastic securing plug can be used to keep it from falling out.

I launched it on top of Sabrina No. 40 as she was hovering about 5,000 feet over Lake Michigan. Pinger-5 had my ships systems picked it up and matched speed to moved Sabrina No. 40 to the point where 62808 just appeared to hover, about a foot off the end of my launcher. It cycled and flashed 3 seconds into the launch I had to walk over to where it appeared to hover above the point where my ships sensors first picket it up.

As I examined it, I noted that there weren't any dynamic forces exerted on it as under Pinger-5's control Sabrina No. 40 just flew formation with 62808. I inspected the airframe to see if there were any thin spots in the fuselage or physical damage of any kind. I all so checked the fins to make sure that all of them were secured. Next came the parachute, I opened it up to make sure that all the shroud lines were intact and still connected to the canopy.

I removed the old used solid rocket motor. I used the blow-gun method of installing fire proof wading down inside of 62808 I noted that the wad of wading had stopped moving just above the rockets very small engine room. I replace it with another A8-3 solid rocket motor. Then I folded up the parachute in a pack small enough to fit inside the open end of the fuselage, so that the shock cord can be added on top.

The last thing was to slide the nosecone onto the front of the fuselage and to make sure that it was not stuck. Then I found a weight and balance check device in the equipment box. This turn out to be fancy name for a 6 foot long piece of string with a closed loop tied in each end. I turned the loop around to make a hard circular lock around the 62808 center of balance to make it hang sideways to my current gravity field.

My last move in the weight & balance check was to gently spend 62808 around my head with the string to note if it was spinning forward. Needless to say if 62808 had spun backwards or sideways a counter weight had to be added to the front of the nose cone and the Weight & Balance test repeated until forward movement is achieved.

My third launch was on the surface of the LEADER. I even filed a flight plan and notified my watch-commander. My first problem was the parachute popped out of the front of 62808 as the airlock de-pressurized.

This moved 62808 out of my hand and caused it to ricochet around inside the airlock, due to the lack of Atmosphere I had to make an extend effort to catch it. It took a while for me to repack it and get it ready to launch again, I had to do my first Weight & Balance test in a vacuum. The last thing I needed to do was to place the end of an igniter in the back of the live rocket motor and to make sure that it is just touching the firing stud in the engine. I even got to use a plastic securing plug to keep it from falling out.

Due to the lack of an atmosphere and the low gravity field, it had a high launch speed lift-off, so fast that it seemed to just disappear. I was smart enough to put a micro locater transmitter on it, so that I could track where ever it went. As it turns out it was in orbit around the LEADER at around the 1,000-mile marker, it amazed me to learn that an object would orbit the LEADER at that distance.

I had to use one of my human maneuvering units to retrieve 62808 from its orbital tract. When I got there it was spinning like a top with the shock cord acting like a piston pulling everything closed with centrifugal force stretching out the shock-cord at the same time. I retrieved it by catching it on my open hand. As soon as I had it back inside of my Command POD.

I inspected the airframe to see if there were any burned spots in the fuselage or physical damage of any kind. I all so checked the fins to make sure that all of them were secured. Then I removed the old used solid rocket motor. Next came the parachute. I opened it up to make sure that all the shroud lines were intact and still connected to the canopy. I used the blow-gun method of installing fire proof wading down inside of 62808 I noted that the wad of wading had stopped moving just above the rockets very small engine room. I replace it with another A8-3 solid rocket motor.

Then I folded up the parachute in a pack small enough to fit inside the open end of the fuselage, so that the shock cord can be added on top. The last thing was to slide the nosecone onto the front of the fuselage and to make sure that it was not stuck. Then I found a weight and balance check device in the equipment box, this is a fancy name for a 6 foot long piece of string with a closed loop tied in each end.

I turned the loop around to make a hard circular lock around the 62808 center of balance to make it hang sideways to my current gravity field. My last move in the Weight & Balance check was to gently spend 62808 around my head with the string to note if it was spinning forward. Needless to say if 62808 had spun backwards or sideways a counter weight had to be added to the front of the nose cone and the weight & balance test repeated until forward movement is achieved.

62808's fourth launch was from the surface of the Earth's Moon I decided to use the smoother Earth facing side, I check my figures and decided to do a trick shot. I launched 62808 towards the east and adjusted its trajectory to make it pass through the antenna farm on the top of my Space Elevators. The last thing I needed to do before launch was to place the end of an igniter in the back of the live rocket motor and to make sure that it is just touching the firing stud in the engine.

A plastic securing plug can be used to keep it from falling out. The launch from the surface of the Moon was a little on the dramatic side as the rockets exhaust blew Lunar Regales in 360 directions at the same time. As usual, I had to use my optical tracker to notice that it had cycled at 3 seconds into the flight the parachute had extended but not opened due to the lack of atmosphere.

Everybody keeps complaining about the time it takes to ride the Space Elevator to orbit. In 62808's case it was waiting for me hanging on one of my communication antenna's by the time I could get there using my Lunar Space Elevator No.3. 62808's fifth launch had a much longer flight time. I was on my way to Mars making my usual replacement stuff flight, Food, Parts, and Personal belongings, with nothing living except me, as I am not old enough for a Commercial Pilots license.

I inspected the airframe to see if there were any thin spots in the fuselage or physical damage of any kind. I all so checked the fins to make sure that all of them were secured.

Next came the parachute, I opened it up to make sure that all the shroud lines were intact and still connected to the canopy. I removed the old spent rocket motor. I used the blow-gun method of installing fire proof wading down inside of 62808 I noted that the wad of wading had stopped moving just above the rockets very small engine room.

I replace the solid fuel with another A8-3 solid rocket motor. Then I folded up the parachute in a pack small enough to fit inside the open end of the fuselage, so that the shock cord can be added on top. The last thing was to slide the nosecone onto the front of the fuselage and to make sure that it was not stuck. Then I found a weight and balance check device in the equipment box, this is a fancy name for a 6 foot long piece of string with a closed loop tied in each end. I turned the loop around to make a hard circular lock around the 62808 center of balance to make it hang sideways to my current gravity field.

My last move in the weight & balance check was to gently spend 62808 around my head with the string to note if it was spinning forward. The last thing I needed to do was to place the end of an igniter in the back of the live rocket motor and to make sure that it is just touching the firing stud in the engine. A plastic securing plug can be used to keep it from falling out. I moved my Command POD to the far end of my upper cargo bay and launched 62808 off the end of my loading ramp of course I was in full space suit mode.

I had the usual problems dealing with a full vacuum. I launched it Sunward. Its parachute cycled at 3 seconds and it went out of sight. I had my ships systems keep track of it. And calculate a continuous intercept angle on it. What amazed me was the solar wind eventually blew it back into my cargo bay as I neared Mars. I did not have to go and get it came back. It made the ultimate solar wind triangle flight of millions of miles. My ships systems intercepted it as it parceled my original course line. I did manage to bend up the fin tips as I had 62808 sitting on the floor in my Command POD as I made a normal landing on the surface of Mars, at my Mars Landing Pad No.one.

My next Launch was on the surface of Mars. I inspected the airframe to see if there were any thin spots in the fuselage or physical damage of any kind. I all so checked the fins to make sure that all of them were secured. Next came the parachute I opened it up to make sure that all the shroud lines were intact and still connected to the canopy. I removed the old used solid rocket motor. I used the blow-gun method of installing fire proof wading down inside of 62808. I noted that the wad of wading had stopped moving just above the rockets very small engine room replace it with another A8-3 solid rocket motor.

Then I folded up the parachute in a pack small enough to fit inside the open end of the fuselage, so that the shock cord can be added on top. The last thing was to slide the nosecone onto the front of the fuselage and to make sure that it was not stuck. Then I found a weight and balance check device in the equipment box, this is a fancy name for a 6 ft. long piece of string with a closed loop tied in each end. I turned the loop around to make a hard circular lock around the 62808 center of balance to make it hang sideways to my current two thirds gravity field. My last move in the weight & balance check was to gently spend 62808 around my head with the string to note if it was spinning forward. The last thing I needed to do was to place the end of an igniter in the back of the live rocket motor and to make sure that it is just touching the firing stud in the engine. Despite my space gloves I used a plastic securing plug to keep it from falling out.

The sixth launch of 62808 was on the surface of Mars. To get away from my base I decided to use my Mars-Cycle. The problem of how to run an air breathing engine on the surface of Mars was simple. All I had to do was give it the engine air to breath from the exhaust end of one of my fuel cells into the standard built Earth style a motorcycle Engine.

The other problem was how to keep my 15 year old body from being splattered all over the Martian landscape. To survive that problem I had to modify my space suit to a form fitting reinforced helmet, knee guards, Upper and Lower Arm Armor Guards, Upper and Lower Armor Leg Guards, reinforced boots, fire proof, gloves, Heavy Leather Reinforced Puncher Proof Riding Suit, with automatic built in flotation devices to help get out of sand trap hazards, the only thing I don't worry about was finding any of the best tasting bugs as Mars has none. I also added a back-up! fire extinguisher as POE to keep me from becoming a mobile fuel fire!

I made sure to know how to fly it before I took off. I treated my motorcycle just it like an airplane. By never taking the Safety out of operating any kind of vehicle where ever I operate it. As I can only afford to operate it safely, by being aware of how the laws of physics act on a motorcycle as well as all the other objects around me.

When operating a motorcycle on Mars the worse problem is all the dust, needless to say it gets into everything. My solution to this problem was to encase my motorcycle inside one of my transparent Cargo Bubbles, and run my cycle around inside of it. This really cuts down on the dust. Just before my next launch I inspected the airframe to see if there were any thin spots in the fuselage or physical damage of any kind.

Also, I checked the fins to make sure that all of them were secured. Next came the parachute, I opened it up to make sure that all the shroud lines were intact and still connected to the canopy. I removed the old used solid rocket motor. I used the blow-gun method of installing fire proof wading down inside of 62808 I noted that the wad of wading had stopped moving just above the rockets very small engine room. I replace it with another A8-3 solid rocket motor.

Then I folded up the parachute in a pack small enough to fit inside the open end of the fuselage, so that the shock cord can be added on top. The last thing was to slide the nosecone onto the front of the fuselage and to make sure that it was not stuck. Then I found a weight and balance check device in the equipment box, this is a fancy name for a 6 foot long piece of string with a closed loop tied in each end.

I turned the loop around to make a hard circular lock around the 62808 center of balance to make it hang sideways to my current gravity field. My last move in the Weight & Balance check was to gently spend 62808 around my head with the string to note if it was spinning forward. The last thing I needed to do was to place the end of an igniter in the back of the live rocket motor and to make sure that it is just touching the firing stud in the engine.

I used a plastic securing plug to keep it from falling out. The sixth launch of 62808 was more dramatic due to the low air pressure, the parachute popped out as soon as I cleared the airlock, and I had to repack it and do a weigh & balance test while in my reinforced space suit.

The lower gravity and thin air made it go supersonic as 62808 cleared the launch rod. A supersonic shock wave is still a shock wave in the Martian atmosphere, the outer air pressure crush 62808 as if one of Sabrina No. 39's landing claw had sat on it.

The flight body was crushed and the fins were torn off, the only thing that stayed connecter was the shock cord to the parachute. However I did produce the first sonic boom that was heard on the surface of Mars.

The now inflight wreckage traveled out of sight and landed on the surface of Mars. The Martian environment buried it on contact with the surface. It was just like my first landing, out of sight and lost upon contact. I would probably still be trying to dig 62808 up if it were not for Spirit and Opportunity.

Ever sense I pulled the rock out of Spirits' wheel they both have been following me around like lost puppies. I used them to document my launch. Due to their own Command Computers that I installed in them, they are as interested as any other of my command ships in small useless human rockets.

I used their data to calculate the touch down point and recovered 62808 wreckage. It also took several hours to remove all the Martian dust from my Mars-cycle's cargo bubble. The rocket fragments were definitely stressed as I noticed that the parachute was in full blossom as it was entombed sideways by the blowing Martian sand. I also noted that 62808's shock cord was stretch to its maxim as I dug it up.

Log Entry #90.
Pinger-5's Vacation:

It has been an interesting week Pinger-5 decided that it was her turn to go on vacation. She had made it all the way to Mars just as the first of her Kuiper objects collided directly over Olympus Mound. She was hovering in her Sabrina No. 40 Space ship waiting for all the snow and Ice to arrive.

I told her it wouldn't work as all the ice entered the Atmosphere as Ice crystals that passed through the atmosphere and buried themselves under several yards of Martian sand. She hardly made a Sonic Boom at the last minute she had her Whale Board morph wheels instead of skies. She did get to belly slide all the way down the full length of the largess Volcano in the Solar system. But the induced drag of all the sand kept her from going supersonic. She was making Whale song all the way down.

That Friday morning I got a "nasty-gram", from the Shedd Aquarium about my food bill. It seems that they had found out about the Beluga's vacation plan, they demanded my personal appearance to pay the food bill. I flew in with Sabrina No. 40 I got to use the old standard approach chart for Meigs Field then made an extended hover to land with my nose landing gear centered on the buildings main door. It was a tough touch down I had to straddle the causeway and put each of my main landing gear underwater with my main starboard landing gear in Lake Michigan and my port main landing gear in Barman harbor. This enables me to have my Nose gear elevator come to a stop next to their main entrance door.

As soon as I enter their main door, I got the shock of my life when I noticed Pinger-5 in their main exhibit whale tank. To top it all off the director of the Shedd came out of his office to meet me and he demanded to see my father, as he did not deal with school girls.

Pinger-5 had retracted her space suit to where it was only showing her control band. I could see that she was trying to tell me something due to her being underwater I had to morph my left space glove into a sonar phone connector and stick it onto the glass surface of the tank with the palm of my hand. Then I transmitted sound throughout the buildings entire structure. As I asked Pinger-5, what she was doing?

This really got everybody attention as the ultra-low frequency sound wave enabled everybody to feel my every word. You should have seen the look on the Directors face when I started to speak Humpback with my puny 15-year-old female human voice. I asked Pinger-5 "How did you get in there?" Then I said, "I know for a fact that the exchange tube is too small for you to use."

"What made matters worse Pinger-5 answered in Human English "Why are you talking Humpback? "She answered back". "I should be talking Beluga" I answered, "If you did you could only say one or two words a day" replied Pinger-5.

It seems that she had made a HALO Parachute Jump into "Navigator's" tank the night before. This had caused the resident Beluga to run for his life, back through the exchange tunnel. Pinger-5 had already eaten her way through all the Beluga's food supply for her night time snack, when I arrived on the seen Pinger-5 was using my communication system to call all the local Hotels for Room Service.

She asked, "Do you know the phone number of an all you can eat sea Food bar that delivers?" As it turned out all the credit card charges for all the food went through without a hitch, it seem that Pinger-5 had learned how to survive along with all the humans on the planet. As it turns out Pinger-5 has a higher credit rating than I did.

The museum director wanted to know that happened to the Beluga whale that was in his exhibit tank. As well as how you got in their instead, he also wanted to know about all the other Octopi and Squids that were also in the tank, I don't think that he will believe me if I tell him that you did a HALO parachute jump from low Earth orbit.

"Pinger-5 answered," I wasn't that high in the atmosphere, I was aiming for the Lake Michigan when I remember that "Navigator had use the HALO method with great success, so I thought that I would give it a try." Does he think I ate Navigator she asked?" "I sent him out to pick up breakfast for both of us, it was a lengthy order, and you know how fast Beluga's talk he probably won't be back until after lunch.

I'm stuck she finally answered" I thought that all the Octopus & Squids were snack food you think they would have said something before I ate them? " "I lost most of my Power supply as I landed, this tank is a lot smaller than it looks, and all I can do is make local phone calls." As I was still in space suit mode right in front of everybody, I power up my extra muscles and walked up the stairs to the top of their whale tank.

Then I stepped into the water only to sink, to the bottom like a stone. The Whale tank was definitely designed for Beluga's. Pinger-5 being a Humpback tended to fill in all the empty spaces. Pinger-5 came back on the sonar phone to remind me that the tank was full of fresh water, so I ballets to neutral buoyancy and floated up off the bottom. I even had time to morph a full set of water thrusters and flippers. All of my He/3 reactors started spooling up as soon as they got wet.

The instant I plugged into the power plug on the end of Pinger-5's dormant flipper. Things really started to change, instantly her space suit returned one layer at a time Silver, Orange then White. As soon as she started to morph ballistic thrusters I warned her that she cannot blast out of the Whale tank without destroying it. She agreed and started to morph her ballistic thrusters into her Humpback Whale size land scooter, with a single over size snowmobile type track on it. Her space suit even formed a clear Cargo POD full of water around me.

She activated her forward drive motors, climbed out of the top of the Whale tank, and started crawling toward Lake Michigan, then she shafted direction and ask if I knew the GPS location of the closest restaurant that had an all you can eat seafood bar. Never mind I told her I would be glad to give you an airlift to anywhere she wanted to go for lunch.

As we reached the halfway point to Lake Michigan our space suit controls activated both of our collision alarm, as I noticed large numbers of fish passing over our location on a trajectory that would land them into the middle of the Whale tank that Pinger-5 was trapped in. It seems the Navigator had put all the young Whales in the Whale School to work launching whole fish from their blowholes into the location where he had left Pinger-5 trapped.

The second we made it to the water Pinger-5 retracted her space suit to make it easier to swim. She made her Whale song and told the entire class to knock it off. I could see from their expressions as they received Pinger-5's instructions, which sent them all scurrying through the water on their way back into the deaths of Lake Michigan.

As soon as I surfaced, I activated my control communications necklace and launched Sabrina No. 40 back into the air. I requested a pick up then hit the automatic button to let my Command Computer do all the work. Sabrina No. 40 landed centered on me, with her forward bottom cargo doors open, I let the water float me up to where I could enter my Command POD, as my morphing system formed Pinger-5's flight tank, I checked to see that Pinger-5 had secured herself in her flight tank, and asked her where she wanted to go. "She replied the Arctic"

"I have a taste for krill" so off we flew a vertical lift off from Meigs with a high altitude climb out to the north with the Command Computer making all the air traffic calls to the Elgin center. The controller at the Elgin Center must have been a nugget as he had a problem with using Meigs as my departure point.

He seemed more confused when I informed him that Meigs Fields lack of runways was not a problem because I was doing an Underwater Ballistic Launch. I was amazed as soon as Pinger-5 took control we did a 3-minute ballistic flight to the North Pole and made a vertical landing around Mach eight. I took control and leveled out before I jammed Sabrina No. 40 into the bottom of the Arctic Ocean.

Pinger-5 launched herself out the bottom hatch to feed, She said, "that the never thought that she would miss the taste of krill." And I let Sabrina No. 40 extended her landing gear, shut down and closed up the Aero-spikes then let Sabrina No. 40 settle on to the floor of the Arctic Ocean.

I left the bottom cargo bay doors open so that Pinger-5 could use it as a breathing chamber, and then settled down in my Command POD to get caught up on some homework. Suddenly the proximity alarm went off, and I checked my cargo bay cameras to discover that it was jammed with Bulge's over a thousand of them. I put more oxygen in the cargo bay and open the other cargo bays only to have them all fill up with more Bulges'. I activated my sonar-phone and asked Pinger-5 what was going on.

She replied instantly that these were the surviving members of the largest Beluga whale Pod in the Arctic, their food chain was disrupted, and they had been trapped inside an Ice barrier until we arrived. They were all starving and being picked off by hungry Polar bears, as they have not been able to get to the open Ocean. Pinger-5 already had several Sabrina No. 40's sister Space ships inbound to transport the entire living Bulge's to Lake Michigan.

It was a first class slather house on the surface, of the Arctic Ocean the hungry Polar Bears had all the open spots on the surface covered, as soon as a Beluga surfaced for air it was attacked by several starving Polar Bears. The only way to stop the carnage was for me to surface Sabrina No. 40 in the largest open air hole, to cut the Beluga's off from the Polar Bears.

This wasn't my smartest move as the Polar Bear instantly started to claw at all my topside hatch covers and at the same time swim under my Sabrina No.40 to try to get into my open bottom hatches. I was able to have my ships systems to trap the first wave with Space-junk traps and drop them into an empty storage spaces, then recycle the trap to get the next one.

As there was nothing a Beluga could do against a band of hungry Polar Bears. Pinger-5 resulted herself and ran most of the Polar Bear strays back onto the Ice. She played them like billiard balls bouncing and tossing them away at will, it wasn't an easy fight as the entire second wave of Polar bears were trying to eat her alive as they all close in on her.

Due to my space suit design, her automatic system repair program was filling in and patching all of the attacking bear claw and bite marks as they happed. Pinger-5's next maneuver was to stack several of my Sabrina No. 40 ships under each other and dock them together to enable all the Beluga's to escape.

As soon as the first ship unloaded in Lake Michigan all the Beluga's made a bee line for the Shedd Aquarium and the exchange tube, every one of them wanting room service. It took a while for my whale medical staff to round them up for processing and medical checkup. My next problem was when I discover that they all had white blank tail flukes, so we indexed them by scars and other wounds.

Pinger-5 really made out on the deal as she found homes for all the hungry Polar Bears at Zoo's worldwide, she treated them like new born kittens, she told me point blank that you cannot give away hungry Polar Bears but you could sell them. She had such a deal going if the receiving zoo complained that the poor starving Polar Bear was on the thin side she, gave them another one for free.

It took less than an hour before Pinger-5 showed up again in Sabrina No. 40's cargo bay she made a big deal out of morphing away her space suit then announced that she was back on vacation. Upon seeing Pinger-5 I asked about the Shedds's food bill as that was the event that caused me to start moving this morning. Pinger-5 replied that it was covered and she had paid all the food bills herself, humans are funny, "I even paid them for nothing." "Nothing," I asked? Yes, she replied "I left a large tip."

Log Entry #91.
Hubble Mission Two:

Pinger-5 and I spent Friday night & Saturday morning, cursing around under the Arctic, melting our way through several thick Ice Jams looking for more stranded Whales as well as hungry Polar Bears.

On Sunday morning before Pinger-5 woke up, I was checking up on current events for my homework assignment when I found a story about N.A.S.A. fixing the Poor old Hubble Space Telescope, Again! N.A.S.A. had really had a fun time outfitting one of their new C.E.V. Spacecraft too capture and repair the Hubble Space Telescope. I checked through all the Sabrina Aviation flight logs and mission reports only to discover that N.A.S.A. had not called me back to inform me that the Hubble Space Telescope had been repaired, and was ready to be dropped off in its original orbit.

I didn't know that N.A.S.A. had forgot about the free delivery from orbit that I had made over a year ago when they first contacted me about repairing it. I had my Sabrina No. 39/9 pick it up in orbit and drop it off at the Johnson Space center for repairs. I figured that I had better put it back before the whole world finds out what had happened, as the last thing I wanted was to get another nasty gram from the N.A.S.A. Administrator.

I tapped into Sabrina No. 39/9's Command Computer and down loaded the mission log for when she snatched and grabbed the Hubble, this was the first time I checked up on it location, I lucked out when I discovered that Sabrina No. 39/9 was still local, moving cargo somewhere around Earth. So I requested Sabrina No. 39/9 to go back to where she had off loaded it a year ago, pick it up to put it back where she had found it. I figured that would solve my problem.

About a half hour later I got a frantic message from Sabrina No. 39/9 complaining that she could not get into the structure where she had unloaded the Hubble object, she had sent me a live picture of the main entrance door with a large written message on the door that said "Base Closed".

So without awakening Pinger-5, 30 minute later I landed directly over Sabrina No. 39/9 as she was parked in the empty parking lot at the now closed N.A.S.A. Facility.

According to Sabrina No. 39/9's GPS she was in the correct location, it seems that N.A.S.A. had vacated this location. I walked over to the door and sat in the aircraft mover's seat, so that I could use its Communications System to wake up Pinger-5 and asked if she could help with a stuck hatch, it only took a minute for her to suit up and get on her Whale scooter, it only took her a couple of seconds to come up with the fix.

Pinger-5 said, "You got to pull it up fast enough to shear off the lock pins without wrecking the rollers." With that, she stuck the end of her tail fluke under the bottom of the doorframe and flipped up, just what every 15-year-old girl needs a 38-ton instant door opener. As soon as all the molecules in the door stopped moving, Sabrina No. 39/9 moved her Aircraft mover over to the spot where she had hung the Hubble Space Telescope from the rafters, and focuses all her work lights on it.

There it was right where I had left it. N.A.S.A. had closed down their operation move off and forgot about it. My next problem was how to get it back, not only to where I had found it but, to the point in orbit where is supposed to be less than an hour from now. While Sabrina No. 39/9 was loading the Hubble Space Telescope, Pinger-5 figured where it was supposed to be in an hour from now when the C.E.V. got to its repair location.

It was quite a show Sabrina No. 39/9 was recovering her aircraft mover with the Hubble Space Telescope hanging from its yardarm, and I was loading Sabrina No. 39/9 into the lower part of Sabrina No. 40 forward cargo bay at the same time. I automatically programmed Sabrina No. 40

where to go, to be at the correct location where the Hubble was supposed to be when the N.A.S.A.'s C.E.V. got there. I asked Pinger-5 to check my calculations only to discover that there was less than 3 inches difference between our aiming points, Pinger-5 was closer.

As soon as I cleared the atmosphere I launch Sabrina No. 39/9 out of my lower cargo bay so that she could reach the drop off point. Without leaving a large exhaust trail, that would eventually catch up to the large section of space-junk that N.A.S.A. had though was to Hubble.

Sabrina No. 39/9 did a beautiful drop and grab maneuver as she delivered the Hubble back to where it was supposed to be. And at the same time grab the oversize piece of Space-junk that N.A.S.A. had been tracking as the Hubble.

I asked 39/9 to stand guard on the C.E.V. for the rest of her mission, and watch over N.A.S.A.'s Crew Exploration Vehicles all the way to its touch down point. I got a blow by blow report as the C.E.V. captured the Hubble with an extendable cradle then, she watched and reported each astronaut's activity as they built an enclosure, her logic board went statistic then the Hubble was no longer visible. Sabrina No. 39/9 really couldn't help herself, after following the C.E.V. in orbit for more than a week, and seeing it not land in Florida due to bad weather.

She trapped it as soon as the repair crew released the now fully functional Hubble Sabrina No. 39/9 waited for everybody to power down and go into sleep mode then she loaded the entire Space ship into her main cargo bay and left it hanging from the ceiling next to the original spot where she had left the Hubble last year when N.A.S.A. asked about my help. She managed to hand it from the Pipes in the sealing of the building, without wakening any of N.A.S.A.'s fines.

Log Entry #92.
Oshkosh the next year:

The next year I did things a little different, because of my overstock, I got a booth in the fly mart just to sell off my space junk supply to the public. I was thinking of displaying the International Space Station but, to do this I would have to link two of my Sabrina No. 40 ships together and land them both at the same time in Pioneer airport.

To do this Pioneer Airport would have to be enlarged, and the FAA would have to allow the helicopter operation to be based in one of my upper cargo bays. Then there would be the rumor that I made a dual vertical landing with the I.S.S. at Pioneer Airport.

On the parking garage operation I left all the units that were used last year submerged in the middle of Lake Oshkosh. As it turned out they were used by the local fish population as a new home. When the Pilot Whales that recovered them from the middle of the lake neglected to remove the water the resulting flood made a real mess out of the parking area. I have personally fixed this problem by informing the Pilot Whale in charge to move the structure only and leave all the water and fish behind.

Sabrina No. 39 got into the act by challenging her drag racing buddy's to a race down the full length of the main north & south runway to include her famous turn, grab, and vertical climb up and away with her prize maneuver. This turned out to be a very popular event as it was held at high noon every day of the fly-in, towards the end of the week the Drag racing guys complained that my Sabrina No.39 was not return any of their losers dragsters.

I informed them that Sabrina No. 39 was only a close friend and that I had no say in her return policies. I recommended that they try trading her something she wanted for in exchange of her winnings. I have noticed that the Dragsters have always gotten faster by adding on horsepower and in some cases a Rocket Motor or two, as they have increased in speed Sabrina No. 39 has to also increase her speed the do her pass and return from the other direction maneuver. Also, Ship Sabrina No. 39/3 has joined the act her job is to pick up the dragsters when Sabrina No. 39 doesn't have the time to make her high "G" turn around.

She also gets to keep most of the loser's dragsters, they both eventfully will transport all their dragsters to the "looser circle" that they created on Mars just south of the main elevator. One of Sabrina No. 39's managed to zoom over the Pyro display the second they fire off the "Fire Curtain" then proceed to use her wake turbulence to blow out all the flames just as they were being ignited by the pyro-chief.

A couple of minutes later on the next attempt two different Sabrina No. 39 ships made a head on pass with a full power pull up to a high speed climb out. During the climb out a large rubber ball full of water was being inflated inside of the connected ships, the ship separate to release the ball of water in flight.

One of the Beluga's who use to be part of a "Sea World Show" along with most of the Orca flight put on a basketball show by bouncing the large basketball shaped object well above 5,000 feet above Airshow center. What was interesting was this object was several hundred feet wide, the whales in their Sabrina No. 40 ships would play soccer with the ball as it fell from the sky over the airshow box, each of the whale flown space ships bouncing it off their outer hulls.

Moved it all over the sky for at least 10 minutes, then at the end of the show. Their "Flight Leader" made a single high speed pass directly through the center of the ball causing it to pop and release its load of Lake Oshkosh water on the crowd of humans watching the Airshow.

All the water fell as rain, I have to remember to try this trick on Mars. I had several complains from the humans, it seems that most of the whales have no concept of having to pay for what they eat. They tend to drive into a food service tent and grab all the human food that was lying on the counter with one large gulp. Luckily, Pinger-5 came to everybody's rescue when she created an open tab for all of the whales at all of the Human food stations.

Another problem was the Orca's decided that they liked hot dogs when they were still frozen so they all raided the kitchen areas and cleaned out most of the freezers, they made it a point to target the ones full of frozen hot dogs. Pinger-5 being the Lady that she is made a point of staying on her Humpback size Whale scooter and did not leave any large cut out grass diverts on the flight line this year, this fixed the problem of having aircraft getting stuck in them then when taxing on the grass.

Pinger-5 managed to develop a taste for Chilly Dogs cooked up in the Chicago format with lots of extra onions and pickles, this also solves the problem of spent zebra mussel shells in her ships waste system. All the new born Whales came into the EAA's seaplane base to meet the humans for the first time, I had a long talk with them and informed them that airplanes had the right of way, this year there was not a single problem with sunken flying boats or sea planes with missing floats, however, there were several events where large numbers, of fish would bombard humans on the beach, not to mention the time when the human announcer at the Airshow was struck by a falling fish during the Airshow. It seems that somebody allowed a Three Stooges movie to be shown in Whale class now all the yearling think that the best way to get a humans attention is to hit them in the face with a live raw fish.

A couple of the Blue Whale yearlings had picked up the anchor of one of the parked floats and pulled it out of the seaplane base to the middle of Lake Oshkosh where they proceeded to push it in the water and make it perform several short distance flights. I discovered them using their blow holes to tossing it into the air as if it were a feather. Upon noticing me in the water they both started to quake, I asked them in my best Blue Whale voice "do you know who I am, they both answered in unison speaking English "YES your Sabrina the Invincible", needless to say I had them put the piper cub back without any damage.

The Flying Whales also got into the act with their aerobatic show using my Sabrina No. 40 series. I also got to do the "Lady with too much Luggage" act. I walked out of the crowd carrying all three of my space suits all closed up in three recharges cans. They were light as a feather to me with my 3 1/2 G muscles, I was handling them all at the same time and asked several of the larger Airshow patterns to help me carry then into my airplane, and needless to say it took several of them to handle just one of the space suit cans. As I was carrying all of them under one arm, after acting out the drama and discovering that this group of big strong men could not help me carry any of my suit cases. I finally placed them side by side then stood in top of all three to start the morph operation, where I grew my own rocket suit and launched myself off the ground, into the stream of passing aerobatic Sabrina No. 40 Space ship. Using ballistics only I flew rings around the line of whale piloted space ships as they pass through the middle of the airshow box, the last ship in-line pops out a Command POD that I fly directly into it.

This is how I get into Sabrina No. 40 during the airshow, as soon as I take command all the new born Whales bail out and do a HAHO parachute jump from Sabrina No. 40 as she clears the Airshow box then they all make an extended parachute flight to the seaplane base. Then I take over and perform my standard show act. As it turned out most of the Whale skydiver were young calf's who were born in Lake Michigan. Sense Pinger-5's big rescue mission started, I found this interesting as they are the Whales first generation that has not been hunted by humans.

When the Marine Corp was doing their "AV-8B" Show the part of the show where the air boss tells the Marine Pilot to stop in midair and then when he proceeds to fly backwards to his starting point, well this really got Sabrina No. 39/3's attention, as soon as her ships systems detect a Jet fighter flying backward, she performed an all-out emergency lift off and caught the backward flying AV-8B in midair. With her Space-junk-trap then carried the Harrier safely away as if it were one of Sabrina No. 39's dragsters.

This got the attention of the other three AV-8B's that were part of the show when they started to rotate their nozzles and vector their thrust to intercept Sabrina No. 39/3. This cause Sabrina No. 39/3 to max out her "G" meter with a series of extremely fast and extremely high "G" maneuvers that allowed her to capture all the other AV-8B"s in flight that were using vector thrust to change their direction.

The end result was Sabrina No. 39/3 got to give the Marine Corp all 4 of their undamaged AV-8B back, and I got to spend the night writing a new subroutine for her Command Computers when other aircraft use thrust vectoring near her.

Log Entry #93.
Last Day around the World Flight:

For the last day of the Oshkosh fly-in, I decided to set the record for flying around the world in an airplane, only a mammal with a brain the size of Pinger-5 could have thought up this event. The requirement is to have an official starting point then over fly Chicago, New York, Paris, Moscow, Tokyo, Honolulu, Los Angeles, and Denver then back to my starting point.

At Pinger-5's Request, I decided to use my last year birthday present. My one of a kind Rutan EZ Rocket Racer, fitted with a few of my special add-ons. I had spent most of my spare time at the Airshow displaying my Sabrina Aviation Rocket Racer, at the Pioneer Airport.

I had added on to the morph program as well as my best effort at an aerodynamic shaped reinforced Cargo Bubble. I also installed my latest He/3 powered Thermal-Ram-Jet-Motor. My Plan was to go for maximum speed inside the Earth Atmosphere. Pinger-5 and I had spent most of the day before bouncing formulas back and forth for the Thermal-Ram-Jet engine operation.

Thanks to the He/3 as fuel there would not be a radioactive exhaust trail. It was one of the Whale Calves by the name of Amelia that came up with the flight plan, when she figured that a very fast moving aircraft flying inside the Earth Atmosphere could navigate vertically point to point as they did a series Polar orbits low inside of the Earth's atmosphere.

To start out I asked the EAA flight line to help me push my now heavily modified Rutan Rocket EZ out to its starting point, I had my Flight Suit morph in to my Amelia Earhart brown jacket with leather flying helmet goggles and all. That's when I announce my plan to the crowed over the public address system to fly around the world in less than half an hour. With my starting point being Oshkosh then Chicago, New York, Paris, Moscow, Tokyo, Honolulu, Los Angeles, Denver, St. Louis then back to Oshkosh.

Then with the aid of the EAA's worldwide radio network to serve as official observers from all of the checkpoints to called in throughout my planned flight path. I climbed into the racer then morph my flying outfit into its Space suit format. Then with the Air boss permission I fired the liquid rocket fuel part of the Rutan Racer and launched myself south towards my first check point Chicago.

I used all of my liquid fuel to just get into the air. I was out of liquid rocket fuel before I got to the end of the runway, that's when I had to switch over to my He/3 Thermal-Ram-Jet -Engine, which made things move a lot faster. I morph my aerodynamic Cargo Bubble into its thermal ram-jet format. As soon as I started to channel my dynamic heat through the compressor the Thermal-Ram-Jet -Engine it increase its thrust over thousand percent.

I shot past the Adler Planetarium so fast that my aerodynamic wake opened doors and knocked over several of their underground exhibits. Then I continued full throttle south, to the Antarctic then back around the earth to New York, where I over flew the site of Roosevelt field which was the starting point for Charles Lindbergh and his Spirit of St. Louis, however it's now a major shopping center not an airport.

Then I used full power to fly south past the Antarctic again then around world again even faster to Paris, France. Due to the small size of my rocket plane I was actually able to fly through the middle level of the Eiffel Tower. I kind of made a mess out of their middle restaurant that was closed at that time of the day due to the early morning hour.

Then I continued south around the Earth again to Moscow, Russia where my wake vortex opened both of the main gates at Red Squire. By then I was really cooking my speed increased too were my airspeed indicator had to skip number to keep accurate. I was traveling a little faster than 500,000 miles per hour inside of the Earth's atmosphere! Let me tell you I had to really work at not being thrown out of the Earth's Atmosphere altogether.

As I continued flying south around the Earth again to Tokyo, Japan I made sure that I did not hit any of the ships in Tokyo harbor, however my wake turbulence did lower their water level as I over flew it. Then I continued south around the Earth again to Honolulu, Hawaii when I was able to make all the surfers happy with the granddaddy of all waves, thanks to my extremely high speed wake turbulence.

Then I continued flying south around the Earth again at maximum speed to Los Angeles, California where I made a point of flying under the Golden Gate Bridge.

I continued south around the Earth again to buzz Denver, Colorado where I don't think that anybody noticed my 500,000 miles per fly over as I continued my high speed flight south around the Earth again to St. Louis, Missouri where I was actually was able to fly through the St. Louis Arch this was not very easy as I was coming in from the north I had to make a hard bank to dodge buildings as well as angling my way through the middle of the main Arches structure.

The manager of the Antarctic base must have thought that I was doing figure 8's over her base. After my last checkpoint over St Louis, I started to shut down my Thermal Ram-Jet. I had managed to slow down to less than escape velocity after my last pass over the North Pole. Then it was simple matter to glide the rest of the way back to Oshkosh, where I made my touch down from the north twelve and a half minutes after my departure to the south, with the Airshow announcer tracking each of my over flight points.

The Air boss was really impressed his first question over the Public Address System was how I got my Rocket Racer to go that fast? I informed him as well as the entire crowd that I had the Swept Wing variant, actually it was all the fancy morph maneuvers that I did with the Cargo Bubble to create my Thermal-Ram-Jet-Engine. Then he was struck in the head by a fish falling from above and knocked off the speaker his speaker's platform.

Log Entry #94.
First official Flight:

Well it s been a long story but I am finally old enough to make my official Solo Flight to earn my FAA Pilot license.

I was using my Sabrina No. 3rd built Aircraft a Low Wing Zenith home build kit plane. That I had earned a couple of brownie points on by fixing its Aileron problem as I put the wings together.

The TRACON folks got more excited than I was when I did not request any high speed or altitude vectors. Pinger-5 as well as several of my other Whale/naut's friends were flying chase for me. They had divided the Airports landing pattern and stood ready to intercept me in the air if I had any problems.

As it turned out the flight was simple and uneventful, I made all the required radio calls as well as a textbook landing.

The local FAA check pilot had some concerns when he noticed that my Pilots license had provision on it for space flight. As well as flights to the Moon and the planets Mercury, Venus, Earth, Mars. Jupiter, Saturn, Uranus, Neptune, Pluto as well as all other know Kuiper object or Dwarf Planets.

Log Entry #95.
War Games UCAV style:

It didn t take long for the first challenge of my Command Commuters to happen, a friend from Grumman Aerospace want to do a fly off. His companies Unmanned Combat Aerial Vehicle, against any of my Sabrina No. 39 spacecraft.

To make it fair I called upon my Sabrina No. 39 herself my one and only prototype. I do not think it was a fair match, first of all Sabrina No. 39 had to fly in from orbit and hover over the aircraft Carrier for over an hour. As she was waiting for the navy to launch a single X-47b that Sabrina No. 39 followed for over another hour.

Her Command Computer put the UCAV in an electronic box that was about a foot larger than its airframe. Then Sabrina No. 39 kept it there no matter what the UCAV did in flight, high speed, maneuvering slow as well as high speed, as it seems the poor little UCAV can't even hover. Finally when Sabrina No. 39 realized that the UCAV had ran out of fuel she grabbed it with one of her space-junk-traps. As it turns out my Sabrina No. 39 spacecraft loves to play with the Navy's UCAV's.

For the next part of the test the Navy launched 94 different UCAV at Sabrina No. 39 at the same time. Sabrina No. 39 went into her full aerobatic mode and captured all 94 of them with her onboard space-junk-traps, in a matter of seconds. Sabrina No. 39 even figured out how to capture more than one of them at a time, without breaking them up.

Finally the navy stopped the test when Sabrina No. 39 tried to land on the aircraft carriers deck just like one of their X-47b's did. As always it took a lot of diplomacy to get her to give any of the X-47b's back. I finally figured out how, all I had to do was inform her that all the UCAV's were Government Propriety and She instantly deposited them all in a nice neat pile on the aft end of the aircraft carrier, as she was still hovering over it. Then she turned on all of her Airshow Smoke System and disappeared vertically back into Low Earth Orbit.

Log Entry #96.
"2003 Q Q47":

On a recent emergency supply trip to several of my Asteroid Ark Ships I finally ended up close enough to the Asteroid "2003 QQ47" that is due to make a very close pass at Earth in 2014.

As I came in close I noticed there was a large bill board type sign advertising a well-known hotel chain, installed on its flattest side. When I questioned Pinger-5 about it, she replied that everything was OK and it was just one of her ongoing business deals, if it falls through.

She would personally angle the asteroid so that none of the humans on Earth would see the billboard from the surface as it made its close fly-by. At the time I was sure that it did not have any tag-a-long want to bees, but as it turns out there was a house size tag-a-long, that found a spot in Russia.

Log Entry #97.
Slider Runs:

Pinger–5 figured how to make sliders runs, she would have to wait until the early morning hours of the night, and then she would call in a Humpback Whale size order, using my Communications System, with her credit card.

To the local White Castle in Des Plains, then she would navigate herself through the maze of caves under the City to surface in the Des Plains River near River Road where she could have her space suit morph into her single track driven whale scooter format.

Then she would pop up out of the river and travel west to the seven eleven to cut through their parking lot to come up beside the restaurants drive through. She would use her suits urban camouflage system to make herself look like a fire truck or other type of vehicle.

She also uses the same methods to get her midnight snack of Chilly dogs at the Super dog drive-in in Milwaukee Avenue and Devon Avenues in Chicago. My main concern it, as she consumes her snack it tastes so good that she tends to pounds her tail flukes on the ground.

This usually makes lots of cracks in the street as well as makes the locals think that it's an Earthquake. I know for a fact that she can get around on the ground and go anywhere she wants. I don't think that she has found her all you can eat sea food bar yet. As far as I can tell it only takes her one visit to cause a sea-food bar to close down and move to another location.

Log Entry #98.
Slow Orbit:

It took the development of the Boeing 787 with its new Rolls-Royce & General Electric Jet engines to make a non-stop around the world flight without being refueled in flight possible. According to my calculations I could modify its Airframe and both of its power plants to do a non-stop un-refueled around the world flight.

I managed to put my Father to work obtaining permission or me to over fly the various different countries. As there was no way that, even I could get my home built 787 to fly over 27,000 feet all by itself. If I did I would be out of the troposphere and out of the record books. To officially break the record I would have to stay in the troposphere and fly at subsonic speed all the way around the Earth without landing or taking on fuel in mid-air.

The Boeing Company had just obtained the Type Certificate for their 787 this is what made it a contender, for the record flight. The problem was they had not set up a production line and they needed the only prototype for their own flight-testing program.

It only took a couple of minutes for Pinger-5 to check her spare parts file to come up with all the basic parts I would need to build my own Boeing 787.

I plan to trace the original Earhart around the world route, by starting the flight in Oakland, California, then tracing Amelia's original route around the Earth near the equator. A total of 24,557 miles non-stop and non-re-fueled,

It only took a couple of hours for Pinger-5 to run down and acquire enough scraped pre-production section of the Boeing 787 for me to build my own airframe as well as engines. All of which was purchased and transported to the LEADER by way of my Space Elevator.

My plan was to assemble all the scraped parts as I was flying between Earth and Mars. I made it a point not to leave a trail of space junk by throwing small bits and pieces overboard. Having a Space ship the size of No. 40 that is large enough to bring along my entire zero-"G" work shop is a defendant plus.

Log Entry #99.
Pinger-5s Parts Plan:

The resale hanger was jammed to standing room only. As it was filled with most of the human ran Aerospace related companies that supplied Boeing with all of their aircraft parts.

I made my fancy entrance by flying my rocket-powered space suit to the middle of the stage. I made a perfect landing next to the speaker's microphone without melting its support boom, and then I morphed all of my flight gear into my official business dress complete with Sabrina Aviation epaulets on my shoulders.

Just as the whole audience started to close their gaping mouths, I noticed that everybody's eyeball were getting larger as the curtain open to reveal a small 38 ton Humpback Whale, in full Space suit mode. There was complete silence in the lecture hall as everybody was focus on the front of the space suits as it open to show Pinger-5's face, as she started to speak human without the need of a translations device.

Pinger-5 said "Hi humans my name is Pinger-5", I want to tell you about my best friend Sabrina. She wants to buy any spare Boeing 787 parts that you have to sell. So that she can build her own airplane.

She wants everything you have to sale, Airframe, Engine, as well as Avionics. As you know Pinger'5's base of operation is the giant underground lake system that she discovered under Chicago as well as most of Northern Illinois, so seeing her around town is not usual.

Yesterday as I going in my parent's front door I noticed myself running down the middle of my street with the rest of the track team from school. It seems that Pinger-5 had an urge for Pizza and was on the way to get some at the Pizza Parlor just north of my Parents' house.

She wanted to know what I thought of her new Urban-Camouflage-Program me running, running north on Oxford Ave. What makes it real interesting was the fact that I have never been on the track team at school. I still have no idea where she obtained the images of me to incorporate into her Urban Camouflage program.

Log Entry #100.
Duson's Sphere:

I had been trying to meet Professor Dyson for a long time. He was the visionary that come up with the idea of developing Space flight to the point where technology wise it would enable any of its citizen to use it like a public transit system.

Which is exactly what I have done? It has been a long and hard trips this time out. I not only had to move emergency supplies to my bases on Mars but to several of my Asteroid Ark Ships that I had in transient. This changed my flight plan to the point where I was able to recover the LM-4's ascent stage that was jettisoned into solar orbit, by the crew of Apollo 10 on May 24 at 10:25:29 UT. Snoopy's assent stage capture was very uneventful as all I had to do was to fly my Sabrina No. 40's lower cargo bay around it in flight and let my loadmaster program store it aboard.

I did make a personal inspection to make sure that Snoopy had burned all of its fuel, as it was in flight more that long enough to have the Sun's solar wind carry all of it away.

The top part of Snoopy did earn 4 records. It is the only one of the real flown Apollo lunar Module's that is still somewhere out in space. LM 4 "Snoopy" up to now is the first spacecraft ever launched from lunar orbit towards the Sun.

"Snoopy" up to now is farthest out in space of all spacecraft. In its heliocentric orbit it is as far as 2 AU's from earth during earth opposition. Apollo 10 and Apollo 12 share the record of the biggest number of real flight hardware objects left over by any of the Apollo missions three major objects.

Apollo 10's Lunar Module "Snoopy", Command Module "Charlie Brown" and S-IVB 505. So, Snoopy really is a quite lonesome record-holder. Having Pinger-5 along made all my navigational rendezvous problems go away.

I had to use extended aerodynamic flight inside of the Martian atmosphere to cook all the carbon fiber aircraft skin. This made the trip longer than usual with this giving me lots more time than usual to take apart all the test stands and reconnect all the parts of the 787's airframe all by myself as I was traveling under zero" conductions.

As it turn out the new generation of jet Rolls-Royce Trent 1000 & General Electric Gen x 53,000 lbs. /235.8 ken engines seems to be made up with a large number large of induction fan blades. I made a note about it to the FAA in my certification request I think it should to be called Fan-turbo instead of a Turbo-fan.

I managed to leave room inside the fuselage for my Command POD as I still plan to connect its fly by wire system to the instrument panel in my Command POD. Pinger-5 got her flippers out of joint when she discovered that I did not leave enough room for her inside the Sabrina 787.

That is until she realized that I could not make any eating stops, this made her declared that she would fly formation with me all the way around the world as long as she could stop at her favorite feeding grounds.

This made Pinger-5 wonder if she could find an open White Castle in Singapore, I informed her that I know for a fact that there was not one at Howland Island.

I had tried for most of this trip to purchase tickets to the Dyson dinner that was being held in Rosemount Illinois. Pinger-5 got me a ticket in a couple of seconds using her personal contacts.

It took the development of the Boeing 787 outfitted with its new Fan-Turbo engines, according to my calculation I should modify this Airframe and its two power plants to do a non-stop un-refueled around the world flight.

I managed to put my Father to work obtaining permission or me to over fly the various different countries. As there was no way that, I could get my home built 787 to fly over 27,000 feet. If I did, I would be out of the Troposphere and out of the record books. To officially break the record I would have to stay in the Troposphere and fly at subsonic speed all without landing or taking on fuel in mid-air.

Boeing had just obtained the Type Certificate for their 787 this is what made it a contender, with all the requirements, the problem was they had not set up a production line and they needed the only prototype for their own flight-testing program.

It only took a couple of minutes for Pinger-5 to check her spare parts file to come up with all the basic test cell parts I would need to build my own Boeing 787. I plan to trace the original Earhart route, a total of 24,557miles all non-stop and not re-fueled. Aircraft construction was not a problem in my zero-"G" workshop. My biggest problem was detaching all the spare parts from their inspection stands then recombine them all into a 787 airframe, the same thing with all the left over test stand parts that I had to place in the correct locations as I put the Turbo-fan engines together.

It was interesting to note the extremely large amount of bypass air that the Turbo-Fan was moving, to make it more understandable I think I will call it a Fan-Turbo instead.

I always laugh when I remember the first time I was flunked on my A&P test because I did not have enough upper arm strength, with a zero gravity work shop I have no problem holding a very heavy part while at the same time attaching it in place. Time building it from all the spare test stand parts that I got to buy from Pinger-5.

Pinger-5 and I were on the way back to Earth, being able to maneuver at extremely high speeds inside the Earth Atmosphere has become routine with established high-speed circular deceleration tracts where my Space ships can have all the room needed to slow down.

When I finally bought the ticket to the Dinner on the internet, I was still trapped in my deceleration maneuver doing very large high-speed figure 8's over the Pacific Ocean.

Pinger-5 figured out how to get them for me as the National Space Society is not easy to deal with. According to my Command Computer, there was no way for me to make the dinner if I stayed on the flight plan so. To make the Dinner, took manual control of the ship and I had to manually fly her through all the changes in the flight plan.

I informed the FAA of my intensions, I also notified the Air Force what I was up to so as not to set off any UFO interceptions. So with a quick flight over the North Pole, then down across Canada to Lake Michigan where I extended my landing gear and adjusted my wheel trucks to skim the surface of the giant lake to cool my airframe and cure my glow in the dark problem.

As soon as the surface of Sabrina No. 40 was at a relative temperature. I extended my lift-fans and started playing helicopter so that I could get into the low altitude helicopter lane that goes directly to Midway Airport, then to manually fly my Sabrina No. 40 space ship to a landing in the dark empty field next to the International Hotel where the NSS Convention was being held.

I stopped my Sabrina No. 40 moving just as I was close enough to put one of my boarding ramps on to the parking garage roof. I modified my urban camouflage mode and made my space ship look like part of the hotel, I usually land close and put my nose wheel elevator down as close as I could to the main door this was not possible due to the extreme closeness of O'Hare Airport.

My friend Dennison had set up one of his Mobile Exhibit that showed the size of everything for real. As I started to morph my Sunday go to meeting space suit in to one of my school outfits then Pinger-5 suggested that I do it up big with a fancy diner gown. What do you think I replied, try this she answered as she stared to transmit directions to my Space suits morph controls?

My top blouse cover started to change into a low cut strapless evening dress, as a nice touch she even gave me a set of command epaulets with

Sabrina Aviation emblems all in black lace. The final touch was when the lower half of my space suit had just finished changing in to a moderately length black skirt with lace hoses, and high heels shoes with enough hold downs on them to mount rocket units, all in black.

Then Pinger-5 said, "I would like to see him to put that in a Dyson's Sphere". I had to force myself to walk normal in Earths 1-"G" I kept trying to fly and float in the atmosphere after all, the high speed maneuvering that I had just finished doing it felt real nice to only have to worry about one "G".

The dinner and lecture were great I even got to meet Buzz Aldron who reminded everyone that he was the second human to set foot on the Moon. It was also nice to hear N.A.S.A.'s plans to go back to the Earth's Moon, and then to Mars. I did not have the heart to tell him about my adventures.

Log Entry #101.
Pinger-5 & Operations:

As soon as Pinger-5 learned how to talk to humans she discovered how useful we can be, she has always had a big problem telling fact from fiction, and she hoped that Star-Trek and Star-Wars were real until she discovered what "a long time ago and on a planet far-far away" really meant.

She did manage to stop the entire Whale Killing operations on the entire Earth just by having all the Whales stay away from their killer boats. After all of the Whaling Companies went bankrupt she bought up all their Killer Ships as well as processing boats and launch them into the Sun, then I asked her why the Sun. She reminded me that it was originally my idea.

Another one of Pinger-5's enterprises was helping the humans in Florida to get rid of unwanted Snakes, Fish and even Wild Boars that had taken over the Everglades National Park.

Pinger-5 had recruited several bands of hungry Polar Bears from my Polar Bear camp then she made an agreement with them to only eat the problem food sources. She would first program extra containment barriers under the full length of one of my Sabrina No. 40 space ships, to keep them from becoming an even bigger problem.

Then she would load it up with several thousand of her hungry Polar Bear buddies, and then Pilot the Sabrina No 40 space ship to the largest swamp in Florida. Only to make a feather soft vertical landing, being careful not to scare any live food source away.

Then she would adjust the landing gear to where the bottom of the hull was just above the surface of the swamp. Then put in place all her containment barriers and release her hordes of hungry Polar Bears into the Swamp just under the space ship.

She maintained strict control and only allowed the Polar Bears to eat the problem food sources. So I had to ask her how it was doing.

Pinger-5 replied wonderful, the Florida Fish & Wildlife Commission pays me $6.25 a pound for each Boa constrictor, $3.90 a pound for each wild Boar, in all it took her almost half an hour for her to tell me her current payment rate.

Pinger-5 said, that to date she hasn't lost a single Polar Bear to Pythons, although several have been wounded by Wild Boars. Pinger-5 deal with the Florida Fish & Wildlife Commission has expanded to there she is using six of my Sabrina No. 40 ships. She is currently having them leap frog their way across the Everglades so far she has cleaned out the Polar Bear camp all by herself it's to the point now where she has to rent hungry Polar Bears from local Zoos.

She said that the biggest complaint was the heat, and that she has a cold chamber where each different Polar Bear can bring their captured prey so that it can be declared foreign as well as weighed before she gives them permission kill and eat it.

As I was making the north to south approach to the top of the Mars Space Elevator on Phobos, my surface scanners noticed a checkerboard square structure on the surface of Mars near its North Pole. So I peeled off from my approach and made a soft landing on the surface with my nose wheel elevator a few feet from the south side of the building. As soon as the Nose Gear Elevator doors opened I recognized the building as the main Operations Building that was at the South Pole.

Where I rescued almost 500 stranded airmen and pilots, a couple of years ago, it still had the claw marks that my prototype docking tube had made on the main door. I made the mistake of opening the main door only to have an avalanche of spent zebra mussel shell came dumpling out onto the surface of Mars. Then I noticed that the entire building was jammed full of spent zebra mussel shells. At a later time when I finally got a chance to ask Pinger-5 about it.

She said that it was OK the whole building as a free-be. I noticed that Pinger-5 was landing lots of equipment high up in the Rocky Mountains in a location that did not have any road for humans for over a hundred miles around. I noticed several hundred of my largest cargo PODs were set up along the top of the ridge line in the usual club house format, as it turned out this was operation "Belly Slide". Where she had built a special resort for whales only so that they could spend the day sliding down snow covered slopes without any humans to worry about.

I started to notice lots of six story abandon hotels with empty swimming pools all located at Longitude and Latitude interception points all over the surface of Mars, in most cases it was the only structure in sight. Pinger-5 referred to them as transplants from Earth, she first started transplanting old hotels that were contracted to be demolished from orbit by her Ballistic Impactor Project. Pinger-5 had figured a way to move the whole building to Mars and place it in a location where it could be used as a navigation aid.

When I asked her why she referenced a Chicago based radio talk shows lengthy discussion about what NASA's latest surface rover operation was going to find as it explored the surface of Mars, up close and personal.

Although I can't fault her last week when a major snow storm closed all the airports in Europe without a seconds notice, instantly there were hundreds of east bound airliners with not enough fuel to go anywhere.

She came up with the best instant fix ever, on her command she ordered all of the available Sabrina No. 40 Space ships to form up in the Atlantic Ocean just west of the Azores she directed their descent and docking them all together to form an instant aircraft carrier large enough to handle 747's and A380's She not only directed each airliner to a safe landing, she also stored them in all the various cargo bays that she could morph.

She even sorted each airliner as to its destination so that when she ran out of aircraft to save. And undocked the space ships where sent to the correct country of its destination, the raging show storm did not even slow her down, on that day most of the Trans-Atlantic human passenger got to where they were going earlier than expected. Of course, she did get most of the Airport managers mad at her, as she filled up all their available parking spaces. On each of their home tarmacs. As well as all of their, closed runways before they had the time to remove any of the snow.

On another hand, I have also discovered that Pinder-5 has gone into business with several PODS of Blue Whales destroying unwanted human buildings with Direct Meteor hits. To make moneyPinger-5 uses large special shaped Water Ice, projectiles designed to hit the exact breaking point on the human made structure.

I also found out about their Space Golf games where each Whale launches a single Golf Ball from Low Earth Orbit to get it to impact directly into the hole of a particular golf course. They give each other extra points if they can arrange for all the Golf Balls to land at the same instant. In all there are seven different types of Whales in my employee, they are the Orcas, Blues, Fins, Grays, Sperms, Humpbacks and Beluga I started out with a few of each.

Log Entry #102.
First Group Out:

As I was talking to the space experts that were at the National Space Societies Convention near Chicago. I though back a couple of years ago to when I moved my first group of space colonist to the Moon.

My plan was for them to get settled at my rocket base in Texas that was located at the foot of my first Earth based Space Elevator. Then when each city became self-sufficient. I would move them up the elevator through the LEADER that was my anchor point in Geosynchronous Orbit.

I am determine not to make the same mistake that humans made when they created Ghost Towns, as in my settlement plan each city will remain mobile as well as under the planet's surface as well as being able to move to mew locations as needed.

From there to a large Asteroid Ark Ship, then off to the Moon to a pre-built location in one of my underground structures near the base of my Lunar Space Elevator shaft that was all ready for new arrivals.

Each Asteroid Ark Ship is a one of a kind structure I gave each one its own model number. The ship that I decided to use for this trip was my 19th Asteroid Ark Ship. She is a potato shaped iron asteroid that's three miles wide two miles high, and two mile long in size.

At the time this was the largest Asteroid Ark Ship that I had, I only had one hole in it, where the docking hatch was located. This was to enable me to pressurize its Atmosphere up to 15 Pounds per square inch so that I could match the Earths sea level air pressure wise.

I had an internal rotating section to Transport Plants & Animals that need gravity to survive. I also build in rotating rest rooms that were fully equipped with regular gravity operated toilets & showers so as not to make life hard on any of my space colonist.

At the time, none of my Command Computers had enough experience too safely move a filly loaded Asteroid Ark Ship, so this made it my problem to fly. This was not the first loaded Asteroid Ark Ship that I had piloted to the Moon however due to the variable numbers of object that would be moving around inside of it as well as the entire colonist constantly shifting personal stuff around inside. I knew from the start that it would have lots of problems maneuvering.

Anybody could move large Machinery like tunnel boring Machines, and Space Elevator shafts sections around in an Asteroid Ark Ship. As luck would have it, I was on the LEADER when I got to word that the first of my settlement cities was ready for transport. Therefore, I unplugged my Command POD, put it into one of my spare elevator cars, and traveled down the Earth Space Elevator, over all it was not a bad trip it just took three days.

We had the first transpiration meeting were I let the whole colony know that their Digestion was "City Alpha". Upon hearing the news everybody cheered, another annoying thing was they all kept asking me if my father was going to do this or that. None of them had a clue that I was in charge.

To prove it I pulled out my communications necklace and called the Command Computer to give the order to move out, there was stark silence when all the elevator cars started to disconnect from its city format and start moving. It took less than half an hour for the first elevator car to start its assent, and then the count up started at every mile marker all 33,000 of them.

Due to the acceleration, everybody was still held at one "G". This is the point in the trip up that I Issued everybody their first Sabrina Aviation Space Suit complete with how to operate classes, my morph controls really got their attention.

The purpose of the morph suit was to save your lives in the event of a depressurization you can also program it to change into any different color of style of clothing that you want.

From that, point on it was like being at a Science Fiction Ball, as I am not into Science Fiction but, if you could name it somebody programmed it into the morph systems control.

For the next 72 hours I helped by making myself available to talk to everybody about living in zero-"G" I made it a point to program a "Snoopy" helmet into all the space suit of all the long hairs, I even made it a priority one command to everybody that had hair longer than mine. I told them that under zero "G" all their personal property that was not held down would move around inside of their living space with the aid of all the streams of air that had to move throughout the Spacecraft to keep everybody from suffocating.

They had to not only to nail everything down but they had to keep it nailed down for the whole trip. I also made it a point to show them where their lost and found box was located in their local air moment system. In addition, I told them that when they lose any of their personal property they would definitely find it in their "lost and found box".

The trip up the elevator was wonderful until I stopped the first elevator car just under the LEADER. When everything went to zero" G" for the first time, which turned everything inside out, I think that first group of space colonist still talk about their first full stop.

It took less than 5 minutes for my Command Computer to populate my Sabrina No. 19 the automated system moved the entire underground "City Alpha" into the Asteroid Ark Ship like it had been doing it for years, the fuel and engine modules were the last to come aboard. I flew in my next in line Sabrina No. 10 space ship and installed my Command POD, then I position two of my Aero-Spike-Rocket motors one on each of the outer doors and started checking the flight control systems.

I charged all of the attitude rockets, with everything working perfectly, I hit the release button and just like that, "City Alpha" was on its way to the Moon. I let Sabrina No. 19 continue on its original trajectory for the first hour just to give everybody time to take care of anything still floating free. The ship had only been in flight for less than an hour. As I moved Sabrina No. 19 forward all the loose stuff hit the back wall and bounced all the way up to the nose of the ship.

This caused a shift in the ships center of mass that caused Sabrina No.19 to do a zero "G" Lomcevak, however it was a very slow speed Lomcevak due to all the mass. As we were still close to the LEADER in geosynchronous orbit we had plenty of room to figure things out. Just like I was doing an Airshow Lomcevak all I had to do was put the correct figures into the flight computer to get the nose of the ship going where I wanted it to go.

The problem was it took me more than one try before Sabrina No. 19 stopped looping with its nose pointing on the correct trajectory towards the Moon. I called everybody together for their first in-flight meeting to have everything fastened down. So that I could perform a simple navigation maneuver with-out hitting somebody with a projectile child or 50 pounds of their toys.

Then the questions really started coming in have you seen this or that? All I do is point to the nearest lost and found box, the most often asked question was "can I space walk on the outside surface of the ship?" and "When are you going to start spinning us to make gravity?" my standard answer was always "No".

It wasn't a full minute until I had to rescue my first long hair from an airlock. It was the usual problem his trailing hair got caught in the workings of the hatch. I had to get into the hatches programming to have it reverse all its workings just to make the hatch let go of some guy's long hair. As soon as the long hair was released, I would personally program a snoopy helmet on his head with a non-removal snap.

It took less than half an hour for the first "lost and found box" to fill up to where it set of its emergency alarm. Then they all started to go off all over the Space Ark at 5 and 10 minute intervals. They would jam up as fast as I could empty them. It took two full days for the Colonists spinal column to stretch, and then all of a sudden everybody started to bang their heads on the hatches.

I know for a fact that if any of my Orca Whale/naut's were in command at that moment they would have just eaten him on the spot, just to get them off the space ship. Despite the fact that humans taste bad, have too many bones, and are covered with cloth.

The pull out maneuver from Geosynchronous Orbit that took Sabrina No. 19 to the Moon was not as bad as I thought it would be, needless to say thing did get better. Four days later when I fire the retro-rocket to slow down to Lunar Orbital Speed, it was hardly noticed.

Later I had to take it very slowly as I docked Sabrina No. 19 at my Lunar Space Elevator number one and down loaded everybody to their new home under the surface of the Moon.

The good news was it only took another 12 hours to move the Elevator train down to its new home, under the surface of the Moon. After all the moving was done and everything had stopped, where it was in the middle of my first Lunar City.

I finally got a chance to check the main lost and found box for "Lunar Alpha". I discover several pounds of nickels, dimes, quarters, and pennies. In 1/6th lunar gravity all the air filter will remain open.

Now I let my rookie Whale/naut's handle this operation. In addition I also require that each city stay in zero "G" after leaving the LEADER for 1 hour just to let everybody adapt to their new weightless environment. For most of my space colonist this was their first exposure to no gravity before their first zero "G" trip.

Log Entry #103.
Knock It Off:

Pinger-5 and I were on the way to Mars when I was at the low end of my acceleration dive when I made a normal request to the closest ground controller tower only to get the reply.

"Knock it off Sabrina you know we can't count that high without using all of our finger & toes. So I used some of my natural born math skills to tell him exactly how fast I was really moving, at this time as well as how fast I would be going as I made my Direct to Mars Maneuver.

I thought that it was real nice of me to help test their machinery.

Log Entry #104.
First Calf Flight:

Pinger–5 and I were having a discussion as to when the best time was to get a Whale/Calf involved in spaceflight school my usual answer should has always been as soon as they can reach the rudder pedals.

Personally I didn't have a rudder pedal problem as I have always known how to build the Pilots seat closer. When I realized that this new born mammal would not have that problem as I was thinking about it my mind wandered back to when.

I was only 8 years old and I was helping the Experimental Aircraft Association to get their Young Eagle program up and running. As the story goes, when the head of the program was explaining it to the Secretary of Transportation. She was intrigued to find out that all that was required legally was the written permission of the child's parents, to get a free airplane ride.

She thought about it for a few moments then she decided to run the problem backwards. With a grin on her face, she asked if "she could have a reverse young eagle flight if she could get her mother to sign the flight form", her answer was yes. So she walked over to the other side of the room and asked her mother a much older woman to sigh the prototype Young Eagle flight form.

This started the ball rolling as the Secretary of Transpiration of the entire United States Government had just turn in the first Young Eagle Flight request form. And requested the first reverse Young Eagle Flight and at the same moment she requested to be assigned her Child Pilot for her first airplane flight.

I could see the panic on the Project Managers face as he looked across the crowed room. Only to look me straight in the eye, then give me the universal hand jester of come over here now! So that he could personally explain to me exactly what was going on.

Then he officially asked me to be the Pilot in command, my answer was that I did not care how old the child was I would be glad to fly her so that I could add her flight to my scorecard. I figured that it could not be worse than flying my own Parents around in Canada, so at the time I was too young to even get into a Pilot's test in the United States.

My next problem was who I could borrow an airplane from that had more than one seat in it, as the only airplane that I had at the time was my single seat Sabrina one, which I had built myself.

With a quick look around the room, we both noticed the president of the Cirrus Aircraft Company standing there with the keys to his brand new Cirrus 20 airplane in his hand. I reach up and shook his elbow when he bent over and looked down at me. I asked him if I could use his brand new airplane to give the Secretary of Transpiration the first young Eagle Ride.

All of a sudden the whole room went silent as all that anybody could hear was the sound of EAA Big Wigs signing the approval slips. I played my part well you should have seen the look on his face when I took command of the first Circus 20 that anybody had ever seen, this was the first production carbon fiber airplane with its very own built in Ballistic Parachute.

Luckily the owner himself, walked us all out to his brand new plane as I had no idea what a Cirrus 20 even looked like, you should have seen the look on his face when I asked him for his flight manual and weight and balance chart. Then I proceeded to do a full regulation walk around and per-flight inspection, due to my small stature checking the Lunkenheimer Valves at the fuel sumps was not a problem.

I just kept reading thing to do from the owners official check list. I had to ask the Secretary of Transpiration her exact body weight so that I could calculate the Cirrus 20's Weight & Balance point. I amazed everybody when I did all the calculations in my head. However the aircraft owner used his official chart too pronounced my calculation correct.

I think that he was amazed that a 8 year old girl could read much less understand all the big words. As we finally got into the cockpit, everybody made a big deal when I turned off the ballistic parachute, as we would not be flying outside of the landing pattern it could not be used.

The flight went off without a hitch, afterwards during the signing ceremony everybody made a big deal when I signed the Secretary of Transpirations flight certificate as the Child Pilot in Command. The answer Pinger-5's Question turned out to be when the Whale Calf could control the spacecraft.

Despite my Fathers best efforts the application of my FAA pilot's license was permanently put on hold until I was old enough, however I was given permission to fly at American Airshows as long as started flying over 50 miles high or in Canada.

Log Entry #105.
Mc-Rib Run:

I finally got an invite from the crew of the International Space Station to stop by for milk and cookies. That is if I would be willing to bring them lunch as well. They even included everybody's lunch order with their message. As I was reading down their list I thought that it was a good thing that the first thing I built on the LEADER was a very large food court, that was open all the time. Fried chicken, Seafood, Chinese to go, even special made up hamburgers.

I decided to do it when I noticed that Mc Ribs were also on their list I knew that I had to make it happen for them. The first thing I had to do was to let my watch-commander know what I was up too. Then with a quick trip to the food court next to the airlock I turned in their order as I floated from Restaurant to Restaurant flashing my ID.

I stored it all in my Cargo Bubble as I paid for everything I even doubled the Mc-Rib order I even added extra milk shakes and extra-large orders of French Fries. I even remember the extra salt, ketchup and pepper packets everything went into my Cargo Bubble one food order at a time.

I noticed that most of my crew members had started to look at me as if I were Pinger-5 going for a night time snack. Finally when my Cargo Bubble was almost as large as I was, I let my operation chief know what I was going to go out for lunch.

I barely made it through the air-lock so that I could check out one of my human maneuvering units, for the trip down to High Earth Orbit where

I personally returned the repaired I.S.S. to its original location. After my repair crews had fixed it after my last visit.

With all the water damage not to mention the large 5 person size exit hole that I had to cut into it, just to get everybody out after it was moved into the "Leaders" main space hanger. I grabbed the next unit out of the Human Maneuvering Unit cabinet. I started to program my well-used flight path as I morph my space suit into operation then opened the outer airlock, stepped out and started my descent down to High Earth orbit.

As usual, the fall away maneuver from the LEADER is a lot more exciting when you don't have a space ship wrapped around yourself. The trip down was as normal as you can get, I had to use my human maneuvering unit's flight computer, as a structure as small as the Space Station, is not easy to see visually until your right on top of it.

This time my approach was a lot safer as the Atomic oxygen cloud as well as orbiting space junk were not a problem. My reprogrammed He/3 scrubbers were working fine as they recovered all the stray gas molecules as soon as the space station expelled them.

As I was getting closer to my destination I could see that all of the solar panels were still in place even though their only use was as radar targets. I could still see where all the electrical fires and electrical short outs were located. All of which were not reparable even with the help of my own repair crews. So I gave them a couple of my He/3 electrical generators to satisfy all their electrical needs.

The addition of one of my docking modules made my arrival a piece of cake. Pinger-5 is still working on the contract but it felt nice to be inside a full pressurized to 15 P.S.I. space station without worrying about an explosive decompression event.

I tethered my H.M.U. outside and transitioned my way through the airlock to the I.S.S.'s main meeting room, where I morph my Space suit into its flight suit format I even had its morph system to start flashing a Sabrina's Space Food service sign on my back. You should have seen all the drooling with the arrival of the Space Station first order out lunch.

All of N.A.S.A.'s finest were gathered around me as if I where Santa Clause on Christmas Eve. Each hungry Astronaut was chanting their food order, and the Mc-Rib eaters were the loudest ones. As all the Astronauts gathered around me the Mc-Rib eaters were most restless, I made sure to feed them first as I passed out all the lunch orders luckily I had remembered the "First Mc-Rib rule of survival always double all the orders when Mc-Ribs are concerned." Therefore, the discovery of lots of extra Mc-Ribs really made their day.

The luncheon reminds me of an Orca feeding frenzy with food wrappers everywhere and all of the lost and found boxes jammed up with small sections of French Fries and spent salt, pepper and ketchup packets. Over all they did fork over some left over space shuttle, cookies as well as a plastic bag full of cold freeze dried milk.

I thought about leaving them a spare HMU then I noticed they didn't have a space suit between them that would make the trip back to the LEADER in geosynchronous orbit. I even hauled back all their trash to the LEADER.

At our next staff meeting I decided to make some kind of messenger service between the LEADER and the International Space Station, as it's always nice to be neighborly.

Log Entry #106.
Amelia's Honor Flight:

At dawn Pinger–5 and I were still in low Earth orbit installing my Command POD and putting the finishing touches on my Sabrina 787. That I was going to use to finally break the around the world without re-fueling record. As well as reenact, Amelia Earhart attempted round the world flight when she was lost in the middle of the Pacific Ocean.

The retractable landing gear was a real pain to put together but I finally made it work. Pinger-5 was a big help when I needed to move my wing and fuselage sections together for final assembly. Having a 38-ton helper is a real plus, as lack of gravity doesn't mean lack of mass. You have got to face it a full size Boeing 787 is a little on the large size for a 16 year old girl to move around all by herself.

I finally sacked out and did not set my wake up alarm, as I wanted to get as much sleep as possible. I knew that tomorrow would be a very real long day. Doing the De-Orbit burn to land at Oakland Airport was a first time experience for my Command Computer so I had to do it myself. I have already calculated that their runway was long enough to get my fully loaded Boeing 787 off the ground.

With the aid of my built in Lift-Fans I made a perfect vertical landing in the empty field just south of their control tower. I set up shop and waited until the Government Officials to show up. Meanwhile, I had Sabrina No. 40 taxi over to the tarmac and lower my Homebuilt Boeing 787 to where its tires could touch the ground for the first time. Pinger-5 promptly took my Sabrina No. 40 back to the original touch down point and activated its Urban-Camouflage-Program to make my Sabrina No. 40 look like a set of aircraft hangers.

As soon as the certification folks for the local MIDO show up, they started to do the full inspection on my home built 787 and issued me my taxi permit I was finely in business. I went through all the flight requirements, I took off and performed all the required maneuvers needed too earned my Sabrina 787 her unlimited flight rating. Their human test pilot was concerned that my fan-turbots were not putting out enough noise as I ran them up to full power for the first time. They were really wanted to know how I had heat treated all of the carbon fiber aircraft skin.

So I told him extended aerodynamic flight inside of the Martian atmosphere. My next problem was buying all the Jet-A jet fuel that I needed to fill up and wet down my wings for the first time. I was nice I even put out a press release telling the world what I was up too.

With everything said and done, I climbed up my air stairs to walk into my Command POD so that I could get everything moving. I retracted my personal air stairs so that the officials could put their personal seals on to prove that I had not landed or exited the aircraft. I turned on my nose camera and started my recording that would prove that I had made the flight. Then I called the Oakland airport Control tower to request my take off clearance and open my flight plan.

The controllers seemed surprise when I informed him that my distention was the Oakland Airport, and that I was reenacting Amelia's last flight. I asked my Command Computer to show me all the weight & balance data as well as the fuel storage plan. So I fired up both of my newly built jet engine, to start my slowest orbit of the Earth to date.

It only took me a few minutes to program all the information in to my Home built 787's Command computer, then only seconds to program it to make all of my air traffic calls to the Federal Aviation Administration. All I had to do was to say the word start and my command computer did all the talking for the whole trip.

Pinger-5 turned off Sabrina No. 40s Urban-Camouflage-Program and launched herself to where she was flying formation with me 200 yards off my right wing tip. My first "Heavy" take off was normal with plenty of room to abort, I retracted my landing gear then turned south west to be on the direct course to Burbank, California a distance of 283 miles.

I set my best cruise speed of 570 mph so it only took 33 minutes to do a low pass down the full length of the Burbank airports main runway, my fuel burned instruments had hardly moved. I've completed the first leg of my Amelia memorial flight. Metro Oakland Airport in Oakland, California to Bob Hope Airport in Burbank, CA. the weather was clear. So far my flight was uneventful, next leg of trip was Burbank to Tucson.

Then off to the Tucson, Airport with a quick pull up and a slight turn towards, New Orleans, Louisiana a distance of 1,070 miles which only took a little less than two hours. With a prearranged and approved low pass down their main runway with a slight turn to the southeast.

An hour later I was doing the same thing to the main runway at Miami International in Florida with nothing out of the ordinary to report except I noticed that my fuel gauge had started to go down. Next up was the leg from Miami Florida to the Luis Munoz Marin International airport in San Juan, Puerto Rico a distance of 908 miles.

This was the first time I got feet wet in my 787 as this would be a two hour flight too my next check point. Pinger-5 decided to peel off and get something to eat in the Caribbean Sea, I cautioned her to make sure that she was hitting a deep spot as she made her feeding dive. She was able to strike the surface of the sea without making a big splash.

A couple of minutes later she called me on my communication neckless to inform me that I had lots of help and to check out the surface at a certain location. As I passed over it I noticed a large number of Whales on the surface of the Caribbean Sea all formed up into an arrow shape pointing the direction of San Juan Puerto.

With a prearranged approach I buzzed the full length of their wet and rain soaked runway. Pinger-5 was still feeding and made a comment about not wanting to fly through the rainy weather and get wet. Then I pulled up to continue south to Cumana, Venezuela which was now less than an hour away.

As Pinger-5 formed up with me we continued to fly formation all the way down the coast of South America. I kept buzzing my way down each of my checkpoints main runways at Mariscal Antonio Jose De Sucre in Cumana, J.A. Pengel International in Zanderij, Suriname, Suriname to Fortaleza, Brazil, Fortaleza to Natal that was still in Brazil. I had just spent six hour flying point to point that Amelia had spent days doing on her flight.

Flying with the South Atlantic on one side of the 787 and all the lush jungle of the Amazon on the other side really got Pinger-5. She kept dropped out of formation to take a close look with all her sensors turned up full power I was amazed when she made the connection that it was like a reef only on land with lots of different animals instead of fish.

As soon as I pulled up from the main runway at Natal, Brazil, I pointed my 787's nose east to Gao, Mali French West Africa 1,130 miles across the South Atlantic, which was only a two-hour jump for me. Pinger-5 finally asked me her first Amelia Earhart Question, "she wanted to know why Amelia was afraid of the water how come she did not have floats in her airplane."

I answered that "I don't think that she was afraid of water she did not have an airplane that could fly very far without adding more fuel." After making landfall, I made my required low pass down their runway #18. Then I turned back towards the east for leg eleven the 99-mile flight from St. Louis, Senegal to Dakar, Senegal we started to have our first bad weather.

So at Ga, Mali I got into Africa, thing started to get dark, ground controller were few and far between the language barriers made my translation computer have kittens and quit. It was a good thing that Pinger-5 was around to translate for me because all the way across Africa everybody wanted me to land and have my aircraft checked for contraband.

Pinger-5 took over and made the talk to all the humans on the ground for me, it seems that this part of the world has always had a language problem if you could not talk to them in their language you were the enemy not to be trusted. So at first contact Pinger-5 started talking to them in their native language without the need of my translator. She kept it up all the way across Africa later I asked her how many human languages did you know how to speak. Her answer was blunt and short "All of Them."

As we did the Check points across Chad, Sudan, Ethiopia and finally to the eastern part of Pakistan a mere six and a half hours for me. Pinger-5 kept hearing lots of radio calls from people who want to escort us to their base for a full ransom, on a couple of occasions Pinger-5 got into a very interesting dog fight with a single engine home built fighter type aircraft.

She had to do some very fancy flying to scare her attacker into ejecting from their fighter plane before she could catch it with her space junk trap. She showed me pictures from her cargo bay to see if I could identify the offending fighter planes. It looked like something I would expect to find in the fly-mart at Oshkosh. I have heard that most of Africa is dangerous to foreigners I don't want to risk getting kidnapped, killed, or robbed by any of their locals.

I could see 'towns' from the air, mainly only with dirt roads, but for the airport runway. I usually had to use my GPS to find the Earhart original runway before I could buzz it.

Pinger-5 was still monitoring all the radio traffic and listening for what was going on ahead of us she kept hearing the same radio commercial about a special dinner that was served locally called Tsehbi sega which is a spicy lamb dish. The bottom line was she had to stop and get some so she made another of her classic food runs at a local restraint. Over all she did not like it because of all the sand.

All I could do was keep doing all the planned checkpoints the rest of the way across Africa, India, Asia, Indonesia, Australia, and New Guinea, Pinger-5 did want to know what happened to the old one. This was the first time that she had made any kind of comment, about the size of the Earth.

She made several more feeding dives after all if I weighed 38 tons I would have to eat as much as Pinger-5 does. As soon as I made my turn back to the northern hemisphere. As I watched Pinger-5 impacting the Pacific to feed again, I decided to take a break and let the command computer fly for a while, I actuality got out of my pilots seat I made myself a late dinner in my flight kitchen checked with my 787 Command Computer then settled down in my pilot's seat for the long dark flight across this section of Amelia's flight path.

Throughout my flying carrier I have always been able to stay in my pilot's seat for the whole flight. As always there was the mid Pacific Typhoon that was tracking around in front of my intended flight path. The large Typhoon had started to move back south and would have been straight in my path when I got to Howland Island the next morning.

Pinger-5 put out the word that "Sabrina the Invincible" was in need of Whale/naut's to attack a large Typhoon storm. She cranked up her communication's system to empty out most of the Whale Calves that were in the Whale School.

Because she needed the whales to figure entrance and exit point to help fly all of the Sabrina No. 39 & 40 space ships that she would need during her Typhoon peeling party. To kill off Typhoon Patty, she got all the No. 39 as well as the No. 40 ships that were available for the job and put them too work.

With the aid of most of the new born Whale/Calf's to punch large supersonic holes in the wall of Typhoon Patty, and then peeling down the sides of her eye to convert Patty back into a Sunny day. Next morning this is why so many of my Whale/naut's were waiting for me at Howland Island.

As soon as I flew past the Earth's Terminator I realized that today I am going to over fly Howland Island. This was nothing new to me as several years ago I first tested my Sabrina No. 40's instrument section during my first attempt to find the wreckage of Amelia's Lockheed 10e. All the time spent planning, preparing and the weeks that I sent in zero "G" building my very own 787 have all came up to this moment. As soon as I sat back down in my pilot's seat Pinger-5 was gone for her breakfast feeding.

She instantly power dove her Sabrina No. 40 Space ship ahead of me into the Pacific Ocean. My navigation system had my exact location pegged down to within inches and feet. As I was looking out over the South Pacific Ocean, with no land in sight anywhere. It gave me a sense of just how small and insignificant my 787 was. I have never worried about getting lost, as I have a GPS and all of my other modern navigational equipment needed to guide me.

However, I cannot imagine trying to navigate the way that Amelia and Fred did using just a clock, sextant, star chart and a compass. As I near Howland Island at 50 miles out, I begin descending as well as slowing down if that's not an easy trick to be able to dive and slow down at the same time.

At 20 miles out from Howland Island, my instrument section finally started to see something other than the Pacific Ocean off in the distance I sighted something. I see a tiny little speck on the horizon that started to get bigger as I closed in telescopic viewing camera. It was slowly growing larger then I saw it had a White Castle Hamburger Restaurant with an oversize sign welcoming Pinger-5 to feed.

I instantly used my communications system to call ahead to make sure that nothing out of the ordinary would show up in my flight film. I was amazed to notice all the flying as well as floating stock that my Whale/naut's flight forces had put around Howland Island. But keeping to my flight plan by the time that I got there, all my nose camera could pick up was just the Island.

I made a beautiful low pass of Howland Island with just the Earhart beacon showing. I flew in over the Southwestern tip of Howland, then made a turn and flew out over the Northeastern corner of the island and continue on my way, to Hawaii. When I pulled up it looked like the whole island started to move as space ship after space ship started to launch from under water all around Howland Island.

As it turned out Pinger-5 was the last Sabrina No. 40 ship to leave due to her loading of her very own White Castle hamburger stand. It was another full work day in travel, Flying North Northeast. All that was left to do was buzz two more runways in Hawaii then fly the rest of the Pacific Ocean.

The low pass down the main runway at Maui airport was next then a single low pass down the main runway at the Kahului Airport. As soon as I was clear of the Hawaiian Island I aimed the nose of my 787 towards Oakland California towards the North East.

Leg thirty-five Maui to Oakland, California seemed like the longest slowest part of the trip. As usual most of my flying stock along with their Whale/naut pilots formed up on me as I came out of the 50th state to fly formation with Sabrina the Invincible herself. One or two at a time my Whale/nauts flew off some dove back into the Pacific Ocean few off then powered up and launched themselves back into Earth orbit or the "Leader."

At my request Pinger-5 flew ahead so as not to get the United States Air Force excited. I made all the radio calls myself as I neared Oakland California, I formed up with several other Airliners that were also on the way to my final touchdown point. The controller in the cab first asked about my on board fuel. After watching my total on board fuel gauge for the last two days a quick check showed that I had enough fuel to make it to my Space Base in Texas.

I replied that I had enough to loiter time for an hour and then divert to my alternate distention. So they directed me to stay in the landing pattern while all the others landed ahead of me.

I called up all the information on my Command Computer and went through my landing checklist. I adjusted my flaps and lowered my landing gear and waited for all the light to turn green, then I set my flaps for slow flight as I brought my 787 over the end of the runway for my official landing. Due to my feather weight caused by my lack of on board fuel I had to really work at it to get my 787 on the ground. I finally brought my 787 to a full stop about two thirds down the same runway that I had used to take off on about two days ago.

After wanting to know why I came to a complete stop the tower directed me to their official waiting area so that the officials from the Aeropause Foundation could check my door seals and informed me that my door seal were still in place and that officially I had not exited my aircraft. I finally finished after flying 25,940 miles in 45 hours and 51 minutes in a little under 2 days I completed my reenactment of Amelia Earhart's around the world flight.

It was a wonderful trip, a fantastic experience and the adventure. Fortunately, there were no major problems anywhere I went. I flew over some amazing places. I also flew a few places that I couldn't wait to leave.

After all the parties and press talks, the airport officials had a problem towing my 787 to a new parking space because of its lack of a tow bar attachment. So I had to duck out of my press conference to move it myself. I'm glad I did it, the next time I think that I will go the other way.

My exit of the Oakland airport was a little more dramatic. I took off with remaining fuel only and performed several fancy Aerial Maneuvers the infamous over-run take off with a vertical climb out, as well as a series of half loops flying the length of the runway inverted the doing it again at the other end of the runway.

To gain altitude while staying over the runway to enable me to exit the airport without violating my home build restricted airworthiness flight certificate.

Pinger-5 toped it all when she launch vertically with her Urban Camouflage Device still active and managed to pick me up in flight home built 787. Several thousand feet above the runway the local yokes though that I had punched it up to light speed and left the planet. Just because I kept up my flight routine until Pinger-5 unloaded me into the main hanger bay on the LEADER.

Log Entry #107.
Next to Longest Trip Around:

Through the use of my Command Computer Amelia informed the control tower that she wanted to do a touch and go. The second her main landing gear touched the runway, she started the nose camera that I had put in my home built 787, to show it all as it happened she made a touch and go at the Oakland, California airport.

Then she kept on going in the same direction all the way around the word across Texas, then down the Mexican coast. Past South America, across the Atlantic, and down past the eastern side of Africa. Across Antarctica, then north to Australia, then across the Pacific ocean and then flew 24,901.55 air miles straight ahead so that she could touched down again at Oakland airport.

Back to her starting point at Oakland, California where she came to a stop on the main runway 43 hours and 9 minutes later. Yes, she is the same blue whale that came up with the idea that I could fly around the word point to point by going from pole to pole and watching my angle.

Her reason for the trip was that she is a growing girl and that next year she would not fit inside an airplane as small as my home built Boeing 787.

Log Entry #108.
Pirates:

On the Pirate side of the human race, the Orcas have taken my personal advice. All of my space ships even if they are being piloted by a Whale/naut could capture the offending human crewed boat via the top cargo bay.

Then insulate them from the rest of the ship with layers of sticky foam. So as not to give the humans a chance to hurt themselves then the Whale/naut Pilot of my ship would deliver the offending humans Pirate ship to the middle of the runway of the nearest human United States Coast Guard Station. All I had to do was make sure that each Base had an ample supply of my Anti-Sticky foam to release them after capture.

As I was inspecting my Sabrina No. 40/33 space ship I noticed that there was a nice looking 40 foot cabin cruiser with several support poles sticking out of its bottom, stored off to the side in the first top side cargo bay.

Upon its discovery I had to ask its Command Whale/naut what was going on with a cabin cruiser on a stick. As her answer was very interesting she calls it her "Pirate Bait. "It seems that she would extend it top side when underwater and use its camera system to watch as other Pirate ships would try to capture it.

When the offending ship would come in from the rear she would open the next available cargo bay hatch and capture the whole boat as simple as putting an egg in its spot in an egg container.

My next question was what if they started shooting guns at you. "Sticky foam" was her next word. She said "Whales had always wanted to go fishing for humans".

Log Entry #109.
Chicago MISO:

Lately Pinger–5 has had her work crews use her tunnel boring Machine collection to connect the massive underground lake system that she discovered under Illinois, Wisconsin and Iowa, that was caused by the New Madrid Fault system.

She made it possible for me to park my Sabrina No. 40 Space ship directly under my parent's house, so without any maneuvering I can extend my Command POD to use it as part of my parent's basement.

I can also stop by the Des Plaines, Aircraft Certification Office without messing up flight operations at O'Hare Airport. All I have to do is move my Sabrina No. 40 over to O'Hare office Plaza Lake and then run my Command POD up to the lakeside door.

It's not as easy as it sounds as I still have to walk all the way around to the main front door to sign in. I don't think that eve I could get away with riding my Mars Cycle around the building.

Log Entry #110.
Problems with Pure Space Gold:

Pinger-5 has been making billions of dollars recovering lost cargo's from the bottom of all of the Earth's Oceans. This is how she discovered that Humans value the element "Gold." With a growing fleet of Sabrina No. 40 ships as well as lots of Whale/nauts to train it did not take her long to run out of lost human treasure too recover.

After checking the internet for information about Gold, it took her less than a full second to figure out that most of the Gold in the solar system would still be on station still locked in its orbital path near the asteroid belt.

This is the news that Pinger-5 used to get me out of my nice warm bed extremely early on a cold Saturday morning. She woke me up by pounding her tail fluke on the roof of the tunnel that ran under my parent's house. Where my prototype Sabrina No. 40 Space ship was parked for what I had planned to be a slow weekend. I was awakening by her ultrasonic call through several hundred feet of solid rock. With the message "wake up and turn on your communications necklace."

It is a good thing that I morph my clothing, as I didn't have time change or to get dressed the normal way. As soon as I aboard my Sabrina No. 40 Space ship, that was always ready to launch. Pinger-5 set us in motion flank speed to the cave systems main exit, up through the water then atmosphere directly into outer space then full throttle directly to the Asteroid Belt.

All I could get out of her was "Gold! Gold! Gold! I know where it all came from". Pinger-5 was so excited that she was shouting it in Humpback Whale Song so loud that it almost put me deaf.

I had to look at her flight program to figure it out on an elemental scale all of the Gold in the Solar system was trapped near the Asteroid Belt still in solar orbit. Pinger-5 made several calculations to prove it according to Pinger-5 the Asteroid Belt is not a destroyed planet. It's a section of the solar systems original spinning disk that did not collapse to form a planet.

As all the different types of mater are still spinning in the same disk they were separated by each other's atomic weight and most of it was still in its original orbit around the Sun at its specific orbital tract.

As such, it took Pinger-5 several second to calculate exactly where all the Gold in the solar System was located, so that she could plot a direct course to intercept it. By her command, I was accelerating to the exact speed that all the rest of the Gold was moving. This will cause my Sabrina No.40 Space ship to drift into the orbiting Gold layer and just scoop it all up.

Using the Apogee method of space flight is as good as any, it took most of the day to travel within 100 miles of Pinger-5's computed apogee point where she expected to pick up all of the Gold that was still in solar orbit. Therefore, with a massive retro firing from all four of my aero-spikes to match the speed of all the microscopic Gold, we started our drift into the targeted area.

As it turn out having the Aero-Spikes close their door really save the day, I turned up my all of my scanners to full and I could not see a thing. I extended all of the built in Space-junk-Trapping blankets that I had designed to cover the entire outer skin of my No. 40 Space ships. As I am extremely tired of having to constantly, keep patching holes in my outer hull. Millions of holes caused by the constant bombardment of the never-ending supply of space-junk.

All I could get out of Pinger-5 "was close closer we are almost there." I had all the space junk recovery blankets running in their constant cycling through the main collection bucket, all of which was showing nothing. Then instantly the collection device fills up to its maximum capacity in less than a second! At the same instant, my communication system went dead as my entire External Antenna Farm was paved over by Pinger-5's incoming space gold strike.

Luckily, this activated my Fail-Safe-System, that I had originally built into of my Sabrina No. 39s, as well as the "First Five" and the Next Ten" space ships. The instant the "Sabina's in trouble light" started to glow red inside of Sabrina No. 39's Command Computer she started moving to save my sixteen-year-old female body. She interrupted her current mission checked the Command Computer system for my last location then she started towards me, at the same instant she commanded the "First Five", then the "Next Ten" to do the same.

Then my personally designed space junk collection system jammed on Sabrina No. 40 filling up the entire system to its maximum and backing up everything all the way to the surface of blanket layers. All of my external cameras went black at the same microsecond. With a quick look at my control panel, I noticed that all of my external cameras were showing black as if all of their lenses were caped.

The only thing I could notice was the brief flash of Gold as the outer lenses cover were opened the camera instantly went black again. I check all of my navigation ports only to discover that I could not see a thing. Then the warning light started to turn red then Pinger-5 started with "We got it all" repeatedly, that is when I discovered that "All the Gold had us."

The next thing I noticed was that a pasty foam like substance stated to come in around all of my internal bulkheads. At first glance, I thought that one of my sticky foam packs had burst open upon close inspection I discovered that it was microscopic flakes of pure gold. That's when I discovered that Sabrina No. 40's micro-gravity field was burying us alive in pure Space Gold.

As near as I can tell under normal conditions, a meteor or comet would just travel through this band of Gold at 30 or 40 thousand miles per hour and pick up a small amount of it as it pasts through. Its specific apogee where as it has been orbiting the Sun sense before the planets were formed billions of years ago. However, thanks to Pinger-5's calculations it seems that No. 40 was now serving as her personal gravity well for several billion pounds of it to fall in on Sabrina No. 40.

Pinger-5 came out of her Gold fever when she discovered that her personal food supply was running low, she even checked out her personal automated on board White Castle Hamburger Stand only to discover that it was out of Sliders. This was the first time that anything that was heavier that Sabrina No. 40 landed on top of her. Much less with enough mass to push its way inside.

Pinger-5 had open one of the bottom cargo bays in her first attempt to load her hoard of Gold aboard. This had caused a quick sand effect as every inch of the cargo bays interior was instantly filled with microscopic space gold! I had to play back the onboard camera report to see what had happened. It looked like a cave in that filled up the entire forward lower cargo bay in less than half a second.

This allowed the Gold to push it way into most of the hydraulic lines on the ship, plugging and jamming every system it hit. My next idea was to fire my Aero-spikes Rockets engines to get me out of this gravity well, all to no avail the entire fueling system was now jammed with pure Gold. According to all of the pressure gauges that were still working, Pinger-5s pure Space Gold problem was pushing inward at several tons per square inch.

I tried to launch several of my remote cameras all with no avail. So this leaves me not only flying by the seat of my paints, but doing it as blind as a bat without radar. Then I released that Pinger-5 could use her echo system to find out how thick of a Gold layer we were buried under.

To do this Pinger-5 had to morph her Space suit back to its basic control band and used only her mass to point herself directly away from the center of her calculation point then she had make her loudest full power Whale Song possible. I had to put a vacuum filled Cargo Bubble around me to keep from going deaf from all Pinger-5s returning sound waves.

This turned out to be the only way Pinger-5 could figure out how deep we were buried and what direction to travel to get away from where we were serving as the center of a Moon size pile if pure space Gold. Together we both figured that what was happening was similar to being buried as avalanche all we had to do was blow it all away as if it were snow.

My next problem was instant Prototyping a heavy-duty snowplow that I could use to push away enough Pure Space Gold to get Sabrina No. 40 moving again. It took less than a minute to come up with a large snow plow type blade to attach the outer surface of my Command POD I had to configure its magnetic track system to surface mode.

As I got started trying to push tons of microscopic pure gold dust around it became evident that I had to build a snow blower type of device that would not only move it out of the way but, throw it over board in a direction that would provide some dynamic thrust as well as.

So as not to have our problem just keep fall back on Sabrina No. 40. According to Pinger-5s, sounding the thinnest layer of Pure Space Gold were located in the rear of Sabrina No. 40 on the elevated mount that I installed the ION rocket motor.

At this point the Gold emergency, it took a while to move back to the ION Engine Section and I had to perform an emergency ejection of my only on board Ion Rocket Engine just to open its outer doors. The Pure Gold Dust provided a driving surface like no other each of my caterpillar tracks started throwing up large roster tails from their first movement. This action turns out to be the maneuver that saved both of our lives as it provided the first push of thrust to get No, 40 moving out of the microscopic pure space gold's, apogee point.

As I ejected the whole ION engine section away it's never fail cable system stopped the whole section at a thousand feet away. It was actually a nice feeling when I noticed that Sabrina No. 40 had slowed a little. As soon as I made it outside, I extended my emergency Communications System and I discover that good old Sabrina No. 39 was just closing in on my last known location from the sunny side of the solar system.

Pinger-5 asked me "why I made a human happy noise" when I discover that Sabrina No. 39's fail-safe was working. There she was several hundred miles back at the point where all of my radio transmissions were cut off when Sabrina No. 40s entire antenna farm was buried under tons of pure microscopic space gold dust. I ordered Sabrina No. 39 to hold her location as I did not want her buried as I was, my gold throwing operation was not as effective as I would like.

It was like trying to plow sand in a sand storm on the surface of Mars. Sabrina No. 39's first communication had a telephoto picture of poor old Gold plated Sabrina No. 40 she looked a lot larger that she was supposed to be as well as quite fuzzy from all the Gold dust. Everybody in the entire solar system had noticed that something was up when all of my original No. 39 Space ships stopped whatever they were doing and started to rescue me.

The entire human race had to know what I was doing. As I had planned to sleep in that morning and have a late brunch with both of my parents. It was not my idea to try to capture all the gold in the solar system I came along because I had a 38-ton friend pushing me all the way.

Together Pinger-5 and I came up with our next escape plan. "The use of a very long towing cable." At my request Sabrina No. 39 launched one of my cabling up PODs to my newly identified location. By the time it got to us it was also incrusted in Space Gold to the point where it had used up its entire fuel reserve just to handle its increased mass.

However, it did manage to successfully deliver the tow cable. I had to constantly keep gold blowing to keep the rear entrance hatch large enough to let the cable POD inside. I had installed this system to cable-up all my Sabrina No. 39's for my world famous acceleration circle maneuver, it was a good thing that it had always had well over a hundred miles of towing cable installed in each one. By this time, Pinger-5 had enough time to come up with a working math formula to enable her to continuously calculate the total external mass that was now a large growing part of Sabrina No. 40.

We came up with a growing figure that was way off my lift able scale. So I gave Sabrina No. 39 the order to start backing off slowly first taking up all the slack, I know for a fact that the cable was strong enough to move any of my space ships under normal conditions, the cable finally firmed up and Sabrina No. 40 started to tremble, as I requested Sabrina No. 39 to gently increase her reverse thrust until something happened.

The first thing that happen was the entire external mass shifted this started an avalanche of gold mass that jammed the Towing POD inside the ION Engine Room causing my Command POD to be jammed through several of my internal bulk heads. The good thing was Sabrina No. 39 managed to pull No. 40 partly out of her self-induced gravity well and away from the sector of solar orbiting Space Gold.

No. 39 had to use all her fuel reserves to move the heavies object in the entire Solar System one 38 ton full size female humpback whale along with enough gold dust to keep her happy for an extended amount of time. As my rescue forces started to arrive from various directions, in the Solar System, two of my No. 39 came in from Jupiter and passed through the Gold barrier from the outside causing both of them to have the same problem that Pinger-5 and myself had. Only a lot smaller due to their flight path as they were coming into the sun.

Sabrina No. 39 was able on her own to launch a Cable PODs into each ship Sabrina No. 39/8 & Sabrina No. 39/9 both of which were in a world of hurt being gold plated as well as put out on communication by the same gold dust problem.

Pinger-5 was able to calculate both the Apagoge as well of the Perigee of her orbiting gold belt. As it turned out if I had not had an active fail-safe Sabrina No. 40 would have continued it gravity well operation. Too eventually form another planet orbiting the Sun just outside of the Asteroid Belt. With a starving 38 ton Humpback Whale and a much stranded 16 year of human female trapped inside of its solid Gold core.

Instantly Sabrina No. 39 started too real in all the cable at the same time the Cable PODs upon connection to the other two Sabrina No. 39 ships let them in on her plan. Sabrina No. 39 transmitted a single word warning "Movement" as all of the Cable PODs ran out of cable at the same instant the massive tug cause when all three of my local No. #39 space ships rebound almost yanked No. 40 out of her gravity well.

Both of us got introduced to the nearest down movement bulk head. With Pinger-5's help No. 39 was requested to keep the cable tough with everything all moving in the same direction until we were well away from the problem Gold Attraction Point. We both made a human unhappy noise when we learned that Sabrina No. 39 was almost out of rocket fuel the other two space ships Sabrina No. 39/8 & Sabrina No. 39/9 were both out of action with their entire surface coated with pure space gold that was several inches deep. So at Sabrina No. 39 request now it was time for Me TOHOB "The only human on board "to go to work.

The first thing was to get my Command POD out of the bulkhead and back outside, this was not possible due to all the space gold dust that I had to move around. I made sure that Pinger-5s automated feeding system was still working. Therefore, I had my Instant pro-typing machine make me a large dusting brush before I loaded out of my Command POD with two spare Space suits and a couple of extra He/3 reactors.

I actually had to morph a shovel blade on each of my hands, to dig my way back to the ION engine mount just too make to make my exit from Sabrina No. 40. This also would enable Sabrina No. 40 to more or less stay on the surface of the Richest

Planets in the Solar system just second ahead of billions of tons of Want-a-bees space gold that is trying to become part of Sabrina No. 40. When I finally found an open passage to the great outdoors the first thing I did was inflate my largest clear Cargo POD and started to morph my human maneuvering unit into operation, It only took a couple of minutes to add on all my extra He/3 power units.

There's nothing like the emptiness of outer space but, this time there was a lot of Want-a-bees gold micro-meteors as planned my newly manufactured dusting brush was my most used tool. I had to constantly keep dusting the gold dust out of my ballistic control system. Moving the hundred miles back to Sabrina No. 39 was a piece of cake. By the time I got there she had reeled in all most all of her cable, and put out her mooring bumpers.

The problem was that each of my ballistic control heads were barely working as I arrived I was coated in a shell of pure gold from one to five inches deep. Sense I was the person who had designed and build each of my Sabrina No. 39 series space ships I did not have to be told where to dig to open up all of their ballistic control ports on both of my Sabrina No. 39/8 & Sabrina No. 39/9.

Of all the space tools that I have at my disposable the best one has to be my finger tip plasma torch, I use it to cut out an Ice cube tray pattern around all of the ballistic control heads. Then I would hit them with my trusty dusting mop, until all the bad old gold bars that were coating the firing head had been cleared away.

It took less than an hour to clean up each ship to the point where they could use their own ballistic control systems. Using the hard docking cargo doors was out of the question because of the extremely large amount of solid thick gold that I would have to remove by hand, just to allow the mechanism work.

Let me tell you I definitely made a human happy noise when I made contact with the rest of my rescue force that was inbound from Earth side. There they were all balled up for maximum speed, collectively they had figured out what was going on and they had plotted their own danger area.

As so they had plotted their own shallow intercept angle. Luckily, the rest of my Rescue Force was in-bound from the Sunny side and the Sabrina No. 39 ships that were on the LEADER when they got my rescue call had the most excess fuel aboard. I can tell you know that all the time I had spent doing pottery class in kinder garden really saved everything, as my latest plan was to have the "Next Ten" cable up with each other to make five of the largest cheese cutters in the solar system.

As I ordered them to make a series of head on passes cabled to each other so that they could cut away large sections of the newly formed gold planet that was following only a second or two, behind Pinger-5 and Sabrina No. 40 trying to catch up and form another planet with a Humpback Whale center.

As soon as both of my Sabrina No. 39/8 & Sabrina No. 39/9 ships could maneuver, they cabled up with Sabrina No. 39. To help tow Sabrina No. 40 faster, the "Next Ten" broke formation cabled up and stared to make head on passes cutting of trillion of dollars' worth of microscopic pure space gold, during each pass.

With the pulling power of three different Sabrina No.39's at the same time the pure space gold would dissipate back into its dust form as soon as it was outside of Sabrina No. 40's gravity well. So with each slice Pinger-5's mass problem was reduced by tons. This cause a bigger problem as we had to calculate mass and movement continuously without errors as our whole towing operation would collapse with the first miscalculation.

As luck would have it, all the now loose microscopic space gold started back to its new solar orbit. It only took a couple of hours to trim Sabrina

No. 40 back to her original size, she was still nothing but dead weight as all of her control systems were still plugged up with billions of dollars' worth of gold dust.

Being caught with my cargo bay open allowed all of her working systems to be jammed full. It took a full day for me to cut away several feet of melted gold just to allow the Sabrina No. 39 space ship with Pinger-5's replacement food supply so that she could finally eat something other than gold.

Sabrina No. 39/8 & 39/9 Pinger-5 made the standard high-speed re-entry to the Earth's Atmosphere to clean off their gold problem and at the same time I used the direct approach the middle of Lake Michigan so that Pinger-5 could feed for herself.

The trip back to the LEADER was as normal as possible, it took almost six months and a series of major "E" checks to get Sabrina No. 40 back into operation.

Log Entry #111.
Throw away Gold:

The last thing Pinger-5 did before Sabrina No. 39 dumped her back into Lake Michigan was to set up a security stop to keep all the humans on the Earth from finding out how rich she was.

She also had a couple of her Whale/nauts set up a series of new earth crossing asteroids that would transverse her newly discovered gold barrier to eventually impact directly over the main entrance to the underwater Whale base under Chicago.

Upon arrival the first thing I did was to isolate Sabrina No. 40's hanger from the rest of the LEADER as the last thing I needed was to get Microscopic Space Gold Dust in all the other machinery on the LEADER.

Not to mention that all kinds of microscopic powder are deadly to all living mammals that used oxygen. As when under "Zero "G"" it will instantly clog up their lungs and cause death.

My first look around was heart breaking, the actual condition of Sabrina No. 40 was far worse than I thought. As I found pure gold jammed in everywhere and in everything, to the point where I seriously though about starting over, with a new airframe.

It took almost an hour to come up with my cleaning plan, Zero "G" He/3 traps rigged for Gold, lots of super-heated water plasma, as it was a good thing that gold has a relative low melting temperature.

I reconfigure several of my He/3 traps for pure gold it had to look like magic to see it in operation, a self-powered floating machine that turns out regulation size 7 inches x 3 and 5/8 inches x 1 and 3/4 inches gold bricks out of thin air.

The Command center finally informed me that the IRS was waiting for me at the top of my space elevator. As I opened the last hatch to my Command Center, I could almost smell the hordes of IRS agents. Who were just being transported up my space elevator to get Uncle Sam's part of Pinger-5's treasure, and then I got the call from my Space Elevator Control Center informing me that the IRS agents had arrived.

The senior inspector was the first to ask a Question, "who are you, how old are you, is this your treasure?" I looked him in the eye and replied I am the Sabrina from Sabrina Aviation, 16 years old, and the treasure all belongs to Pinger-5, a personal friend of mine I did not have the heart to tell them that she was a 38 ton Humpback Whale.

I shudder to think what that they would do if they knew that I had thrown away enough gold to make a small planet just to get Sabrina No. 40's mass down to movable. As soon as the IRS discovered that the gold in question belonged to Pinger-5 the whole accusation team made a sigh of relief because she had been paying her taxes all along.

I also informed them that Pinger-5 would personally contact them as soon as she had an idea of what she owed them. She eventually had her Whale/ naut force cover the entire outside of the Washington Monument with regulation gold bricks, 7 inches x 3 and 5/8 inches x 1 and 3/4 inches all of which weighed 22 and a half each. Then she politely asked the IRS for her change. I don't think that even the IRS can write a check with that many zeros in it.

Log Entry #112.
Dog Fight:

It finally got to the point where I had to replace my space suits re-charger just to get rid of all the Gold Dust. Needless to say I have been working the Mechanic parts of my DNA very hard.

I got a request from my old friend the now 23-year-old Raptor pilot. It seems that Captain Lynda Lou Love was due a long range patrol mission and she want to know if I was up for lunch over the South Atlantic Ocean. This time I changed into a-non-gold contaminated space suit, I was still having electrical problems with Sabrina No. 40. So I call on the services of my original Sabrina No. 39 Space ship.

Needless to say it felt good to move Sabrina No. 40 back into the vacuum of Outer Space. About this time Sabrina No. 39 showed up and I requested her to come into Sabrina No. 40 upper cargo bay so that I could interconnect her Command Computer into Sabrina No. 40s operational system to find out was wrong.

It only took a second for Sabrina No. 39 to take over poor old Sabrina No. 40's operational systems, and bring up the master list of systems it was a real pleasure to see most of the warning lights turn from red to green. With Sabrina No. 39's Command Computer in charge she was maneuvering lots faster than normal. The re-entry into the Earth's Atmosphere was as awesome as always. Plus all of the out streaming of now molten Gold nodules dripping out of all her landing gear wells.

Once we got low in the Earth's atmosphere Sabrina No. 40 started doing deceleration tracks over the South Atlantic. I picked up Lynda's Raptor flying several hundred thousand feet below me, Sabrina No. 39's command system instantly got into her flight computer and displayed a copy of her instrument panel on my viewing screen I could tell that she was about to pounce as soon as I flew straight into her gun sights. I told Sabrina No. 39 to move my Command POD aboard, and launch out of Sabrina No. 40's upper cargo bay. I did a high speed loop and let No. 40 continued her deceleration circle. I made radio contact as I flew up behind her transmitting "GUNS, GUNS, GUNS" and had her dead to rights.

Despite the fact that I did not have any operational guns. I was falsely accused of using Sabrina No. 40 as a decoy. As I started to fly formation my exterior camera system picked up a most horrifying look on Lynda's face when she noticed how large No, 39 was next to her puny little F-22.

Sabrina No. 39 automatically went into her airshow mode and put a location box around Captain Love and her Raptor. I informed Lynda to announce "Fight-on "when ready. Then she discovered that I had her pinned, no matter what she did I had her cold for the better part of a full minute, then she went to full power in a vertical climb, she did not even get to change her orientation in the Airshow box.

Suddenly Lynda called "May-Day" as both of her jet engines jammed up and destroyed themselves. Then I noticed that Sabrina No. 40 was doing the old blackbird anti-missile trick by leaving a trail of molten metal in her exhaust wake in this case one hundred per cent purer space gold.

Sabrina No. 39 had to fire her retro-rocket to slow down fast enough to instantly capture Lynda's dead Raptor, and pull it into her port main docking hatch. I had to laugh as this set off my Command Computers emergency alarm when I noticed that it took one of my own Space-junk traps to get Lynda out of her capture box.

I asked Sabrina No. 39 to recover all of us back to the LEADER. Lynda had stayed inside her cockpit until I arrived as usual her Raptor was a mess I loved teasing her about all the F-22 glider time she was going to have to enter in her log book, all 33,000 miles of it.

She was a little confused to learn that she was now 33,000 miles away from where we were doing a dog-fight. I was a little concerned to discover that she had passed out because of all the movements, Sabrina No. 39

is programed with my human parameters so as not to injure me when maneuvering.

I guess that 23 year old fighter pilots are not as tough as us 16 year old EAA types. I had my medical sensors take a close look at Captain Love to make sure that she was A-OK, by that time my FOD gold team guys were on the job cleaning off all her newly added exterior gold plating.

As usual, both of her jet engines were totaled by very heavy pieces of molten gold. As Lynda eyes started to focus she made an interesting distress sound and put both her hands over her eyes as my Gold retriever pulled a solid Gold mold of the entire front end if her F-22, off all of its leading edge surfaces and started compressing them into a regulation gold bars. I pick up one of my He/3 power gold recover machines to get it started to melt the pure gold molded shape of the front of Lynda's F-22 into 7 inches x 3 and 5/8 inches x 1 and 3/4 inches regulation gold bars.

I told her not to worry Pinger-5 had won several F-119 engines in a poker game and had given them to me as souvenirs. At this point in the mission, I noticed that Lynda was changing back to her normal color as we started floating towards the closest Food Court.

She snapped back to normal as soon as she stepped onto the food courts main gravity wheel and the movement instantly stuck booth of us to the floor. As if we were standing in a shopping mall anywhere on the surface of the Earth. Lynda's mouth was opened as wide as Pinger-5s as she took a good look around at all the different places to eat. I knew she had made a total recovery when she made a beeline directly to the onboard "Golden Arches" and order two Mc-ribs, with a large order of fries and a large diet-coke. I will have to be the first person to admit it. I would never have pegged Captain Love as a Mc-Rib eater much less a two at a timer. I had a cheese burger happy meal, with milk, and cut apples Lynda started to smile when she noticed that it had a pre-built model, of an F-22 inside as a prize.

She reminded me that I should have specified that the prize was for a girl when I ordered it. I looked her in the eye and informed her that it was a girl's prize. We both made small talk for the rest of the meal, are rumors true were you really trapped in the Asteroid Belt and had to call for help. After lunch both of us went back to Sabrina No. 39s space hanger to find out that the Gold FOD teams He3 power gold retriever was just finishing up producing another 7 inches x 3 and 5/8 inches x 1 and 3/4 inches perfect gold brick

Lynda look kind of shocked when she noticed an inspection card on each spare F-119 engine that said save for Captain Lynda Lou Loves next visit. It took less than 20 minutes for me to replace both of her blown F-119 jet engines, I even got too talk to her on board maintained computer to make sure that everything was plugged into the correct plug. Lynda was just floating around inside the cargo bay watching me work. Less than an hour later I dropped her off near her base, this time I remembered to ask and adjusted my flight path to acuminate her estimated time of arrival.

I did have a slight problem when Lynda went to full power she splattered several hundred pounds of molten gold nuggets into my Sabrina No. 39's cargo bay wall.

Later I discovered when at drag races due to the larger size of Sabrina No. 40 as soon as her nose passed the finishing line, she would zap the still fast moving losers-dragster with a space-junk-trap then make a Sabrina No. 39 type vertical climb out, as she reeled it in. I still have to do more work on her programing to get her to return the driver.

Log Entry #113.
Lake Front Airshow:

Amelia my Blue Whale friend has spent more time flying my homebuilt Boeing 787 than I did when I re-enacted Amelia Earhart's attempted round the word flight. She made such a nice request to fly it as long as she did not break I it.

Amelia's specialty in heavy aerobatics, nothing fancy just the same old maneuvers, loops, left and right handed hammerhead stalls. The first part of her act usually would consist of one of my Sabrina No. 40 series space ships surfacing just off Chicago's North Avenue Beach, as soon as the show announcer noticed this large Spacecraft safely floating on the surface of the Lake. It would flatten out its top side to morph a long enough runway for Amelia the blue Whale to make a safe normal take off, then she would instantly start into her aerobatic show act.

At the end of the act she would find out that the runway on top of the Sabrina No. 40 ship was too short, at every attempted landing, Amelia would have to go to full power and climb out to keep from going off the end of her morphed runway into Lake Michigan.

Finally after all else failed another No. 40 Space ship shows up to catch Amelia in flight with a very large Space-junk-Trap, and carries her aircraft out of the airshow box. Needless to say Amelia's air show trap is just a prop as she is a good enough pilot to make a useful recovery any time she wants.

Several minutes later the Space ship that had just captured Amelia in flight surfaced inside the airshow box and launch her airborne again. If I did not mention it she is flying a homebuilt 787 the whole time. By using her dominant flippers control band.

Log Entry #114.
Mid-Atlantic Rescues:

I got another call from the Air Force it seems they had misplaced several of their aircraft again somewhere over the Atlantic Ocean. They wanted to know if I could help, find them locating both the downed pilots as well as the aircraft.

Officially, this part of the Earth is out of sight of the "Leaders" camera system. It's times like this, when I seriously think of building another Space Elevator on the other side of the Earth. Pinger-5 has always l liked this idea, as it would make it easier for her to move Whale/naut's, on and off the Earth.

As usual, it was a dark Moonless night with several mid Atlantic Hurricanes happening on each side of Greenland at the same time. Pinger-5 answered the call by loading several different Sabrina No. 40 Space ships with as many Whale/naut's as possible, as there is nothing a Whale likes better than a rough Hurricane stirred Ocean.

Needless to say, this flushed out every available space ship that was on the LEADER as well as the Chicago Cave Base. Several of the Sabrina No. 39's managed to locate as well as pick up several different aircraft in flight with the aid of their Space-junk-Traps. As soon as Pinger-5 noticed that, several of the human aircrews were down in the Greenland glassier, she got her Polar Bear act in to the rescue operation.

For aircrews that actually bailed out over water she used her Whale pods of Orca Whale/naut's that dependently did not like to eat humans. With Sabrina No. 40 series ships making supersonic vertical impact landings to pick up pilots down in the water. Over all the Whales loved all the massive turbulence as that past directly through the massive Hurricanes.

Then launching their Whales/naut's to the required search grid to grab the poor lost human pilots as they were bobbing about the freezing Hurricane stirred Atlantic Ocean. Only to be grabbed from beneath and hulled several hundred feet under water into the waiting cargo bay of their Sabrina No. 40 Space ships where they were officially weighted and rescued.

Over all it cost Pinger-5 big money to run her rescue operation not to mention having the saving mammal being paid for by the pound. I would have given anything to see the look in the Pilots faces when one of Pinger-5's trained Polar Bears grab them by the scruff of their necks and hauled them into a hovering Sabrina No. 40 Space ship.

Pinger-5 also got a lot of goody points from me when she gather up all the aircraft wreckage and gave it to me, so that I could patch it all back together and build my very own squadron of Raptors. So that the next time I wanted to play Dog-fight with Lynda, I could do it better, if I had my own fighter plane.

Pinger-5 was a little disappointed when she found out how slow they would fly as the poor little airframe could only do a little over Mach two and did not have any kind of ballistic control systems. She did make a comment as to the airframe having many outward opening cargo areas where I might install better power plants.

Log Entry #115.
"Weird Raptors" :

A month later, it was finally my turn to make the "Milk-Run" between Earth and Mars. Because I am the Sabrina of Sabrina Aviation, it is my choice to get first crack at everything. My trusty sidekick Pinger-5 makes it a point to keep her schedule open, as all she needs is a communication line and she is good to go anywhere anytime.

If an unplanned mission happens, I have the first option to step in at the last minute and do it. If I am already on a mission this job falls to the next most qualified astronaut team of humans and Whale/naut's. As it is always easier navigational wise to just let the Whale/naut do it. Which is the only way I know how to maintain all my vast resources?

For lack of a better term, it also a mail run as unbelievably as it sounds I still have personal that will not use e-mail. Then on the other hand, everybody keeps ordering stuff off the internet. In addition, if somebody doesn't keep everything moving. The LEADER would just fill up sometimes I think that it could do it overnight.

The milk-run part of the trip as always is first jump from the LEADER to the crossest space elevator on the Moon. Then to the closest Asteroid Ark Ship what is interesting is, I get to stop at both incoming as well as outgoing vessels. On this trip when Pinger-5 and I departed my Lunar Space Elevator No. 3, my workshop bay was loaded aboard.

I found all the Raptor wreckage rolled up in one big cargo net floating inside, the same one that I used to build my home built Boeing 787. Then its Pinger-5 job to calculate the speed and direction to the first rendezvous as the plan is to end up flying formation with the other Asteroid Space ship.

Pinger-5 likes to see how close she can come to matching up docking hatches, without having to use maneuvering thrusters. To save fuel my ship gets to do the slow coast maneuver, this give me lots of extra time to work on my aircraft building operations. I am getting smarter in my old age as I am almost up to 17 years old.

The first thing I did was request Sabrina No. 40 to contact all the still living onboard computers to find out how bad things were as well as to create an instant list of what was still operational in the cargo net. As usual when an airframe strikes anything even at the low speed of Mach 2, the airframe tends to come apart.

Patching the airframes back together was not a problem in zero-"G". My biggest problem was shrinking down my standard Command Computer so that it would fit inside the already existing avionics boxes. I wonder what one of my Command Computers would do installed in an airframe that could not fly into outer space or for that matter go no faster than Mach two. The only thing that I came up short on was operational instrument panels and cockpits at zero-zero ejection system really makes the cockpit live hard.

I had lots of spare parts and pieces my first thought was too combine fuselages sections. Everybody knows that if you combine two P-51's you end up with an F-82. However, what do you get when you put an F-22's and an F-35's together. Or for that matter combine everything to see what turns out. A Bi-plane or even a Tri-plane version of the Raptor I wonder how well it would maneuver in a dogfight. Retractable thermal ramjet motors in the missile bay, retractable floats, underwater fans, the extra add ones were endless.

I even had enough left over parts to make an updated version of the German World War II Mistel. All I had to do was convert chunks of several Air force F-35's into the Marine V.T.O.L. variant. After all what good is an F-35 if it can't hover. Then build a mother ship out of several F-22 fragments.

In all I made 3 rendezvous with Asteroid Ark Ships before I made it to the Martian space elevator. As usual I used the Martian atmosphere to decelerate just enough to pop out of the Martian atmosphere with just enough forward inertia left to drift over to the main docking port on its now much larger Moon Phobos.

After exchanging Cargo PODs, which only took a couple of minutes to change incoming mail for outgoing mail, it only took a couple of commands to finish business. Then with a full power blast from my aero-spikes, I was on the way back to Earth. On this trip, back I still had the same three rendezvous on the way back to Earth. This gave me lots of extra coasting time to finish my new collection of "Weird Raptors".

During Re-Entry of the Earth atmosphere I kept Sabrina No. 40 flying inside of the Earth's Atmosphere Flying in her deceleration pattern for as long as I could. Despite all my very hard work Sabrina No. 40 still melts out about a million or so dollars of pure space during atmospheric re-entry.

To top it all off I almost collided with a couple of the Whale/naut's In front of the main underwater entrances, to my under Chicago Base, it seem that they were picking up several Gold incrusted Meteorite fragments for Pinger-5.

You should have seen the look on the new MISO guy's faces when I walked into their office the next day. They both were a little alarmed when I asked them to come with me out their closed exit door to "Lake Rogers" they were quick to noticed my builder bay surfacing in the Lake just south of the door next to their office in the 2300 Building.

I really impressed both of the new guys, I got both of their eyeball to widen as well as jaws to drop, they both made a human Oh! Oh! Sound when my rebuilt gimmicked up F-22 became a Bi-plane, and a repeat performance when the third set of wings popped out of the side wall missile bays. It took them almost an hour to check out my modern F-22/F-35 Mistel. I plugged all the Modern Mistel electrical system in to my work shop's He/3 power source, to make sure that everything was working as advertised. The F-82 variants of my dual fuselage F-35 really blew their minds after my inspection was over I gave the commands to have my shop module pulled back under water into Sabrina No. 40's cargo bay.

Log Entry #116.
Lake Front Airshows:

After Sabrina No. 39 made her usual airshow entrance and I had slowed to sub-sonic speed I moved my Command POD to my lower rear cargo bay, so that I could get into my home made F-22/F-35 Mistel and launch from Sabrina No. 39 along with all my new built- ups, as my new Airshow act.

This enabled me to fly formation with myself. The purpose of the new act was to give the audience a real good look at my home built F-22/F-35 homemade Mistel. Flying the closest formation ever, because they were physically attached to each other. As I do the first part of my Airshow act? When then I made my break a part maneuver all the Whale/naut's could hear was the human audience makes a human happy sound.

Then after a few standard aerobatic stunts, the F-22 part of my act would start its wounded bird act, and make a standard ditching maneuver coming to a full stop in front of millions of people on the surface of Lake Michigan just off Chicago's North Avenue Beach. Then it would proceed to sink out of sight under water.

After a couple of very long wet minutes the Sunken F-22 would then inflate and extent its retraceable floats and come bobbing to the surface. Then my F-35 would change into its non-produced V.T.O.L. Marine Corps variant and proceed to make a vertical landing on top of the now wet bobbing F-22. Then I would re-attach itself, to the support rack on my now floating F-22's retractable floats, to enable both now joined aircraft to make a normal hydrofoil take-off. With just using the engine from the F-35 as thrust.

We always get a cheer from the audience as both of the waterlogged F-119 engines on my re-built F-22 re-ignite and go to full thrust as my "Modern Mistel" makes a vertical exit of the airshow box. Sabrina No. 39 comes back into the middle of the airshow box where I would hover into the lower cargo bay to keep Sabrina No.39 from having to snatch and grab me with a space junk trap. Then is on with the show.

Log Entry #117.
Alaskan High Mountain Rescue:

Pinger–5 and I were orbiting down in Low Earth Orbit with Sabrina No. 39 intercepting large clouds of space-junk. I was trying to update an old idea of mine, a space junk net, so far, it was not working, as the first sharp point would cut the net to allow the targeted space-junk to escape.

This also causes all of the fragments to dramatically change their orbits. It finally got to the point where I had to call it quits to allow all the Space-junk time to stabilize themselves in all of their new orbital tracts.

Another one of my fighter Pilot friends had gotten herself in a pickle of a problem she had gotten herself separated and lost during a training flight. She had tried to land her F-22 to save her aircraft, only to have to do zero-zero ejection as she failed to make a survivable landing.

She had escaped her crashing aircraft without a scratch only to have the moving high speed air currents of the Alaskan mountain range to carry her up and away high into the largest vast mountain ranges of Alaska. After spending several hours of being trapped on the surface of the Earth she managed to locate her communications necklace, and call me.

That's when my Communications System patched through an urgent communications necklace call from my friend Captain Jackie Love. After her usual amount of small talk, she asked if I had heard of her problem. "No I answered I'm not even on Earth right now ", I answered.

I patched into the commercial television frequency to hear the news about this poor luckless Rapier Pilot that had ejected from her damaged jet fighter after she had tried to make an emergency landing. She was trapped on a mountainside high up in the mountains of the Alaskan Range well above the snowline. Miles and miles away from anybody or any other kind of help, the local mountain rescue teams had ran out of everything.

A local television reporter announced that all would be lost with the coming dark of night that would make the rescue location as dark as the backside of the Moon.

Well that's all I needed to hear, instantly both Pinger-5 and I started computing my atmospheric re-entry angles as well as the most useful deceleration circle needed to keep this rescue sight from going dark. Finally after repeated attempts to locate Jackie's Rapier, my Communications System finally locked in on to the computer of their only operational rescue helicopter.

I started to fly a 10-mile wide circle around it using my re-entry fireball as a light source for that part of the mountain range. As soon as I was flying slow enough I extended No. 40's wings and, turned on all my exterior lights. I even focus all my on board spotlights where they would go the most good. As I slowed to a hover I extended my lift-fans.

My first though was to make one of Pinger-5's Salvage Mountainside Landing over the target. By angling the landing gear too, match the terrain, so that a hard landing on top of the Rapiers' crash site would be possible and I would be able to lifting everything aboard with my loadmaster program.

This idea went out the window as soon as I could see that I was dealing with a vertical cliff. My next idea a vertical landing next to the cliff was out due to my rocket exhaust patterns. As it turned out my only option was to open both of my mid top side and bottom rear cargo bays, then land on the pointy tip of the mountain top, then to have it impale Sabrina No. 40 through both her main top and bottom cargo bays. I was able to attach it through Sabrina No. 40's load master program, too make everything become stable.

I open my forward lower cargo bay, to use to lower equipment down the face of the vertical cliff. I also remembered to keep the lights on. As soon as their only surviving helicopter landed the rescue, team in the newly morph hello-port in No. 40's forward top cargo bay. The rest of the rescue was a breeze despite all the unpredictable high winds Pinger-5 bailed out using one of her Whale size parasails to locate as well as recover the wreckage of Jackie's Raptor.

I parked all the Rescue team in my spare Command POD, I even got to power up it ballistic control system to use it as a stable platform. Then I lowered the whole rescue team down the sheer cliff in my Command POD to pick up Jackie.

Upon arrival, we had our hands full, due to Jackie's extreme downward momentum she had been crammed into a rock crevice like a rock climbers piton spike her extraction would have been impossible without the ability of my Command POD to Instant Manufacture a Pneumatic Jack-Hammer to break the face of the cliff away from both of Jackie's trapped legs.

As I was helping out with the finer details of the rescue, it's always nice to help out the older pilots, as sooner or later I will be in my late twenties also. I could not help to see Pinger-5 belly sliding down the near vertical cliff face on her way to the final resting place of what was left of Jackie's poor beat up F-22.

After Pinger-5 extensive recovery efforts, she deployed her Up-Chute to enable her to fly all her recovered wreckage back into No. 40's cargo bay carrying several section of Jackie's lost F-22 with her. When No. 40 got everybody to the closest hospital, all I had to do was hover while my ships systems lowered my latest saved friend down to the local Hospital Helicopter-pad. I also saved the entire mountain rescue team as they had used so much of their helicopter fuel that they were "Bingo" to fly to anywhere.

The main reason that this even happed was the fact that I did not have a Space Elevator in operation on the other side of the Earth. I already know of several suitable asteroids in the belt that would be perfect for this task, in all this rescue operation was not quite as bad a mining asteroid but, it was close. The bottom line was that Jackie was a little banged up and had to spend some time in the hospital, a nice quiet military hospital on the surface of the earth.

Log Entry #118.
How Smart Are They:

I keep getting asked that question, by everybody I meet as soon as they find out that I personally know a live Whale. The first thing you have to realize is that whales are usually friendly at first contact especially if you do not try to kill them at first sight. The major problem has always been communications.

Frankly, it hurts humans to even try to talk any of their languages. As none of them have ever been written down until now. Not to mention the fact that none of the whale species has ever been able to wright anything down on paper until I lucked out and got Pinger-5 to talk to me through my basic translation program that I built into my first communication system.

It is always interesting to know that once Pinger-5 learned that we poor dumb humans could speak to each other, she took it upon herself to learn all of the various languages that we humans use. She did it pretty much overnight she even figured out how to do human ascents. On several different occasions I asked Pinger-5 about her ability to talk to other animals. She answer that she could not really talk to another species like Polar Bears but she could listen in and in some cases change the subject that the Bear was complaining about.

She also recruited a small army of Polar Bears and employed them to eat problem food source reptiles as well as mammals in Florida, and figured out how to get humans to pay her for this service literally by the pound. She hasn't gotten rid of all the Earth bound Whale Killers ships but she is buying them up one ship at a time as soon as their company goes out of business. Also as far as a safety Issue Pinger-5 has my personal permission to launch each Killer Ship into the Sun, just to get rid of it.

If knowledge is power a Whale has to the most powerful mammal on the Earth. Their best comparison would be to compare them to the nomadic tribes of Native American humans that existed before the European invasion of 1492. Each tribe has their own language as well as favorite food sources. Even an uneducated Whale could figure out how to use celestial navigation all by themselves.

Each whale has a superior memory letting them remember everything they hear or see, and with a little help the ability to recall all data as needed. All historical facts as written in history books really gets any of the whales' attention, ask her to verify a historical event and she will quote hundreds of references for any event that you want to know about. Quoting each reference line by line, you should see what she does when she finds a historical wrongs especially when it in any kind of school book.

Pinger-5 has a real mad on for the History Channel, every time she catches them in a mistake she sends all their producers the photos of the correct ship or aircraft along with all of her correct facts to back up her statement. As far as I can see, the only reason that Whales do not rule the world already is because they don't have hands therefore they can't use tools.

Over all whales are fearless on one of our latest adventures Pinger-5 figured out where all the Gold in the solar system was located and went after it all. The problem was she had no idea of how much of it there was, as it turned out we didn't get it, it got us. Upon our safe return Pinger-5 has come up with several different strategies to safely recover Space Gold in much smaller quantities.

Log Entry #119.
Modern Mistel Special:

I have had lots of fun with my home built F-22. I surprise my friend Lynda with my latest gimmicked out Raptor at first she didn't believe her own eyes, their Lynda stood wide eyed with her mouth open like all the other Pilots in her squadron. I called ahead to request a public meeting on her own home tarmac. No. 39 and I made a perfect V.T.O.L. landing on her home base and off loaded my latest homebuilt F-22.

As soon as my nose wheel elevator doors open, I drove my Mars Cycle with its extremely large over-size sand tires. I powered it up and drove it over to my parked home built Raptor. As Lynda and her commander were taking a close look at my latest handy work, I stopped my Mars-Cycle under the nose of my home built Raptor and ordered its Command Computer to load it aboard, to use it as a cockpit.

The big empty space under the canopy really got their attention. The first question on the tip of their tongue was how I can use a motorcycle to fly an F-22. The bottom line was all the F-22's original cockpits were destroyed by firing their pilots firing their ejection seat charges. And my Mars Cycle has enough instrumentation for both. So after a few morph commands I had installed a fully operational cockpit.

I walked up to Lynda's Commander and officially asked if she could come out and play. As regulation boarding stairs suddenly open up to create a set of stairs to climbs up into the cockpit level. At first glance it looked like any other F-22 until it started to morph into its regulation Sabrina Aviation metallic red gold paint scheme with the official FAA N-Numbers and all. The first commit was why only one Pilot seat, then I gave the command to my on board Command Computer to morph my F-22 into a two-seater, as another cockpit started to show up, as the canopy finally open I politely asked if she wanted to be the Gale in the Back or for me too. Being a much older Fighter Pilot she took the rear cockpit. I even morph a copy of the cockpit of the last aircraft that I knew she flew.

During pre-flight she even remarked that her instrument panel was working, of course it works I answered do you think I would morph you a fake one. Because of my re-build my Sabrina Aviation Raptor had more on hand power than the standard Air Force variant, with Lynda in command we used a taxi-way to get airborne on. I think this scared Lynda to where she instantly surrenders control to me, as I leveled off at 40 thousand feet. I called her air traffic controller for a vector to the training area.

Lynda's next question was what did you do to the engines, nothing much I replied this airframe can't stand mush over Mach two, I answered. Have we flamed out she asked due to the quiet operation of my Twin Baby Aero-spike rocket engines, I started to slow down to show how I can do super maneuverability.

Lynda was screaming "she's going to stall" when I extended my parasol wing and made my home built Raptor into a Bi-Plane while still in-flight. Lynda's next question was worth millions "Hay we just grew a set of wings "and when I extended the hidden set of wings from the old side-wall missile bay. "Wow were flying a tri-plane" next was the aerodynamic cleanup of the century, with the inflight conversion of a Tri-Plane into a supersonic Space ship that started to zoom climb all the way up to low Earth orbit.

That is until I ran out of liquid rocket fuel this caused me to have to do a back slide into a full stall feather maneuver. I was still trying to raise Lynda's air traffic controller for a vector with my communication system, I will have to admit that my communication system was working perfectly. From several hundred miles up during the long slow fall back down to the surface of the Earth, Lynda made a lot more comments as she thought we had been shot down.

During my power-less controlled descent, Lynda made several interesting commits as well as tried to eject a couple of times, needless to say it took the complete control of my falling airframe to make sure that when my F-22 hit the surface of the Earth, it did it on a deep wet spot.

So we ended up at the bottom of Lake Mead, sitting gear up at about 800 feet under water. At the last second before impact I managed to make my world famous nose over maneuver to enable my F-22 to slip underwater without making a big splash.

So Lynda though that it was a very big surprise to be just sitting on the lake bottom of Lake Mead, it took Lynda almost a full minute to realize that she was still bone dry. She really liked the altimeter that was showing negative numbers.

It only took a few minutes for my onboard Oxygen/Hydrogen separators to get to work so after a quick refueling from all the available water my homebuilt F-22 was ready to go again. With a quick inflation of a set of retractable floats that I had built into the bottom missile bay, we both bobbed to the surface without any problems.

Except we had a set of flooded engines, due to Lynda's added mass both of my aero-spike engines igniters were underwater. "What are you going to do now call the flight Line Chief for a jump start cart" Lynda Asked. Don't tell me your pet whale is going to show up and move us to shore.

Something like that I answered. Without word of warning there was a tremendous splash as Pinger-5 entered the water and surfaces next to us as we were floating dead in the water. How did she get here Lynda asked? A swan dive I answered she has to fly the F-35 into its docking pins, I replied as if we had done this maneuver a 100 times already.

About this time my homebuilt V.T.O.L. F-35s showed up and started to hover directly above us. As we were floating aimlessly on the surface of Lake Mead. With an instant extension of my built in Mistel support rails. It was very interesting to watch the changes in Ping-5's eye ball as she gently guided the F-35 that she was remotely piloting into its docking pins.

As soon as everything was locked my F-35 reoriented its engine to enable it to start pushing both of our now connected airframes across the surface of Lake Mead. As soon as we were up on step-2 both of my combustion chambers were dry enough to light off both aero-spikes, enabling me to level out and fly Lynda back to her base, as a tri-engine layout.

So where is your Whale buddy Lynda asked? She has been flying the F-35 for over an hour, I replied. Pinger-5 has been shadowing us sense we took off from the Lake. I heard Lynda moaned as she finally noticed Pinger-5 in her newly morphed rocket powered whale maneuvering unit.

Lynda's return to her base was a little on the dramatic side, first with a maximum high speed run a couple feet above the surface of her bases main runway low enough to set fire to all the left over skid marks.

Then I pull my F-35 / F-22 modern Mistel into a hover as I extended lift-fans as well as opened up my bottom thrusters to make a perfect landing in the same spot that I had first used. Lynda was a little shaken but not stirred. As I was walking her back over to where her commander was standing Sabrina No. 39's remote aircraft mover quickly loaded everything back aboard and gave me her clear to depart call. I marked my test flight as a success and made planes for several improvements.

Log Entry #120.
Shuttle Shuffle:

It had been an uneventful day I got a head start on tonight's homework. I was hard at work in my Command POD when all of a sudden I got a call from the Administrator of N.A.S.A. Due to the latest government cut-backs things had to happen now or never. It seemed that upon the retirement of the last operational Space Shuttle all federal funding had been removed to maintain their airframes, they didn't have enough money to keep the seagulls off their airframes.

As of now, there wasn't even money allocated to keep the lights on in their hangers. The administrator of N.A.S.A. had heard rumors about my moving the "Last Bird" for the EAA and he was hoping that I could do the same thing for N.A.S.A. To make matters worse two of the delivery points were not anywhere near a runway that was long enough to land a 747. Also, their only operational Boeing 747-123 mother-ship had already been sold to a cargo hauling company.

To top that off he had orders to move two of the three as soon as possible to three different museums throughout the country. As an added glitch the Shuttle Enterprise, currently on display at Steven F. Udvar-Hazy Center in Virginia will have to be swapped for the Shuttle Discovery.

Then picked-up and moved the Enterprise to the Intrepid Sea, Air & Space Museum in New York. The Space Shuttle Endeavour will go to the California Science Center in Los Angeles. The Shuttle Atlantis will be displayed at the Kennedy Space Center Visitor's Complex in Florida.

As such I was not allowed to touch it. This one I was going to do myself, along with the help of Sabrina No. 39. I checked all the data and determined that No. 39 could adjust her lower forward cargo bay too fit in two of the space shuttles at the same time with inches to spare. That if I loaded one of them aboard facing backwards. To make it work I would have to retract all three of the space shuttles landing gear myself, or fly with the bottom hatch open.

At this point while he was still on the phone I told him that I would be glad to take the job. I put my largest aircraft loader on board in the lower aft cargo bay.

Then I made all the safety checks pulled No. 39's program up on line made sure to put myself aboard Command POD and all. I transferred Sabrina No. 39's control to my PODS flight computer closed all her hatches. Morph my primary Space suit in existence then I used my controls to move Sabrina No. 39 out the hanger door to put Sabrina No. 39 into a vertical dive. Directly to Florida 33,000 miles below needless to say it felt good to have nothing on my 360 degree viewing walls except the vacuum of outer space.

As usual, I made contact with the local FAA as soon as I had descended to below 100,000 feet. I started making all the radio calls myself during the long glide to the Kennedy Space Center. I used aerodynamic breaking to save fuel. I landed in front of the shuttle serving building without getting anybody's attention. As soon as I came to a complete stop I gave the order for Sabrina No. 39 to start changing her cargo bay to hold two space shuttles at the same time. I had to morph my space suit back into its flight suit format, and un-load my aircraft mover, so that I could drive over to their only security guard to have him open up the locks to allow me into the building.

The only Security guard had to go back on patrol just to keep up with his security rounds. The distant lack of live humans was scary to say the least, as it seems that the only human around was the only security guard that I had to personally locate myself. Sure, enough the electricity had been turned off. Then I made all the connections to enable Sabrina No. 39 to take control of my aircraft mover, and use it to pull open the shuttles hanger doors as N.A.S.A. could not spare the change to pay their own electric bill, to open up the door much less turn on the lights.

Sabrina No. 39s Command Computer was working very hard figuring out how to use my aircraft loader to open the Space Shuttles hanger doors just enough to get the now retired Space Shuttles out one at a time. I caught my aircraft mover just as it was coming out side with the Shuttle Atlantis. It took a lot of very stern voice commands but I finally got Sabrina No. 39s Command Computer to put the Atlantis back where she found it and not to consider it to be one of her Looser Dragster.

As Sabrina No. 39's command computer finally drove the aircraft mover out of the main shuttle hanger with the Endeavor on board I noticed the first glitch. Even with Sabrina No. 39's landing gear extent to its maxim height the shuttle rudder was too tall to slip under the lip of Sabrina No. 39s lower cargo bay to load aboard.

Therefore it was time for plan B, I ordered the mover to bring out the shuttle Discovery and to place them side by side facing the other direction. Then I had Sabrina No. 39 take off and make a vertical landing with her cargo bay open, loading both of the shuttles all at once as she touched down. It only took a couple of minutes for my load master programs to pick up and secure both shuttles in the forward cargo bay.

I had to relocate my Command POD to get into the Space Shuttles cockpit to push the release button that will allow me to physically pick up the landing gear struts. I consider the space shuttle to be an inferior design. Because of its ability to fly like a rock, being equipped with non-wing warping control surfaces. And now I get confronted by its poor designed landing gear system, that depended on used gravity to lower it and floor jacks to retract it. Not to mention the fact that I had to push a manual locking pin in the cockpit to move it in any direction at all.

But, first I had to get into each shuttles cockpit to do anything. So there I was standing at the end of my Command PODs gang plank, when I reached out and open the shuttles main hatch, when it fell in on me and pinned me to my boarding ramp. I realized that it weighed over 500 pounds and to lower it without damage or throwing me off my gang plank. I would have to be able to carry it in my bare hands, I don't know about you but most 16 year old girls cannot lift 500 pounds cold, without a warning of any kind. Luckily, my space suit registered the stress in my arms and instantly made adjustment on my artificial muscle department enabling me to just lower the 500 pound hatch slowly without allowing it to tear off the airframe of the space shuttle.

Needless to say this added a new wrinkle in the relocation problem but, nothing a 16 year old girl with her powered space suit could not handle. I lucked out when I discovered that the safest way to pick-up and close the hatch was to power up my Space suits extra muscles and use the hatches main handle.

I can tell you for a fact that the nicest sound the space shuttle can make is the click when its hatch locks closed. It took me over an hour to secure the shuttles landing gear by manually retracting all their landing gear struts. I had to have the aircraft loader pick up each gear strut one at a time. The exhausting job of actually closing all the landing gear doors had to be done by me, by pushing close all the landing gear doors with a large over size push broom. Who said that 16-year-old girls don't have enough upper arm strength?

As soon as all six landing gear of both space shuttle wheels were retracted and landing gear doors closed, then I was able to close Sabrina No. 39's main cargo doors with a single command from my communications necklace.

As soon as I was back in my command pod, I called the control tower and requested a vertical takeoff from the parking lot, with a vector to the north. The flight to Udvar-Hazy Museum was normal my only problem was the Local runway controllers refused to let me land in the parking lot they made me use the main runway just like all the other airliners. And they even ordered me extent the wheels & tire parts of my landing gear trucks to taxi. Therefore, it took a little longer to drop off the Discovery from her last flight.

I did have a problem lowering her landing gear. I had to get out of my Command POD and climb all the way to the shuttles main hatch. Where I powered up the motorized part of my space suit to just lower the main hatch, then climb into the Discovery's cockpit to push the manual gear release so that gravity could lower the shuttles landing gear for the last flight. I still can't figure why N.A.S.A. would build a spacecraft that used gravity as the only means to lower its landing gear? Just like in Florida I got to use my space suits built in muscles to simply close the main hatch, I had to vertically launch with the cargo bay doors open to leave the Discovery behind It only took a couple of seconds for my electronic load master to set the Discovery on her own landing gear.

As soon a Sabrina No. 39 was high enough off the ground to enable me to move the Discovery without knocking off the top of its rudder. I picked her up with my on board aircraft mover and drove over to the Udvar-Hazy Museums main door. Sabrina No. 39 landed back in her original stopping point to wait for my return with the Enterprise.

In the back of my head I was wondering what they would do if they found out that because of my tender loving age I only had a student driver's license. As soon as their main door opened my jaw dropped as nothing on the museums floor had been re-arranged to allow me access to the Shuttle Enterprise. So my next job was to park the shuttle Discovery in their west parking lot and move everything around myself, it was not a problem with my aircraft mover as it could re-ornate itself to pick up everything in the way, and move it out into west parking lot along with everything else. I was amazed when I finally got to pick up the Enterprise of how light it was then I remembered that it was only made out of plywood and not space worthy. I moved it into the other end of the main parking lot and left it so that Sabrina No. 39 could load it aboard and have my load master program secure it for it last flight to New York City.

Now I could finally pick up the Discovery and put it in its official parking place inside of the Udvar-Hazy Center. I even took another couple of minutes to put everything else back where I found it. By this time my load master program had the Enterprise loaded, except for the retraction of it landing gear. This time I was ready I moved my Command POD around and set the end of my loading ramp, reach out and open the Enterprises main hatch only to discover that it was made out of plywood.

Needless to say my Space suit automatic adjusted itself for its lack of weight. I lucked out when I discovered that it had the same landing gear release buttons as all the other shuttles. This was my job just like in Florida I had to use the jacks that were built into my aircraft loader to retract both the nose as well as both main landing gears. I luck out as there was an automatic lock built into the main strut, all I had to do was manually push on the release and have my aircraft mover pick it up. As in Florida the final solution was a very long handle over size push broom that I had to use to finally close-up all the landing gear doors all by myself.

I knew that flying into New York without a lot of special permits would be a problem. Not to mention its location, I checked on the internet only to discover that they published their Aircraft Carriers location. I also luck out when I discovered that I had to be 16 years old to visit their museum without having one if not both of my parents along with me.

This was not good news as I did not have time to fly all the way back to Chicago and pick them up. I finally found their location on Google Earth, there the Intrepid was located it was docked at Pier #86 in the Hudson River on the west side of Manhattan Island just west of 12th Avenue, W 46th Street and 12th Avenue New York, NY 10036-4103. This was all my Command Computer need to know as Sabrina No. 39 instantly plotted the safest flight path to this location. I checked with Pinger-5 who had done a lot of business with the humans that live in New York. She has been running a salvage operation by bringing in all the sea going plastic, that we humans have left floating in the Atlantic Ocean just east of their state. In a few of her words all these nickels add up in a hurry.

At the Intrepid Air and Space museum but she had always used one of my Sabrina No. 40 Space ships to make the delivery by using my Urban-Camouflage-Program to make her Space ship look like a sea going barge.

This was not good news as Sabrina No. 39 does not like to get wet. I vertically launched and flew east and out to sea then north east to the southern tip of Manhattan Island. I had been hovering for less than a minute then I detected one of my No. 40 ships coming in from the Atlantic Ocean under water moving several thousand miles per hour despite being submerged I could plainly see her hydromantic controls as she extended her speed brakes and slowed to a stop about 100 feet below the surface.

Sabrina No. 39 used my Communications System to inform Sabrina No. 40/78 that it was her job to surface as she did not like to get wet. Instantly No. 40/78 popped to the surface of the water at the mouth of the Hudson River and morphed into one of Pinger-5's instant Urban-Camouflage-Program making herself look like one of the passing garbage barges that were moving up and down the Hudson River.

Sabrina No. 39 did not even think of reducing power until Sabrina No. 40/78 had surfaced all the way. All of a sudden the middle of a garage barge turned into an empty spot and Sabrina No. 39 instantly reduced her flight speed extend her wings and turned on her lift-fans and made a V.T.O.L landed in the extremely well light empty spot like she had performed this type of maneuver every day.

To a person watching it looked like Sabrina No. 39 disappeared into an empty spot at the mouth of the Hudson River. Then with a very slow cruise up the Hudson River to 46th Street I could not get close enough to just connect up to the Intrepid Flight Deck. Also, the Flight Deck was already covered with aircraft the only empty spot was on the front of the ship. This new wrinkle made me glad that I had built Sabrina No. 39 as she was the only aircraft on the planet that had the raw power to hover over the flight deck of the Aircraft Carrier Intrepid and lower the Space Shuttle Enterprise directly onto its final resting place on her bow just west of the Hudson River Greenway.

All she needed was my permission to proceed on my command the urban camouflage slowly faded into the middle flight deck of No. 40/78, Sabrina No. 39 extended her wings and turned her lift-fans up to full power. Before launch Sabrina No. 39's Command Computer automatically called the local FAA control tower to get permission for a vertical assent from our present location. Sabrina No. 39 convinced them that she was a helicopter as we lifted-off we hovered and transitioned directly into the closet helicopter taxi lane. Manhattan Air Traffic Control controller center automatically gave me a vector to fly over to the Intrepid Helicopter-pad.

Sabrina No. 39 was smart enough to just come to a hover over top of it with the lower cargo bay door open. I relocated my Command POD next to the Enterprises main hatch so that I could enter the cockpit and manually lower the Enterprises landing gear for the last time. I finally I got to use gravity to let all of the landing gear struts just fall into their permanent down position, as I moved back into my Command POD I looked down and noticed the sign that read, "Please note – all guests under the age of 16 must be accompanied by an adult for entry into the museum – no exceptions.

Guests under the age of 16 unaccompanied by an adult will not be permitted to enter the museum. "I quickly re-orientated my Command

POD to my nose wheel, and then extended it to where my nose wheel was parked just in front of the Enterprise's nose as she sat on the steam catapults on the bow of the USS Intrepid. I rode my nose wheel elevator all the way down, and move as quickly as I could to put its forward as well as aft wheel shocks under each of her tires as the last thing I wanted to do was have her roll on to the Hudson River Greenway.

This also opened up a lot of old programing where Sabrina No. 39 wanted to land on the deck of an Aircraft Carrier that was launching lots of X-47 drones at her. I personally made a sigh of relief when my leave now request put the idea of her personal landing out of her logic boards programing. By this time the FAA had figured out what was going on, as my communication system had picked up hundreds of different I-Phones that were transmitting live photos of her hovering over the USS Intrepid on the internet, in some of the closer shots even I could plainly see me through my open cargo bay doors with the Space Shuttle Endeavour still secured in the other half of the lower forward cargo bay.

I chuckled as I wonder if I would be bombarded with questions as to why I was hauling it backwards in the cargo bay. With all the confusion Sabrina No. 40/78 just slipped under the surface of the Hudson River and went back to her mission. I let my Command Computer do all the talking as the FAA finally gave me permission to make a vertical climb out from my present location with a vector to the west.

So then with my permission Sabrina No. 39 did one of her best turn-around, climb and close-up everything maneuvers that was ever photographed on the internet. Some of the photographer must have had very powerful zoom lenses as they were able to maintain their full frame close-up view of Sabrina No. 39 as we transition from hover mode to space ship, as I close my lift-fans and retracted my wings. As soon as I had enough altitude I fired up my aero-spikes and put on the speed to get to California as soon as I could according to my helicopter flight plan time it would take me 4 hours to get to the California Science Center in Los Angeles, in reality it took me less than 10 minutes, that's pretty good considering I stayed in the atmosphere the whole time.

Thanks to complete FAA automation they still think that Sabrina No. 39 was a helicopter, they even authorized my vertical landing at the main gate of the California Science Center in Los Angeles. Sabrina No. 39 made a perfect vertical landing in their parking lot with the aid of her retractable lift-fans she put herself down just behind their DC-8. Their gate guard did get a little excited when Sabrina No. 39's main landing gear misted his guard shack by less than foot.

I had to move my Command POD next to the Endeavour's main hatch, lower my boarding ramp and walk all the way to endeavor's main hatch. For this operation my space suit remembered what to do and set all its controls automatically. Finally for the last time I had to climb into her Command Pilots seat to push the button that makes Earth's gravity dramatically lower all of her landing gear at the same instant. Then it was a simple matter of lowering Endeavour for her last landing. The last thing I did was closed the shuttles main hatch with my bare hands thanks to my space suits built in muscles. As usual Sabrina No. 39 had to perform another of her vertical lift-off and close-up maneuvers just to get the Endeavor out of her cargo bay. She closed up and made sure that her vertical launch exhaust did not blow away the guards shack.

I made the day for the Los Angeles Air Traffic Controllers when I request a vertical assent with a high speed acceleration to Mach 26, as I flew east to my space elevator shaft and followed it all the way home. The rest of the day went off without another hitch.

I did hear about a very interesting television news program about a top secret supersonic heavy-lift helicopter that the government was experimenting with. In all this job only took 4 hours and I did manage to get a few new push brooms or two out of the deal.

Not to mention being the last person to fly the Space Shuttles, three of them at the same job. I just realized that I am now the first Pilot to land the Enterprise on an aircraft carriers deck, the fact that it was a full stop and docked to the 46th street pier in New York, only make it harder to figure out for the record books. I all I spent more time playing house than I did flying.

Log Entry #121.
Summer Intern:

I spent the summer working with the nice folks at the Boeing Phantom works in California at Edwards Air Force Base they are the ones that are working on the latest X-plane. It's nothing new to me their trying to convert a poor old navy F/A-18 Hornet fighter plane to be aerodynamically controlled with a wing warping control system.

Similar to how the Wright Brother kept control of their 1903 airplane. I offered to convert it for them myself but they would not let me transport it to my own construction hanger that I keep on the "Leader." I was kind of interesting for the Air force not to allow anybody to take a navel aircraft out of California.

Not to mention not allowing me or any other of my team member to even think of flying it as a Pilot in command. So we did it the Earth bound way in the desert heat and blowing sand I helped my Phantom works team to hollow out a perfectly good F/A-18. Then to install a wing warping system that would allow it to do an aerobatic display at any supersonic speed, problem was it just barely made it up to Mach 2. If it was my project I would have had it finished the first day in my nice cool sand free zero "G" work environment on the "Leader." When on breaks I started going into the ladies room and ordered my Space suit to morph up to cool me down too my normal 72 degrees. Needless to say when working by myself I kept my Space suit on with its air condition system turned way up.

I really lucked out when the company's safety officer ordered everybody into Hazmat suits. This made my day with a few simple commands to my morphing controls I had it made. I could get away with wearing my space suit all the time all I had to do was use my Urban-Camouflage-Program to make it look like a standard Haze-Mat-Suit. Being in a one "G" environment my built in extra muscle also came in handy caring around heavy aircraft components.

As I was looking out the window of my dorm room I noticed a large pile of F-35 fragments. I thought that it was left overs parts from the Air Forces target practice. It turns out the whole pile of fragmented parts was from Pinger-5, who though that I could re-build the entire fragment pile into flyable airplanes over night.

As if I had my zero "G" work shop on my key ring. Sabrina No. 39 loved it also, as Edwards Air force Base is her favorite location, the fact that it's the first place in California that she was programed to find, only makes it better. Given the wide open spaces all she needs is a little of my Urban-Camouflage-Program and she is not to be seen anywhere. Sabrina No. 39 did manage to load up all of Pinger-5's F-35 fragments so that I could deal with them on my own.

This proves the fact that all Sabrina No. 39 needs to be happy is an operational aircraft mover and an Urban-Camouflage-Program set too, "sand." Come to think of it Pinger-5 did make an interesting deal for lots of extra external water tanks to hold all the liquid needed to make the Wing Warping Mechanism operate.

During our tour of the official United States Air Force Astronaut Test Pilot School, on a dare I was allowed to take the final written test that all of the military astronaut have to pass, it had the same old questions with a lot more math than usual. I managed to pass the written test with a score of 100 percent in less than half an hour.

Log Entry #122.
Weather on the Gas Giants:

I am afraid it's true and it's my entire fault. Look on the bright side so far we have only made holes the great red spot on Jupiter. As a matter of fact I have been to the outer gas giants as often as anybody. Saturn has its rings but Uranus and Neptune are not worth the trip.

I can calculate the penetration points to use Jupiter's Atmosphere as an aero brake to be able to dive into the atmosphere too spend emergency and slow down just enough to pop out the atmosphere at the exact point needed to automatically get trapped in the orbit of any one of Jupiter's Moons you care to mention.

Extending the hover fans and trying to play helicopter just doesn't work inside of Jupiter's large gravity field. The problem of speed inside the Atmosphere my Space ships are tough but not indestructible, to crash into water at supersonic speed is nothing compared to flying around the inside of Jupiter's Atmosphere.

The problem is how to fly slow lower in the Atmosphere on a planet that has no surface. To do this I decided to convert the middle top cargo bay to expel a single giant blimp shape envelope that is large enough to carry the weight of the whole Sabrina No. 40 Space ships as it would operate deep inside the gas giant Jupiter.

This enabled my Whale/naut's to use their oversized up-chutes to make extend trips away from the now stationary Sabrina No. 40 so far nothing as show up for them to eat or eat them. So far due to my school actives I have only had the time to travel to Jupiter several times myself.

Now it's everybody else turn to go and see for themselves. Pinger-5 latest venture is to send small Kuiper belt object through her newly discovered solar Gold dust section of the asteroid belt, on a free trajectory to land in front of the main entrance to Pinger-5s under water Chicago base.

My Whale/naut's have kept thing going they have piloted pioneering research space flights as well as everyday re-supply flights. They are actively searching the Asteroid Belt for key special shape asteroids suitable to use as a Space Arks.

I am toying with the idea of making a "Fingers and Thumbs" controllable set of human hands that any of my Whale/naut's can work themselves.

And they are out there now still looking and planning for bigger and bolder space programs. After listing to them talk to each other and looking at their math equations I think that they are planning to put together their own planet or Giant Space Ark. Thanks to their exploration flights the list of recoverable comets are over 100 pages long. But they still depend on humans to build and repair machinery I am referred to as "Sabrina the Invincible" or just "Fixer" in conversations between each other directly in personnel conversations.

Another name that confused me at first was "Hats" as it turned out it refers to all the different type of work that this lonely 16 year old human female can do at the same instant. As in their eyes I am the only human capable of wearing more than one hat at a time.

Over all they are fair enough when working with other humans other that myself, however with the first failure of a system they call for me "Sabrina the Invincible". To fix whatever the problem was for the first time and forever.

Log Entry #123.
JOO2E3 Rendezvous:

I got a phone call from the head of N.A.S.A. it seem that he had revived several inquiries from the public about the possibility of finding 5 lost S-IVB's from old Apollo Moon missions. S-IVB-503N used during the Apollo 8 mission on December 21, 1968 they think that it's in a solar orbit. S-IVB-504 used on Apollo 9 on March 3, 1969 all they know is it's in solar orbit. S-IVB-505 used on Apollo 10 on May 18, 1969 was left in solar orbit. S-IVB-506 used on Apollo 11 it was used on July 16, 1969 it was left in solar orbit and last but not least. S-IVB-507 used on the Apollo 12 mission on November 14, 1969 it was left in Solar orbit it's believed to have been discovered as an Asteroid in 2002 and given the designation JOO2E3.

This is the first time that I have received an incoming communication from N.A.S.A. that identified what they wanted by space frame number. His next question was if I knew where they are now. I asked if he knew any of their last location, speed, and directions of flight. He gave me a list from different years, and directions, as well as different speeds. Being able to calculate like a whale is definitely a plus it took me less than a second or two to give him all of their exact locations in the solar system.

He made a hissing air sound when I told him that most of them were on the other side of the Sun. As well as that none of them were anywhere close to landing in his back yard. He was very excited to know that I knew where he lived. When he asked how I knew where he lived I had to tell him about my Christmas card list.

My next question was if he wanted me to pick them up for him. As at this precise moment I had over 20 of my space ship that I could divert to pick up all of their solar targets. One of the lost S-IVB-503N was only 20 hours and 15 minutes away from one of my Asteroid Ark Ships. He was really worried about the S-IVB that was due to hit the Earth in 2012, I told him that he would not have to worry about it as Pinger-5 would have sold it on E-bay long before the year 2012. I called home to get permission for an unscheduled leaving of the planet.

My father's first question was how long of a mission it would be, I instantly answered 5 years as on Earth a year is one orbit of the Sun and I would have to do at least one for each pick up. He reminded me that this was not science fiction,

The director of N.A.S.A. wanted their lost boosters located and retrieved. It only took me less than a minute to calculate each location. I decided to make in my responsibly to recover all the lost S-IVBs. As always getting there was the problem Sabrina No. 39 and I launched off the LEADER within the next hour. My first thought was to do this the easy way with one intercept per orbit. However, after Pinger-5 studied all the flight paths she came up with an interception plan as well as an intercept point that I could use to catch three of the four on the other side of the Sun.

As always the only hitch was this rendezvous would happen this Thursday on the other side of the Sun. I decided to pick up the S-IVB that was currently closing in on the Earth. It was child's play for me to plot my interception course. As soon as I got there, I was amazed to find a very concentrated fuel cloud with my targeted S-IVB at its center.

So I ordered Sabrina No. 39 to stand off as I flew in close with a towing cable using my Human Maneuvering Unit. Long duration space flights are always a little on the weird side despite the fact that N.A.S.A. ordered the complete use of all of the S-IVBs liquid fuel, the mass of the small 3rd stage booster still siphoned a large portion of its spent exhaust plume into a very large microscopic fuel cloud problem.

This caused lots of control problems when maneuvering near its space frame in outer space. It really gummed up the surfaces of my human maneuvering units, not to mention all the extra thrust every time I fired one of my maneuvering rockets. Needless to say first I had to clean up the orbital sight and recapture as much of the micro atmosphere as I could get.

The first thing I had to do was to use one of my oxygen/hydrogen collectors to capture all the collected rocket exhaust. As soon as Sabrina No. 39 pulled it into one of her empty cargo bays she made a note to me stating that my race car did not have any wheels on it, and asked if she should keep looking for all of the others.

As it turned out I had captured S-IVB-503N that was used during the Apollo 8 mission which had been in flight for more than 40 years. Needless to say getting to the rendezvous point was not a problem for a space ship like Sabrina No. 39.

As Sabrina No. 39 has always been able to go faster, as we were closing in on the targeted area I could see the other three S-IVBs on my scanner as they came into view from around from the other side of the Sun. It was not a problem for Sabrina No. 39 to just fly to the rendezvous point and start flying formation with the closest S-IVB. It was my job to spacewalk out to, it and hooks on a tow line so that Sabrina No. 39 could pull it into her open cargo bay and installed it next to the first capture. Just as with the first capture there was a microscopic exhaust problem as the microgravity of the S-IVB had pulled most of its exhaust plume around itself. Once again this gummed up my space suit and caused lots of problems when I fired my ballistic control rockets.

The good news was it did not set fire to itself or cause an explosion. I barely had time to exchange my primary space suit for my back up Space suit before No. 39 was once again flying formation with S-IVB number three. This time Sabrina No. 39 seemed to rush me because my back-up Space suit was still morphing. This time I played it safe and did not use any of my ballistic controls inside of it microscopic spent fuel cloud. I had to do a lot of bouncing and pushing offs of the surface of Sabrina No. 39 but I finally got the tow cable hooked without firing a control rocket.

This old spent booster rocket pulled in enough ionized gas to set off No. 39s cargo bay sensors. The good news was as Sabrina No. 39 fired her Aero-spike-Rocket motor to catch the next S-IVB she inertly set the fuel cloud on fire causing a pretty had kick in her pants.

I had barely gotten out of the airlock when we had rendezvous with the next S-IVB. After surviving the last dentation I decided not to let Sabrina No. 39 come as close as last time, so this time I had Sabrina No. 39 spool out all hundred miles of her tow line. I used my human maneuvering unit to pull it all out then I got to invent space skiing.

It was very interesting to be towed up beside an S-IVB booster that had been in flight since the 1960s. And coming close enough to reach out and connect a towing cable on the first pass. The second I connected up to the S-IVB No. 39 started to reeled me and my big catch into her aft cargo bay. As soon as I was aboard I had Sabrina No. 39 made a Bee Line to the fifth and last S-IVB on my list.

It was a simple matter to figure it location and to top everything off it was on a direct tangent back to Earth. I played it safe and went space skiing again, it became old hat for me to be let out on a 100 mile long tow cable. I lucked out and hooked on the first time, so just like that I had all five of the missing S-IVBs. In all I did Five years of flying in less than 72 hours. My mother did get a little excited when she found out that I was in the other side of the Sun but there was nothing to it.

Log Entry #124.
Grabbing the Eagle:

I secured a small storage area on the LEADER to tuck away all of my recovered S-IVBs. At last I had all 5 of N.A.S.A.'s lost S-IVBs floating next to each other. Ever since I was a little girl I wanted to build my own Space ship from old rocket parts. As it turns out N.A.S.A. did not want any of the S-IVBs back. Pinger-5 had a few nibbles from several museums but nothing came of it. As I was inspecting them for scrap I discover that all of their avionics were still working including the very old television camera that took and broadcast the historical picture of the separation from the SIIC while it was still low inside the Earth's Atmosphere.

I started planning my Apollo space-tug I had five still operational J-2 rocket motors that ran on hydrogen and oxygen the same fuel that I have always used on my space craft. So with everything up and running I could not get anything to work with my fly-by-wire system the bottom line is a needed some old technology that had a computer in it. As such I realized that I had to find and capture one of the two missing Lunar modules that were abandoned by N.A.S.A. in the 1960's as I remember the problem was not finding one but being able to recover it.

As the recovery problem has always been the fact that each of the surviving lunar module assent-stages are spinning as fast as they can, on all three of their control axes, if I were try to just grab on to it, it would tear itself into millions of very small fragments. As it turn out the answer to the recovery problem very simple, all I had to do was submerge the out of control vehicle in liquid water then freeze it into a ball of ice, big enough for me to grab onto and stop.

Then with all the pitch, yaw and roll problems under control all I had to do was melt away the Ice then pump off all the water. So with this plan in mind, Sabrina No. 39 and I went after what was left of the Eagle the spacecraft that first landed men on the Moon way back in July of 1969, and then was abandoned in lunar orbit.

Over the years in flight the gravity wells of the Earth, Moon, and the Sun had caused the very fragile throw away space ship to spin on all three of its axes, faster and faster. Just like when I was a child pumping the swing in my back yard it would increase its speed, of Pitch, Yaw and Roll on every orbit. Making it impossible to pick up and recover.

So plan "A "was to rig Sabrina No. 39s forward ballistic control rocket to squirt water. This is something that Sabrina No. 39 did not want to do. It took all of my programing skill and lot of re-plumbing of her control system to make it happen. I knew I could make this idea work as soon as Sabrina No. 39 complained about her running nose. I let my lunar manager know that I wanted to hunt down and recover what was left of Apollo 11's Eagle.

I had performed this trip a number of times so Sabrina No. 39 already knew the way having performed all the different orbital maneuvers need to park herself directly behind the "Eagle" as she has been in lunar orbit since 1969. As usual Sabrina No. 39 tried to abort her interception because of the targets movements. It only took her seconds to break down the Lunar Modules pitch, yaw, and roll movements only to tell me that the "Eagle" fragment was still spinning too fast to be recovered.

As she did not want it bouncing around inside any of her cargo bays. So I took over the controls and inched my way in closer and closer with Sabrina No. 39 setting off alarm after alarm as we got closed to squirting range. It was impossible to program all the variable into a computer so all I could to was adjust the stream of water and chase the "Eagle" around as it started to pick up mass and dance around in lots of different Lunar orbital tracks.

It took several hours of extremely intense piloting to really give the "Eagle" a real dunking. It was quite interesting to watch as layer after layer of water formed up into a solid ball of pure wet water ice. After the big wet down the problem of getting the still spinning but very wet "Eagle" captured. But first everything had to be frozen solid, so all I had to do was to keep

Sabrina No. 39s shadow covering the spinning ball of water until in turned white.

This took a while once again an extremely low orbit around the Moon, finally "Eagle" passed into the Lunar night part of its orbit, where its temperature instantly dropped to 250 degrees below zero, this caused all the water to freeze solid finally just before Lunar dawn I decides to give it a try.

I open up the top cargo bay doors and positioned Sabrina No. 39 cargo bay around the still spinning "Eagle" and closed the cargo bay doors. My cargo bay seniors instantly started giving me readings as the direction and speed that the "Eagle "was moving. It took the morphing of oversized rolling balls that I plan to keep moving in closer until contact was made with the now glass smooth Ice surface.

I started shrinking the size of the cargo bay, until all six rollers walls made contact and then I started to use the roller braking system to finally bring the "Eagles" movement relive to that of Sabrina No. 39. As soon as my home built de-celebration system started to work Sabrina No. 39 started the trip pack to her hanger on the LEADER.

Log Entry #125.
Apollo Space-Tug:

I most definitely had to do a lot of flying around to gather up enough parts but I can finally start building my Apollo Space-Tug. Not to mention the fact that old used Apollo parts are hard to come by.

The first thing I did was to create a movable morph capable space ship. In the past I have been hampered by the size of my cargo bay doors. If I can't get it inside of my space ship I could not haul it structure bulk heads.

I plan to send my Space-Tug out into the asteroid fields and have it expand its self to where the whole space ship would just swallow any large size asteroid that I want, then expand the tugs size to where it would fit inside of it. I plan to mount each of my captured S-IVBs, on a control mount on each corner control would be maintained by changing the orientation of each separate S-IVB.

To be able to control the old Apollo boosters I needed the computers from the Lunar Module to fire as well as monitor the operation of each S-IVB. It was a simple matter to freeze dry the salvage "Eagle" assent stage and install one of my Command Computers to keep track of everything.

At first the poor little assent stage was not designed for continues use I had to install a very low power He'3 reactor for electricity, once reactivated all the ships systems can back on line. The cockpit was very small by anybody standard, with no seats or any kind of pilot's seat. To top it all off the poor little Lunar bug was full of hole where hundreds of very hard micro meteorites had shot it full of very small as well as very long through holes.

As usual working by myself in my Zero "G" work shop rebuilding the "Eagle was a piece of cake, I had all the control systems clean out and refueled in only one day. The next day the Eagle was moving itself around my repair shop. She even flew herself to her new roosting spot in the Apollo-Space-Tug.

Log Entry #126.
This is a list of all of Amelia Earhart's Achievements with a few of my commits:

One of my early assignments in school was to compare myself to Amelia Earhart. On June 17-18, 1928 Amelia became the first woman to fly across the Atlantic Ocean in an airplane it took her 20 hours & 40 minutes flying as a crew member aboard a Fokker F7, Friendship. My first crossing of the Atlantic Ocean that accrued during my first around the world flight only took 12 minutes. During my first flight to the planet Mars, upon my first return from Mars I flew the Atlantic Ocean length wise in less the 7 minutes.

In August of 1929 Amelia placed third in the First Women's Air Derby, aka the Powder Puff Derby. This is when she upgraded herself airplane wise to a Lockheed Vega. I have not got into the Air Racer operation yet as I am having enough problems with Sabrina No. 39 drag racing operation.

In the fall 1929 Amelia was elected as an official for National Aeronautic Association and encouraged the Federation Aeronautique Internationale to establish separate world altitude, speed and endurance records for women. I have tried to communicate with the French Government however for some reason they think that I still build airplanes on the roof of my father garage.

June 25, 1930 - Amelia set the women's air speed record for 100 kilometers with no load, and then with a pay load of 500 kilograms.

July 5, 1930 - Amelia set speed the official record of 181.18 mph over a 3K course. I have built as well as flown Space ships with larger cargo bays.

On April 8, 1931 Amelia had set the woman's autogiro altitude record of 18,415 feet, while flying in a Pitcairn Autogiro. I - hauled a Pitcairn Autogiro to Mars to see how well it would handle in the Martian atmosphere.

Due to the low air pressure I calculated that I would have to increase the rotor span to at least 150 feet just to get it to lift off the surface. On May 20-21, 1932 Amelia became the first woman to fly solo across the Atlantic in a time span of 14 hours & 56 minutes. This was also the 5th anniversary of Charles Lindberg's Atlantic flight.

Amelia was awarded the National Geographic Society's Gold medal from President Herbert Hoover. Congress awarded her the Distinguished Flying Cross. 1932 - She was the first woman to fly solo nonstop coast to coast she set the women's nonstop transcontinental speed record, flying 2,447.8 miles in 19 hours and 5 minutes. I flew 25,675 miles east for just over an hour before I was in Grade School. All I got out of it was a nasty letter from O-Hare Airport about burring off rubber skid marks with my landing skids.

In the fall 1932 Amelia was elected as the first president of the Ninety Nines. A new women's aviation club which she helped to form. I had to beat that speed record just to get into Low Earth Orbit, not to mention the speed necessary to travel to the other Planets on our solar system.

On January 11, 1935 Amelia became the first person to solo the 2,408-mile distance across the Pacific Ocean between Honolulu and Oakland, California, this was also first flight where a civilian aircraft carried a two-way radio. After an 18 hour flight, she landed at Oakland, with thousands of cheering fans to welcome her. To help save the Whales I created a continuous airlift operation between Honolulu and Chicago, I designed and constructed Space craft that can haul live Whales a full family pod at a time, and I also built a Command Computer that enables the Whales themselves to operate the airlift.

May 8, 1935 Amelia became the first person to fly solo nonstop from Mexico City to Newark, New Jersey in 14 hours & 19minutes. To this very day I still have no need to fly to Mexico City. I don't know how to explain it but I know that I have something to do with Amelia Earhart. Somehow I have always known that someday I will get to meet her in person. Who knows someday I might even offer her a Job.

Log Entry #127.
Eagle Space-Tug:

As I was saying the "Eagle" whom was abandoned in Lunar orbit in 1969 was my interface with all the control systems of the five different S-IVBs that I recovered from solar orbit.

Because it was designed to fire its landing rocket engine while on the dark side of the Moon, the Eagle was the first operational Space ship to have a built in computer. So it was a simple matter for me to add one of my command computers to its operational command system. Granted it was not a very smart computer but it could communicate. Once my command computer took over the Eagle started to think for itself.

She would have been a real help during the time when Pinger-5 and I were entombed alive by billions of tons of microscopic space gold. As my Apollo space tug can expand its main body large enough to hold several of my Sabrina No. 40 ships at the same time. So with its five operational S-IVB booster rocket boosters to use as variable control self-contained rocket motors it had the power to move anything that was left to move in the solar system.

I eventually named her as my Sabrina No.100 a one of a kind structure that I sent out into the Asteroid belt in search of large iron asteroids that I might be able to use an Asteroids Space Arks.

Log Entry #128.
I am now at M.I.T.:

I have been invited to dinner at Kirkland House but, I am visiting Harvard Physics first. I just finished my first full week as a sophomore here at M.I.T. I have a dorm room at The River Boston View on the top floor. So far the most exciting thing to happen here was Hurricane Irene!

The school lost a lot of floor space to the rising storm water when the Charles River backed up and stayed, in some of our buildings up to the third floor. Sabrina No. 39 sat out the worst part of the storm parked on my dorm roof, with the aid of her Urban Camouflage program I had her made up to look like a standard roof top air conditioning unit.

She still does not like to get her insides wet. I still remember the last time I parked her on the roof of my dorm when she got to save the day by flying me and my school administrator away as a level five Tornado destroyed the whole campus. Despite all her complaints she stood watch over me during the whole storm.

Just in case I did have her instruct her loadmaster program to install a travel POD for each of the on hand students and facility in case the building started to collapse. She even extended my Command POD down into my secret passage ways. It was quite interesting to see exactly how many Whales live in down town Boston, as their whale scooters were the only vehicles that were still operational in 30 feet of flooded Ocean water.

All the rain was wonderful especially for a person like me that has spent time on the surface of Mars. I had to call off Pinger-5s Hurricane party when the Irene's Eye moved inland over heavily populated areas with lots of very tall building. Although, a couple of days later when Hurricane Irene had finally moved a safe distance out to sea, I allowed No. 39 to punch all the holes in Hurricane Irene's eye that she wanted.

After all it's not nice to keep a super storm working on the surface of the Earth. Life at M.I.T. will not be the same as when I was at school at I.M.S.A. for openers the first year I have to go to classes on the surface of the Earth. I cannot tune in from my PODs classroom and make 100% on the entire test in advance anymore.

I will have to show up in person and go to class like everybody else. Of course there will be official field trips that will not have to be-on planet.

Log Entry #129.
My New Roommate Lorynda:

Life with roommates is a new thing for me as I always seem to run out of living space in my Command POD in a hurry. Answering personal questions such as "How did you get past me in the elevator", or "how come you stay inside your closet all the time". When it's really the secret entry point to my Command POD whose boarding ramp is placed behind my closets sliding door.

I have to face it my old bed in my Command PODs always the most comfortable. My new roommate Lorynda who is a much older person in her late teens, is hard to figure out she wants to know everything about me. How come she never catches me studying or using the dorm rooms' computer? I wonder what she will say when she meets Pinger-5. How come every time I need something it magically appears, how come this and how come that, how can I change my clothing so fast and where did I get that new outfit or school uniform. And of course the latest how can I stand outside on the Veranda during Hurricane Irene without getting wet.

Also how can I freeze dry my wet textbooks instantly? After personally recovering all of them from my three stories deep flooded out hallway locker. I will have to keep my space suit and Cargo PODs a secret as long as I can. After all I would not want her to think that I was a Martian or that I had lived on Alien Planet.

To top it all off Lorynda is not a pilot or a mechanic, and I know for a fact that she has never had a Young Eagle Flight. She's a standing member of the Flat Earth Society and believes that when she is standing still on the surface of the Earth she is not moving. However Lorynda is a computer expert, she has built several smart machines so far nothing that I would trust to fly with. I have already picked up a few pointers from her as to how I can improve may command computers.

Log Entry #130.
Earth based Class Rooms:

I have to admit it was a real change for me to have my own hall way locker. To actually have to walk and move, room to room, and to have to sit in a desk or chair. I had to re-discover exactly how hard the seat of a school desk was under the force of one Earth Gravity.

You guessed it on the first day of Photography class the subject was "Sunrise" that's it one word. "Sunrise"! That night Sabrina No. 39 and I managed to make it up to Low Earth Orbit where I activated my forward censors and filmed sunrise every time it came around I brought in all the available data and displayed it on my portable school rooms round screen. The small Computer Chipped camera that I was issued worked like a charm.

All I had to do was park the camera in thin air without a tripod and set the timer. I just let it float in the Zero "G" environment of my Command POD, next time in class the professor wanted to know how I had seen 18 different sunrises in only 24 hours. I told him that in Low Earth Orbit there is one every 90 minutes. That is at the standard speed of 17,500 miles per hour.

If he wanted to make the next assailment "Earthrise" I could get him some new photo of that. Later when the entire class was doing abstract stop motion, the instructor want to know how I had taken so many detailed photos of tiny pebbles in flight, I told him that the rocks were Asteroids several miles across. Of course I did manage to get some very nice photographs of "Earthrise" as well as several lunar craters as I was recovering the Snoopy descent stage.

What was most interesting was that Snoopy appeared as a multi-color-spinning-sphere on the film due to its rapid spinning rate over all my Photography Instructor seemed to like my Snoopy descent stage shots the best. I had another problem with my Math Teacher. It seemed that I made a yucky face when she passed out the advanced Caucus Books, which was a reprint of the same math book that I had in my advance math class in Jr. High School.

She wanted to know why, I didn't like the book, so I showed her where all the mistakes were, a lot of the formulas were useful enough but they were all mixed up. The formulas for one problem was displayed with the wrong proof page and one problem seem to be created just to use all the math symbols in creation without making much since.

We both even had a laugh or two when I showed her the pages that were printed upside-down and backwards to make the calculation proof look correct. The rendezvous problem on page number 310 works but it only gets me close enough to see the other space ship not close enough to reach out and touch it.

If I had to depend on this level of math I would still be on the other side of the Sun trying to catch lost S-IVBs. I did not tell her but I will ask Amelia the Blue Whale if she can come up with a better example of a human math book. Not to mention that there was not a single calculation in the entire book that would enable me to squirt a liquid forward to enable it to be pulled into the gravity well of a spinning Grumman Lunar module assent stage.

So far my worse problem had been in history class when the history professor asked me if I knew how many humans had walked on the surface of the moon. I don't think that he believed me when I answered 3,097 humans 931 Whales, 309 Grizzly Bears and 837 Polar Bears.

Due to my 3"G" muscles I have to be very careful not to be drafted by the M.I.T. gymnasts team the kind that does not use airplanes. I can still run faster, longer, farther, and carry more dead weights than any other 16 year old girl.

As Lorynda and I were talking in the Gym I causal reach out and gripped the side of the gym bar. Then with only using one of my wrists I pulled my entire Earth weight straight up as I did a one arm hand stand, balancing myself upside down under only one Earth Gravity.

This was the first time I made Lorynda go Bug-Eyed. I told her that that is how I passed the physical strength test to earn my A & P rating. I know that I can pull it off and only make an "A" in Gym class.

Another problem is that M.I.T. looked at long range human survival the bottom line is it's impossible to grow enough plants in outer space to make enough oxygen to do anything. For plants to hold their own against humans it take close to 18 acres of plants to make enough Oxygen, for only one human, a small very inactive human at that. Personally I have had enough problems trying to grow enough plants just to eat in outer space.

As the main problem is lack of gravity as all the plants have to stay in contact with the soil to grow or produce any amount of oxygen. Personally I have lived by hauling large amounts of water with me to chemically strip it apart and use its Hydrogen and Oxygen for rocket fuel then to run fuel cells to make electricity that runs more machinery to filter out Co/2 from the ships atmosphere and replace it with oxygen from the striped water supply. Of course in space flight the only way to get more water is to find locate and capture Comets.

Log Entry #131.
Catching the Snoopy:

I have known about old left-over lunar landers parts that were abandoned in lunar orbit for all of my life. The Snoopy Descent stage's primary job was to support a powered landing and surface extravehicular activity. When the lunar excursion was over, it served as the launch pad for the ascent stage. Octagon-shaped, it was supported by four folding landing gear legs, and contained a throttle-able Descent Propulsion System engine with four hypergolic propellant tanks. A continuous-wave Doppler radar antenna was mounted by the engine heat shield on the bottom surface, to send altitude and rate of descent data to the guidance system and pilot display during the landing. Almost all external surfaces, except for the top, platform, ladder, descent engine and heat shield, were covered in amber, dark reddish amber, black, silver, and yellow aluminized foil blankets for thermal insulation.

The front landing leg had an attached platform informally known as the "porch" in front of the ascent stage's EVA hatch and a ladder, which the astronauts were suppose used to ascend and descend between the "L.E.M's" only cabin to the lunar surface. The footpad of each landing gear contained a 67-inch long surface contact sensor probe, which signaled the commander to switch off the descent engine. The probe was omitted from the number 1 leg of every landing mission, to avoid a suit-puncture hazard to the astronauts, as the probes tended to break off and protrude upwards from the surface.

Equipment for the lunar exploration was to be carried in the Modular Equipment Stowage Assembly, a drawer mounted on a hinged panel dropping out of the left hand forward compartment. Besides the astronaut's surface excavation tools and sample collection boxes, the MESA contained a television camera with a tripod as the commander opened the MESA by pulling on a lanyard while descending the ladder, the camera was automatically activated to send the first pictures of the astronauts on the surface back to Earth.

The official mission American Flag for the astronauts to erect on the surface was carried in a container mounted on the ladder of each landing mission. The Early Apollo Surface Experiment Package later the Apollo Lunar Surface Experiment Package was carried in the opposite compartment behind the LM.

An external compartment on the right front panel carried a deployable S-band antenna which, when opened looked like an inverted umbrella on a tripod. This was not used on the first landing due to time constraints, and the fact that acceptable communications were being received using the LM's S-band antenna, but it was used on Apollo 12 and 14. A hand-pulled Modular Equipment Transporter, similar in appearance to a golf cart, was carried on Apollo 13 and 14 to facilitate carrying the tools and samples on extended moonwalks.

On the extended missions Apollo 15 and later, the antenna and TV camera were mounted on the Lunar Roving Vehicle, which was carried folded up and mounted on an external panel. Compartments also contained replacement Portable Life Support System batteries and extra lithium hydroxide canisters on the extended missions.

I remember charting their orbits on my computer since I was in kindergarten. As a matter of fact their orbital tracks had a lot to do with the locations that I had picked for all three of my Lunar Space Elevators. Over the years I had made lots of flight data entries as I have constantly checked their lunar orbital tracts and for that matter I have personally rendezvous with the Eagle's Assent stage and Snoopy's descent stage on hundreds occasions just to see if their recovery was possible.

Only to discover that they were both spinning faster on all three of their control axes, with no way to latch on to it and capture any of them. Over the years of flight the gravity well of the Earth, Moon, and the Sun had caused the very fragile throw away space ship to spin on all three of its axes, faster and faster. Just like when I was a child pumping the swing in my back yard it would increase its speed, of Pitch, Yaw and Roll on every orbit.

Thanks to Pinger-5's math formulas it was child's play for me to figure Snoopy's assent stage exact location at any time. Finding Snoopy's descent stage was not the problem figuring out when to capture it was. Throw-out is flight carrier it had circled the moon more times than I could count using all of my fingers and toes. Sabrina No. 39 still had her watering nose problem, and I was looking forward to all the maneuvering needed to keep a constant stream of water going into the spinning Snoopy descent stage, then freezing it solid and capturing it as if it were a Comet Core.

I discovered that it was not in danger of being thrown out of lunar Orbit and that it had almost crashed into the surface of the moon hundreds of times. I have read lots of written reports from my lunar prospectors as too what happened when the lower half of Snoopy came in low and doing enough high speed maneuvers to sell tickets and start changing the crowds for the Air Show.

So now is the time to recover Snoopy's descent stage the same way that I had grabbed the Eagle, problem was Snoopy's lower half was in a very erratic Lunar Orbit. Needless to say Snoopy's lower half had been on my things to do list for most of my life. Sabrina No. 39 made all the maneuvers to end up on the tail of Snoopy's descent stage a trip that she had done many times in the past.

So just like that Sabrina No. 39 runny nose and all was on the tail of Snoopy as she was still locked in her lunar orbit since N.A.S.A. abandoned her in place. The higher altitude part of Snoopy's orbit was pretty normal except when it came close to any of my space elevators. All it would take was any kind of collision and Snoopy would be vaporized, or spin itself into millions of very small pieces of space-junk.

I started the water moving as soon as Sabrina No. 39 was in range, a nice slow direct stream from Sabrina No. 39s most forward ballistic control thruster. Just like with the Eagle despite all the spinning I finally got Snoopy's lower half soaking wet. When considering the distance and the speed at which we were traveling I had to perform a zero error tailing job just to keep the stream of water on tract, needless to say I did not spill a drop of liquid despite all of Snoopy's odd changes in direction.

Due to the much larger descent stages landing gear I had to make a much larger ice ball just to save the landing pads. Flying extremely low lunar orbits are second nature to me but to do it at several thousand miles per hour will get anybody's attention.

To come zooming across the face of the moon and still be able to look up at the top of the taller craters will definitely help keep you on your toes. As soon as I could, I used Sabrina No. 39s shadow to start the freezing process. Sabrina No. 39 set off most of her collision alarms as we orbited closer to Snoopy's descent stage as well as the lunar surface.

Due to Snoopy added mass she was now descending a little faster than normal this caused several lunar ground strike that actually helped the smoothing water ice operation. The hard part was keeping Snoopy's lower half covered with Sabrina No. 39s shadow. Together we waited until the ascending part of Snoopy's orbit to trap her in the cargo bay where my deceleration devices were morph and ready to start working.

As soon as Snoopy's descent stage was finally closed into the dark cold of my cargo bay, I started the capture process by shrinking the size of the cargo bay to fit the exact size of Snoopy still spinning trapped inside of its Ice-Ball. Then Sabrina No. 39 gently closed in with her decelerators and gently slowed all of its gyrations to match her speed and direction. I could hardly wait until the Ice ball melted; I knew everything was going well as soon as Sabrina No. 39 started to complain about all the water in her cargo bay floor.

I really lucked out as both Modular Equipment Stowage Assembly bay were full of Apollo artifact for weight and balance purposes. The bay was full of vintage Apollo Equipment for the lunar exploration was carried in the Modular Equipment Stowage Assembly, a drawer mounted on a hinged panel folding down out of the left hand forward compartment.

Besides the astronaut's surface excavation tools and sample collection boxes that contained a television camera with a tripod. The Early Apollo Surface Experiment Package. The instrumentation and experiments that comprise A.L.S.E.P. were decided in February 1966 to transport a Passive Lunar Seismic Experiment, Lunar Tri-axis Magnetometer, Medium-Energy Solar Wind, Suprathermal Ion Detection, Lunar Heat Flow Management, Low-Energy Solar Wind, and an Active Lunar Seismic Experiment. The

A.L.S.E.P. was built and tested by Bendix Aerospace in Ann Arbor, Michigan.

The instruments were designed to run autonomously after the astronauts left them on the Moon's surface and to make long term studies of the lunar environment.

They were arrayed around a Central Station which supplied power generated by a radioisotope thermoelectric generator to run the instruments and communications so data collected by the experiments could be relayed to Earth. A compartment on the right front panel carried a deployable S-band antenna which, when opened looked like an inverted umbrella on a tripod.

A hand-pulled Modular Equipment Transporter, similar in appearance to a golf cart, was later carried on Apollo 13 and 14 to facilitate carrying the tools and samples on extended moonwalks.

After I made it back to my dorm roof, Sabrina No. 39 kept ringing her systems alarm until I re-plumber her most forward maneuvering rocket cluster not to spurt water. I had to sneak up to Sabrina No. 39 to crawl around inside of her while under one full Earth Gravity.

To fix her runny nose problem, as she was parked on the roof of my M.I.T. dorm room, to keep all of my other roommates from constantly hearing Sabrina No. 39s system alert alarms going off louder and louder! It did not take me very long to get both the now capture descent stage back together with the assent stage. After all a girl can never have enough charms on her bracelet.

Log Entry #132.
Finding the Aquarius:

I also confirmed that N.A.S.A. though that Intrepid, Antares, Falcon, Orion, Challenger were all crashed into the moon way back in the 1970's. Although according to the flight data Apollo-13s Aquarius most definitely was thrown into a very erratic solar orbit after it bounced off the Earth's Atmosphere.

Now it's my job to find it, so that I could retrieve it. For this job I requited not only Pinger-5 but several of her Whale/naut's as well as a couple of history graduates from the latest whale school. At our first planning meeting in the Main Whale Tank on the LEADER, I started with the detailed history of Apollo-13, its inflight explosion and all the trajectory changes caused by all of its outgassing. At this point the youngest Whale/naut, who was named "Doris" made the Comment about" Herding Comets".

At the time of the Command Modules re-entry into the Earth atmosphere the service module was reported to have burn up over Illinois on a due south trajectory. There was not a thing recorded about Aquarius after it was kicked loose from the Apollo 13 Command Module. As usual with N.A.S.A. as soon as they throw something away it doesn't exist anymore.

My first question to the group was does anybody have any information about The Aquarius trajectory instantly three of the resent Whale school graduates answer they started to sing the coordinate as a Whale Song. All at the same instant with each different whale adding a new series of calculations when it became their turn to sing.

Was it thrown into our Solar System or into the Sun, according to Pinger-5 it went backwards in the Earth Orbital tract? As it traveled around the Sun the planet Venus caused its first gravity assist that enable it to very slowly orbit a little higher than the Earths solar orbit still traveling backward away from the Earth. At several different times it got a gravity asset from both the planets Venus and Mercury on the other side of the Sun. As it worked out The Aquarius had been zipping around the interplants since April 17th 1970.

The whales started sing "where - Oh where can the Acquires be - Oh where - Oh where can it be", Singing as if they both were humans over, and over again in human English as they continued to chant over and over. "Oh, where oh where can the Acquires be - Oh where – Oh - where can it be"? Finally after going over the entire celestial data file for the better part of an hour we came up with the answer.

Considering all its movement the Aquarius was still locked into a solar orbit about two thirds the ways back into the Earths orbital track. If we were to wait another Hundred twenty seven years, nine months, twenty nine days four hours, and thirty-nine seconds it would impact the surface of the moon 227.56 miles south of my space elevator number three, on the back side of the moon. This gave me some breathing time so I put the job of recovering the Aquarius pick up on my things to do list.

Log Entry #133.
Lunar Eclipses:

I was amazed that N.A.S.A. had erased all the views of my space elevators One, Two, and Three. As well as any photos of the surface of the moon that shows the extent of my actives in its surface. I can imagine that I did scare lots of the not so intelligent humans on the Earth then they noticed that the man in the moon face was wearing glasses.

Caused by the lunar shadows that were caused by my lunar space elevators. I did make an effort to hide them from human view from the surface of the Earth. Also, during a lunar eclipse anybody with a small telescope can count the number of Asteroid Space Arks that I have in Lunar Parking Orbit.'

As I like to keep them insight as much as possible. However most of my lunar surface structures are on the back side of the moon so that I can use the structure of the higher lunar mountain ranges as radiation shields. I am also building a space traffic control center at the moons geographic north pole where the top of the Shackleton Crater is located.

All of my activities at this location can be seen from the surface of the Earth during a Solar Eclipse. I have a special interest at the lunar South Pole because of the occurrence of ice in the permanent shadowed areas of its surface. At the lunar south pole where I can have my staff view the entire surface of the Earth from a single point. The South Pole has a larger area that remains in shadow it's much larger than that at the moons north pole. The lunar South Pole craters are unique in that sunlight does not reach the bottom.

So far my Whale/naut's are having fun using Pinger-5's tunnel boring machines to hollow out an empty space large enough to swim in. As well as building Whale size Belly Slides.

Log Entry #134.
Mission Planning 101:

As everybody knows M.I.T. had been trying to fly to Mars and back since before the end of World War two. Over the years their flight plan has changed for the better or worse with lots of idea changes and deigns studies.

As soon as I was on the Mars team the first thing I did was fill out and send a FAA form 8110.1 to the local Federal Aviation Flight Standards Office, requesting to install the first nuclear rocket engine on to the back of their best looking singe stage to orbit space plane design.

When my father contacted the Atomic Energy Commission about my first nuclear powered rocket they decided that because it was constructed and being installed off planet on the LEADER, they did not have jurisdiction. Their only request was that I not use it inside of the Earth atmosphere. So far this it a request that I have always been able to keep.

However it still would be the FAA's job to approve the installation of a nuclear rocket engine in an aircraft that powered itself from the surface of the Earth and back. I did summit the first written request to the FAA to build a Nuclear Power Aircraft.

Another historical quart is an old M.I.T. design for a space ship that was thought to replace the old Apollo program. A nuclear powered rocket powered spacecraft that was thought to be launch with a heavy lift booster, and then flow throughout the inner planets. All work on this project was stopped by the Atomic Energy Commission way back in the 1960's. However, because none of my operations are not on the Planet Earth, as such the Atomic Energy Commission has no control, so Pinger-5 bought up the design and gave it to me to fix up and up date.

Then launch them up to the leader through my space elevator without operating a nuclear rocket engine inside of the earth's atmosphere. This spacecraft eventually became my Sabrina No. 50 design.

Log Entry #135.
Sabrina No. 50 Resurrection:

Sometimes Pinger-5 really floors me! She bought the design rights for this old 1960s space ship design from one of the older spaceflight instructors at M.I.T. that had hoped to have been launched as an S-IVB from a Saturn V booster.

She wants me to fix all of its problems and equipped each one with my own Nuclear Powered Rocket Engine Design. After I took over the design I re-named the design to "Sabrina No. 50". Because I was still out of Saturn V Booster Rockets, I had to make a few changes. First of all the Sabrina No. 50 space ship had to fold up to be the same size of one of my space elevator cars.

Most of its mass was extendable as fold outs from the ships main fuel farm. Pinger-5 set up a manufacturing sight at the base of my space elevator in Texas. After she gets a couple of hundred of them built she plans to rent them out to rich humans that want to get out into outer space and see things for themselves.

Over all the basic design was sound enough for the 1960s Sabrina No. 50's Space ships were not designed to fly inside an atmosphere. But due to its extreme long range it could easily be used to explore the surface of Mercury, or any other object in outer space that does not have an atmosphere. It could orbit any of the Gas Giants, and could supply a safe platform to take a nice long look down into their Atmosphere. I shudder to think what several of my class mates could do with a Sabrina No. 50 Space ship in or around a cluttered place like the Gas Giant Saturn.

Pinger-5 plans to stage Space Races with them for human spaceflights to Jupiter and beyond. Pinger-5 also wanted me to up-scale a version so that she could use one herself.

For test flights I installed my updated Command Computer and requested their first ten to check out the Kuiper Belt for me. They were each sent up the space elevator as soon as they were manufactured and quietly sent on their way. I even used some of their data when I made my first Jupiter trip.

All the Sabrina No. 50s were equipped with a full set of zoom cameras as well as high power telescopes. Along with my standard electronic data gathering package. As an add on extra Pinger-5 even included a Control-POD that could be docked back to back with each other or docked at two different locations on the Sabrina No. 50 Space ship.

The Space-POD could also be used as the Sabrina No. 50s cockpit when it was in travel mode. For high speed acceleration maneuvers all six of its Engineering, Green House, and Living sections can fold back behind its main base for shielding. Of course the First-Ten did not have any humans or plants aboard, so they used both of these onboard areas to house my Command Computer and Communication System.

With a little help from the Space-POD it can even replace its nose cone that also can be used as a meteor deflector. The first thing we discovered was that it had to fold down it Green House, and Living sections to accelerate or decelerate as there was no way to reinforce it design to keep all its space wings from being torn off during even a small burst of thrust from is Nuclear Rocket Motor. A definite case of too much rocket power and not enough space frames. Needless to say it did not take long for the first Sabrina No. 50's to start showing up, launching them from the LEADER worked like a charm.

Log Entry #136.
First M.I.T. Stand Down:

It been a very full week at school after all it's not nice to get hit by a super-storm while I was stuck Earth side. I did enjoy standing out in the rain although my space suit would not let me actually feel the water as over a hundred mile per hour rain drops would tend to be not so good.

After spending any amount of time on the surface of Mars I think that my body has reprogramed itself to seek-out water. With lack of electoral power and the sudden flooding of the lower three stories of my dorm building was very exciting. I did my best to blend in and not do anything that would get attention.

As a cleanup force my whole class was down in the water doing what we could to save anything. We formed human chains to pass all the library books up to the top floor, during the worse time of the storms initial flood. I did manage to have some of my smaller Whale friends help by closeting off water lines and turning off the building electrical systems as the water came up.

They also kept abandoned street vehicles from piling up at the entrances when they were underwater. Pinger-5 herself swam up the stairway to my third story railing just for her very own bragging rights. As luck would have it my locker was on the first floor, so it went under first and fast, later that night I retrieved all my lost equipment and school books.

It always amazes me how fast a textbook can become outdated, then discarded but, in this case I did not get a chance to open it even once. But I pulled a trick that I learned on Mars as how to use a Cargo POD to freeze dry wet books to save them, if I could get it cold enough and then vacuum off all the water. The book will open without any of it pages sticking together.

Pinger-5 also got going and recovered several of the off shore World War two U-boat kills that took major damage from the Hurricane. As usual once she had loaded the entire kill sight aboard one of my Sabrina No. 40 space ships.

She would fly the whole sight up into low Earth orbit, once weightless all the polluting mercury could easily be picked up by my converted He/3 grabber devices.

Then she would return the wreck sight to its original location on the sea bottom where it will serve a perfect non-poisons living sight for lots of nice tasting bottom dwellers.

Log Entry #137.
Roommates Night Out:

I had not been able to get away from Lorynda at all. So after a very long day of hard schooling we finally got to get some long sought after sleep. All of a sudden it sounded as if all the alarm bells in the world had started to go off at the same instant. The sound levels were so loud that it broke the communications mirror on the door in front of the secret entrance to my boarding ramp. My room telephone as well as my communications necklace both started ringing at the same instant. Needless to say this also woke-up Lorynda.

I answer my communications necklace first it was the Regional FAA duty officer asking if, I was Sabrina. Seeing me on my communications necklace Lorynda picked up the room phone and screamed it's the duty officer from the French Aviation Control Center wanted to speak to me it was an emergency. So she put the room phone up to my other ear.

It seems that all the time I spent talking to whales was not wasted, in one ear I was hearing French and in the other I was hearing in English and I could understand them both at the same instant. It seems that two different Jumbo-Jet airliners a Boeing 747-800 and an Airbus A380 Jumbo-Jet had clipped each other wings in flight over the middle of the Atlantic Ocean. Both aircraft were still flying they had both lost engines as well as fuel that was still in the aircrafts wing sections. Both damaged airliners do not have enough fuel to reach dry land in any direction.

The A380 was damaged worse, as it was losing altitude and will have to ditch in the mid-Atlantic in less than 25 minutes. The Boeing 747 was a little better off as it was holding altitude but could only remain airborne for another hour and a half with its remaining fuel. I activated my space suit as I got out of bed and started walking over to my secret door, with the fragmented mirror I had to rip it off it mountings to get into my Command POD.

I did not even think about Lorynda until she bumped me from behind as I enter my Command PODs pilot's seat, when she asks "where do I sit?" Needless to say I did not have time to throw her overboard.

So I place my bark-up Space suit on her lap and activated it, as my Command POD was being reeled up inside of Sabrina No. 39. As she extended her wings, and launched herself off the roof of my college dormitory building the second that my Command POD was in its flight position.

Due to my floating suspension system we hardly felt any acceleration at all. However acceleration forces did manage to pin Lorynda to the Command PODs back wall. The second that my cockpit wall activated and started showing me the outside view from Sabrina No. 39s external camera system, I notices that she stiffen up as we started to move faster. I couldn't hear her screaming after her helmet formed.

I had to laugh as Sabrina No. 39s last jester as she re-programed my back-up Space suits name tag was to make it say "Lorynda." By now Sabrina No. 39 was accelerating in a straight line and had climbed up to the edge of outer space all of which was showing on all six walls of my cockpit. I put in a call to my watch commander on the LEADER to find out why the FAA called me out in the middle of the night. She informed me that Pinger-5 had launch out of the Atlantic Ocean and was ready to send on seen photos.

I know for a fact that an A380 airbus will not fit inside of any of my Sabrina No. 39, at that instant I received the live feed from Pinger-5 and her very loud gravely Whale voice speaking Human English we both could hear her talking over the Communication System. As Pinger-5 wanted to know if the now a clipped wing span of the A380 was now small enough to fit inside of Sabrina No. 39's cargo bay. With a quick look I could plainly see that it had lost its number one engine as well as everything else out to where its wing tip should have been.

I could also see a un-stop-able fuel fire streaming from it rip point trailing a fire plum for over 5 miles. Meanwhile Lorena was still pined on the wall staring wide-eyed looking straight ahead, I know for a fact that this was the longest time in the last 10 days that she hasn't asked me a personal question. As soon as my ships camera system picked up my flying bond fire, my communication system locked on to theirs and I started to receive flight data directly from their on board computers.

The good news was the fire would not burn its self out because the aircrafts main fuel farm was in the part of the wing that was torn off, so all the remaining fuel tanks were draining directly into the fuel fire without any way to turn them off. The only good news was that the fire would go out as the A380 ran out of fuel and hit the surface of the Atlantic Ocean. But at flight speed the A380 would break up into lots of very populated pieces.

At the same time Pinger-5 was Piloting Sabrina No. 40 underwater at supersonic speed trying to position herself directly under the Boeing 747 and take it aboard the second it quit flying. Meanwhile Sabrina No. 39s Communication System locked on to the location of the stricken A380 as always it was nice to see that it was still flying. The five mile long flame plume that was coming off of its torn wing made it easy to find. I could see Sabrina No. 40 coming up from under the water as Sabrina No. 39 turned on all of her dorsal external landing lights.

When I extended my speed brakes Lorynda was moved to the forward part of my cockpit. I think she thought that I had ejected her into the Atlantic Ocean. I extended Sabrina No. 39 lift fans and started to fly close formation with the stricken A380. The actual pick-up maneuver was simple for me to fly Sabrina No. 39 down over the big wounded bird and have my automated load master grab on and stored it inside of No. 39s forward lower cargo bay.

The flaming blow torch was extinguish as soon as the lower cargo hatch close and cut off all the available oxygen, the massive trailing flame hardly measured on Sabrina No. 39's heat shield thermal indicator.

The bad news was all the remaining jet fuel spilt all over Sabrina No. 39 main cargo bay floor. I don't know how she did it but Lorena started to complain about the offending fuel smell. The ships systems program easily plugged the wounded wing with sticky foam allowing the actual fuel spill to be drained back into Sabrina No. 39s main Aero-Spike-Rocket motor section that put it to some good.

I stopped their decent and was holding level flight the couple of seconds it took to stow the now leaking fuel three engines A380. Needless to say the three running turbo-fans all flamed out due to the lack of available air, as pilot in command I got to fly everything fire leaking fuel and all.

What happen next had to blow Lorena mind. Sabrina No. 39 despite all the extra thrust from leaking jet fuel she managed to extend her lift-fans all the way and go into a full hover as Sabrina No. 40 under the Command of Pinger-5 surfaced underneath us. As we hovered in the dark over the glass smooth pitch black Atlantic Ocean as Sabrina No. 40 finally opener her top side forward cargo hatch to allow Sabrina No. 39 to land inside of her forward topside cargo bay.

This proved to be the quickest way to get me "The Sabrina" aboard Sabrina No. 40 so that I could fly the next Interception Mission, to catch the damaged soon to ditch in the vast dark Atlantic Ocean Boeing 747. Lorynda saw everything, as she was struck wide eyed and speechless. But, the show was not over as Sabrina No. 40 made a nice slow hydrofoil take-off from the surface of the Atlantic then turned to intercept the other victim of this mid Atlantic mid-air collision.

The pilots view was displayed throughout my cockpit as before, as soon as I was the pilot in Command. The Boeing 747s aerial pick-up was a lot easier as the folks at Boeing are smart enough to put their fuel transfer system in a location where it cannot be torn out by the loss of a large section of its wing. This is what saved the day as it gave the 747 enough fuel to remain airborne for over an hour.

The wounded 747 was a lot harder to find due to its lack of a large plume of flame. In fact coming in from above in the dark I had to look twice and count all three of its remaining engines to make sure I had the correct aircraft. According to my communication system they were just flying along fat dumb and happy minus a turbo-fan engine and a lot of wing. All I could say was the "You have got to love that fly by wire system".

I did a perfect Interception and flew Sabrina No. 40 to a point in the air where my load master programs could load and secure the poor damaged three engines 747 inside of Sabrina No. 40s forward lower cargo bay. It was getting to be late and I had to fly the Atlantic to get back to M.I.T. and the rest of a good night's sleep. Pinger-5 had arranged the off-loading location to be at a large RAF base in England. I made sure that several Command PODs were connected to each recovered jumbo airliner to help maintain their atmosphere.

As soon as we stopped moving Pinger-5 took charge of the offloading. Once again Sabrina No. 39 reminded me that I was in charge of lowering the landing gear. I laughed real hard as I answered when do think that I learned to speak jumbo-jet. It took a while for Lorynda to come out of the Command POD only to start talking again. Its daylight she said "Yes I know "It's already tomorrow morning here in England" I answered. "England!" She echoed back. The outside view clicked off as I mover my Command POD over to the A380's pilots door. Where I politely knocked and waited for the First Officer to open the door.

As we both entered the head steward wanted to know if I was the same young girl that saved a Japanese Airlines A380 from a mid Pacific Typhoon. I answered "Yes" then he gave me the unpaid bill for the VIP dinner that was served to me as well as all of my crew members. This started Lorynda asking about the cost for a full course breakfast. The Captain was glad to learn that he was in England and at least 2 hours ahead of his flight plan.

After paying my tab for dinner we went back to my Command POD and were lowered to the ground to see how Pinger-5 was doing with her un-loading of the Tri-Engine Boeing 747. Lorynda walked past Pinger-5 twice before she realized that she was the live mammal in charge I don't think the she noticed that Pinger-5 was a Humpback Whale. As soon as the clipped wing Boeing 747 was towed away Sabrina No. 39 quit wasting time she opening Sabrina No. 39s bottom cargo bay doors and started to lower my first catch the slightly cooked Airbus A380.

Lorynda jumped a foot into the air and jammed her finger tips into her ears as she heard the sound of the A380 snapping its landing gear down and locking it in place all by itself. The next thing that happen even shocked me as all twenty of the escape slide activated. It was quite a show there was nothing either of us could do expect just stand there and watch.

At this point Sabrina No. 40 opened her top cargo bay doors. As No. 39 extended her hover fans and at the same time my lowered Command POD was ready to be retracted all the way back up through Sabrina No. 40s opened structure.

I chuckled to myself as Sabrina No. 39 was complaining that its boarding ramp was still on the ground, so that we both could enter. As we re-entered my Command POD Lorynda asked if tonight was normal for me. I answer yes and had my space suit morph out a red cape with a large "S" on it.

As soon as I back in my Pilots seat I call the local control tower. They had no problem authorizing my departure to a hundred thousand feet with a vector to the west. I made a textbook Vertical Lift-Off out of Sabrina No. 40s forward topside cargo hatch and headed due west. I turned up the speed, so in less than a half an hour Sabrina No. 39 quietly lowered my Command POD back to its "Sabrina at school location".

Lorynda was so tired that she went sound asleep around the mid-Atlantic point of our return flight. I did not have to use the extra mechanical muscles in my space suit to carry her in my arms as if she were a baby all the way down my boarding ramp and tucked her into her bed. I recovered her Space suit and left it laying in its container on our rooms lamp stand. I had to instant manufacture a new control mirror before, I morph mine back into it sleeping bag format and then called it a night.

The next morning I discovered that on the way back home Pinger-5 had stopped and recover both of the lost turbofans as well as all the metal in both of the lost wing sections. Who knows there may be enough, left overs to make a business jet or two. As it turn out Pinger-5 eventually purchased both aircraft the Boeing 747 as well as the Airbus A380 for scrap. Then she made a point to put both of their repairs on my things to do list.

After all Amelia the Blue Whale is still a growing girl calf and she will not fit inside my home-build 787 for very much longer. I am looking forward to seeing her do an inside loop or for that matter a hammerhead stall while flying my repaired Airbus 380. Lorynda also inform me that she had the wildest dream ever last night. I asked her for details but she said that I wouldn't believe her. Sabrina No. 39s latest problem was that the ships automation system did not clean up her cargo bay floor well enough to suit her program.

So it became my job to clean up the A380s fuel spill, to the point where Sabrina No. 39 was satisfied. I knew for a fact that Lorynda was not interested in helping me to shine any of the floors in Sabrina No. 39s main Cargo Decks.

Log Entry #138.
What to do with Junk Cars:

Charley who is one of my Whale/naut's whose job in his Orca Whale Pod is to come up with new ways to attack the enemy. It seems that he has discovered the Military Channel, yesterday he was observing a program where a group of humans were shooting Anti-Tank Missiles at this poor old shot-up Army Tank.

Every time the missile hit its target, Charley expected it to be completely destroyed, and every time it wasn't it really started to get his goat. Finally just to help out the Army he arranged for the targeted tank to be completely put out of its misery by five direct meteorite hits. To top it off we have ran low of local want-to be Meteors, would you believe that with all the Orbital Golf Games small Meteors are getting hard to find.

To make matters worse regular Earth Rocks are not as useable because of their microscopic water content. They heat up from the air friction they all tend to vaporize before they have a chance to become regulation meteorites. This didn't even slow Charley down as he changed his ammo to old automobiles from one of Pinger-5s junk yards.

It was kind of funny as the next morning the Army could not find any of their favorite target tanks to shoot at. According to Charley due to their different types of metal and plastic. So each of his old Junked cars made a beautiful Re-Entry Fireball and smoke trails as they all fell from Low Earth Orbit. It seems that Charley's favorite ammunition turns out to be old mini-vans the kind that has sideways opening back doors.

Log Entry #139.
My S.A.T.-Test:

Lorynda and I are still trying to bond I lucked out then she thought that my latest adventure with two Jumbo-Jets was just one of her dreams. She had been bragging about the 94% that she had made on her S.A.T. Test as well as being finally stopped by the tester, who had to physically taken her test form back when the time limit was up.

It took a while and a lot of prodding but I finally told her my S.A.T. Score was 100% and that at the time I was only one of eleven students that scored that high. I had kept changing the test date, because I was away from the school on a long trip, I did not say anything about Mars, and having to fly around a large meteor storm, as I have firsthand knowledge of Martian meteor storms.

I had to fly in directly from this side of the meteor storm just to make the last chance I had to take my S.A.T. Test. Sabrina No. 39 had problems finding a close in parking spot a location to put my nose gear elevator down next to their main door. So I bailed out using my space suits rocket flight system, after I landed I had a problem morphing everything back into my school outfit Number 6 and ended up with a large heavy winter coat to carry into the testing room.

The testing official made me hang it up on the rack in the back of the room. It was so heavy in Earths one "G" that it pulled the coat hook off the wall and thumped on the floor as under Earth's one "G" it weighed over four hundred pounds.

Over all the S.A.T. Test was very simple, one of the questions dealing with the distance of each planet orbiting the sun was very interesting as I remembered to fix the exact time that I was taking the test calculating to inches and feet. I proved out all the math problems I had to figure very small to get all of my formulas in play.

I marked each question as I went down each page of the test, checking off answers as I went. I could tell that it was the newer test as when they wanted to know the names of all the planets in our solar system there were only eight places for answers. I lucked out as they did not want a complete list of all the known Kuiper objects.

Finally after 20 minutes I stood up and started to walk to the back of the room to pick up the rest of my space suit. The testing examiner ran over and snatches the now finished test out of my hands and informed me that he would have to grade my test at this time and that I would have to live with the score for the rest of my life.

He marched me over to his grading computer, with me still carrying the four hundred pound winter coat and all. He scanned it in! The score came back with 100%! I asked for my official grade slip, as soon as I had it in hand I place it on my chest and started morphing my space suit around it.

Rocket lift-motors, finger-tip-control rockets, and everything else that had to morph instantly started forming around me. He just stood there and watched as my heavy winter coat re-fomented back into my space suits ballistic lift system.

I made it a point to just smile back at him as my boot mounted rocket motors started to form, as this cause me grow taller, almost up to his eye level. I was a nice 16 year old girl and walked outside before I fired any of my assent rockets to fly back to my still circling Sabrina No. 39.

I had to fly through several different white fluffy clouds before I found the one that had my hovering Sabrina No. 39 hidden inside. Needless to say I did not tell Lorynda all the details.

Log Entry #140.
787 Orientation Flight:

As soon as Boeing 787s were operational. The Boeing Company flew my entire class in their latest airliner the 787, this one was especially designed to fly humans. They picked us up in Boston and flew everybody to their museum in Evert Washington. Everybody got the VIP treatment, they answered to all of our questions as if we were children.

The company pilots would not let me or any of the other students fly their airplane. They barely let us stand at the cockpit door and drool. To me it seems kind of dumb to have standard flight instruments when the aircraft is equipped with glass cockpit system. It did make me feel better when I realized that I could fly the 787 from my passenger seat with my communications necklace that is if the cockpit were to fall off all of a sudden.

Lorynda thought it was wonderful, eating pounds of oversized shrimp and other tasty treats. She seemed to eat more sea food than Pinger-5. I found the flight long and boring as their 787 was lots slower, louder, and definitely not rated for aerobatics. The VIP tour was OK but I have a better and more diverse manufacturing operation on the LEADER that turns out two or three of my Sabrina Number 40 space ships a week as well as keeps the rest of my space fleet operational.

I even have space to repair and rebuild about anything else that flies. With this thought I managed to slip away from the tour group and called Sabrina No. 39 for a ride back up to the LEADER. I got to spend some time working on some of the current projects where I am repairing and modifying both the Boeing 747 and an A380 airbus so that whales can fly them at airshows. Where I got to help with the re-winging of Amelia the blue whale's new Aerobatic Jumbo-Jet.

It had been a couple of weeks since I had a chance to use the A & P part of my DNA. To be able to float in zero "G", move and, repair equipment, the pleasure of just floating around inside a wing structure as large as a 747s re-attaching everything that was torn by its high speed collision, and then to reinforce the wings to the point where Amelia the blue whale can do Aerobatics.

Overall I spent the return to college flying time working on several of my Zero"G" reconstruction project. I even got around to manufacturing a new fuel farm for my clipped wing A380 I personally removed the "Sky Line Restaurant" out of my A380 old flamer as I do not think that Amelia the Blue Whale would find a use for it.

I beat the whole gang back to the dorm by 30 minutes. I even got a comment from Lorynda because I beat her to the computer. So far nobody noticed that I made it back to Boston on my own.

Log Entry #141.
Mars Cycle M.I.T. Style:

Because of all the long lasting storm damage it didn't take long to get permission to use my motorcycle, as walking has never been one of my hard points. My problem was how to get it out of Sabrina No. 39 and down to street level.

I also had to remove all of the add-on features that I had to put on it to operate in on the surface of Mars. The first to go was my Cargo Bubble, and then the oxygen system as it still had its internal combustion engine. I lucked out when I notices that after converting it back to its original Earth operational form it would easily fit down the stairway.

As it turned out I was not the first female student in my dorm to have her own pet motorcycle, I was surprised to learn that most of the student cyclists keep them in their bedrooms. It wasn't 15 minutes until Lorynda ask me how come such an extremely clean motorcycle had such a high mileage numbers on is odometer, and exactly where did I have it hidden until now.

I told her that it was just delivered and that both of the tires had just touch the surface of the Earth for the first time. Needless to say riding a motorcycle on Earth is a lot harder than on Mars it's also a lot wetter.

Lorynda and I really got into it because she had just become the president of the flat moon society, stating that all the moon landing were fakes. I walked her into my closet, up my gang plank to inform her that I would personal show her.

I put one of my spare space suits in her lap and activated it. That when she shouted "It was not a dream!

Latter when I had to prove to Lorynda that Apollo's 11, 12, 14, 15, 16, and 17 had actual landed on the surface of the Earths original Moon. And we had an occasion to search for lost Apollo lander parts. She was a wide eyed as always during the flight up from my Sabrina at school Location. After landing in the Sea of Tranquility we both had a laugh when we tried exploring the problem of trying to walk on the surface of the moons one sixth gravity.

We both decided to use my motorcycle to move around the lunar surface. It only took a couple of minutes to convert it back to a non-terrestrial vehicle status. I would give anything to have a picture of her face as I re-attached the oxygen generator as well as the Cargo Bubble. We both morph into Space suit mode and got into the Cargo Bubble. I gave the morph command to add all the extra motorcycle safety gear.

Helmet, knee, leg, elbow, as well as shoulder pads then open the port side cargo bay door, and zoom out into the airless lunar surface. The trick was to remember that I did not have any ballistic thrusters and the only time I could maneuver was when the Cargo Bubble was actually on the lunar surface.

As we were sitting in the bottom of the crater that one of my impactors had made when it landed a couple of year ago as I was trying to win one of the X-prizes by landing a camera on the surface of the moon to send back a photo of the Lunar Modules descent stage. Which it did the only problem was I scored direct hits. I got photos but I struck the Lunar Lander directly at an impact speed of over 50,000 miles per hour.

The way I figured it I got a gravity assist from the Moon itself. We got tired of all bouncing and maneuvering so I finally morph out the ballistic control system to make a stopped in the middle of the Eagles Descent Stages impact crater possible.

After all the moon dust settled both of us could plainly see small fragment of metal that had been driven into the walls of the crater that I had made out of the Apollo 11s descent stage. We spent the rest of the day traveling to all of the other Apollo landing sites. When we were checking out the Apollo 15s landing site Lorynda noticed the Moons Grand Canyon.

I was easily able to jump the distance with distance to spare. As we were leaving the Apollo 17's location I managed to use one of the Moons taller craters to make a high speed low gravity motorcycle jump high enough into low lunar orbit so that Sabrina No. 39 could catch us in flight. With this adventure I got Lorynda to resign from the Anti-Moon Landing Society.

Log Entry #142.
Mc-Rib time of the Year:

As soon as Pinger-5 ran out of thing to do off the Atlantic Oceans shore line she contacted me to help her run down a supply of new Mc Donald's restaurants Mc-Rib sandwich for her personal feeding containers. After a quick sampling Pinger-5 started to make a yucky face, let me tell you, you have not seem a yucky face until you have seen one on a Humpback Whale.

As somebody had changed the recipe and the Mc.-Rib now tasted completely different. I already had firsthand knowledge of her addiction to slider and Chicago Chilidogs but this is a first for Mc-Ribs! Luckily Red Lobster was running an all you could eat shrimp special, it took a little doing to get a table beside an open window. I got a table for two and I informed the waiter that my guest Pinger-5 due to her weight problem was outside in the van that was really Pinger-5 in her Whale scooter with my latest urban camouflage program that even made Pinger-5s tongue look like a human hand with arm attached. This worked great for the first fifty refills and Pinger-5 went through all of their shrimp specials recipes, and was still starving as it took a lot to fill up a thirdly eight ton Humpback Whale.

I don't think that Pinger-5 was ever completely filled up, as she has always been ruled by her stomach. It did not take long for us to get kicked out of the restaurant they do not believe that a full grown Humpback Whale was eating at one of their tables. I lucked out and they considered Pinger-5s partial feeding a college prank.

All of this made Pinger-5 want to fly back to Des Plaines, and hit up her favorite White Castle feeding point. I reminded her that there was a McDonnell's on the other side of River Road, from her favorite feeding sight that might be able to supply her with a regulation Mc-Ribs.

Pinger-5 did it again, It all started on Halloween she was soaking on the surface tanning herself as she was floating of one of the connecting lakes that are located in Northern Illinois. Lots of people call them old strip mines to explain their extreme depth, but they were formed by the extremely violent New Madrid Volcano.

As the report goes on she detected the beeping sound of several of the humans long flying rockets that had drifted away from their launch points. Last year she was convinced that they were trying to communicate with her she even tried to run the location transmitters beeping pattern through the translation metrics of my communication system.

This caused her to check out then launch into the air with a Sabrina No. 40 space ship with its urban camouflage system set for "Clouds". This enable her to fly as close as she could get to the passing "small useless human made projectiles." Using the ships location system Pinger-5 was able to locate all the "small useless Rockets" that had not been recovered after their brief low speed flight.

She spent the afternoon zapping them with space-junk recovery traps, then reeling them onboard for her personal examination. I wonder what Lorynda would do if a doghouse size structure would fall from the sky and grab her rocket away from her then reel itself back up into nice fluffy white cloud.

While she was on station the smell of regulation Mc-Ribs got her attention with a quick scan the smelled out the location that was determined to be the Mc Donald's Restaurant in Princeton, Illinois they not only had regulation Mc-Ribs but was selling the second on for only a dollar.

Needless to say Pinger-5 almost landed Sabrina No. 40 on top of the restaurant. She did land her Sabrina No. 40 just outside of town to launch her expedition Mc-Rib into the town of Princeton, Illinois.

Pinger-5 did have a few problems with the local terrain when a 38 ton Humpback Whale on a camouflaged Whale scooter runs over a concrete bridge that is only rated for 22 tons lots of bad thing start to happen. Meanwhile, Pinger-5 scooted into town and proceeded to buy up as many Mc-Ribs as possible. Her first order of 25 made the restaurant manager wonder what was up, as Pinger-5 sampled his version of the Mc-Rib, after successfully tasting Pinger-5s purchased all their remaining Mc-Ribs in lots of 1000.

She did not tell me how she made out with sliders. I made it a point to send in my repair teams to replace all the shattered road bridges that Pinger-5 had driven over during her recovery process.

By using my Martian designed equipment to replace all of the concrete bridges that Pinger-5 had run over near Princeton, Illinois on Earth was a piece of cake, compared to doing it on the surface of Mars.

To keep Pinger-5 happy I promised her that I would come up with a machine that can make regulation Mc-Ribs upon her demand that is capable of launching them into a hungry whale's mouth as fast as if they were machine gun bullets. I think that I will name the machine a Bet-ty-Ja-ne.

Log Entry #143.
Happy Halloween at M.I.T.:

Let me tell you I have had better times being stranded on the International Space Station. First Hurricane Irene, then floods and now a major snow storms that has about starved everybody who was part of the M.I.T. student body to death.

What a time to be stranded on Earth as the snow got deeper and started to pile up we began to run out of everything except hungry students, it was almost like being stranded in the Andes Mountains we were only joking about eating the dead. This morning the only thing left to eat in the college dorm cafeteria was warm chocolate milk and dill pickles slices, hardly anybody was eating the sliced dills.

I helped out the best I could by having Sabrina No. 39 wired one of her He/3 generators into my dorm buildings electrical system and supplied electrical power to the whole building. Of course I did not tell anybody that they were getting electrical power from a He/3 reactor. Sabrina No. 39 was not a happy camper as she realizes that snow was wet and she did not like water. So after not having anything to eat for lunch except snow cones made out of real snow. We all gathered together and talked about all our favorite foods the food that we were not getting to eat.

Needless to say the menu was endless I started to feel like Pinger-5 and I did not weigh anywhere near 38 tons, as it got later everybody realized that all the local restaurants were closed. As if 40 inches of snow would not affect their operation. To make matters worse the out of business College Dorm Cafeteria even ran their last call to dinner bell. Then Lorynda announce that we had misted the dinner bell and that the College Dorm Cafeteria was now officially closed.

That's when I decided to go into action I got my most serious look on my face and asked everybody if they could keep a secret. After they all said "Yes", even Lorynda, I told everybody that I knew of a place where the food courts never closed, or ran out of anything and that I had a safe way to transport everybody there without going outside in the Raging Blizzard.

At this point I told Sabrina No. 39 to start warming thing up and to inflate enough Transportation PODs for everybody, as well as to start lowering the Transport Tube to my secret door.

What was most interesting was that Sabrina No. 39 automatically lowered the operational He/3 generator that was supplying power to my dorm building leaving it on the roof.

Then I envied the whole gang to my room for a late night feast. As I started moving into my room it was worth it to see Lorynda jaw drop as I open my closet door and started climbing up my boarding tube into Sabrina No. 39s main cargo bay. By this time all the ships systems were on line complete with plenty of operation heated restrooms that were instantly put to use as most of the plumbing in the dorm building had been frozen for days. Most of my fellow students could not help to notice the molded tie down points for the Aquarius that was hanging over the main cargo bay. "What are you going to do with that they asked", as well as the other big question where did I get it. I told them that I plan to recover the Apollo 13's Lunar module Aquarius during Christmas vacation and that the molded tie down was to keep everything intact during my Aero breaking maneuvers.

It was quite interesting to watch as one of my Passenger Pods morph out of an empty deck "As soon as everybody was seated. As I sat down I started to fly Sabrina No. 39 from my Communications Necklace. After all what good is a fly-by-wire system if you don't use it. By this time Sabrina No. 39 had de-Iced herself and was ready for a quick direct flight to the LEADER.

I had Sabrina No. 39 make all the air traffic radio calls as all she had to do was extend her lift-fans and release her landing gear clamps. So that she could act like a helicopter and hover all the way out of Boston.

It took a couple of seconds for my watch commander on the LEADER to call me and ask what was up. By this time Sabrina No.39 had transition into her space ship mode and was closing in on the LEARER. I informed her that there would be a couple of hundred more mouths to feed this evening at the full time food court and that I would need to dock at its closes airlock.

I allowed Sabrina No. 39 to keep, her one "G" acceleration program running as we orbited the Earth higher and higher, all the way up to the LEADER. I did myself proud as I flew Sabrina No. 39 to the requested docking port with only the use of my hand held communications necklace.

I extended her landing gear and had her clamp onto her standard three point perch. As soon as we docked I extended and guided the Transpiration Tube to the outside of the main docking hatch. All of a sudden everybody started to notice the distant lack of gravity.

There were a few screams as soon as everybody noticed that we all had a "Little Orphan Annie Hair Dues" as every hair on everybody head was standing straight up. Due to everybody's lack of food nobody got sick. I made the official announcement "Remember to use the hand holds" as I started to lead the whole pack of fellow starving students up through the boarding tube into one of the "Leaders" large 24 hour a day food courts.

Where I had built all the different Restaurants of Earth on a large rotating wheel to simulate gravity. Everybody hair went back to normal as soon as each of my starving school mates jumped onto the Food courts main rotator. All of their jaws dropped as soon as they noticed that every type of restaurant in the world was open before them and ready to serve all their favorite foods everything except take outs.

Needless to say the mass feeding began and went on for hours. It took a while to round up the whole gang and get them loaded back into Sabrina No. 39 luckily the only place they went to was food court #6. I took it easy on the way back to school as everybody was filled to their gills with lots of their favorite foods. They all seemed ready to pop at the least provocation.

Boston was still buried alive with lots of wet cold extremely deep snow. It was still night and so Sabrina No. 39 didn't have a problem passing herself off as a helicopter that was landing at the Sabrina at school location.

Everybody was so full with food that they all moved like zombies as they made it back to their own dorm rooms. I noticed on the landing monitor that Sabrina No. 39 recovered her He/3 generator before she retracted her lift-fans or folded down any of her aerodynamic control surfaces.

She even remembered to activate her Urban-Camouflage-Program and disguised herself as a snow covered air-conditioning unit. The last thing that I noticed before I close my eyes was Lorynda sound asleep with a well feed smile on her face.

Log Entry #144.
M.I.T. First Thanksgiving:

Thing got colder and the snow piles deeper the people of Boston started to bury their dead. The dorms cafeteria restocked and I stopped the nightly food runs up to the LEADER. Most of my "next ten" landed on top of all the major hospitals as they ran out of their back up-power systems, most of them didn't find my gift of an operational He/3 generator mixed into their hospitals emergency power system.

I even powered up several hospitals that did not even have a back-up power system. I'm not worried about it as Sabrina No. 39 has a list and she is checking it twice each day, so that all of my loaned out equipment will be recover as soon as it was not needed.

Lorynda had become the much older little sister that I did not want to have. It did not take her a very long time to realize that I could transport myself as well as anybody else to any location within our solar system anytime that I wanted to.

My standard reply was that all of my technology is experimental I have not taken a single step towards having the Federal Aviation Administration certify that any of it was safe enough for me to start selling tickets. I am still building up my safety record as I am barely old enough to legally fly my airplane all by myself.

To that statement Lorynda Said "You have your own airplane"! Yes I replied I even built it myself it's currently aboard Sabrina No. 39. The bottom line is I cannot fly anybody not even stow-a-ways Lorynda asked, not even charter flights until I am 21 years old and become old enough to get my Commercial Pilot rating.

Lorynda discovered where the worse airport in the world was a place called Lukla it is the closest airport to Mt. Everest in Nepal. The runway is extremely short and runs up and down hill at a 15 degree slop that makes it steeper than most ski slopes. Not to mention the elevation at the lower end of the runway was 9,860 feet above sea level.

My communication system translated Lukla to mean the place with many goats and sheep as a note it also one of the few places on Earth that happens to be supported 100% by an air-bridge meaning that everything has to fly in and out of their single downhill runway.

The next day Lorynda introduced me to 10 of my fellow M.I.T. students that were stranded for the Thanksgiving Holiday. Due to travel problems their collective commercial traveling problems have kept them from going home for the Thanksgiving Holiday's for as long as they have been M.I.T. students. It was impossible for them to even send food packs home because of the Air bridge problem as most of their stuff would not fit on any size aircraft no matter what.

As we talked Lorynda politely let me know that they could all use a free flight to Nepal. Ok I said "don't tell me their closest airport is Lukla?" my next question was "where they all packed and ready to go?" With that statement Lorynda open the door to show me all the other students in my dorm all lined up toe to toe holding a holiday food gift that had been stored for lack of transportation in some cases for more than 3 years.

It looked like they had cleaned out a toy store, Lounge Chairs, Bicycles, Tricycle's, Beds, there was even several Baby Buggies, and of Course Strollers, all load to the hilt with food and Christmas Presents. All I could do was activate Sabrina No. 39 and have her lower her transportation tube to its usual location.

Then all the students in my class helped to load everything into Sabrina No. 39s main lower cargo bay. As soon as it all was aboard I wanted to know who would off load it all at Lukla Airport. With that statement everybody chanted, "we will" so I had the load master program start to inflate personal Travel PODs one for each student. Sabrina No. 39 wanted to know where we were going, when I told her it took a couple of seconds longer than usual for her to find it and plot her course and file her flight plan.

The local FAA did question the arrival point when they thought that Sabrina No. 39 was a helicopter but, when they noticed our dentation was Lukla airport in Nepal, they must have figured that using a helicopter was the best bet.

The flight over the North Pole and quick descent over China was not a problem, in that part of the world was the big problem my GPS system had everything located before we launched. Little things like weather and altitude did not mean a thing to Sabrina No. 39. So it took less than a half hour before I made a vertical landing on the main as well as only runway at the Lukla Airport.

I had my instant prototyping unit start making oxygen hoods for any of my fellow students that were having problems breathing due to the extreme high altitude of our touch down point.

As soon as I depressurized and opened up Sabrina No. 39s lower cargo bay. I made in a point to keep an eye out for anybody that collapsed or started to turn blue. I could not find the main door in the dark so I put my nose wheel elevator square on the only marking #24 that I could find. The only problem I had was that I had to retract Sabrina No. 39s nose wheel to level the cargo bay for a quick off-loading.

Sabrina No. 39 used her terrain landing program to angle and clamp both of her main landing gear onto the mountain side just out-side of town. The Airport was so small that Sabrina No. 39 barely fit on it. Having my whole student body along for the trip really helped as we instantly formed a human chain and moved everything up into the airport's main lobby, that happened to be closed at the time as we were not expected. I will admit this was the first Earth bound airport terminal that was pressurized with its own built in airlock.

The first thing Lorynda notices was that it did not have any locks on their doors. It was also the smallest building in town. After the terminal was filled it took up most of the airports parking space just to pile up all the cargo Sabrina No. 39 hauled in that night. As soon as her cargo bay was empty Sabrina No. 39 informed me that it was time to leave, it took a couple of minutes for everybody to climb back aboard, and minus the 10 locals that were M.I.T. Students evidently they all wanted to stay.

After all the excitement was over and all of my returning class mates had boarded. I powered Sabrina No. 39 up and went into a full hover despite all the extra lift-off thrust from the lift-fans and other loud noises. I became the first pilot to take off from the Lukla Airport while flying backwards as I did not want to blow the entire town away. So I had Sabrina No. 39 hover as she backed down their now down-hill runway and applied full power after I was off the end of their runway.

This airport had a few good points as it was impossible for me to flip over parked cars with my lift-fans, because there was not a single vehicle in town. It took a little longer than a half an hour to fly everybody back to M.I.T. as I kept Sabrina No. 39 in a climbing hover until we had cleared the entire mountain range. By this time with everybody breathing the pressurized sea level air inside of Sabrina No. 39s cargo bay everybody had changed back to their normal color.

Another reason that leads to the success of this mission was the large slug of 15 PSI pressurized air was dumped as my lower cargo bay doors opened. I also lucked out as my Space suit did not automatically morph itself into existence due to the altitude of the landing location. Sabrina No. 39 made all the radio calls needed to park herself back in her "Sabrina at school location."

Later at dinner time everybody did have a wonderful dinner in the Dorms Cafeteria. I found out later that there was a large military presents at the Lukla Airport who main job was to keep the local Bandits out of town. They were not a problem as they were all out of town the whole time we were on the ground in Nepal.

Fourteen days later one of Pinger-5s Pilot Whales by the name of "Pete" made a stop-off to picked everybody up. In the middle of a high altitude blizzard due to the White out Blizzard at the airports Location, as well as the runway length. "Pete" played it safe by going into an extremely high hover and having Sabrina No.40/24 lower a cargo pallet outfitted with Transportation PODs.

All that had to be done was to put down a cargo pallet next to Airports Terminal building. It was kind of comical I think the operators at Lukla thought that No. 40/24 was a Dirigible as all that "Pete" could do was lower a cargo pick up pallet and direct all the stranded M.I.T. students to sit on the Passenger PODs.

Then when everybody was finally seated it was snapped up inside of nice white cloud. As soon as everybody and their luggage were safely aboard. He made a perfect flight to my Sabrina at School Location. Where I had him lower them into Sabrina No.39s top cargo deck.

Log Entry #145.
Capture of the Aquarius:

It was Christmas break before I could get away from M.I.T. long enough to make a fast trip to Mars on a priority Christmas cargo run. Sabrina No. 39 was loaded so full of cargo that I had to leave Pinger-5 behind after all despite the distance, direction, or the extremely large amount of mass that had to be moved, the mail has to get there as soon as possible.

In case you're worried about it I don't have a contract to fly the mail but as a company Sabrina Aviation can legally move its own mail around when ever and where ever it wants to. It was finally my turn to do it again.

I made it a point to come back on a trajectory that would put me within 50 feet of the know location of the Aquarius. It took Sabrina No. 39 almost three hours to finally bring me to the point in outer space where we were quietly flying formation with the Aquarius.

I chuckled to myself when I realized that it had been in flight since 1970 always traveling away from the Earth and now I have come from the other direction to capture it and bring it home.

Due to its unique shape the solar wind had caused it's top to point towards the sun as if it were a badminton birdie in a wind storm. Its landing gear had acted as fins to keep it from spinning and the solar wind had carried away all of its atomic oxygen clouds. All of its solar shielding was gone as well most of its black paint.

The RTG was still in place but my radiation warning light was not worried about it. Two of the landing pads were missing as was the main doors of the Modular Equipment Stowage Assembly. With all the lunar experiments that were inside missing. I also noticed scaring on its surface that must have been caused when the ill faded oxygen tank in the service module popped like a toy balloon.

It only to a second or to, too morph my Human maneuvering unit into operation and space walked the last few feet to the Aquarius. As I could not bring her aboard until all of my safety protocols were answered and I had removed all of the un-used liquid rocket fuel.

My heart skipped a beat when I noticed that the Assent Engine had not been activated. My next move was to check out its Bell Aerospace fuel sealed packaging that would have opened the fuel valves on the Valve Package Assembly. The valve assembly still had its safety pins so that both the fuel and oxidizer tanks were still filled to their 100% capacity.

Liquid bi-propellant rocket fuel it real nasty stuff it was used to make a lunar Launch guaranteed, as all it had to do was drain into the lift-off-engine with the aid of the moons gravity. It contained its own Ascent Propulsion System engine and two hypergolic propellant tanks for return to lunar orbit and rendezvous with the Apollo Command/Service Module.

The Ascent stage contained the crew cabin with instrument panels and flight controls. I decided to bring her aboard it must be a reflex from Sabrina No. 39s racing days as soon as she grabbed the Aquarius with her space-junk-trap she instantly made a pull up maneuvers pointing us straight back towards the Earth.

As soon as my cargo bay doors closed I stopped the pressurization process as I was afraid that full pressurization would crush the Aquarius as if it were an empty pop can. Sabrina No. 39's ships system program moved the molded tie down that I had specially built to lock it into position to keep Aquarius from bouncing around. I first filled the cargo bay 100 per cent with a .00000001 atmosphere, and then I waited a couple of minute's too double it and recalculated to see if anything inside of the Aquarius was pushing back. As it turned out there were so many microscopic holes throughout the Lunar Module that pressurization would not be a problem.

I slowly allowed the cargo bay to pressurize all the way up to 15 P.S.I. I morphed my space suit back to its flight suit mode as I entered the cargo bay to take my first good look at my recovered prize my first thought was what had happen to it during its more than 50 years of space travel. The Aquarius had greatly exceeded its design requirements by maintaining life support for 3 Astronauts after an explosion damaged the Apollo Service Module. I floated over to the bottom of the EVA ladder and became the first person to travel up it. Just like it says in the history books Aquarius did have the wrong lunar plaques with Ken Mattingly still listed as command module pilot.

However, I suppose that an original Richard Nixon autograph must be worth something. Once on the front EVA porch the first shock was the missing lunar entrance hatch it was popped off by the high speed atmosphere that had to pass through the cockpit as it bounced off the Earth's atmosphere. As I moved into the interior of the cockpit the first thing that I heard the whistling sound of atmospheric gasses being pulled back into long empty container tanks.

I also had to contain the Aquarius' Reaction Control System that was used for attitude and translation control, which consisted of sixteen hypergolic thrusters similar to those used on the Service Module, mounted in four quads, with their own propellant supply that I had to remove. I made it a priority to move all of its un-used fuel into Sabrina No.39's operational systems. I made it a point to use two different hoses to move the fuel and oxidizer separately.

The next thing I noticed was the "mailbox." that was a Geri-rigged arrangement which the Apollo 13 astronauts built to use the Command Modules lithium hydroxide canisters to purge carbon dioxide from the Lunar Module. As it turned out this was the first devise to be built in outer space. Pinger-5 plans to have it duplicated so that she can sell thousands of them on E-bay. Of course everybody knows that it was designed on the Earth at mission control but it had to be constructed on the Aquarius.

I still use lithium hydroxide to scrub Co/2 from Sabrina No. 39s atmosphere as well as my own Space suit. I could help but noticing the calculations that were use still on the windows that Astronaut Lovell used to adjust his flight path without the aid of a computer, as I ran his original calculation through my head I could plainly see that the Aquarius never had a chance to burning up in the Earth Atmosphere.

I was wondering what happened to all the little Knick knacks that were abandon inside both the Snoopy and Eagle. Then I remembered that mission number 13 came up short on mass when the lack of 300 pounds of moon rocks made the crew strip the Lunar module for what they could get to make up for their extreme shortage of Moon Rocks.

Considering all the mileage on her space frame the Aquarius was not in that bad of shape. She is definitely a patch up and keep project as I don't think that I could get much of a trade in on her from the Used Space Ships for Sale Lot.

Yes, I threw the old beat up RGT unit into the sun it should to hit its chromosphere in about a year. A forward EVA hatch that provided access to and from the lunar surface, while an overhead hatch and docking port provided access to and from the Command Module. Both had been lost then the Aquarius bounced off the Earth Atmosphere. Internal equipment included an environmental control system; a VHF communications system with two antennas for communication with the Command Module, a unified S-band system and steerable parabolic dish antenna for communication with Earth, an EVA antenna resembling a miniature parasol which relayed communications from antennas on the astronauts' Portable Life Support Systems through the Lunar Module.

Primary and backup guidance and navigation systems as well as an alignment optical telescope for visually determining the spacecraft orientation its rendezvous radar with its own steerable dish antenna; and an ice sublimation system for active thermal control. Electrical storage batteries, cooling water, and breathing oxygen were stored in amounts sufficient for a lunar surface stay of 75 hours.

The Descent stage's primary job was to support a powered landing and surface extravehicular activity. When the Lunar excursion mission was over, it served as the launch pad for the ascent stage. Its Octagon-shaped, was supported by four folding landing gear legs, and contained a throttle able Descent Propulsion System engine with four hypergolic propellant tanks. A continuous-wave Doppler radar antenna was mounted by the engine heat shield on the bottom surface, and used to send altitude and rate of descent data to the guidance system and pilot display during the landing.

Almost all external surfaces, except for the top, platform, ladder, descent engine and heat shield, were covered in amber, dark reddish amber, black, silver, and yellow aluminized Kapton foil blankets for thermal insulation. The # 1 landing leg had an attached platform that was informally known as the "porch" in front of the ascent stage's EVA hatch and a ladder, which the astronauts would have used to ascend and descend between the cabin to the surface of the moon. The only remaining rear footpad of the landing gear contained a 67-inch -long surface contact sensor probe, which signaled the commander to switch off the descent engine.

The probe was omitted from the number 1 leg of every landing mission, to avoid a suit-puncture hazard to the astronauts, as the probes tended to break off and protrude upwards from the surface.

All of the equipment for the lunar surface exploration was carried in the Modular Equipment Stowage Assembly mounted on a hinged panel dropping out of the left hand forward compartment. Due to the very close call with the Earth Atmosphere as well as all the "bucking maneuvers" that occurred just after the oxygen tank exploration. All of the astronaut's surface excavation tools and sample collection boxes, television camera with a tripod, and American flag were missing.

The Early Apollo Surface Experiment Package was supposed to be carried in the opposite compartment behind the LM. An external compartment on the right front panel was to carry a deployable S-band antenna which, when opened looked like an inverted umbrella on a tripod. A hand-pulled Modular Equipment Transporter, similar in appearance to a golf cart, was carried on Apollo 13 to facilitate carrying the tools and samples on extended moonwalks. All of which was missing. The last thing I did was to put her in her special made molded tie down and secured her in the cargo bay.

Despite my detour I made it back to "The LEADER in time for Christmas Dinner. As planned I met both of my Parents in the main Lounge of "The "Leader's" Food Court Number One. As I had decided to surprise my parents with a full course VIP Christmas Dinner at the "Leader's newest Restaurant the "Sky Salvaged Dinner".

That I was able to remove from one of my latest catch a flaming Airbus A380 and install it back with all the other fancy eating locations that were already in business on the "Leader's Main Food Court." I had my communications necklace send morph direction to each of our space suits to form into formal Ball Attire for me and my Mother as well as a Tuxedo for my father.

Log Entry #146.
Supersonic Helicopter:

Eventually the local FAA Inspector came around the college looking for M.I.T.s supersonic Heavy Lift Helicopter. To top it off M.I.T. did not even have a helicopter, much less a high speed one. I was not concerned as my entire class was sworn to secrecy.

During this morning's announcements the president of M.I.T. wanted to know if any of his students had a Supersonic heavy lift helicopter hid on campus. As everybody knows helicopters are not airplanes, the only way that a helicopter can leave the ground is because it beats the air into submission to get a helicopter to fly at higher altitudes you have to have enough air to beat. As for high speed flight forget it, due to the rotor stall problem, even if you play around with the shape of the rotor blades the rotary winged flying machine cannot get much above 200 miles per hour forward before the rotors destroy themselves on a very spectacular way.

Also, the longer the blades the slower the forward speed can to be. I have tried to fly auto-gyros on the surface of Mars, without much success; so far the first Spacecraft or aircraft for that matter that had successfully flown around inside of the Martian atmosphere was my Sabrina No. 39 series spacecraft. Which is equipped with retractable lift-fans used for vertical-take-off or landing operations?

I also have variable wheel trucks that can morph into any type of landing gear needed. In some cases Sabrina No. 39s had to be driven back to the nearest Martian base as surface vehicles, when local Martian weather makes it impossible to fly inside of the Martian atmosphere.

So far nobody's noticed the massive air conditioning unit that is sitting in plain sight on top of my dorm that does not have any kind of a built in Air-Condition System. I can tell you for a fact that the idea of flying a Helicopter, Gyro-Copter, of Auto-Gyro on Mars is the worst kind of Science Fiction. As Mars does not have enough atmospheres to operate any type of rotary wing aircraft.

Log Entry #147.
The Astro-Bug:

I found a notice on the bulletin board about a local scout troop that wanted somebody with rockery experience to help out at their next rocket launch. So I volunteered as they were flying small useless human rockets that had no chance of making it into outer space.

The problem was the Scouts could not get them to make it to inner-space either. The good news was despite all their efforts they have yet to launch a single rocket. As usual everything was all wrong the major problem was lack of safety as nobody knew anything about the National Rocketry Associations basic safety rules.

So at the next meeting everybody got introduced to the safety rules, and informed that they were all to be used and lived by. Rocket wise everybody was attempting to fly a different rocket kit and a few of them had interchanged their parts and left off their recovery systems. When I asked what type of recovery system they were using the usual reply was gravity which is not a recovery system.

As they have not heard of a Parachute, Streamer, Aerodynamic, Autogiro, or Tumble. It took several meetings to get the same Rocket Kit for everybody, an Alpha III. I took the advice of my much older friend Dennison I had to organize everybody into rotating flight teams. With each launch having five different jobs, pilot, pre-flight, launch, safety, and recovery. Then we acted out several mock launches with everybody rotating all the jobs.

After a couple of meetings everybody was ready to launch. Another thing that happened was the lack of knowledge as to the "Path of flame" I seems that the melting of a parachute was normal as nobody used the blowgun method to make a pressure seal to save the life of their poor parachute.

The only problem was one of the scouts' younger siblings showed with a pay loader that was crewed by the largest meanest looking Wasp that I had ever seen. He called it his Astro-Bug and wanted to fly it, from the angry sound that was coming from the pay Loader the Astor-Bug did not want anything to do with it. So I told the child to forget it according to the Rocketry Safety rules we cannot fly anything that's alive because of the "G" factor at launch tends to pull enough "G's" to kill the average mammal at lift-off.

As luck would have it he came back with the old Boy Scout manual that had a rocketry cargo list and bugs were on it. By this time the Astor-Bug wanted to leave due to lack of food in the capsule, and was starting to hum.

Despite all my hope the young child just bypassed me and proceeds to launch his bug several times. The next time I got close to the Astor-Bug was when a recovery person bought it in because of all its buzzing it was trying to chewing through a hole in the side of the pay loader.

It had discovered that the plastic was thinner on the nose cone and had tried to sting the recovery person through the nose cones thin skin. The Astor-Bug was making a mush louder as well as much more of a threating sound was very mad and attacking anything that it could get at.

I quickly put a layer of tape over all the newly opened stinger holes where it had tried to sting everybody that held the Cargo-Pod. Just then the younger brother showed up to calm his Astor-Bug along with the rest of his rocket. Along with his Parent, I gladly gave it to them and requested that they deal with their extremely angered Astor-Bug themselves.

The next time I saw them both, they were at the first-aid-station tending multiple Wasp Stings. The bottom line is no matter what, we have to live with the safety rules. Every payload that is launch has to have at least one recovery device. So to fly an Astro-Bug it would have a Streamer or Parachute attached to it. Also remember that "G" means gravity on acceleration and decelerations even the weight of a small bug could make it heavy enough to be thrown out of an unsealed pay loader.

Even though the bug has wings accelerating it to over 500 miles per hour puts it in a high speed flight envelope that the poor little bug cannot deal with all that speed.

Log Entry #148.
The Follower:

This time they made the announcement at school another large Asteroid had just come out of the Suns Atmosphere and it was heading straight towards the Earth. On a trajectory that would cause it to make an all at once vertical landing in the middle of Lake Michigan.

I definitely have to arrange for a full time series of patrol ships that will be stationed on the other side of the Sun. This Asteroid was larger than the LEADER not to mention the fact that it was almost on the same trajectory. After a quick first look at its first long range photos it had earned the name "Follower." As it was a 10 miles wide, 14 miles high, and 20 mile long Potato shaped Asteroid that had millions of smaller various size Want-a-bees Meteors trying to become one with it.

This was the same problem that I had to deal with when I only had one Sabrina-IX space ship operational. Checking back on its trajectory I should tell that it was originally a very large un-numbered asteroid that was safely parked in its orbit in the Asteroid belt. When it was knocked out of its orbit by Jupiter's long reaching gravity well. When it aligned with Mars and Earth this started it moving just enough to collide with another large Asteroid as they tried to combine with each other they started their power dive towards the Sun.

They both just missed landing square on its surface by less than the thickness of a human hair as it passed through the Suns Atmosphere where it was cooked into a gravel pile. When it came up and away from the sun it was a lot smaller, moving lots faster and accompanied by all the little pieces of burnt or broken meteors.

Millions if not billions of them all trying to orbit the Follower trying to land on its surface, the main problem was it would collide with the Earth in a little more than 100 hours.

It only took a couple of minutes for both of my Parents to call me to casually mention that I have their permission to go off planet. So with a quick stop at the President of M.I.T.'s off to get permission to leave the school grounds, then with a quick stop at the M.I.T. cafeteria to stock up on rations I launch of the roof of my dorm in broad daylight to capture the Follower.

But, first I had to get a close up look for myself. As soon as I was airborne I called for my First Five and the Next Ten to join me as soon as possible. I lucked out this time as the Follower was out of missile range just passing the orbit of Mercury.

As Sabrina No. 39 and I were closing in, all the small Want-a-bees started to show up on my navigation system I hadn't seen so many meteors in flight since, I was shot down over Mars several year ago. This time I was smart enough to not let them sneak up on me. When I first saw the extent of the problem it took more than a full minute for my instrumentation system to make a complete chart of all the Want-a-bee's movements.

The Follower literally had its own built in Meteor storms, several layers deep as several Meteors had tried to orbit it and were broken up by other larger meteors moving in a another direction at different altitudes. This created lots of different moving meteor storms all constantly colliding with each other changing the size, speed, and direction of everything.

The final picture was not very pretty as of now I could see all the work that I had to do to save the Earth for the second time, and I had a little less than 100 hours to do it. My next task was to plot a safe course to safely fly all the way down to the Followers surface. Needless to say this was the job of the best high speed Pilot on the planet me!

By this time Pinger-5 had received my transmission and knew the location of all the incoming want-to-bee Meteors this enabled her to plotted a safe course through all the moving meteors fields to enable me to land on it and move it out of the way.

But, first all six of us had to get to the Followers surface. This would have to be the trick of the century as the only thing my Computer could see was a Large Asteroid with Billions of small various size want-to-bee Meteors trying to orbit it, as it smashed into the Earth in 99 hours.

By this time Pinger-5 and most of her Whale/naut's that were on Earth to launch themselves into outer space even her Whale school bus. The Orca's attack force had a field day going after all the larger house size Meteors fragments that were still trailing the Followers gravity field.

The initial capturing of millions of small Want-a-bees Meteors made all the Humpback day as now they could play orbital gulf all they wanted. Pinger-5 finally plotted a safe course to the Followers surface, and transmitted it to me as I was still flying the Sabrina No.40 space ship that was closest.

At first glance I thought that Pinger-5 had sent me a drawing of a loop of electrical wire, as it overlaid the data from the Followers so just like that I had a course to fly around and through each flight of meteorites as we would penetrate each level of Want-a-bees Meteors.

On my command Sabrina No. 39 and the "First Five" extended all their surface level space junk traps. I marked each ships touch down point on their Logic Boards.

Instantly the first five reported that they were ready to follow, so I started the most exciting trip that I had ever flown in Outer space, it was like driving on the express ways in Chicago, with lots of constant very close and very high speed merging.

Which was a lot more exciting than riding a run a way roll-a-costar? The Follower had lots of layers of what-to-bee meteors all traveling in random orbital tracts around the Follower. Lots of high speed driving, acceleration as well as deceleration and of course lots of high speed cloverleaf intersections.

It was like being passed from both sides at the same time by streams of double bottom Semi-Trucks going over a hundred miles per hour then pouring on the speed re-passing the same group of Semi-Tractor Trucks. Then speed in front of them both only to instantly exit from the right lane into a very tight Cloverleaf turn to accelerate in front of another full line of Semi-Trucks. With all the lanes full on a very crowded express way traffic.

On several occasions I had to stay in the safety of the Cloverleaf when there was not any space left on the main orbital tract to merge.

After a while my hand started to hurt from all the constant throttle on and throttle off action. It was a good thing that I finally have a drivers permit. On several occasions I had to loupe a city block size meteor and use it as a turning point. It took almost 6 hours to run the gullet and land all six of us, at the proper locations on the Followers surface. As soon as the first five set their landing anchors I was ready to move it anyplace I wanted go.

At 92 hours before impact I stopped the clock as I pulled the "Follower" out of line and moved it forward of the swarm of Want-a-bees Meteors. This caused the swarm to collapsed and fall in on themselves. We did have a problem with the waves of sand size Meteors that filled up the space-junk traps as they passed all the anchored Sabrina No. 39s as we moved out ahead of the swarm. Then with a hard left turn and a little retro rocket action I slowed the Follower so that most of the Want-a-bees meteors impacted on its port side when they were pulled down into its gravity well.

At this point in the mission all the Want-a-bees had reformed themselves into a single column that was still on its original Earth bound trajectory. To fix this problem all I had to do was start the Follower rotating, this enabled the stream of Meteors to be wound around the surface of the "Follower" as if it were winding up a rope.

The Whale/naut's pulled all their Sabrina No. 40 ships in close and loaded themselves up with full loads of meteors and hauled them away as soon as their He/3 collector cleaned off all of its surfaces.

With a quick refueling from some of Pinger-5's, Sabrina No. 40 space ships. I had no problems moving the Follower to Earth. Now that I have captured it I think I could use as the top of a new Space Elevator sight on Earth. I became the big winner as soon as I parked the Follower in its new permanent Geosynchronous Orbit over the Island nation of Madagascar in the Indian Ocean.

So that I can build my other side of the world space elevator. Needless to say I did all the math calculations for all the maneuvering in my head as it was needed. Sabrina No. 39 and I made it back to school with minutes to spare and I got to keep my perfect attendance record.

Log Entry #149.
Madagascar Space Elevator:

I lucked out as it was the Rainy Season in Madagascar at the time of the Followers arrival over its present location. So I figure that it will take several months before any of the local's notice it parked directly over their heads.

I originally thought about landing the bottom of the space elevator in the Indian Ocean but, according to the Whales, it has too many underwater fault lines to worry about. Pinger-5s Tunnel boring machines were still hard at work establishing the original docking ports and landing the more of her tunneling machines to start the converting operation.

I also requested my personnel on Mars to convert the big square box that I left docked at the top of the Phobos Space Elevator to be converted into a manufacturing location to make standard Five Tube Space Elevator shaft components as of now I am in need of another 33,000 miles of them.

Amelia the Blue Whale Calf who happens to be my youngest Whale/naut's took it upon herself to rundown and recovered several of the original Space elevator components that were damaged in transient on their way to Mars for their first Space Elevator. Believe it or not several of them were struck by unknown Meteors or Comets on their way to Mars, and were severely damaged.

Amelia's plan is to recover them and repair them for the Madagascar space elevator. I suppose they will do for a starting point.

Log Entry #150.
Space Elevator Parts:

The call to action was answered with full force. Amelia the Blue whale located and captured all the known damaged Space Elevator components that I had lost during the transportation of the original Parts to the Phobos space elevators.

Under Amelia directions the First Five Sabrina No. 39s recovered everything and moved it into the big empty box located at my Phobos Space Elevator. As soon as each of them had been repaired they were sent back to Earth to be used at the Madagascar Space Elevator Site.

I think that my Other Side of the Earth Space Elevator over the Island country of Madagascar will be operational sooner than I thought not only are we manufacturing components on site but at several other locations on the Earth's Moon and Mars as well.

My most interesting enterprise was to convert the Follower Asteroid to a full time Space elevator shaft factory

Pinger-5 first job was to make room for the fulltime work crews, then hollow out custom size space elevator shaft size area along with several elevator car space cities aboard to house all the construction crews. So my only problem was funneling in all the raw materials.

Log Entry #151.
"Chucked"!!!!:

I woke up in the middle of the night as I was having a dream about my friend Captain Lynda Love. I could see the startled look in her face, her eyes would get real big and she would get this real scared look on her face as she would pull down her helmets visor. Then I would wake up, instantly siting straight up in my bed with a start I would order my Communication System to put me in contact, with her. Then Lorynda would roll over in her bed and say "That did you say".

Then I would fall back to sleep only to have the same dream happen over and over again, the next morning all I heard from Lorynda was who is this Captain of yours. As soon as I could make it into my Command POD I set a record for having my Communication system linked to her Communications Necklace.

After all I had given all four of my Typhoon Ravaged fighter pilots a Communications Necklace that even managed to save Jackie's life when she had crashed her F-22 out of view in the middle of the Alaskan Range.

I had not heard from Lynda in a while, so I finally had my Communication System give her a call, "Just to say High". My Communication System instantly located all four of my Typhoon Busting Buddies. It was nice to learn that Jackie was back with her squadron as it looked like they were all close enough to be in the same cockpit.

As usual the first thing to focus in was a picture of what was in or around them the problem with a necklace camera is that it usually shows the photo from under the outer layer of clothing. I got the shock of my life when I switched the camera to Infra-Red Mode only to get a close up view of the mouth of a very large Crab chewing on something that was still trying to get away.

After a couple of seconds it beeped and started the report, the GPS showed that they were all on an Island in the Western Pacific Ocean, and that all four of them were stationary, on its north side beach. I could hear the sound of the waves breaking over rocks and of course there was the unmistakable sound of very large live crabs feeding.

My next call was to their squadron commander, only to find out that all four of them were away at survival school for the next six months to a year. I called a few of my own contacts in their personal section to check their pay records to discover that all their pay had already been signed for all four of my friends, this confirmed that they had been "Chucked".

I had met General Chuck Yeager several times when I was a Young Eagle and I have also studied all of his personal history books, so I instantly knew what was happening. All four of my friends had been roped into a year-long training program designed to find out how they would survive when they are captured by the enemy.

They were put on this island in the guise of it being a short length roughing it type survival program. If they left or were driven off the Island by the live crabs they would be court martialed for desertion. And thrown in the worse possible prison location and forgotten about for six mounts to a year before being rescued or until they escaped.

This is what the Air Force does with Pilots when they don't have enough Fighter Planes. The bottom line was my friends were in for the worst year of their lives if I did not stop them. I ducked out of school as soon as I got out of my last class of the day, and made it back to my dorm room. I used my Communications System to check my facts. Then with a quick and quiet launch off the top of my dorm building, with Sabrina No. 39 making all the radio calls herself.

As soon as I was over the Atlantic Ocean I transition from Hover-Fan mode to space ship with a quick acceleration south down the old Atlantis missile range and a high Speed turn to the west, just north of South America. I was flying at Mock 50 inside of the Earth Atmosphere the whole time I was zeroing in on my friends location. I was in such a hurry that I had to use Sabrina No. 39s Aero-spikes as retro rockets.

I had Sabrina No. 39 Land on top of their camp on the training island with all three of my landing gear centered nose gear as well as well as both of my main landing gear mains on their exact location. The Island was so active with moving Large Crabs that Sabrina No. 39 just wanted to hover and not touch down.

She made sure that all of the animal screens were in place and I made sure that they were all double locked. As soon a Sabrina No. 39 stopped moving she automatically activated her Urban Camouflage program, which was not very easy as she had to start looking like a beach full of thousands of moving live Horse Shoe Crabs. I lowered my Command POD and stood at the end of my boarding ramp to finally look into the very tired bloodshot eyes of Lynda, Doris, Jackie and Kathy, all of which looked dirty, smelly and about to kill me on sight.

As usual it was raining, dark, extremely hot, the entire Islands surface was claimed by a colony of very aggressive large horse shoe crabs that upon my arrival were inviting Lynda to be a late night snack.

As I set my foot on the surface of the island a large horseshoe crab tried to eat my Space boot as well as my foot that was still inside of it. The hungry Giant Crab even caused my space suit to activate its Auto-Repair-System. Now with everybody accounted for I expanded one of my clear Cargo Bubbles around the end of my gang plank and invited everybody to sit down and talk.

Instantly the entire surface of the Cargo Bubbles was covered with hundreds of Crabs several layers deep all trying to feed on all of us with me included. There was an instant look of relief on everybody's face as this was the first time in weeks that my Pilot Friends were not trying to be eaten. The first thing Kitty did was to pull out her gun and shoot the largest Crab at point blank range, only to have three other smaller Crabs instantly eat him. Without a second though Lynda Said "Don't worry about it her Space ship will fix the bullet hole all by itself.

With that she looked at me with some discus and said "How come you rescue us now on the last day of the survival test. I answered "What

Survival Test you have all been Chucked!" None of you are about to be rescued, if anything you're about to be captured by your enemy and forgotten about in a prison cell for about a year.

Did any of you actually read General Yeager's book cover to cover line by line? With that Statement everybody came aboard to live in my Command POD! My next move was to morph 4 complete decontamination rest rooms with at least 100 gallons of hot water each. Due to my high speed flight inside of the Earth Atmosphere I had plenty of hot water to spare.

I goes without saying that due to their lack of clothing I had to issue them Sabrina Aviation space suit's, set to the flight suit mode. I did get several comments as well as questions about my sowing ability, as the replacement flight suits were all perfect fits as well as having regulation nametags and rank.

I reminded everybody that I also was an A & P Mechanic and that one of its requirements was that I had to know how to use a needle and thread to make flight gear. I wonder what they would do if I morph them all a formal mess dress uniform. As soon as we all were cleaned up and crammed together inside of my flight kitchen I decided to test my prototype "Bet-ty Ja-ne".

As it was activated this this time, it was about as large as a small tomato juice can. As it morphs into operation it grew to a machine that was about 6 by 8 inches large. Then it started to expel an endless supply of regulation hot ready to eat Mc-Rib Sandwiches one after another taking less than fifteen seconds between each Sandwich. Needless to say all four of my Fighter pilot friend wanted a "Bet-ty Ja-ne" for themselves.

Log Entry #152.
War Games Sabrina Style:

At this point I turned on all my sensors to look for their pick up aircraft. At the same time I had my Communication System talk to the flight computer of any local aircraft or ship. With nothing showing up friendly in contact range for hundreds of miles around. I asked the whole gang to explain what was going on, all four of them answered in unison "Survival Training"! They were dropped out of the back of a C-130 a week ago and had lost most of their equipment before they made the Beach. My next question to all of them was had they volunteered for a long term study dealing with being captured by the enemy? To that question I got a very large "Negative" from all parties concerned.

Over the last couple of weeks my survival students had notices small boats passing their location but none were flying a national flag or flashing the proper day code. Most of their time was spent trying to get away from millions of hungry Crabs. The best attempt was to use what was left of their Rubber Raft to make a crab proof barrier that only lasted almost an hour. That is until the local crabs learned how to climb as well as eat rubber.

Meanwhile, all four of my Fighter pilot friends were getting cleaned up and better fed. As I was running out of "Bet-ty Ja-ne's" as we set there during the rest of the morning we saw lots of small boats with military figures start to show up on the beach. What was most interesting to note was that none of the Horse Shoe Crabs even made a pass at any of them.

My Communications System had been talking to several of Pinger-5s Mid-Pacific Whale/naut's, it seems that several of their Whale/calves wanted to meet "Sabrina the Invincible" in person. We sat there and watch as the human invaders scoured the beach area picking up all the stray survival equipment that the girls had lost during their survival ordeal.

As we read their body language we all agreed that none of them were the least bit interested in rescuing anybody. All of our worse thoughts were confirmed when I zoomed No. 39s camera system in on the aft deck of one of the larger ship to see an large Iron Bar Cell full of other captured prisoners just sitting ready and waiting for us.

About this time one of the Beach Patrol picked up Lynda's communication necklace the one that the large crab was wearing. Upon sensing its movement Sabrina No. 39s Command Computer instantly launch a Space-Junk-Trap, to capture the luckless Human that was holding Lynda's located necklace in his hand.

This caused him as well as all the others on the Beach, to be instantly zapped with Space-junk-traps and recovered into my lower forward cargo bay. I waited until we all had gathered around the airlock before I had the now occupied Space-junk-Trap lifted out of the airlock. For our personal interrogation Lynda was the first to speak as she requested her necklace back.

The Landing party's Beach Master was very talkative He confirmed the worst of my fears as his capture party had been sent onto the beach to capture not rescue all of my Pilot friends. To top it all off He didn't even know the correct friendly contact password. Being a tough guy He demanded our surrender to him, upon hearing that I had him instantly encased in sticky foam up to the bottom of his chin.

By this time several of my Sabrina No. 40 Space ships in submarine mode had position themselves just off shore. According to Pinger-5s attack plan, the first thing my Sabrina No. 40 ship would do was put up its bait ship a relative good looking 20 foot long speed boat on a pole, then the Sabrina No. 40 would slowly move away from their intended target to get them to chase them down.

As soon as the targeted enemy little boat was decoyed over an open top hatch it was allowed to fall inside to be captured and have all humans aboard sticky foamed up to their necks. Just like filling up an empty egg carton the Whale/naut's in charge had divided her top cargo bay morphing system into enough rooms to capture more than 20 little boats each.

Sabrina No. 39 was button up so tight that not even a crab could get in much less an attacking human. Without giving away our position we kept still and just watched. It did not take very long for the other side to come back and see what happen to their original capture force. She had already call in the "First-Five" and the Next "Ten" whom were defiantly inbound to our location.

Upon discovering an empty beach, they sent in the second capture team. If you can believe it, two fast moving OV-22 Ospreys zoomed over the beach looking for anything other than live crabs.

Then came several high speed low passes by AV-8c, I check each aircrafts serial number with my Communications System as they shot past us. As we all still sat camouflaged on the beach watching all the attack runs. I made it a point to ask Lynda what type of aircraft they were. She replied that they were the rebuilt AV-8c models, with up graded avionics Fly-By-wire system.

I asked all my fighter pilot friends if they knew what the bad thing about a Fly-By-Wire System was. So I told them that the nice thing about having a fly-by-wire system is there is not a direct control link to anything, so having a more powerful, faster thinking, computer system like one of my Command Computers I can take all the fun out of it. It was a simple matter to have my communication system to overpower and take control of the other side's entire AV-8c attack force. Then I had them repeat the Oshkosh AV-8 show, Doris loved the part where they all hovered backwards in mass formation and spelled out the message:

SURRENDER NOW

On the beach In front of us in block letters as each AV-8c vertically landed using each aircraft to form elements of each letter. It was heartwarming to see each of their fighter pilots jump out of their aircraft as soon as it touched down in the sand, to run up and down the beach passing each other.

I could see on my plotting screen where the "Next Ten" had a field day catching every one of the OV-22s in flight. The Osprey is a special case due to safety concerns Helicopters are off the Space-Junk-Trap hunting list, however when in airplane mode a capture from behind is possible. My only problem was making enough space inside the Sabrina No. 39s cargo bay.

My on board loadmaster program had suspended them vertically by their tails and applied a layer of sticky foam around each one to keep all their humans aboard. The next part of the show was a little more intense as two of my Sabrina No. 40s surfaced in the Ocean with one on each side of my Location on the externally crab infested beach. They both extended their landing gear and adjusted their gear trucks to drive up on the beach, stopping with both of their nose cones over my location.

Then each ship open their bottom cargo bay doors and dropped out all of their very sticky foamed covered, captured little boats directly on to the Crab infected beach. All of their captured humans were sticky foamed up to their necks and installed on to a pallet that was sticky foamed to the top of one of their aircraft movers.

Their ships system did keep all the caged humans confined. I made sure to drive it fast to keep the larger of the hungry giant Crabs from trying to feed on my next set of captured humans. The island was not that large, so Sabrina No. 39 spent the next hour pin pointing and Space-Junk-Zapping each of the loser AV-8c pilots. A couple of the other sides pilots even tried to fly away with their over controlled airplanes.

It took a couple hours to sort out who were the good guys as well as the bad guys. Needless to say the bad guys were all sticky foa med up to their necks. It was getting late and I had to get back to class tomorrow. So I started making plans for the bad humans that were stuck in sticky foam, too be transported to my Secretary Force on the LEADER.

When Sabrina No. 39 picked up an entire naval task force on her plotting board on a direct inbound course to our crab filled island. I definitely did not want to be out numbered on the ground so I ordered a mass launch. Both of the Sabrina No. 40 extended their wings and Lift-Fans-Fans.

To make a vertical take-off at the same time. Sabrina No. 39s communications system took charge of all the captured AV-8c and had them make a mass vertical take-off and fly formation as we proceeded to intercept the incoming fleet.

Both Sabrina No. 40s made a vertical impact in the nice deep Pacific Ocean on both sides of their convoy. As I started to fly all the captured AV-8c automatically around inside the carrier's holding pattern all under my control.

What happen next even impressed me as both of my Sabrina No. 40s proceeded to surface directly under the task forces only Aircraft Carrier, to enable Sabrina No. 39 to place both of her main landing gear trucks on their hulls, as the aircraft carriers deck was too small for Sabrina No. 39 to actually land on. I put my nose wheel as close to the center of their flight deck as I could get it then adjusted the height of my nose gear strut to make Sabrina No. 39 level to their flight deck. The Task Force Commander was the first person that I saw as my nose wheel elevator door opened. I could tell from the expression on his face that this was the first time during his life that he had to deal with a 16 year old girl that just happens to be a college student.

We both demanded each other surrender, upon assessing his salutation he had one of his Aegis Destroyers launch a missile directly at Sabrina No. 39 as she set on my newly captured flight deck. My communications system took command of it in flight and then had it sky write:

Sabrina Wins

Directly overhead until it ran out of fuel. Then it fell harmlessly into the water without a parachute or any other type of recovery system in operation.

To counter this I had five of my Sabrina No. 40s surface with their nose cones all pointing directly centered at the Task Force Commander. At this point in our conservation the Commander asked me if I knew what an attack submarine looked like.

In the past Whales have always had to laugh at us poor humans that wanted to play Whale? Every now and then a human manned submarine would show up in a few of their Whale songs. Now under the new war-game situation, I had requested the whales to intercept and capture the human manned Submarines, a request that only took minutes for my Whale/naut's to perform.

According to their capture report several of my Sabrina No. 40s had just, chased down and captured their entire Submarine force without giving them a chance to maneuver. So I had no worries as I walked my counterpart over to the side of my newly captured flight deck to show him the view directly down into the now open cargo bay of one of my Sabrina No. 40s. To see several of his Attack Submarines all high and dry with their human crew standing on their deck covered up to their necks with sticky foam.

I could tell from the expressions on their faces that the Grizzly Bears as well as the Polar Bears on the "Orc Tact Team" had a fun time tearing the hatches on each submarine open and running its entire human crew up on their main deck to be sticky foamed in place. With his next Command all of his Aegis Destroyer started to aim their Gun Turret as they were finally pointed in my direction. On when I politely asked the Command Whale/naut on each of my submerged Sabrina No. 40 space ships to start making them disappear one and two at a time.

One of the Destroyers Captains must have been a Klingon as he launched every one of his ships missiles as he was being pulled down inside one of my Sabrina No. 40s. This caused me no problem as all Sabrina No. 39 had to do was reinforce the sky writing program, I wonder how the Task Force Commander can write off the cost of millions of dollars' worth of one way missiles, just to sky write: "Sabrina Wins"

In the sky until every one of them ran out of fuel and crashed into the surface of the Pacific Ocean. At this point in the battle I decided to introduce my friend the Task Force Commander to a pack of ballistic M & M's all of which impacted his flight deck with holes sever inches deep.

Charley the Orca Whale had his weapon of choice impact surrounding the exact location where, the Task Forces Commanders ships use to be with sever hundred flaming mini-vans. Judging from their flame and debris trails, this must have made the other side worried.

It didn't take very long for their side to run out of Aegis Destroyers. About that time my 'First-Five' Sabrina No. 39s all flew past my captured Aircraft Carrier, doing their airshow act, coming close and closer and flying faster on each pass. Finally the first captured AV-8c ran out of fuel and drop into the Pacific Ocean.

As the first AV-8c hit the water the Task Force Commander surrendered, I put my next pack of M & M's away to save for the next time.

Then it was time to settle up. I put all the humans that the Task Force Commander returned aboard Sabrina No. 39 in all I took charge of over 150 older military personal, Pilots, as well as Flight crew members, all of whom had no idea of what was going on. Several of them recognized me from my adventure in Antarctica a couple of year ago. I had Sabrina No. 39 start putting my sticky foamed prisoners on his Flight Deck, as his AV-8c landed and his flight deck crew recovered them. They discovered that they were full of Very Large Hungry Crabs.

Just as I was ready to give Sabrina No. 39 the thrill of her life by giving her the request to launch herself offs the deck of an Aircraft Carrier. My ex-counterpart personally came running over to my nose wheel elevator to ask how he could get his troops out of my Sticky Foam. So I dropped a case or two of Anti-Sticky Foam spray on to his Crab Infested Flight-Deck as I had Sabrina No. 39 use her Lift-Fans to vertically launch herself off the back of the Task Force Commanders Aircraft Carrier.

As soon as I had departed with Sabrina No. 39 the "First-Five" and the "Next-Ten" took their turns hovering over the Aircraft Carriers Flight Deck to lower each of their sticky foamed Ospreys. All of my Sabrina No. 40s first surfaced them released all there little Destroyers at the same instant. Sabrina No. 39 requested an open landing bay for Sabrina the Invincible to come aboard.

"I did get to inspect both of my Sabrina No. 40 and have several new born Whale calves actually meet "Sabrina the Invincible" in person. All of my freed prisoners as well as my original four victors were transported back to the LEADER for processing.

I launched back to school for the rest of the night sleep, Sabrina No. 39 managed to park herself back in her Sabrina at school location without getting anybody attention. The training Island was the first location that I had the new camera system locates on the earth side of my Madagascar Space Elevator.

Log Entry #153.
New Employees:

I have yet to advertise for personnel all of the humans as well as the whales joined my space flight operation through word of mouth. I also have lots of medical, weather, as well as storm chasers that want to study the weather on Jupiter. Space Pioneers as well as their entire families all coming from other humans in Space organizations.

So I have yet to show up at a Carrier Fair looking for employees. So I expect a call from Lynda, Doris, Kathy and Jackie about becoming Sabrina Aviation Employees.

However, I did not expect to be contacted by all the other humans that did not like the vacation plan their Commanding Officers decide to send them on. I had E-mails from all of them detailing their experience as well as their last survival school. It was interesting to know that all of their personal propriety was put in long term storage and forgotten about the second that they departed for their last week long survival course.

I hired the whole group on the spot, and issued them their first space suit it took a while to run everybody through the "LEADER's" operational center, as several of them had to spend time healing up from Crab Bites in my Zero Gravity Hospital.

As "Sabrina the invincible" it was up to my various department heads to worry about housing as well as pay vouchers. For something to do I decided to see if they could operate my Sabrina No. 50s Spacecraft Program. I had operated 10 non-manned space ships for over a year, without having any life threating happen and I had worked out all the bugs, as well as Crabs.

All four of my friends still had my Sabrina Aviation Flight suits in their personal possession. As a matter of fact Sabrina Aviation Flight suits were the only clothing that they had. I began to worry as soon as I noticed that their flight suits were changing color, meaning that they were in need of a recharge. I reached in my pocket and pulled out a hand full of my micro-chargers.

I toss each of them one and had them put it in the left epaulet of their flight suit. Instantly all four of their Flight suits changed back to their original color and clean themselves of all dirt and stains.

The time was running short as I had to get back to school. I welcomed everybody aboard and started to tell them about my Sabrina No. 50 project. I have two main reasons for getting the Sabrina No. 50 series spacecraft up and working. The first reason is safety I can tell you from experience when you run out of space ship it really help to have another one handy.

The other thing is to have a way to move key personal as well as the company mail. To maintain human occupied Cities anywhere, there will always be the need for an alternate means of transportation. So in a nut-shell my new fleet of Sabrina No. 50 space ships will serve as a space born lifeboat, as well as a small space craft doing High Speed, Rescue, or Cargo ship, to serve my expanding fleet of spacecraft.

In the past it has always been the job of the Military to step in and help during emergencies, to stop a threat, even if it's a large storm or Asteroid or Comet. I am always honored to have a person around that will put the mission first.

My only problem is that as of now I only have about 150 experienced humans that I have picked up from this adventure.

Log Entry #154.
First Sabrina No. 50 Space Camper:

I flew in from school on a special trip just to welcome my new employees aboard just to tell them that, my plan for your group of Aviators is for you to take over the old space ship designs that Pinger-5 had purchased from M.I.T. After I fixed its design and made it work I named them my Sabrina No. 50s Space ship Project. I described the program and stated that their job would be to train as well as serve as personal pilots to take Science and Research teams throughout the Solar System.

This spacecraft has a Command Computers similar to the ones in my Sabrina No. 39s and 40s all capable of flying the space ship all by themselves. The Sabrina No. 50's teams main job would be to put humans aboard and to make sure that they know enough to stay alive.

But, first if they were interested everybody is welcome to take a short shake-down trip to the Moon and back. As we looked out the conference room window we could see the Space Hanger Crew pulling one of them out of its storage case.

Such a nice quote little space ship floating there in zero gravity with her meteor deflector nose cone pull up to protect all of her observatory equipment. At first sight the folded up Sabrina No. 50 Space ship looked a lot like a grain storage tower with set of built in gas tanks. It's a lot larger than one of the old Saturn S-IVBs that I recently recover from Solar Orbit.

Its main hatch was open to make sure that its internal pressure matched the main space hanger. I morph into my space suit mode and jumped over to the open hatch. I looked back to notice that all of my new Ex-Fighter

Pilots friends were hanging on to the airlock hatch as well as each other for dear life. I had to get aerobatic to jump back to the main hanger wall and just stood there with both of my space boots attached to the wall.

They all stood up and I pointer to the button on their flight suits center pocket that caused each of their Flight Suits to instantly morph into their Space suit for the first time. With that taken care of they all jumped off the hanger wall and followed me over to the closest Sabrina No. 50 Space Camper.

As I passed through the main hatch I said Hi the Sabrina No. 50s Command Computer and asked it to activate her space ship. I also requested the life-support system to adjust for 150 humans. As everybody was looking at the telescopes and all the other gadgets in the ship observatory, I had the Command Computer start its pre-launch check. I squeezed myself into the Control POD, to launch the ship out into outer space for our first reverse Young Eagle Ride. I extended the Nuclear Rocket motor and activated its reactor, and then I unfolded the nose cone to activate the ships navigation system. As soon as everything settled down, I closed the nose cone/meteor deflector, finally with everything in the green. I launched my Sabrina No. 50 on its way towards the moon.

As soon as we were under way I extended the ships six gravity wings and started creating gravity the only way that I could. For a bunch of Earth bounders it was not that bad of a trip for all the pilot types to get into zero gravity Aerobatics.

We made a close pass next to one of my out-going asteroid ships, and then came in low for a good look at the surface of the Moon, followed by a fly-by of all three of my Lunar Space Elevators. By using the Nuclear Rocket Engine to speed up as well as slow down I had all of us back at our starting point on the LEADER, in less than two hours. Where I close down the Nuclear Reactor retracted the engine, and had the Sabrina No. 50 fold herself up and goes back into her storage box. The fly-by went well, everybody agreed to work for me and do whatever was necessary to get the project up and running.

Log Entry #155.
Orca T.A.C. Team:

It was a comment from Lynda that first gave the Orca Whale/nauts the idea of forming a Rescue Force whose main job was to save any human for a reward from Pinger-5. Several of the Orca Whale/naut's have banned together with several of my Sabrina No 39s to go into the Commando style rescue business.

By having my Communications system to track the location of conservation, they could instantly locate both ends of their Communications. As soon as they learn the location of a kidnapped victim they mount an instant rescue mission.

Then with a ballistic landing anywhere on the Earth within a 15 minute time period. By moving fast and faster they have the ability to move in to make a land fall then with the aid of several fast moving Orcas as well as Dolphins. All on whale scooters knocking down doors and make holes in walls as need to get the kidnap victim out of harm's way in a hurry.

For all their bad-talk, they got more business looking for lost hikers and mountain climbers. Charley the Orca is also part of the team and I understand that he has lots of fun impacting his junk mini-van projectiles in the bad guys as needed. Local humans have complained as its, hard to explain how there can 25 or 30 instant chain reaction car wreck can happen, even when there are no roads Pinger-5 had made a point to also employee her civilized Grizzly & Polar Bear force as needed for both tracking as well as extraction. As Pinger-5 puts it as soon as we touch down it the White Bears job is to track down the targeted human and it's the Gray Bears job to take down human made barriers.

Log Entry #156.
Flying Oversize Fish:

When Pinger–5 heard about the Asian Carp problem in Chicago she decided to do something about it for profit. As soon as she discovered that the Army Corp of engineer was spending 40,000 dollars a month in electricity just to run their electronic barrier.

Pinger-5 came up with a better way to keeping Asian Carp out of the Great Lakes. First off the Illinois River is not the only waterway going into Lake Michigan. Thanks to the New Madrid fault line there are hundreds of not thousand's of underground Lakes and Rivers that run into just Lake Michigan alone.

However she considers them just a part of the available food sources. When her gourmet Polar Bears gets tired of eating Python and Wild Boar she substitutes Asian Carp.

She utilizes large troops of Polar Bears to consume the large number of Asian Carp as all she has to do is troll around with one of my Sabrina No.40 with the bottom cargo bay doors open, to let the genetic altered fish jump directly into the waiting hungry Polar Bears mouths.

And to top it all off she gets paid for it by the pound, from the Illinois Department of Fish and Game. I have also read reports that she has a troop of Grizzly Bears intruders that she got from her Conservation Friends High up in the Rocky Mountains.

She also rents out the mouth of the Illinois River too several different Pods of Orca Whales as a vacation site. I understand that she has quite a waiting list.

Log Entry #157.
Meteor Storm Rescue:

I should have stopped this mission in the first place. Several scientists got assigned to Doris to go meteor prospecting. Somehow they got the Idea to flying formation with a meteor storm, this is not very easy as there is usually a microgravity problem that makes it real easy to get boxed in and crush between several different chunks of solid rock at the same time.

I think Doris had problems with the term Pilot in Command, as her passengers wanted her to keep getting closer. The problem was she got too close and crashed her Observation equipment section two or three levels deep into one of the pointy ends of a house size meteor.

This was how I found out that my Location necklace works off planet. Doris had lucked out as just like in billiards her Q-ball had moved her captive asteroid away from the swarm.

Keeping her damaged space ship from being crushed into dust by other meteors in the storms micro gravity was the problem. My Sabrina No.39/85 who was the closest space ship answered the call. She was only 2 hours away when she picked up their call for help.

What makes it interesting was the only antenna available was the communication chain around Doris' neck. I received several interesting E-mails about it as to where to make the entrance cuts. As the Sabrina No. 50 had to be brought into a full pressure Cargo Bay before the human crew could pry the house size asteroid out of in observation section.

What happen next was comical as all that Doris had to do was open up the Sabrina. No. 50 that was already aboard Sabrina No. 39/85 activates it, and then has her crew move all their personal equipment aboard and continue their mission.

So in less than 4 hours after her collusion Doris was back to her Rock Carving Activates inside of the local meteor storm. My four fighter pilots, stayed with me for the rest of their lives. Lynda, Kitty, Doris & Jackie as Sabrina Aviation employees operates at all locations throughout the Solar system.

Log Entry #158.
Here is a list of my space ships to date:

As you can tell from my list my Space ships started out using Roman Numerals, I had to give up when the Roman Numerals got too complicated.

Sabrina No. I   Was an Airplane that I build myself in grade school It was original a Zenith design that I fixed this enabled me to call it my Sabrina No. I, It also was the airframe that I used for my first official FAA Flight.

Sabrina No. II   Was pieces of several Cessna 150s that I rebuilt to fly myself this was how I fixed my rudder pedal problems as I learn how to build them close.

Sabrina No. III   Was my first jet aircraft it was a little larger than a Bede Jet and power by my first generation turbojet engine. Its main use was to test fly my early jet and rocket engine designs.

Sabrina No. IV   Was also an airplane piston engine mono-plane that I used to make touch and go. Flights I used her to develop my ability to snitch and grab soil samples off the surface of the Earth, or Mars.

Sabrina No. V   Was my first Aero-Spike powered rocket-plane that I used for my first around the world Flight. She is hanging in the Smithsonian.

Sabrina No. VI	Was a larger version for lack of a better term she was an operational space plane, capable of single stage to Low Earth orbit.
Sabrina No. VII	First Command POD it was built it.
Sabrina No. VIII	The first spacecraft with wing warping high speed control system.
Sabrina No. IX	Was the space ship that I used for my first touch and go flight to the planet Mars. Removable Command POD
Sabrina No. X	Was my first design for meteor recovery space ship. As such she had several hundred copies built; her most unique feature was its ability to turn its self-inside out to make it easier to load meteors in space. I also expanded to ships work shop areas and made is useful to fix space-junk wounds on larger spacecraft.
Sabrina No. XI	Mover of Space Elevator Shaft Components
Sabrina No. XII	The first conversion ship with its own Tunnel-Boring-Machines
Sabrina No. XIII	Mover of Space Elevator Shaft Components
Sabrina No. XIV	Conversion Ship with its own Tunnel-Boring-Machines
Sabrina No. XV	Conversion Ship with its own Tunnel-Boring-Machines
Sabrina No. XVI	Mover of Space Elevator Shaft Components
Sabrina No. XVII	Un-manned model supply base, I designed it to have whatever we need. I like to think of her as a portable grocery store.
Sabrina No. XVIII	Asteroid Ark Transport.

Sabrina No. XIX   My first Asteroid Ark Space ship that I deck out for comforts with simulated gravity wheels and she was pressurized to the Earth sea level. At the time she was the largest Solid Space Rock converted.

Sabrina No. XX   Large solid Impactors

Sabrina No. XXI   Asteroid Ark Transport.

Sabrina No. XXII   Small Asteroid Ark Transport.

Sabrina No. XXIII   Small Asteroid Meteor farmer equipped with 25 Sabrina No. Xs

Sabrina No. XXIV   Large Asteroid Meteor farmer equipped with 50 Sabrina No. Xs

Sabrina No. XXV   Asteroid Ark Transport.

Sabrina No. XXVI   Medium size Asteroid Ark Transport.

Sabrina No. XXVII   Asteroid Ark Transport.

Sabrina No. XXVII   Asteroid Ark Transport.

Sabrina No. XXVIII   Asteroid Ark Transport.

Sabrina No. XXIX   Asteroid Ark Transport.

Sabrina No. XXX   Asteroid Ark Transport.

Sabrina No. XXXI   Asteroid Ark Transport.

Sabrina No. XXXII   Asteroid Ark Transport.

Sabrina No. XXXIII   Asteroid Ark Transport.

Sabrina No. XXIX   Asteroid Ark Transport.

Sabrina No. XXX   Smallest Asteroid Ark Transport.

Sabrina No. XXXI	Asteroid Ark Transport.
Sabrina No. XXXII	Asteroid Ark Transport.
Sabrina No. XXXIII	Asteroid Ark Transport.
Sabrina No. XXXIV	Asteroid Ark Transport.
Sabrina No. XXXV	Luxury Asteroid Ark Transport
Sabrina No. XXXVI	Long Range Human and Whale Transport.
Sabrina No. XXXVII	Asteroid Ark Transport.
Sabrina No. XXXVIII	Asteroid Ark Transport.
Sabrina No. 39	She was my first generation Space ship First one designed to Land and Launch from Mars. She also had to fold up small enough to be taken under ground on Mars for loading as well as maintenance. This was the point where I decided that Roman numerals were getting too messy.
Sabrina No. 40	She was my second generation space ship built to go to Jupiter's Moon IO. 4 time the mass and double the power, with the capability of working underwater. Has lots of extra internal space for cargo as well as workshops.
Sabrina No. 41	Asteroid Ark Transport.
Sabrina No. 42	Asteroid Ark Transport.
Sabrina No. 43	Luxury Asteroid Ark Transport
Sabrina No. 44	Luxury Asteroid Ark Transport
Sabrina No. 45	Luxury Asteroid Ark Transport
Sabrina No. 46	Luxury Asteroid Ark Transport

Sabrina No. 47	Luxury Asteroid Ark Transport
Sabrina No. 48	Luxury Asteroid Ark Transport
Sabrina No. 49	Luxury Asteroid Ark Transport
Sabrina No. 50	Is an eleven person Nuclear Powered Space camper that folds up and is storable on any other Asteroid Ark Ship intended to be launch able for extended search and observations.
Sabrina No. 51	Asteroid Ark Ship Tender for Sabrina No.50 series spacecraft
Sabrina No. 52	Conversion Ship with its own Tunnel-Boring-Machines
Sabrina No. 53	Large Asteroid hollowed out to use a Space elevator manufacturing site.
Sabrina No. 54	Asteroid Ark Ship
Sabrina No. 55	Conversion Ship with its own Tunnel-Boring-Machines
Sabrina No. 56	Asteroid Ark Ship
Sabrina No. 57	Asteroid Ark Ship
Sabrina No. 58	Asteroid Ark Ship
Sabrina No. 59	Asteroid Ark Ship
Sabrina No. 60	A Noah's Ark for real- a special rotating asteroid ship intended to move live farm animals off the Earth, the Ark ship is designed to keep spinning constantly.
Sabrina No. 61	Asteroid Ark Ship
Sabrina No. 62	Asteroid Ark Transport.

Sabrina No. 63	Asteroid Ark Ship
Sabrina No. 64	Asteroid Ark Transport.
Sabrina No. 65	Hollow Garden of Eden a nuclear powered green house where only grow plants their only mission is to grow more seeds for other space colony ships. My larges space ship to date that was not an Asteroid.
Sabrina No. 66	Asteroid Ark Ship
Sabrina No. 67	Luxury Asteroid Ark Transport
Sabrina No. 68	Luxury Asteroid Ark Transport
Sabrina No. 69	Luxury Asteroid Ark Transport
Sabrina No. 70	Extremely large Hollow Asteroid this was my first attempt to build my own Duson's Sphere. With the main point on Humans with a few Whales.
Sabrina No. 71	Slightly smaller Hollow Asteroid this was my second attempt to build my operation self-sustaining Duson's Sphere. With the main point on Humans with a few Whales.
Sabrina No. 72	Very extremely large hollow Asteroid this was my first attempt to build my own Duson's Sphere. With the main point on Whales with a few Humans.
Sabrina No. 73	Hollow Asteroid ship used as a Water mover. I like to refer to them as Liquid Comets.
Sabrina No. 74	Hollow Asteroid ship used as a Water mover. I like to refer to them as Liquid Comets.
Sabrina No. 75	A solid rock asteroid with a tunnel boring machine and a blunt nose Pinger-5 planned for it to fly into her Microscopic Gold's Orbit and see if she can

get it to form a Gold Planet that she can deposit in several of her Earth bound money Banks.

Sabrina No. 76	Hollow Asteroid ship used as a Water mover. I like to refer to them as Liquid Comets.
Sabrina No. 77	Hollow Asteroid ship used as a Water mover. I like to refer to them as Liquid Comets.
Sabrina No. 78	Rock engine powered hollow Asteroid Want-a-bees Magnet
Sabrina No. 79	Hollow Asteroid ship used as a Water Mover. I like to refer to them as Liquid Comets.
Sabrina No. 80	Hollow Asteroid ship used as a Whale colony Mover. I like to refer to them as Whale Pods
Sabrina No. 81	Luxury Asteroid Ark Transport
Sabrina No. 82	Luxury Asteroid Ark Transport
Sabrina No. 83	Luxury Asteroid Ark Transport
Sabrina No. 84	Hollow Asteroid ship used as a Water mover. I like to refer to them as Liquid Comets.
Sabrina No. 85	Luxury Asteroid Ark Transport
Sabrina No. 86	Luxury Asteroid Ark Transport
Sabrina No. 87	Luxury Asteroid Ark Transport
Sabrina No. 88	Luxury Asteroid Ark Transport
Sabrina No. 89	Luxury Asteroid Ark Transport
Sabrina No. 90	Luxury Asteroid Ark Transport
Sabrina No. 91	Luxury Asteroid Ark Transport

Sabrina No. 92   Luxury Asteroid Ark Transport

Sabrina No. 93   Luxury Asteroid Ark Transport

Sabrina No. 94   Luxury Asteroid Ark Transport

Sabrina No. 95   Luxury Asteroid Ark Transport

Sabrina No. 96   Luxury Asteroid Ark Transport

Sabrina No. 97   Luxury Asteroid Ark Transport

Sabrina No. 98   Luxury Asteroid Ark Transport

Sabrina No. 99   Luxury Asteroid Ark Transport

Sabrina No. 100   Expandable Louvered ship that can expand or
                           shrink up to fit mission requirements powered
                           my 5 S-IVB

Log Entry# 159.
Glossary

A & P – Airframe & Power plant- basic entry level aircraft mechanic

AMARC Aircraft Maintenance and Regeneration Center

APU—Auxiliary Power Unit

C.E.V. – Crew Exploration Vehicle, meant to replace the shuttle, to expensive

EAA—Experimental Aircraft Association

FOD—Foreign Object Discovery

HALO—High Altitude Low Opening

HMU--Human Maneuvering Unit

IAU--International Astronautical Union

IOU— I OWE YOU

IMSA—Illinois Mathematics and Science Academy

I.S.S. list (TTFOOTISS)—Things that fall off of the International Space Station

M&M's - Candy coated chocolate delights that can be used as very small extremely fast moving ballistic projectiles.

MIDO- Manufacturing Inspection District Office

Mistel- two aircraft put together to make one aircraft, Mistel German word

M I T – Massachusetts Institute of Technology

PAM-- Pluggable Authentication Modules—add on rocket motors

POD Personal Orientation Device

RTG—Radioisotope Thermoelectric Generator- obtains power from radioactive decay

RTW-- Round the world flight

S.S.R.F.S. - Space Suits Rocket Flight System

T.C.A.S.—Traffic Collision Avoidance System

TIGHAR- The International Group for Historical Aircraft Recovery

T.O.L.H.A--The Only Living Human Aboard

TRACON- Terminal Radar Approach Control

UCAV—Unmanned Combat Aerial Vehicle

V.T.O.L.—Vertical Take-off or Landing

Want-a-bees - Small Meteors that are being pulled my larger meteors.

WD5- Name of a Meteor that hit Mars

Zero "G" Zero Gravity Weightlessness

Printed in the United States
By Bookmasters